Freedom in My Soul

Shauna Reilly

Freedom

University Press of Colorado

Shauna Reilly

in My Soul

a novel

Copyright © 1998 by the University Press of Colorado
International Standard Book Number 0-87081-503-2

Published by the University Press of Colorado
P.O. Box 849
Niwot, Colorado 80544

The University Press of Colorado is a cooperative publishing enterprise supported, in part, by Adams State College, Colorado State University, Fort Lewis
College, Mesa State College, Metropolitan State College of Denver, University
of Colorado, University of Northern Colorado, University of Southern Colorado, and Western State College of Colorado.

The paper used in this publication meets the minimum requirements of the
American National Standard for Information Sciences Permanence of Paper for
Printed Library Materials. ANSI Z39.48-1984

Library of Congress Cataloging-in-Publication Data

Reilly, Shauna.
  Freedom in my soul / Shauna Reilly.
    p.   cm.
    ISBN 0-87081-503-2 (alk. paper)
    I. Title.
PS3568.E4849F7   1998
813'.54—dc21   98-8849
                                                            CIP

07 06 05 04 03 02 01 00 99 98   10 9 8 7 6 5 4 3 2 1

Freedom in My Soul

Shauna Reilly

chapter

one

Ever since I was a little girl, I knew I had freedom in my soul. Still, it took a long time before I could make a run for it. My family and I chose a muggy summer night in 1850 when our Chickasaw owners' personal concerns demanded their attention. By the light of a fading moon, we planned to start southward over Oklahoma Territory.

"If we survive that," I'd told the others, time after time, "we'll cross the hellfire and brimstone of Texas to reach free Mexican soil."

When the big evening arrived, my scheme started out as slick as I had devised it. We all kept calm through supper at the grub table, although that wasn't hard. Everyone was so exhausted from their days in the field that no one had much to say.

As we walked back to our cabin Mammy said, "Go on. I'll catch up with you. I'm going to check Mose and Amanda's cabin."

"Hurry, Mammy," said I, my stomach jumping into my throat. "We don't want to draw attention to ourselves this night of all nights."

Mammy—whose given name was Chloe—cast me a scornful glance. "I want to leave that cabin as free of bugs as I found it."

Mammy had chased Mose and Amanda away by pointing out some crawlers—that she herself had smuggled in—on the wall, then offering to cleanse the cabin of bugs. Just as they promised, Mose and Amanda had gone straight to their daughter's cabin after work, so there was no sign of them.

After Mammy squashed the few crawlers she could find, she called out for my pappy. His name was Isaiah, but most everybody called him Ike. I just called him Pappy.

Pappy had already turned part of the spring to run between our cabin and Mose's and Amanda's, and had the grass stripped down bare in that plot of ground—to keep the fire we planned to set from jumping from our cabin to theirs.

"I'll just throw a few buckets of water on their walls," he told me. "I'd hate to set Moses and Amanda's place to burning."

"Go on, Pappy," I told him, "but don't be long."

When Mammy and Pappy came back, we all dressed in our traveling clothes and went to bed. Only Samboy and Pappy slept, because they were so tired from the fields. Mammy and I stayed on the alert, along with Dog.

"The quarters are settling down fast tonight," I whispered.

"Everybody's falling into their bunks, too tired to mind our doings," she agreed.

After an hour or so, I crept near our cabin's front door. "You sleep some," I told Mammy. "I want to watch the moon so I'll know when our running time comes."

Even though cloud cover blanketed the sky, I could see the moon's shine here and there. We'd agreed to stay in our cabin until the moon peaked. When it began to drop, we'd make our bid for freedom. That left me with several long hours to wait and worry.

Within minutes, I found my mind spinning back over the years leading up to this moment. My younger—and only—brother had set off my recollecting earlier that evening. "Please, Mammy," he'd said, "don't let Samgirl cook on the runaway trail."

My brother hated my cooking because I believed garlic was the key to nearly every dish, including some desserts. My love of garlic started during the 1830s back in northern Mississippi, where I grew up watching Mammy split those fat bulbs with her hammerlike thumbs. She'd just grab those cloves and bust them open, and the smell would wash over me like a scent straight from heaven.

"My mammy is the best cook around," I'd brag to anyone who would listen. By the light of a pine-knot torch, she roasted ears of corn in the ashes of the fire, then scraped off the kernels and fried them. She boiled all kinds of greens that she collected from the woods and mixed them with deer or wild turkey meat, or sometimes with fish from the creek or turtle from the swamp. On Sundays, she made grits with pounded hickory nuts in it.

"I don't care about learning the fine points of cooking," I often told Mammy. "I'm more worried about freedom." To myself I vowed one day I would get me some.

I believed I could free myself because I had certain abilities. I've always been clever and I was well educated. My brother sometimes taunted me, "That's a mistake our Chickasaw Indian owners made, educating you right along with their own offspring."

The main trouble with getting freedom was my blackness. Even as a girl, I was very black; you might say ebony black. If I had been light, maybe quadroon color, and talked as good as I talked, freedom might have been easier to come by. Maybe I could have grabbed my chance and sashayed down the streets of town along with other free blacks, most of whom were light-skinned. But for me, freedom could only come the hard way; my blackness marked me much like Abel marked Cain.

Still, even though I was black as black could be, I was beautiful black. My skin shone like it had been oiled. My hair stood out like a fierce bush around my head and my eyes glittered like quartz. My cheekbones were high and my lips like petunia petals, just waiting to be kissed.

My brother, who was named Sam just like me—Samuel and Samantha—would split his trousers laughing if he ever heard me describe myself. He'd surely say, "Our Chickasaw 'family' gave you too many fancy ideas, Samgirl."

Of course, the Chickasaw took white folks' ways, including Christianity, right into their hearts long before I came on the scene. Still, I admit they passed a few ideas on to me.

Despite all their fine ways, the Chickasaw sure lacked imagination in the name department. To distinguish me from my brother, they called me Samgirl and him Samboy. I once asked Mammy, "Why not just give us two different names at the start of life instead of making it so confusing down the line?"

"I didn't have any say in the naming of my own children," Mammy replied.

Although the Chickasaw treated their slaves like people, they sure wanted to be there first in the matter of naming slave babies. Now that I think of it, our Chickasaw owners weren't too good at Indian names either. The pa went by John Stands-in-Timber and the ma by Nellie Mad-Doe. The children were a passel of apostles: Paul, Simon, Peter, with an Esther and a Rebecca thrown in. No wonder they ran out when it came to naming my brother and me.

Samboy could be right. Maybe I did get some unnatural notions from old John and Nellie. I had it easy growing up—that is, as easy as growing up in slave quarters gets. I ran barefoot and buck-naked with John and Nellie's youngest for a summer or two, then Mammy made me a tow smock. I was still barefoot, and naked as a bluejay under the smock.

Sometimes I waved a straw fan over old John and Nellie's guests, or fetched water for them or a snack to eat. Mostly I was free to climb trees, play marbles with pebbles, and torture the old rag doll Mammy had made for me. That doll had charcoal eyes and red thread worked in for the mouth, and was my only real toy.

Next thing I knew I was eight years old and going to school every morning regular with old John and Nellie's brood. That was when one of the little apostle fellas, Paul, said to me, "I own you. Ma and Pa gave you to me for my eleventh birthday because I'm the oldest and have to learn how to manage slaves. I especially asked for you."

That boy was only three years older than I was, but already his evil side showed. He was a sneak, less than a credit to the man who sired him and the mother who bore him. I worried about the change in my ownership, but was too innocent to know what it really meant. It took me years to find out how much suffering Paul's owning me could cause.

It started to come to me when I myself turned eleven. I had a yellow mutt who had taken a shine to me and followed me around the quarters.

I fed him scraps of food when I could and he slipped away to peruse the big house's garbage when I couldn't. I could count his ribs through his spiky yellow fur. He always appeared lopsided to me because he had lost most of one ear in a fight he probably didn't win.

I loved that dog with a fierce passion. "I want to call him Samdog in honor of me and Samboy," I told Mammy.

But she said, "That'll only muddle everything more. Think of somethin' else." My family also seemed to lack imagination for naming, because we finally ended up calling him just plain Dog.

Paul, who always seemed to be hanging around me, hated Dog. Paul disliked anyone or anything that got between me and him when he wanted to use his rights to me. Just about twilight on my eleventh birthday, Paul dawdled his way down to the quarters and gave me a lace handkerchief—a bit frayed around the edges, but lace nonetheless. He also glided me behind a thick oak tree and ran his hand up my shiny black leg farther than I thought he should.

"My mammy and pappy will be looking for me, Paul," said I as I slipped out of his grasp. I headed for our cabin, but Paul snatched my arm and held fast.

"Too bad for them," he snapped. "You're mine and I can take you where I want." Paul planted his feet in the loamy dirt and fixed his eyes on mine.

I wiggled my arm, trying to get loose. He held on tight, set on getting his own way. "But it's my birthday," said I, with a twisted logic I hoped would fluster him.

Paul blasted right back, "And I brought you a birthday present, so you owe me something in return." He grabbed the front of my dress and tried to pinch where a breast should be. Because I was only eleven he came away empty-handed.

That was where Dog came on the scene. I squealed and Dog, ever my protector, bared his teeth and had the temerity to growl at Paul. Like the original apostles, Paul smote his enemy smack between the eyes. Instead of having the good sense to retreat, Dog actually had the gall to snap at Paul.

I seized Dog by his good ear and ran for the cabin, hauling him behind me. My departure sure frustrated Paul, in both the breast-pinching and dog-smoting arenas.

"Come on, Dog," I urged as I dragged him into our cabin. "Get in and stay in, if you know what's good for you."

Being that our cabin didn't have a door, and Dog was male and therefore lacking sense about fighting and enemies and such, he snuck out sometime during the night. Although I could hardly credit it, Paul must have waited outside for me or Dog to appear. The next morning I heard Dog whimpering on the bare boards we grandly called a porch.

Dog sat crying, held in place by a rope tied around a huge rock, his good ear completely gone. Dried blood caked over the side of his head like dark mud. A few trickles of fresh, red blood made tiny streams through the dried black blood. I was down on the boards in a flash, with Dog's butchered head in my lap and the acrid smell of blood going up my nose.

I buried my head in Dog's bloody fur and let hate for Paul rise up the back of my throat until it almost choked me. I must have groaned something fierce because Mammy and Pappy ran onto the porch and dragged me and Dog, a tragic spectacle to be sure, inside the cabin.

"Get that creature inside," Pappy bellowed, "where your mammy can care for it."

The upshot was that Dog lived, thanks to my mammy's doctoring. Dog never went near Paul again, and I tried to keep my distance, too. At the time, I kept my silence about these happenings, but I tucked them away in a back corner of my mind. Many nights I hugged Dog to me, even when he was smelly and dirty from running through the swamp all day. I cried myself to sleep, some tears for Dog's ear and some for me as being owned by Paul.

Despite this and other troubling events, it took me another two years to figure out what Paul's owning me was leading to. "What does that Paul want with me?" I would ask Mammy.

She would shake her head and once let a small tear dribble out of the corner of her eye. "You'll know soon enough, Samgirl."

It hit me hard when I was thirteen and Paul started to lie in wait for me, behind the oak tree, along the road to the big house, or wherever his warped imagination landed his sassy ass.

I managed to dodge Paul. I was always busy, going here and there and keeping lots of folks around. That is, until one Tuesday morning. I remember because Mammy was up in the big house starching and ironing with her work partner, Becky. They'd drag the irons off the stove, land them with a thump on Master's Sunday shirt or Mistress's petticoat, and slam them back on the stove. Then they'd grab other fresh, hot irons and make the clean-clothes smell go right into the air again. Around and around they'd go, dragging irons from stove to shirt and back again. No wonder folks called them sad irons. They sure made Mammy and Becky sad every Tuesday morning.

Anyway, I was in our cabin putting some beans and fatback and a bunch of garlic to soak when Mister Paul—that's what he made me call him—poked his head in the open door and announced, "We're going for a walk in the woods."

I glanced around for help, but Pappy and Samboy had gone to the fields at dawn. Dog cowered under the table. I should have known I wasn't safe anywhere, even in my own cabin. I snatched the first feeble excuse that came into my head. "I have work to do, *Mister* Paul," said I, but he grabbed my hand and dragged me off.

"I own you," he told me, in a sharp tone that lit a flame of fear in my chest and reminded me of the occasion on which Dog had lost his second ear. "If I say we're going for a walk, then you walk. Understand me?"

I couldn't help thinking how little Paul resembled his daddy. Old John was scrawny and dark-skinned and kind. His bright, piercing brown eyes almost always had a sparkle to them and his black hair hung in his eyes like a little boy's hair. Even though Paul was scrawny too, his muddy brown eyes—sort of the color of animal dung—gleamed with hate most of the time. He spoke in a tight, sharp voice and kept his hair slicked back from his forehead so that his pointed features stood out on his red-brown face.

I couldn't picture old John commanding or abusing any of his slaves, but Paul fancied himself a modern Chickasaw. In my opinion, Paul spent too much time running around with the white boys in the neighborhood. They gave him downright un-Indian ideas about slaves.

To make matters worse, old John let Paul do whatever he wanted, seeing as how Paul was the eldest son and the favorite and all. I thought old John put too much store by Paul's being the oldest. "Maybe it's some Chickasaw way we know nothing about," I told Mammy. "Or maybe old John learned it from the white planters in Mississippi."

That morning Paul asked me, "You're thirteen now, aren't you?"

"Yes," I answered with a chill dancing up and down my backbone about what was coming next.

"Then you should become a woman," Paul continued.

"You're going to do this for me?" I sassed right back.

Paul blinked and glanced sideways at me. "Yes, I am. Today, up in the woods."

"I kind of figured it," said I, my chin sticking out and my shoulders high. My breakfast oatmeal stood high in my stomach and threatened to come roiling out.

"Good, then it's settled," Paul muttered and kept on striding, me stumbling along behind.

I wasn't a stupid girl. My mammy had talked to me about making babies two or three years ago. Besides, we lived in a tiny one-room cabin that wasn't much. The roof was shake and the walls plank with a mud mixture shoved in between the cracks. Other than that we had a fireplace with a stick-and-mud chimney, some wooden stools and a table, and homemade beds nailed to the wall, with rope springs and corn-husk mattresses. "I was right there," I liked to brag to Samboy, "to see you born, coming out all red and squeezed between Mammy's legs."

There was plenty of other plain evidence of where babies come from. I saw pigs do it and later have piglets, and cows do it and later have calves, and so on. I knew Becky and her man, Eurias, did something real regular because at one time they had fourteen children, though only eight were alive now.

Of course, I lacked particulars. Even though I could hear Mammy and Pappy moving around and moaning sometimes at night when they thought I was asleep, I didn't know exactly what they did. A couple of times I even hung my head down from my bunk—I had the top one because Samboy worried about falling out—but I couldn't see anything. There was no window in that cabin to let in the moonlight.

I did better with young Tate—a handsome, strutting buck—who fooled around with every slave gal he could get near.

"Let's follow Tate behind the barn tonight," Samboy suggested one moonlit harvest night.

"All right. I'll go along," I said, not wanting to look a coward. When me and Samboy snuck up on young Tate, we saw him heaving and panting over some gal he had pinned to the ground.

So, that Tuesday morning I pretty much knew what I had in store for me. I was happy I'd escaped it as long as I had. I'd never forgiven Paul for what he had done to Dog, but, at the same time, I knew I had no one to protect me. Old John and Nellie had given me to Paul. As Paul often reminded me, I belonged to him. Besides, old John seldom, if ever, curbed Paul.

Paul didn't make it any easier on me, or on himself either.

"Follow me," he ordered.

He pulled back his bony shoulders and marched into the woods like he was Satan leading the way straight to Hell. When I hung back, trying to scrape the nettles off the hem of my dress, he caught my hand and yanked me on toward a huge old weeping willow tree.

"We're there now," he said.

Paul parted the willow boughs like a curtain and dragged me through. "You been here before?" I asked.

"What do you think?" he said as he pointed to a small cache near the willow's trunk.

I spotted a blanket or two, a pillow, a comb and mirror, and what looked like a sack of clean underwear. "You mean you've been here with another gal?" I asked, my eyes round and unbelieving.

"No, I've got better places to take girls of my own kind. I fixed this especially for you—and me."

"I appreciate your trouble," I began, "but I don't think I'm ready for—"

Paul's lean hand shot straight out, grabbed the neckline of my dress, and tore a strip out of it right down the front. I clutched the piece in place and headed for the hanging willow boughs. "This ain't a good day for me," said I.

This time Paul caught me by the back of my dress, causing the damaged front to give way and the whole thing to depart from my body.

So there I stood naked, except for a pair of drawers made from the same material they used to make cotton-picking sacks. Paul also ripped off the drawers, pulling with his talon-like fingers from the waist down.

He stood in front of me like a prizefighter and began undoing his belt. "So you think this is a bad day, huh?" he asked.

I folded my broad hands across the few strands of pubic hair I had managed to grow and nodded. "It's a real bad day."

Paul's hand blasted out again, this time aimed at my face. I felt the sting of his blow even before I knew his fist had connected with my jaw. Paul's jab caused me to bite my tongue. I spit blood on the ground near his feet, but, thank goodness, no teeth with it.

"It's going to be a worse day if you don't stop your whining and resisting," Paul hissed. "Remember, I own you and I—"

"—can do anything you want with me," I finished for him.

Wham, his hand jinged out again and left me with a bloody nose. I couldn't see why he would want to mess with a girl with blood oozing from various parts of her face, but I figured he didn't plan on doing much more with my face anyway.

I was right; Paul got right down to business. He spread a blanket and pointed to it and said "Lay," so I laid. When he got the rest of his clothes off, he plopped down beside me. He fooled a minute with my breasts, which had grown near to nothing since the last time he tried when I was eleven. He gave that up and stuck his fingers up me instead.

"Quit wiggling and turning," he said.

Then he rolled over on top me—like me and Samboy saw young Tate do that night—and rooted around awhile, just like I'd seen male hogs do. Next thing I knew, it was over. Now I bled from three places.

Paul rolled off me and rested on his back for a second or two. Then he leapt up and started to get dressed. "Clean yourself up and get home," he ordered me. "From now on, when I say 'meet me at the willow,' you hightail it up here and take your clothes off and get down on that blanket."

I felt sassy because I had lived through the ugly ordeal and because Paul seemed considerably spent. I sat upright and stared at Paul mean and hard. "Oh, yeah?" said I. "I've got work to do. How'll you explain to your ma when my kitchen work isn't done?"

Paul sank down on the blanket next to me and his narrow shoulders slumped. "Ma could be a sticking point, that's for sure. How about if you just work a little harder and faster."

"What you'll give me if I do?" I bargained.

That turned him nasty. "I'll give you another bloody nose if you don't," he said.

"Don't you think your ma will object if I'm beat up all the time and can't do my work because of it?"

Paul turned thoughtful and his forehead furrowed just like his daddy's fields. "What do you want? I haven't got much."

That's for certain, I thought to myself. My mind plotted ways I might gain something from all this. Out loud I said, "I don't want much. Bring me an old newspaper or a book borrowed from your daddy's library."

Paul let out one big sigh of relief. "Done," he said and fled through the willow curtain.

I sat there for a minute with my head resting on my bent knees. "Mammy," I murmured. "Now I knows."

I seemed unable to cry, which is what I almost always do in times of bad trouble. Instead, I pictured the weeping willow shedding its tears for what Paul had just done to me. I thought a bit about drowning Paul in the nearby stream, or maybe complaining to Nellie or the girls, but I already knew that it was useless to resist. I thought to myself that even Nellie would probably take Paul's side.

Pretty soon, I pulled myself together and used my ripped-up drawers to clean up the blood and other mess Paul had left behind. I noticed I smelled funny, like young Tate reeked sometimes. I put on my torn dress and wrapped the blanket around my wide shoulders like a shawl. Then I squared my shoulders and straightened my back. I arched my neck and held my head high.

It ain't as bad as it could be, I told myself. At least Paul gets it over with quick. No matter what anyone says, he's going to use me the way he wants, so if I can get a newspaper or book out of it I'll have something. It won't be near enough, but at least it will be something.

chapter two

At this point in my recollecting as I lay by our cabin door, I tried to throw off my memories. They were too galling; I still hurt in my heart as I did on the day Paul first took me to the willow. Yet somehow I felt I had to recall everything that had happened over the years.

"Memories," I told myself. "It's the best way to get up steam for the trip ahead." I stared at the moon and pulled from the reaches of my mind what had happened next.

After Paul left me, I hurried back to the cabin, grabbed my only other dress off its wooden peg on the wall, and threw the dress on. I shoved the torn, bloody dress and the blanket under Samboy's bunk. I washed my face and put a thin layer of black mud over my bruises to hide them. Even though I knew I'd have to tell Mammy, I wanted to wait for the best time.

What I wanted flew right out the door when Mammy walked in. She took one look at me and said, "Child, you had a bad day for yourself." She plopped down on a wooden stool by the table and said, "I'm waitin' for particulars."

Mammy was not a fearsome woman. She was short and soft all over; not fat, just curved and rounded. She was a gold-brown, like tree leaves in the fall, and her mouth nearly always smiled. Her wide brown eyes darted around and she didn't miss much of anything. But she could also fix her eyes on just one thing, and that's what she did now, the one thing being me.

I went to Samboy's bunk and squatted on the floor and pulled the wadded dress and blanket out. I knelt in front of Mammy and spread the mess out on the dirt floor at her bare feet. Then I gazed at Mammy expectantly, waiting to see if she was as smart as I thought.

"Child, child," she shook her head, "Paul got you at last." Her brown fingers clasped and unclasped in her lap.

I nodded my head and a silver tear slid down each bruised cheek from my sorrowful eyes. "I made him promise to bring me a newspaper or a book, so it's not a life-or-death tragedy," I said, with pluck I didn't feel. Paul had hurt Dog and now me. I didn't want what he did to me under the willow to hurt Mammy any more than it had to.

Her eyes turned to fire in the dusky cabin light. "You want to have his bastard baby?"

I hadn't thought about any baby. I hadn't even gotten my women's monthlies yet. "No, I surely don't," I shook my head at her. Fear goose-pimpled its way across the flesh of my arms and shoulders.

"That bein' the case," she said in a harsh voice, "we're goin' to get over to Aggie, the doctor woman two plantations down—and we're goin' to get there good and fast."

In matters of importance, Mammy always acted swiftly, but in this instance she moved more speedily than usual. After making faces at Pappy all through dinner, she lit out for the big house after the meal and left us to clean up by ourselves. Samboy and Pappy were both good workers, whether it was in the cabin or in the fields. Although they were both black like me, they stood tall and muscular, with taut faces and stubborn, hard heads to match. Of course, Samboy wasn't near as big as Pappy and he was a bit awkward yet, all legs and arms. Pappy said that Samboy was like a puppy with big paws, that Samboy had to grow into his hands and feet and then he would really be something.

On that night, the three of us worked away together. Although the smoke from the cooking fire hung in the cabin and made it smell musty, I could also catch a whiff of the greasy leavings on the plates. I was sniffing and woolgathering when Pappy broke in.

"So," Pappy said, "you've got yourself a problem, Missie Samgirl."

I spun around, shaking and startled. I saw that Pappy's eyes shone dark and kind in the dimness. He was trying not to make too much of my dilemma. His mood calmed me a bit. Still, I was surprised. I didn't know Pappy could learn all that just from Mammy's twitchings and frownings. I saw in his wise, mahogany eyes that he knew, all right.

"I've got a problem, but I'm doing the best with it I can, Pappy." Even though I forced a smile onto my lips, it didn't reach my eyes.

At that moment, Samboy piped up, "What problem? How come no one ever tells me anything?" His face looked like a nosy little coon's, his eyes bright and seeking.

"Because you're only nine," said I and play-banged Mammy's old iron pot on that child's curly head.

Samboy pouted and acted insulted. He refused to talk to me. Pappy had already said what he had to say, so we finished the rest of the chores in fast time. We spoke not another word about the matter until Mammy popped in through the wood-framed door.

Mammy smelled of the night air and her sienna skin glistened with sweat. She stared right at me and said, "We're goin' to see Aggie this coming Sunday, right after Missus Nellie gets done givin' out the rations. I got us a pass from Marse to cross the roads between here and two plantations down."

"Chloe," Pappy asked in a low-down voice, "what did you tell old John?"

Mammy's eyes turned cagey and she grinned. "I told old John I think I'm pregnant. Since he sold away our midwife last month, I've got to see Aggie fast. Old John patted my back and smiled, thinkin' about that free baby I might make for him. He handed me a pass and said take all the time you need. Yes sirree, take all the time you need, he said."

Pappy burst out laughing. "What a lie to tell," he said, "when you're really goin' to the doctor woman to stop a free baby from comin' to this farm."

I started to laugh too, thinking on what we were about to put over on old John, young Paul, and all slave owners who want black women to make more slaves at no cost to them.

Samboy seemed addled. "I don't know why you're all laughin'. How come no one ever tells me anything?"

"Because you're only nine," Mammy said as she landed a loving swat on that child's backside. Even though Samboy was more curious than put out, he still refused to say any more about anything for the rest of the evening.

Sunday was slow in coming. When it finally arrived, Pappy and Samboy lined up in front of the big house to get our rations. Except for special rations-givings, only a few people from each family went to the big house. The rest stayed in the quarters to do personal chores, like washing their clothes or cooking up food for the week to come. This particular Sunday, me and Mammy stayed behind to make preparations for our outing.

The way most Sundays went, old John and Nellie parceled out the slaves' supplies from the porch of the big house. They came out not yet dressed in their Sunday clothes. Usually a pair of overalls hung on old John's bones, while Missus Nellie always wore a plain, cotton dress of checks or plaids with a sturdy white apron over it. Being that Nellie was kind of plump, on windy days she looked like a boat about to sail off to sea. But her eyes were always gentle and her hands worked fast giving out such victuals as coarse flour, a measure of corn for cornmeal and hominy, fatback bacon, potatoes, rice, molasses, beans, peas, and milk.

"Take a little more," Nellie would say. "You've got lots of work to do. And a mean Mississippi sun to do it under."

Sometimes we also got a little pork. We had to make our rations last for a week, adding to them what we grew in our vegetable patch—such as okra or cabbage or squash—and the rabbit or coon Pappy might have time to bag. Twice a year, we received some tow to make clothes, a pair of homemade moccasins each, and some cheap shoes for the men.

"Thank you, Missus," we'd always tell Nellie, although we wished her handouts were even more generous.

Afterwards, old John and Nellie and their children went inside the big house, where they dressed up in their Sunday best and held a Sunday service. Sometimes they traveled to a neighboring plantation where a real preacher came to minister to them all. A huge dinner always followed, whether they were at home or away, so that some slave cooks and table servers somewhere had to work part of each Sunday.

This Sunday after rations-giving, Pappy took Samboy with him to hoe our vegetable patch. Mammy whipped out the pass Marse had given her. "Come on, Samgirl," she said. "It's time."

Off we went up the dirt road, as proud and sassy as two white women walking in the sun and breathing in the clean-smelling country air. Dog followed a couple of paces behind, his head down just the way it'd been ever since he lost his second ear. I swear that dog felt ashamed of his sad looks.

Mammy waved her pass in front of her, just waiting for a slave patrol to stop her. Then she'd tell them good. But we got two plantations down without even seeing a white man.

Things turned a bit more muddled when we tried to find Aggie. "Aggie's delivering a baby," a woman who looked like a dwarf told us. "You go over there. Sit and wait for Aggie. She'll be along soon."

Mammy plunked down on a stump outside Aggie's door, spread her legs so that her skirt made a tent, and smiled to let all in the vicinity know she was open for the gossip business.

We didn't have long to wait. A young, brownish gal about my age sidled up and took my hand, pulling me off to join the other youngsters. "Come and play."

Hard on her heels came her mammy and grandmammy, along with an aunt and cousin or two, all feverish to find out what my mammy knew that they didn't. Soon the buzz of conversation outdid the bees in the flowers and the flies on the garbage.

From where I sat under a tree, half-listening to Polly, I watched the knot of women. When I heard them laugh out loud, I knew Mammy had told them how she'd fooled Master about the pass to come see Aggie and how she hoped Aggie would help us fool Mister Paul. "I can't play," I told Polly. "I'm too, um, old."

Polly smirked in my face, her chubby cheeks shining and her mouth sarcastic. "You don't look too old to play. You is just scared of strangers, that's all."

I backed away from Polly and the others. I hid behind an oak tree, all the time watching Mammy and the other women.

Eventually Aggie came striding through the crowd, her fat face still perspiring with the sweat of bringing a child into a world of anguish and pain. "Let me through," Aggie grunted as she pushed her bulk against first this one and then that one. "Surely someone's gone and died while I was away."

I saw Mammy stand right up and offer Aggie the piece of fatback she'd tied in the corner of her apron that morning before we left. To my surprise, Mammy and Aggie seemed to know each other. They slapped each other on the back and rubbed cheeks. "How you been, Chloe?" Aggie boomed out in the humid, heavy air no longer lightened by voices.

Pretty soon Mammy called to me. Aggie sized me up and down as I walked toward her and I wished the thing with Paul had never happened. I saw that Aggie's eyes seemed kindly—even sympathetic—so I girded my loins and turned myself over to her hands. "How do you do, Aggie?" I said in my best company voice.

Me and Mammy followed Aggie into her dark cabin. Herbs hung drying from the ceiling and the place smelled like a field in springtime. Aggie sat me and Mammy on a wooden bench and then went about making her preparations. "This is goin' to take awhile."

Aggie tied a bright red kerchief over her thinning hair and put some strings of greenish beads around her plump neck. Those beads jumped all over Aggie's huge bosom as she worked.

That hot afternoon Aggie burned a candle, moaned some chants in a rough, low-down voice, then burned another candle. "Ah-who, ah-wha," was all I could remember.

At the end, Aggie showed Mammy how to mix and brew these special herbs of hers. We finally left, Mammy carrying a package of herbs in her hand and me sucking on a molasses candy stick.

I headed toward the road, but Mammy pushed me toward the trees behind the quarters. "If I remember right," she said, "there's a path along the river that leads us back home."

"But, Mammy," said I, "what about the pass? We got the right to use the road." I had looked forward to strutting along that road as bright as brass.

Mammy had her own ideas. "Hush, child," she said. "You've got to come to Aggie's every few weeks to get more herbs, so you better be learnin' this secret path."

We found the trail, a nasty thread of gumbo mud with tree branches and Spanish moss waving over the top. Even though it was still afternoon, that old path was dark and dank. The air hung thick and heavy and mouldy smelling.

Dog sloshed along, his bony hips swaying back-and-forth, back-and-forth, while I thought of asking Mammy again about the pass and the road. I forgot that when another idea struck into my brain like a lightning bolt through the middle of that heavy air.

"Mammy," said I, jumping around with excitement, "you know this path because you've been coming to Aggie's for herbs yourself. That's why you only have me and Samboy."

In the half-light I saw Mammy's face go rigid and stubborn, not like my Mammy at all, but like some creature of the swamp, half woman and half monster. When she finally spoke, her voice hissed out of her lips: "There's more than you and Samboy, child. Before old John bought me, I belonged to a mean man named Lamar Quimby Camp. When I was your age, he told me to go keep house for Rufus. That Rufus was a bully and I didn't like him. When he tried to get in the bunk with me I knocked him back out with my feet and threatened him with my sewing scissors. Then Missus Camp said she expected me to have portly children with Rufus. So you have a half brother, Albert. He was such a troublemaker that Marse Camp sold him away somewhere. As I watched him go down the lane I cried the whole time. I've never seen Albert since. And you had a half-sister named Adeline that died of the cholera when she was a baby. I guess my children weren't portly enough for Marse Camp because he sold me to old John."

Tears jumped to my eyes at the thought of Mammy's pain. The tears spilled over when I realized I had a brother and sister I would never know and that Mammy had kept them secret so long. "How come you never told me about them?" I asked in a low, sorrowful voice filled with accusation.

"I was waitin' till the right time came and it came this very hour." Mammy kept going on the sticky path, unwilling to accept the guilt I was trying to dump on her shoulders.

I pondered Mammy for a few minutes, still trying to keep up with her and Dog. Gradually, Mammy's toughness braced my mind and I started thinking more clearly. "So that's why you decided you didn't want any more babies, because you lost Albert and Adeline."

"That's right," she said, spitting her words now instead of hissing them. "After old John bought me, I met your pappy. I'm older than your pappy. I don't know the year I was born, and he doesn't either, but I know I'm older. We had you and then Samboy. Even though we love you, me and your pappy didn't want to bring no more children into a slave world. After I had Samboy, I got in the family way one more time. Aggie took the seed of a child right out of my body, then she fixed me good. I'm never goin' to have more children. But you, you're different. You might want to have babies someday so we got to trust to Aggie's herbs. Lots of folks disbelieve Aggie's medicine, but, God willin', it'll work for you."

"Humph," said I back, "I'm agreeable to trusting Aggie. Being you're such good friends with Becky, you should tell her about Aggie."

Mammy's round face softened. "Becky is older than me. She had most of her babies before I knew her. Her master gave her a new dress and extra rations for every baby. Besides, Becky don't believe in Aggie. She calls her a witch woman."

"I believe in Aggie," said I. "After all, she's the only thing I have between a flat belly and bearing Paul's bastard baby."

We spoke not another word, just huffed and puffed our way across that path, tangled as it was with vines and undergrowth. We got back just in time for the Sunday evening service that old John and Nellie always held for their slaves. This week they had the visiting preacher at their place. He came out on the porch of the big house to read from the

Bible and give us a sermon. He was a scraggly looking man with grey hair flowing over his collar. That was probably a good thing—from the looks of him, his collar was probably none too clean and at least his lank hair hid it from view.

Despite his high, whining voice, all the slaves from the quarters swayed with his preaching and said "hallelujah" now and again. But then he shouted, "I take my text, which is: Nigger, obey your master and mistress because what you get from them in this world is all you'll ever receive. You're just like the hogs and other animals; when you die you aren't no more, after you've been buried in that swamp hole," and the slaves rustled and whispered.

Sudie, the oldest slave in our quarters, saved the situation. She piped up and covered the rustling by hollering, "Praise the Lord."

Meanwhile, I thought about Mammy and our trip to see Aggie and how we intended to fool our master and mistress. Even though I knew the preacher would blame me for doing it, I couldn't seem to muster up any guilt.

After that, we did some singing and more praying. Twilight had dropped down when the preacher finally limped back into the big house. We fell into a loose formation, like a gaggle of geese going back to the pond. We shuffled back to the quarters singing low:

> I heard the voice of Jesus callin'
> Come unto me and live
> Lie, lie down, weepin' one
> Rest thy head on my breast.
>
> I came to Jesus as I was
> Weary and lone and tired and sad,
> I found in him a restin' place,
> And he has made me glad.

In my mind, I wondered about the two-faced preacher who talked about Jesus's love, yet supported slavery. I knew some folks said slavery existed in the Bible, but Jesus also taught that we should treat other humans as we treat ourselves. "I would never treat anyone to slavery," I muttered under my breath. "Not even Paul, as horrid as he can be."

I also wondered about when Jesus might come to earth to set us free. I didn't have too much hope for that in the near future. I concluded I'd have to take a mighty hand in my own freeing. Mostly I was just relieved to hurry home and eat supper and get some sleep before another work week began.

During the next few weeks, the whole business of getting to be a woman brought more trouble and excitement than I was ready for. I hardly counted the time under the willow tree with Paul. In my mind, I'd made Paul into a flyspeck on a wall, and I kept my loathing of him in a separate part of my brain. "I don't want to poison myself with the venom of hate," I told myself, "but I want it there, ready and waiting, in case I need it for one reason or another—such as running away."

I found it much more interesting that I had older siblings I had never heard of. It was downright stirring to find out that Mammy and Pappy had fought slavery in their own way, by having Aggie fix Mammy and by buying me a handful of magic herbs that would keep me from producing any slave babies.

I thought about Mammy's resistance to having any more slave babies for a long, long time before I broached the subject to her. One Sunday afternoon we were alone in the cabin, the men having gone again to work in the vegetable patch.

"Mammy," I began, my chest swelled with determination, "I have to talk to you about something important."

To my horror, Mammy sank down on the hearthstone and buried her head in her apron, moaning, "No, no, no." When I realized she thought I was going to tell her Aggie's herbs hadn't worked, I threw my arms around her shoulders and murmured, "Mammy, it's not that. I'm not with child. It's something even more important."

That brought all five feet of Mammy right back up into a standing position, curiosity lighting her eyes and making them shine in the dusky cabin.

"You and Pappy fought slavery," I started out, "by refusing to have any more babies. But did you ever think," and I dropped my voice to a whisper, "about running away?"

"Child, child," she shook her head and muttered, "what's on your mind?" She let her eyes pierce right into the innards of my very soul.

I trembled and quaked yet I stood tall and answered, "I'm going to be free someday, that's what."

Tears rose up in Mammy's eyes and splashed over on her cheeks. "Your pappy tried to run away once when he was young. That's how he got that cobweb of scars on his back that he don't ever talk about. Albert tried to run away again and again, though he wasn't very old. That's what convinced Marse Camp to sell Albert. Me, I never thought about runnin' away since I met your Pappy and had you and Samboy, which tied me here for good."

Mammy spread her splayed, bare feet wider apart on the ocher and black hearthstone. She put one hand on each hip. The flames of the fire jumped behind her, making her look like a witch woman herself, and turning the cabin smoky and rank. She peered square into my eyes and said, "I'll tell you straight, child. If you were ever to run away from your family, it'd break my heart. I'd lay down in the straw on my bed and never get up again."

My eyes bugged out. I backed away from Mammy a few steps. I'd never heard her make that strong a speech or look that savage. "Yes, Mammy," I gasped before I turned and ran from the cabin.

After that, I thought a lot about running away. I realized that Mammy was right; family was all I had. For most slaves, family was the core of life itself. We didn't have a school or any church to speak of. We didn't have dances and shouts. We didn't even have much ceremony for weddings, births, and deaths. And we certainly didn't have jobs we had chosen and liked. I decided I'd better stick with Mammy and Pappy and Samboy, at least until I was grown.

Dog too was important to me, although he was probably getting old. We didn't know when he was born and he'd acted old since Paul had swiped his ear, so there was no way of telling his true age.

That thought led me back around to Paul. Even though he was a liar and a scoundrel in most matters, he kept his bargain and always brought me a few pages of the Mississippi *Constitution* or parts of an old magazine.

"Thank you, Marse Paul," I would say.

I acted so pathetically grateful for whatever he gave me that he sometimes threw in a piece of licorice or a scrap of dress goods. I guess he figured it was a small price for my silence and easier than bruising my face. I didn't once think he used the papers and gifts to salve his conscience, because I didn't believe for one instant that he had a conscience. He just didn't want old John to learn about his misdeeds. Not that old John would do anything about it.

I didn't like the idea of trading my body for bits and pieces, but I reminded myself that Paul would make me come to the willow tree anyway, and getting something was better than getting nothing. "At least," I often told myself, "as a lover Paul is swift."

He stayed pretty much on the same level he began on. As my breasts grew, he sometimes spent a few seconds on them, but I bet the whole thing didn't take eight minutes from the time my backside hit that blanket to the moment he jumped up to get dressed.

Too, Paul only bothered me once a month or so. I chalked that up to my demand for presents. Even someone as sneaky as Paul must have found it difficult to get away from the house without anybody noticing the booty he carried.

As time passed, Paul turned a little gruff about my failure to get pregnant. For one thing, he thought if he could tell old John a free baby was on the way, old John would not only excuse Paul's treatment of me, but would also praise Paul for making a future slave. Old John had been mighty disappointed when Mammy reported that she had miscarried her "baby," and he was always happy to see one of his slave women in the family way.

Gradually, Paul turned downright nasty that I didn't produce anything from his fine seed. Paul frequently grumbled, "You've always been an obstinate bitch."

I finally convinced him I couldn't block a pregnancy with just my mind. Of course, I never mentioned Aggie's herbs. Eventually, Paul wiped the matter from his thoughts. "Samgirl," he told me one day, after a six-minute interlude under the willow, "I doubt you'll ever bear my child because you're obviously as barren as the Sahara Desert." He held his head high and poked his nose into the air. "I'll breed, and breed nobly, when I couple with finer stock."

"Whatever you say, Paul," I replied, a wide smile on my lips and a simple look in my dark eyes. Mammy taught me that. "Look dumb," she said, "like you don't understand and they'll leave you alone." She told me she'd used that look to get out of plenty of hard jobs.

I wasn't about to let Paul aggravate me into telling about Aggie's secret herbs, so I gave him one of Mammy's simple-minded looks. "I'm sure those gals of your own class will appreciate you more than I know how," I added for good measure.

Paul shot me a sharp glance. Apparently, he decided I was too mindless to know how to insult him. Pity his poor wife, I thought, when and if he gets one. The eight-minute marvel will have the poor woman pregnant before she knows it, unless she has her own version of Aggie's herbs.

Actually, I spent too much time and energy on my own doings to waste much time worrying about Paul or his petty insults. First of all, there were the newspapers he brought me. I remembered from our schoolhouse days that Paul had never been much of a reader or a thinker. In school, Paul did as much work as the teacher forced him to and no more. Because he had never formed the habit of reading newspapers and magazines, he didn't have a hint of the treasures he put into my waiting hands.

You can believe me when I say I nearly fell over with shock to find out that some white South Carolina women named Grimké had run away from home and had gone to Philadelphia where they joined folks called Quakers in fighting slavery. "I had no idea," I mused out loud, "that any white people, especially from the South, objected to slavery." Yet these sisters, who went by the names of Angelina and Sarah, traveled around writing and speaking against what they called the "evils" of slavery.

I could tell the Grimké sisters a few things about the evils of slavery, I thought. I pictured Paul and the willow tree at the back of my mind. I thought too about Mammy getting herself fixed so she couldn't bring any more slave children into the world. I envisioned Samboy as he followed Pappy off to the fields every morning as dawn was breaking over the hills. And I remembered Dog dragging around the quarters with no ears.

I kept on reading and wasn't surprised to learn that the state of South Carolina had burned Angelina's pamphlets and put an order out for the sisters' arrest should they ever return home. I finally checked the date to see how long this had been going on. "This is old news," I spat out. The year on the paper was 1839; it was now 1844. "That scamp Paul must have stolen the newspapers lining his dresser drawers to give to me."

After that, I kept better track of Paul and made him bring me fresh papers. I must have put an added burden on Paul, who now had to pretend an interest in his Daddy's reading matter so he could get part of it before it went to the kitchen for shelf-lining or garbage-wrapping or fire-starting. I know Paul still didn't read the papers before he gave them to me, for he never would have let news like that fall into a slave's hands.

I read about a fire-eating abolitionist named William Lloyd Garrison and his journal, *The Liberator*, and about the American Anti-Slavery Society, and World Anti-Slavery conventions. My favorite thing was reading about the white and free black women in Philadelphia and Boston who fought slavery. Of course, the editor of the *Constitution* thought they were awful women and only wrote about them to warn Mississippians of what he called the "terrible perils" growing day by day in the North. I was tickled as could be that those abolitionist women frightened the editor, because the more upset he became, the more he wrote exactly the news I wanted to read.

Pretty soon the editor started printing accounts of what he called slave insurrections. I guess he intended to get slave-owning Mississippians good and scared so they would watch their slaves carefully and enforce all the rules governing slaves. Anyway, imagine my astonishment when I discovered that a Mississippi slave down in the Yazoo-Mississippi delta had run away and hid in the woods until nighttime—then she returned and set everything from the big house to the ginning shed on fire. In my eyes, it was a minor detail that the authorities had caught and hanged the woman. "Surely," I told myself, "if a smart slave could keep from getting caught, she might do a good deal for the abolitionist movement up north."

I also learned some discouraging things. I came across a notice warning all free blacks to carry their passes at all times. That sure threw a crimp into my thinking. "I didn't know free blacks had to have special passes," I muttered several times each day. "I thought they just walked around as they pleased."

This knowledge caused a near-crisis for me. "How am I supposed to get freedom and a pass, too?" I asked myself. Obviously, the thing I was scheming demanded long-term planning.

I also discovered that the Cherokee and Choctaw and Chickasaw people frequently went west and carried their slaves off with them. If the local government there didn't like slavery, folks who took slaves to the West simply called them indentured servants. Even if western states opposed slavery, that didn't mean they would let whites and blacks get together and do things like get married. Why, Iowa had already passed a special law against that.

I looked up the name of that law in Paul's daddy's dictionary. It was a dusty, dirty, decrepit volume that Paul had obviously rescued from the trash bin and brought to me as payment for his monthly pleasure. I hid that book under Samboy's bunk, and whenever I could, I pored over it like the Bible.

This time I looked up *miscegenation.* I mouthed out the words: "marriage or interbreeding between people of different races." Antimiscegenation laws were supposed to put a halt to such goings-on. I figured what Paul did to me under the willow tree fit the interbreeding part. I couldn't see how anyone could ever stop white men from doing that to the black women they owned. People being what they were, and sex being what it was, I didn't believe any legal mumbo-jumbo could bring interbreeding to a standstill.

I pondered everything I read, balancing the good and the bad and forming a conclusion. "All in all," I thought, "slavery has pretty well spread over most of the country in one form or another, and the abolitionists make more noise than progress."

I tried to look on the hopeful side of all this. I was glad that someone objected to slavery, but I wasn't about to sit around waiting for freedom to come to me. "I will," I vowed, "seize it for myself."

chapter three

Paul didn't seem to know it was against the law to give such things to slaves. I knew, so I kept my scraps of newspapers and magazines well hidden.

My trips over the slave trail to see Aggie were supposed to be secret as well, but my visits there opened such a whole new world to me that I couldn't help but talk about it, at least in the quarters. "I've got some gossip," I would say, in words and tones mimicking Mammy's.

Now that I look back, I know Aggie's world was a limited one, but at the time, it was vaster and richer than anything I'd ever known.

From the time of Mammy's and my first trip to Aggie when I was thirteen, I went regular to Aggie's every month. Mammy and I tallied the days on the cabin wall by the fireplace so I wouldn't miss. Mammy couldn't count any higher than the five cuts she had to spin when she worked in the loom room, but she always came up with the piece of charcoal for me to do the marking. "Fourth week coming, Mammy," I'd tell her.

That Saturday evening, I'd slip out of our cabin about dusk. Mammy and Pappy and Samboy would sit down to supper just like always, knowing that no one from either the quarters or the big house would bother them during Saturday supper. Just in case, they rolled a blanket in my top bunk and put another over it so they could say I was in bed sick in case anyone asked.

No one ever did. I slid across that swamp as neat as you please, eating the piece of cornbread Mammy had tucked in my pocket. When I reached Aggie's she sat me down to eat at her scarred wooden table. Of course, I always brought a gift from Mammy and a little something else as payment for the herbs.

Best of all from Aggie's point of view, I brought news from our plantation right to her cabin. "Sit yourself down, Samgirl," she would say, "and tell me what you know."

Aggie never let anyone else in the cabin while me and Aggie and her wizened mother ate supper. Aggie wanted exclusive rights to my news so she could hold forth later to the other slaves in her quarters.

That was fine with me. Aggie was a good cook and a generous woman who could whip up a Saturday night supper out of almost nothing. "Sure is a good meal," I'd assure her.

Most times, though, Aggie didn't have to cook from nothing, because her midwifing and doctoring business brought her in everything from greens to possum, squirrel, and catfish. I could catch the odor of dinner cooking before I even got out of the swamp. Although I never told Mammy, Aggie's suppers outdid even hers.

Aggie's old, wrinkled mammy never talked during supper. Come to think of it, I never heard that woman speak during any of my visits there. She seemed to communicate with her eyes, which sparkled or dulled or closed entirely depending on the topic under consideration. She took part in each conversation and revealed every emotion anyone could imagine without saying a single word.

In between stuffing my mouth with everything on Aggie's table, and sniffing to see what else she had cooking, I'd talk enough to make up for Aggie's mammy and two more. "You want to hear about the newest baby?" I'd ask Aggie. Or, "This week someone got married. Want to know about it?"

On our plantation, we used a strange marriage ritual that blended Indian and African ways with Christian customs. Afterward, old John would write the names of the couple in his leather-bound book and slam it shut. He'd say, "Now that's done and I don't want to hear anymore about it," and stomp off for the big house.

Or I might tell Aggie and her mammy about who had died and how the corpse had been helped on its way to heaven by the chants—sometimes low and mournful, other times lilting and lifting—that the folks in our quarters sang for the dead. "We crooned all night," I said. "In the morning, the men wrapped the body in whatever rags the women could spare, along with an old picking or ginning sack."

Aggie and her mammy would wait for me to go on, their eyes fastened on my face so they didn't miss a word. "We all marched to the swamp with some of the men carrying the corpse on their shoulders."

Of course, we'd go in just a short ways because most slaves feared the swamp. Some of the men would then dig a pit in the oozy ground. We'd put the body in and the men would cover it with elm bark.

"Then we each walked by real slow and careful and threw a wildflower in on top. The men spaded muck over the body and we all headed back to the quarters."

Sometimes after such a ceremony we'd eat and drink, but most times it was a workday, so everybody would go right to the fields or the big house or wherever. After all, it was only another slave life gone, to be sucked right down into that swamp. Slave owners only seemed to care that there was one less hand to do the work, but we did the best we could to mark that soul's crossing from this world to the next.

Of all my stories, the ones Aggie and her ancient mammy liked best were those about sassy slaves. Being that old John and Nellie had a small plantation as those things went, they only kept between forty and fifty slaves. Out of those forty or fifty, a number were always up to devilment. When I told Aggie how Mammy saw a table servant put some lime juice in the lemonade before he took it to table, Aggie and her mammy about exhausted themselves laughing.

"The folks in the big house had company that evening," I explained, "so nobody wanted to say anything tasted bad. They tried to drink that lemonade but their noses twitched and their faces twisted up like persimmons and they put their glasses back down. Finally, Nellie saved the situation. She said, 'I think we'll have our coffee now, Nero,' and off he went to get the coffee and tell the kitchen slaves what he had done. Everybody laughed except Cook, who worried she'd get blamed.'"

Granny didn't say anything to this, but Aggie chirped up right away, "Is that Nero fella married?"

Aggie was always looking for a husband to take some of the load from her shoulders. She liked a man with some punch to him. Aggie never had a man that I knew about, but in those days there were lots of things I didn't know. Mammy told me Aggie got away with things other slaves couldn't—like living alone with her mammy—because of her ability at doctoring and midwifing. Aggie even delivered white babies and doctored white folks, although any pay she received went right into her master's pocket.

I knew slaves could hitch up with someone on a neighboring plantation, as long as the owners went along with it and the woman's cabin could accommodate the man on his Saturday night visits. Although Aggie's cabin had enough room, it wasn't Nero she'd be accommodating. "Nero already has a family," said I, "but I'll keep watching out for a man for you, Aggie."

Another time I told them about a slave gal named Cordelia on our plantation. Cordelia stole the sheets from the guest bed. Although Cordelia wasn't working that day in the big house, she had to go there for an errand. On her way out, Cordelia saw the sheets lying all alone in the downstairs hallway. She grabbed them and wrapped them around her body under her loose dress and scampered back to the quarters.

"Missus Nellie went looking and looking," I told Aggie and her mammy, "but she couldn't find the sheets. While Nellie looked, Cordelia snuck into the quarters and stuffed the sheets into a cooking pot. Then she started a fire going; pretty soon the water boiled. She threw in some ground hickory shell and some live oak bark and pulled the sheets out with a wooden stick. They had turned a nice dull brown, but that wasn't good enough for Cordelia."

I took a deep breath and went on. "Cordelia set to winding and twisting them, then dunked them in another kind of dye she made from dandelions or something. When she untied the sheets, they showed brown and yellow side-by-side in curving and curling patterns. After they dried, Cordelia cut them up and made dresses with them."

"That Cordelia," I said. "Even she wouldn't dare to wear those dresses in front of Nellie, who might recognize her own sheets despite the brown and gold dye. So Cordelia used them to trade."

In fact, Cordelia sent one of those dresses over the slave trail with me to repay Aggie for some doctoring Aggie had done a few weeks back. At first I felt like a thief, then I held my head up proud that Cordelia had been so clever in the face of want.

You see, we never received any money for our work, only our cabins, our vegetable patches, and our Sunday morning rations. We had no money to buy extras or even things we needed, like doctoring, which old John wasn't supplying since he sold the midwife. If we wanted extras, we had to furnish them ourselves and that's just what Cordelia had done.

In our own quarters, I never told anyone outside our family about the herbs. I simply said, "I have to go see Aggie whenever I feel sort of sickly—which is plenty often."

I had no gal about my age in our quarters to confide in and I never found an auntie among the older women. I'm sure Mammy told Becky, but Becky was close-mouthed about personal sorts of things. Besides, Becky didn't have much faith in Aggie. "One of these days," Becky told Mammy, "that Samgirl's stomach is goin' to swell up."

I took special care around Serena. Because Serena was the washwoman for all the clothes and tablecloths and such at the big house, she had arms like hams. "You stay away from that Serena," Mammy had told me. "She's a bully. She browbeats anyone who'll let her get away with it."

Serena must have weighed as much as a couple of big sacks of cotton, and she threw her weight around. She lorded it over the other women and told them what to do.

Serena once poked her nose right into my face and said to me, "You're sick a good deal, child. What's ailin' you?"

I stared Serena right in the eye and breathed on her real heavy and responded, "It seems like I got some regular ailment. Aggie says only some people catch it. And only some people can catch it from me."

That kept Serena at her distance after that. I was just as glad. I didn't need some ruffian woman trying to find out things about my life. Pretty much though, folks in the quarters didn't question why I followed the slave trail to two plantations down; they just wanted to hear what I learned on my journeys.

At first I didn't have much to report because Aggie kept me so busy eating and talking. Pretty soon I caught on and pumped Aggie for tidbits of news to bring back to the quarters. Aggie didn't mind; she loved to be the center of attention. She was as good a talker as I was. No wonder her mammy had lapsed into silence somewhere along the line.

One night Aggie told me, "On this here plantation we got white owners, not Indians. Things is stricter here. Only house slaves can go into the yard of the big house. The rations-giving is done in the barn by the driver and his wife. If slaves want to tell Marse or Missus something, they have to go to the side gate at high noon on Sunday. Then they have to wait for a house slave to come take their message into the big house."

I couldn't imagine old John and Nellie cutting themselves off that way from their slaves. I was smart enough to know they didn't want to hear about Paul and his antics with me under the willow tree, but I knew they listened to other things, like the time my mammy went to get the pass so we could go to Aggie's.

Sometimes Aggie told me things that spoiled the meal for me, no matter how delicious and fragrant the food. On her plantation, Aggie said, the white driver punished lazy and disorderly slaves by laying them over a barrel and whipping them with bullwhips until the blood dripped on the ground.

"One time," she said, "the driver stropped a slave named Jim so hard he couldn't work. The following morning they found Jim hanging from a tree back of the quarters. He'd hung himself to escape all his pain and misery."

I couldn't stomach Aggie's molasses cake after hearing that.

After awhile, Aggie let some women come around to talk to me after supper. Even though she still didn't want me telling gossip to anybody but her, she allowed me to listen to theirs. That's when I heard the worst stories of all.

One night, Polly, the girl who had befriended me during my first visit to Aggie's, turned up her bare feet so I could see the soles. They looked as bad as my pappy's back, all meshed with scar tissue.

"Once," Polly explained, "we were making soap and some little chickens ran into the fire burning under the soap kettle. Missus Betty, who oversaw the soapmaking, blamed me. Betty smacked me over the top of my head with the butt of a cowhide whip, then she made me walk barefoot, back-and-forth, back-and-forth, through the coals of that fire." Polly paused for effect. "She only let me get off the coals when my smoking skin made them all cough."

Polly also told me about other times when Missus Betty beat her with a whip, then rubbed salt in her wounds. "My mammy can't do anything about it," Polly added, "except grease my wounds and put wet cloths on my face to try to bring my fever down. After I walked in the coals my fever lasted for a whole week."

When the men learned that the women told me such tales, they wanted to get their share in too. A big buck, maybe twenty-five years old and new to the plantation, carried on about the slave auction where Aggie's master had bought him. "They stripped us down to the waist and oiled our skin," Ralph said. "Then we had to ripple our muscles to show our strength. The auction man even opened our mouths to show our teeth."

I sensed Caty simmering and burning while Ralph talked. Although she was a tiny woman who seldom spoke, she seemed set on doing so now. She pushed her way to the front of the group, her eyes glaring and her mouth puckering with hate. All five feet of her quivered with indignation.

"Let me tell you about that greasin' down business," she began. "This white auction man, he came into the slave pen and started rubbin' goose grease all over me. I was already naked so there was no need of him takin' my clothes off. The grease smelled pretty bad and the auction man smelled worse yet, all lard and sweat and tobacco."

Caty stopped to let folks catch their breaths. Not one of us looked at each other. We just waited for Caty to go on, which she soon did.

"That man, he got himself so excited greasin' me, he jumped me right there in the pen. He pushed me down in the sawdust and went right to it."

My mouth hung open; I made an effort to shut it. I couldn't shut my heart against Caty's suffering, though, no matter how hard I tried. It was clear that Caty hadn't finished, so I listened hard to the rest of her words.

"That wasn't the worst," Caty said. "When they put me on the block, the auction man, he *told* what he had just done to me. They all laughed. Then he pulled my legs apart and pointed to his seed drippin' down. 'See, boys,' he shouted. 'You could be buying a wench who is already in the family way.' "

Paul wasn't so bad after all, I thought. I put my arm around Caty's shaking shoulders and gave her a hug. "We all love you, Caty," I whispered.

The other women crowded around Caty to give her some encouragement, while the men stood apart, their heads hanging down, humiliated by their helplessness to defend their women.

As I slipped off to the slave trail, I carried Caty's shame on my back and the men's disgrace in my heart. I sure couldn't take any more storytelling that night. I had no more feelings to give, no more in my well of emotions to draw up for the folks who have been degraded and put low by slavery and what abolitionists called its "evils."

Those stories burned themselves into my brain like a brand. I know I'll never forget them for my whole life. Maybe I'll remember them after death as well. I suppose I shouldn't have encouraged Aggie and the others, but, for the first time, I saw a part of slavery I knew little about. I already hated and feared slavery. Now I became obsessed with learning the extent of the harm it did to human beings—other humans like me who worked and loved and endured and eventually died.

In one way, the cruel things I heard made me prize my situation more. At least, I appreciated gentle old John and chubby Nellie. Maybe they were kinder because they were Chickasaw, not white folks. "I can even tolerate Paul," I assured myself. I had come to think of him as a pesky mosquito who stung me every once in awhile and flew on his way until the next time. "Even though Paul is bothersome, he isn't life-threatening."

In another way, those tales of heartlessness made me think even more about freedom. In fact, I began to make freedom the goal of my entire existence. I would lie in my bunk at night knowing I should get to sleep, that in the morning I would regret every minute I stayed awake. When that heavy bell in the big house yard gave off its mournful peals at dawn, I would be one sleepy slave.

I couldn't help it, though. I thought and thought, especially about Mammy and how she refused to have more slave babies. "Old John let me alone about havin' babies," she told me, " 'cause I've already given life to four children."

Mammy couldn't help it if one child turned out so wayward he had to be sold and another died. Besides, old John had me and Samboy. And old John felt bad about the baby Mammy had supposedly miscarried that first time we went over to Aggie's. Mammy toted around some guilt about her lie to old John until Pappy said in a sharp voice, "If old John didn't have slaves to begin with, you wouldn't have to lie to him."

Thinking about slave babies made me remember every story I ever heard about slave women and their children. I recalled the yarn about a slave mother named Fannie, who had kicked and even bitten her mistress. When the woman threatened to sell Fannie without her child, Fannie said she'd kill her own child rather than be sold without it. Knowing Fannie's temper, Fannie's mistress gave in. She sold Fannie and her child together.

Another gal I met over at Aggie's, a scrawny girl by the name of Martha, told me how her mother had begged her master to whip her instead of her girls. After a few bloody beatings, the man gave up. He no longer whipped either mother or daughters. "My mammy," Martha added, "also taught me and my sister to get out of work by acting sleepy or stupid."

Martha's story reminded me of Mammy and her feeble-minded look. That must happen on all plantations, I thought. No wonder most slave owners judged their slaves dense. Really, it was the owners who were dull-witted. They couldn't see what went on under their own noses. They just blamed the slaves for being slow and simple and went off and found someone else to do the work. The owners were too full of themselves to see that slaves could be clever enough to outsmart them, of all folks.

After that, I developed my "feeble look" to a high art. I could see the usefulness of such a ploy both now and in the future. I had three levels of stupidity. I could appear sort of thick when I wanted to get out of chores. Of course, this never worked with Mammy, only with Missus Nellie or one of her girls. Next, I could look stupid and like I might fall into a fever when I wanted someone to leave me alone. I discovered that, once in a while, I could pull this on Paul. If I acted fevered, I could cut him right down to two or three minutes—or chase him away altogether.

My highest level was looking moronic. This was difficult to use around our plantation because everyone knew I wasn't an idiot. It was even hard to practice because someone or other would rush up and ask, "You having fits, Samgirl?" So I got to where I practiced my moronic look only on the slave trail or in bed at night. Even though I wasn't quite sure what use I would put this to, I wanted to be prepared when the right time came.

But I always came back to stories about slave women and children. One night Aggie told me about something that had happened three plantations down from hers. That would make it five plantations down from old John's and Nellie's. "The owners stuck a mammy and a pappy," she said, "in the baracoon. They intended to sell them at market."

Right away, I had to interrupt and ask, "What's a baracoon?"

Aggie glanced at me like I was stupid and muttered, "Don't you know anything from that Chickasaw plantation of yours? A baracoon is a black hole in the ground where bad slaves go. They get no food—only water—and some of them die in there."

"Oh," said I, never having seen such a thing at old John's and Nellie's. I shook my head at the shame of it all. In my eyes, old John and Nellie seemed downright kind next to other planters. They had a scale of lashes they adhered to: one for this, two for that, and so on. If a slave did something really awful, old John or Nellie cut his rations, but Nellie didn't like doing that. "How's that boy going to work on that tiny bit of food?" she scolded old John whenever he punished young Tate with cut rations.

Anyway, Aggie wanted to continue, so I paid strict attention. "To make matters worse," she went on, "the overseer told the mammy and pappy in the baracoon that they'd would be sold without their children. Never again were they goin' to see their little boy and girl."

I opened my eyes wide and stared right at Aggie's glistening face. I was beginning to see the wisdom of my mammy and pappy in avoiding future children, but I kept quiet so Aggie would go on.

"One moonlit night," she said, "some slaves came and loosened the thongs holding the wooden roof over that pit. Sure enough, the mammy and pappy crawled out and stole to the cabin where their children lay sleepin'. They took the children down to the river and drowned them. Then they threw themselves in and drowned themselves. The next morning the master found his slaves bobbin' up and down. Caught in the rushes they were and no good to him on his farm or on the auction block, either one."

It took me a few minutes to absorb the immensity of the parents' deed—and of their love, in choosing for the family death instead of further suffering as slaves. When my mind worked its way around to it, I felt mighty glad that my mammy and pappy had never been driven to such an extreme.

The worst story came when one of Aggie's friends, a pinched-looking, sticklike woman named Lina, told me about her cousin. It seemed that Lina's cousin, Emma, had tried to overprotect her baby girl—at least that's the way Emma's white mistress saw it. Emma didn't want the girl to work and her mistress did. Emma and her mistress even had hair-pulling contests over it. One time, Emma's mistress smacked her with a fireplace poker, leaving a lump in Emma's head that never went away.

At her wit's end, Emma's mistress demanded that her husband sell Emma—without her girl. "The master," Lina explained, "agreed because he was so tired of hearing his wife complain about Emma, and of watching the two women fight. So he took Emma to auction and left the child back at the plantation. Even though Emma never spoke a word, her mind caught it all. Her eyes smoldered and sweat poured from her forehead."

"Go on," I urged. "What happened next?"

"Well," Lina drawled, "Emma's owner shoved her in the slave pen. He took a front row seat just waitin' for Emma to come up on the block. As he sat and waited, he heard some shouting from the pen. He knew it was Emma. Sure enough, Emma had kicked the white auction man smack between the legs when he tried to grease her down. By that time, the auction man was madder than a rabbit who'd lost its tail, and he dragged Emma onto the block. When bedlam hit that hall, the auction fellas got rattled and careless. They ran around the stage like possums in daylight and left their tools layin' when they fell."

Lina dabbed at her eyes before she continued. "Without waiting for quiet, the main auction man started the bidding: 'What'll you give me for this feisty bitch?' "

" 'Rip her loincloth off,' one of the men in the audience shouted back. The auction man stripped Emma bare. He turned back to the crowd. He still shouted for bids."

We all sat breathless, waiting to see how this gruesome tale would end.

"Emma bent down," Lina said. "She scooped up an ax one of the pen men had been using to bust slaves free from their chains before they went on the block. In less than a second, Emma chopped off her right hand against the floor. She stood up and flung the bloody hand right in her master's lap. There it sat, smoking, its fingers still twitching. The man jumped to his feet, shrieking."

We moaned and groaned so that Lina couldn't finish her story in any detail. Emma's white master had had to take her home and reunite her with her daughter, who was too young to sell. But no one seemed to know what Emma suffered as punishment, or if her master eventually parted her from her child.

That night I not only felt sick of listening to stories, but as if I carried the weight of more wisdom than even my broad shoulders could bear. On the trail home, I slid along in near darkness, choking on the meanness of slavery. Just before I reached our plantation, I retched my dinner, along with the tang of such incredible viciousness, onto the swamp ground.

As smart as I got about the ways of my world, it wasn't smart enough. I could see life from a wider plane now, yet I couldn't seem to apply common sense in my own life. Take the day Samboy came to me with this idea about smoking.

"Old John smokes and chaws both," he told me. "His boys try it on occasion, too." Samboy gave me a sidewise smile, begging me to join him in mischief.

"So?" said I, not willing to make it too easy on him.

"So, I want to try it." Samboy pulled out an old pipe and some home-cured tobacco and held them under my nose. "I borrowed these from Mose. He says we can hide in the barn and no one will know anything about it."

Being a mite curious myself and ready to try something new, I threw up my hands and said, "Let's go."

Once in the barn, we picked the darkest corner and wiggled down into the hay. Samboy lit up and took a puff. He gave me the pipe and I took a puff. We gazed at each other. It was clear neither of us liked it. We tried again. And again. We didn't have much to say to each other. Instead, we tried to choke back our coughs and look content.

In the meantime, it grew real quiet and Pappy missed us. "What you two troublemakers up to now?" he said right outside the window where we sat. We said not a word.

Pretty soon Pappy stuck his head in the barn door and sniffed the smoke hanging in the heavy barn air. He heard the crinkling of the hay as we wormed our way farther down.

Pappy swooped down on us just as a spark dropped into the hay and lit a tiny fire. Mind you, it was just a small fire, but Pappy acted like it was a bonfire. "What're you two doin' in here?" he yelled, as if he couldn't see that for himself.

Pappy stomped out the tiny fire. We sure were lucky Pappy wore shoes that day. Pappy threw the hot pipe right out the barn window. "You two are the devil himself," he yelled.

Next, Pappy made a grab for Samboy and caught him by the seat of his pants as Samboy tried to get away by crawling through Pappy's legs. With Samboy in one hand, Pappy clutched me by the nape of the neck—hard. If you think my pappy wasn't one strong man, you're mistaken. His hand felt like a death grip on my neck. "Let me go, Pappy. You're hurting me."

Pappy just grabbed all the harder. He dragged us to the center of the barn where he proceeded to put plenty of fire on our backsides and to make us see lots of smoke. We bawled a little and acted sorry. Finally, Pappy dropped us on the dirt floor. We sat there like two sacks of seed corn and waited to see what would happen.

"Never again," Pappy growled as he glared down on us.

"Never again," we promised and meant it.

It wasn't that I didn't learn lessons from such incidents. It was more that the learning never seemed to carry over to the next thing. Like the time me and Samboy got so hungry for chicken we could hardly stand it. Even though we always had enough to eat, after awhile beans and greens and fatback proved less than satisfying. We craved some real meat.

Me and Samboy put our heads together. "Let's steal a chicken from the chicken yard," I suggested.

"A real chicken," Samboy agreed. "And all ours."

We figured old John had plenty more. We planned to cook that bird over a fire and stuff ourselves, so we hid some firewood and a flint behind the vegetable patches in preparation.

The afternoon came. It was a Thursday when Samboy didn't have to go to the fields and I didn't have to go the big house. We had pick-up jobs to do around the barn that day. Because we'd worked real fast, we finished our chores early. The quarters were quiet because everyone else still worked, most in the fields, the loom room, or the big house.

"Ready, Samboy?" I asked. I shut Dog in the barn so he wouldn't give us away. "We'll bring Dog some chicken later." Of course, we didn't plan on bringing any chicken to Mammy and Pappy, who would be troubled about us stealing a chicken. Instead, we slunk off without giving a hint of our plans.

We watched the chicken yard from afar until Dixon, the chicken-keeper, went off to refill his feed sacks. Samboy had brought a piece of rag, which we pulled over the head of a smelly old chicken, who was stupid enough to stand on the edge of the chicken house near our reach. Even though that chicken squawked, we ran fast into the woods toward the vegetable patches. That chicken, blinded by the rag, screamed and clucked. Samboy stumbled and nearly fell.

"Keep going," said I, "or we'll be dead right along with that chicken."

Breathing hard and running scared, we finally tumbled into the vegetable patches. Because no one worked in the patches on a Thursday, we had the place to ourselves. I took the rag off the chicken's head and looked at Samboy. "All right, Samboy," said I, "wring its neck."

Samboy put on an indignant face and replied, "What do you mean, wring its neck? You wring its neck. Mammy always does it at home."

That was how we discovered that neither of us knew how to kill a chicken. We studied the chicken, trying to remember how Mammy did it at home. As far as we could recollect, Mammy broke a chicken's neck with her bare hands. We spent some time bending this chicken's neck, but it sure didn't break. Once the chicken got away from us and ran around squawking and yelling. We ran after it but tried to be quiet with our squawking and yelling.

"I remember," I finally shrieked. "Mammy spins a chicken around in the air and gives its neck a crack."

"Yeah," Samboy said. "Spin that old chicken. You can do it, Samgirl."

I tried and tried until the chicken went flying. It landed headfirst against a tree trunk. When we picked it up, it was finally dead.

"Whew," Samboy said, "that was harder than I expected."

Next thing, we had to get the feathers off that dead bird. I remembered how Mammy dunked a dead chicken in boiling water to loosen the feathers, but we didn't have a pot for water. I decided that heat was what loosened the feathers from the bird, so Samboy held that chicken's feet and I held its head and we passed it back and forth across the puny fire we had going. Instead of loosening the feathers, the fire singed them and made a terrible stench.

When little puffs of smelly fumes went up from the fire, we got scared. We laid the smoking chicken down in the dirt by the fire and studied it.

I had pictured the bird cooking on the green wood spit Samboy had carved with his little work knife, but I'd forgotten the part about getting the chicken ready for the spit.

"We need a real knife," Samboy said. "Then we can cut the feathers off along with its feet and head."

"Where're we going to get such a knife?" I asked.

A long brown hand came from above. It held a bone-handled knife with a real sharp edge. A deep, male voice intoned, "Here's your knife."

Me and Samboy froze on the spot. Both the hand and the voice belonged to Dixon, the chicken-house man. He had come right to that scorched chicken smell. "March," he said. "We're goin' to see your mammy and pappy."

Dixon took us home along with the sad-looking chicken. "You put this in the pot and cook it," he told Mammy. "You eat it, but not a morsel goes to these children. At dawn tomorrow, no breakfast for them. They'll come to the chicken house to help me feed chickens and collect eggs. And no lunch, they're goin' to help me clean the chicken house. By suppertime, they'll no doubt think more kindly of their own victuals. They won't ever again mess with old John's chickens."

I couldn't tell what Mammy thought. One half of her seemed mad that her children would do such a thing, but the other half seemed sorry for children who pined so for chicken. Because I couldn't tell which way Mammy would go, I looked around for a way out.

Samboy must have thought the same because, at the exact same moment, we remembered Dog locked in the barn. We made our excuses and went to free him. We took our time explaining to Dog about the chicken and why we hadn't brought him any. We also idled in returning to the cabin.

When we got back, Pappy stood behind Mammy looking sorrowful. Mammy and Pappy said not a word about the chicken. We sat down to supper—beans for me and Samboy, chicken for Mammy and Pappy. Me and Samboy sniffed that rich chicken odor and wished we were eating chicken right along with them. I noticed they had a hard time enjoying it, even though they agreed with Dixon about our punishment.

The following morning we helped Dixon and again at noon. "I sure don't want that man's job," Samboy whispered to me.

"Me neither. Chickens smell bad and act silly."

By suppertime, we were real hungry. We got beans again. We were surprised to find some small pieces of chicken underneath. When me and Samboy glanced at Mammy, the darkness in her brown eyes told us to keep eating without saying anything. Dog also seemed happy with his grub.

As far as I know, Dixon never told old John and Nellie about that scorched chicken, but he was sure right about one thing. Me and Samboy never messed with old John's chickens ever again.

chapter
four

It must have been 1846, when I was fifteen, that I started to hear grumblings from Aggie and her friends against old John and Nellie. "Those folks of yours ain't white like ours are," Aggie told me one day. "Your folks are Indians."

At that, I threw my chest out and stared at Aggie in a real aggravated way. "I don't suspect they ever told anyone they were white," I defended old John and Nellie. "Except for Nellie and maybe Esther, they sure don't look like white folks."

Aggie reacted with spirit and, I thought, some meanness. "Yeah," Aggie snapped, "but they sure do try to act like white folks. My mistress says no Indians have a right to live in the Mississippi country anymore, that it belongs to whites now."

I left Aggie soon after, agitation bouncing through my mind and making me rattled. I slogged along the slave trail and tried to shut the heavy night smells out of my nose. As I blocked the eerie hee-hee of night birds and the slither of snakes from my ears, and the burning gold eyes of owls from my eyes, my thoughts jumped back to the only book Paul had ever given me, his pappy's thrown-away dictionary.

That dictionary may sound like a funny thing to be thinking about when a scorpion skitters across the path in front of you, and you can hardly see the trail because the black, skeletonlike arms of trees hide the moon, but I wasn't thinking about the dictionary as much as the letter I'd found in it. By the time I found it, the letter had turned yellow and brittle around the edges and smelled musty. It was dated 1833 and was from old John to his brother, but old John had never mailed it. He just stuck it in the pages of that dictionary instead.

"Dear Bro.," the letter began in old John's scrawly handwriting, "I hope you will someday forgive us for not moving west to Chickasaw Nation lands with you."

Of course, I'd never heard of Chickasaw Nation lands, so I hurried to read the rest. The niceties of etiquette in our home didn't include keeping your nose out of other people's mail, because no one received any mail. Anyway, I read on. John wrote to his brother:

> When the Chickasaw leaders signed the Treaty of Pontotoc Creek last year, they didn't ask us how we felt about it. As you already know, the treaty allows us to stay in Mississippi if we adopt white names and live like whites. We've already been doing that for years, especially seeing as how we already have some white blood in the family on Nellie's side. We practice Christianity and talk English in our home, so it's far easier to stay here than to move westward.
>
> Our neighbors accept us as we are and nobody cares about our land, being as it's on a creek nobody ever heard of and producing as little cotton as it does. Someday we'll come to the Chickasaw Nation tract and visit you and your family.

The signature was "Your loving brother, John Stands-in-Timber." Nellie had scribbled an unreadable message at the bottom.

Naturally, I was curious. I bided my time and eventually asked Paul if he had any uncles living anywhere. "What do you want to know that for?" Paul demanded. He seemed suspicious about what kind of scheme I had in my head now.

I shrugged and tried to act pathetic. "I'm just puzzled about families, that's all. I don't have much of one and wondered if you have any I don't see right off."

At that, Paul softened a bit and said, "I had an uncle a long time ago, but he died going west to the Chickasaw Nation land. His family died with him. The others weren't even allowed to stop and bury them. So many people died that buzzards and wolves followed those people all the way to the Chickasaw Nation."

"That's terrible," said I, understanding at last why old John had never mailed his letter, but had shoved it into the dictionary instead. As I hesitated a moment, trying to bring my thoughts together and decide which tack to take next, Paul lost his interest in the subject of family and who had died where. Paul's mind went right back to the matter at hand. That was all I learned about the rest of his family, but it etched itself a place in my mind.

As I went down the slave trail, all of this came back to me. I began to connect a lot of things. Paul seemed lonely lately, I thought. The young white planters didn't want his friendship anymore. The girls seemed to have found other young men to spend time with. I remembered noticing too that Esther and Rebecca stayed home more than they ever had. Their beaus had stopped calling and bringing nosegays. It was oddly quiet around the big house these days: no wagons full of young people coming and going, no laughter scaring away the night birds, no pranks to startle old John and Nellie and the house slaves.

From my schoolroom days, I knew that Mississippi had been a state since 1817. Old John's letter had told me that the Treaty of Pontotoc Creek was signed in 1832. That meant that most of the Chickasaw people must have moved to the West during the 1830s. "It seems a little late," I muttered, "to be worrying about a few leftover Chickasaws living far from Mississippi's rich delta. All they do is grow themselves a bit of cotton and corn on scrub land. Old John and Nellie can't be much of a threat to anyone."

I puzzled around for an explanation for the sudden outrage toward the Chickasaw. In my memory, I turned over everything I could remember from the papers and magazines I had scrounged from Paul, but little came to mind. I had the feeling that whites had gotten downright grabby, fighting with Indians in the West and with Mexicans south of that somewhere. Even though the newspapers called it Manifest Destiny, I called it flat-out greed.

I searched my mind some more, trying to figure out what peoples' new way of feeling about old John, Nellie, and their family might mean to me. Maybe old John would be leaving Mississippi after all, I thought, although no brother waited for him on that faraway Chickasaw Nation land. Maybe old John and his family would have to move west and settle in Indian Territory, whether they wanted to or not. Maybe old John's and Nellie's slaves would have to go west as well, whether they wanted to or not.

As soon as I reached our cabin, I tried out my new theory on Mammy and Pappy. Mammy fixed supper while Pappy carried in the firewood that Samboy and I had forgotten. Neither of them seemed too eager to learn upsetting news. Still, being me, I broke right in. "There's something funny going on," I started.

"Yeah, like what?" Samboy asked. Mammy and Pappy barely glanced up. Either they thought this was another bit of Aggie's gossip, or they didn't want to hear anything troubling.

"People in this neighborhood don't like old John and Nellie anymore, that's what," I threw back at him. I felt proud and satisfied. I had real important news here. "They say John and Nellie are nothing but Indians and don't have a right to live in Mississippi alongside white folks."

I saw Mammy stare at the ceiling above the fireplace and heard Pappy sigh deep in his chest. "We've been expectin' this," Pappy said in a gloomy voice. "We remember when the other Chickasaw moved. You were a teeny thing then, Samgirl. And you were no thing at all, Samboy."

"So what happened?" Samboy clamored. "Why didn't John and Nellie go too?"

Likely Samboy wasn't pleased about being reminded that he was the youngest of the bunch. Lately, he'd taken to standing up tall and puffing out his chest to show he was getting to be a man. Now he tried to look bold, like he was determined to be part of this family discussion.

"How're they goin' to go?" Pappy retorted, knocking Samboy down at once. "They're not white folks born and bred, but they took on white ways so as to keep their land and blend in, so to speak. Now they're cotton planters and slave owners. So how're they goin' to move? They ain't suited to live somewhere in the wilderness with wild Indians and so."

"They may *have* to go," I busted in, frustrated at being shut out of a conversation I'd started. "Aggie says white folks is talking and growling a lot about it. They want old John and Nellie out of the— "

"Child, shut your mouth," Mammy broke in. Annoyance had turned her eyes dangerous. "Didn't your pappy just tell you old John and Nellie have no place to go? They no more know how to live out in the West than we would."

Now I felt real put out, so I didn't tell them about the old John's letter to his brother. I didn't tell either how Paul had said that his uncle and family died on the way west. I just stuck my nose in the air and walked away from the whole discussion.

Samboy was no dummy. The next morning he found me alone and started pumping me to see what I knew. Samboy had turned eleven and had real worries about his future. He had been doing more thinking about slavery and freedom than I could've imagined.

"I don't want to be a slave like Pappy all my life," he told me that fine Sunday morning. His words took the sweet flower smell right out of the air. My heart hung heavy about what he might have in mind.

"What are you going to do about it?" I asked. I told myself that this boy was only eleven and just blowing off steam that didn't have much fire beneath it.

Samboy stood up real straight. I noticed he was almost taller than me. He gave me a haughty look and said, "I'm going to run away someday."

I grew cold and wrapped my arms around myself to warm up. I remembered how Mammy had acted when I talked to her about running away. Now I understood her feelings.

I knew I had to do something to calm this boy down. I sat Samboy down on the wood stacked in that shed where I was supposed to be getting fuel for our breakfast fire. I told him what Mammy had said to me the day I talked to her about running away. I reminded him how important family was and that, as slaves, we had little else. At this, Samboy nodded his head in understanding. At the same time, he appeared discouraged and like he might cry.

Then Samboy rallied. He sounded like a honking goose as he swallowed his unshed tears. "Maybe," he rasped out, "there ain't no slavery in the West. If old John and Nellie have to go west, and if they take us with them, then— "

"That's a lot of ifs," said I, feeling as sympathetic as could be for Samboy. I decided to reveal some of my own feelings about running away. "I was thinking some myself. I know there *is* slavery in the West, but it seems that it'd be a mite easier to wiggle out of it there than it is here."

Samboy looked at me, a grin spreading over his wide mouth. He was almost back to normal, but more aware of how serious a matter running away might be. "What else have you been thinkin'? What more do you know about all this?"

I told Samboy about old John's letter and what Paul had said about his uncle and family dying on the way west. Those bits of news depressed Samboy considerably. Although I felt bad about that and wanted to go on, I heard Mammy calling for the firewood. To cheer him up a bit, I continued another minute or two telling Samboy about the abolitionist movement in the North that I had read about. "There are white people up north who actually fight against slavery."

"You mean to tell me," he said, "that some white folks are tellin' other white folks to give up their slaves?" His eyes had grown as big as Mammy's white crockery bowls, the ones we used for porridge or cornmeal mush in the mornings.

"That's exactly the way of it," said I, just before I saw Mammy marching on the woodshed with lightning in her eyes. I plunked three pieces of wood into Samboy's arms and pushed him out the door smack into Mammy. While they tried to get untangled, I ran by with an armload of wood and headed right for the fireplace. I had that wood in the fireplace's belly before Mammy came through the cabin door.

Still, Mammy seemed plenty annoyed with me and Samboy. She started on me first: "Where have you been, child? Your pappy has to eat his breakfast. He's got to help with the rations-givin' today."

"I'm sorry, Mammy," said I with innocent eyes. "It's Samboy's fault for bothering me when I'm doing my chores."

Like I knew she would, Mammy sighed. I always blamed Samboy for everything and he did me the same way. She gave up right there. Instead of carrying on any longer, she said, "You two can pester each other all you want because you have to work the vegetable patch together this afternoon."

At that, me and Samboy flashed each other a look of understanding. We knew we'd be able to talk about the West and the strange idea that some white people had about other people's slaves. We were anxious as could be for vegetable-patch time to come.

That afternoon, after a small meal of grits and greens, Samboy and I set off to the vegetable patch without one reminder from Mammy. I thought about bringing some of my newspapers to show Samboy, but he could barely read. About the time he should've been sitting on the schoolroom's hard benches, it was getting unpopular in Mississippi to educate slaves even a little bit. Even though old John and Nellie had shaken their heads over the new rule, what could they do about it? Nothing.

As a result, all Samboy had learned he'd learned from me. That wasn't a whole lot. What with the chores Nellie kept loading on me as I grew older, trying to help Mammy at home, keeping Paul still, and fitting in reading time for myself, I didn't have a whole lot of time left over for Samboy.

When I did, though, he proved a fast learner. If it was nighttime, we curled up by the fire so as to have some light, or, if it was daytime, we went out in the sun. Dog always came along and got in the way, because he liked to lay his earless head on the very page we were reading from.

Anyway, I decided not to take my papers with me. It was just as well, because we ran slap into Paul on our way to the patch. He would surely have been unhappy to see me parading through the quarters with the forbidden reading material I got from him. As it was, Paul didn't look too pleasant. Samboy said nothing and Dog cringed behind him.

"Where're you going, Samgirl?" Paul asked, ignoring my companions.

"It's Sunday, *Mister* Paul, so I'm going out to work the vegetable patch with Samboy here." I dropped Paul a little curtsy and waited for his response.

Paul's eyes clouded over. He got my meaning. On old John's plantation, on Sunday nobody bothered slaves, except cooks and table-
servers, unless there was an emergency. Paul didn't like being reminded,
that was clear. "Someday I'll make the rules on this farm," he grumbled
as he stomped off toward the big house.

"Why's he always hanging round you?" Samboy asked. "Where do
you go with him when the two of you disappear?"

My face started to burn and the roots of my hair went to prickling.
I glanced sideways at Samboy, not wanting him to know how surprised
I was that he'd noticed my doings with Paul. "It's the way of masters and
slaves," said I. "I'll tell you more when you're older and can understand."

"I understand now. It's just like the pigs in the barnyard, or the
cows in the fields, or young Tate, ain't it? Paul hangs around because
you're a she and he's a he."

Again, I shot a sideways glance at Samboy, thinking a slave boy has
to learn far too much way too fast. "Yes, that's how it is," said I real soft,
my voice stuck way down in my throat at having to tell my baby brother
such a thing about myself. "What do you think of that?" I said, shame
slurring my words.

Samboy smiled, obviously tickled to be asked for an opinion. He
puffed out his chest and spit out his words. "I think Paul stinks. He
believes he can do anything with you that he wants because he owns
you. I know you wouldn't have nothing to do with that pig if you were a
free gal."

I stopped stock still in the path, turned toward Samboy, and captured his gangly arms and shoulders in a big hug. Samboy, being eleven,
fought his way free as fast as he could. "What was that for?"

"That's because you're an eleven-year-old man instead of a boy,"
said I. My compliment brought a grin to his lips and a swagger to his
walk as we started toward the vegetable patch again.

"Then you're goin' to tell me all you know about this aba— this
abolitionist business?"

"Yeah," said I. "Let's hoe hard, then we'll sit in the shade and talk
hard."

Samboy and I attacked that vegetable patch and made weeds fly in
every direction possible; then we plunked down under a tree where

Dog already snoozed. Me and Samboy drank the lemonade Mammy had put in an old brown jug for us and enjoyed the whispy Mississippi sky for a few minutes. A bee buzzed around the flowers at our feet and made us feel lazy.

Samboy didn't stay distracted for long. "Now, about them abolitionists," Samboy began.

I told him about the Grimké sisters and the abolition societies and William Lloyd Garrison. Then he wanted to hear some more, so I went on about free black abolitionists like David Walker. Samboy got real excited. He never thought blacks could be powerful enough to work for the emancipation of their own people.

"When do you think they'll be comin' to get us out of slavery?" he asked. His eyes had gone to glistening and he licked his lips, so I hated to disappoint him.

I started slow, like I was pondering his question. "I think we better not wait for them. We're way down in Mississippi and they're mostly up north."

"How far is that?"

I drew an outline map in the dirt and showed Samboy where the North was, the South, and the West. I scratched some wriggly lines where Mississippi was and put a bitty star at its top for where we sat. Samboy asked some more questions; his lack of geography shocked me. I swore I would spend more time teaching him some of the things I had learned, especially reading and geography.

Finally, we got to the matter of miles and how many miles separated the abolitionists from us in our vegetable patch in Mississippi. I told him it was about a mile from the vegetable patch to the big house and back again. "If we made one hundred of those trips we'd be mighty tired, wouldn't we?" I asked him.

Pretty soon, Samboy marked in the dirt alongside my map. He made separate bunches of numbers and he said to me, "Thousands of miles would take months for those abolitionist folks to cover, maybe more if they walked instead of ridin'."

I was real surprised; I suspected Samboy was a natural mathematician. "Who taught you to count, boy?" I asked, wondering who would be teaching him besides me.

"Nobody taught me. I taught myself by listening to the head man count the bags of cotton each slave brings in."

I questioned Samboy more. I realized he had caught the logic of the ten-by-ten system. Pretty soon he counted right along with the head man. I figured that with his counting ability and my talking skills, we could get far. I said to him, "You serious about running away someday?"

"I'm serious," he said. He bunched his forehead into a frown. "Why?"

"What do you think about us running away together? And maybe Mammy and Pappy too?"

"I think it'd be harder for four folks instead of one, but when you got where you were going you'd still have a family."

I resisted the urge to hug Samboy, but snuggled my shoulder closer to his. "I'm sure glad you're my brother."

"If that's the case," Samboy said, looking a little shy or maybe embarrassed, "why don't you tell me everything you know?"

"Like what?" I asked. I worried about what else he knew, or thought he knew. Again, he surprised me with how much he had figured out, or maybe overhead.

"Like about Aggie and what else Mammy told you when I wasn't around and all." Samboy seemed satisfied that he had set me back a bit.

I thought about it for a minute and felt pretty ashamed to tell my own brother about the herbs and Albert, who was probably alive somewhere, and Mammy having Aggie fix her good. Still, I figured that if Samboy was going to be my partner he'd better know the details. I didn't know how to go about this, so I decided to be matter-of-fact and maybe even a little curt.

"Don't be asking a bunch of questions and slowing me down," I warned him. "Let me tell what I know, then you can ask what you want."

Samboy prepared to listen to all I had to say. He pulled his knees to his chest and put his arms around his legs. I told that boy about Paul and Aggie and the herbs and Albert and all. I could see my story go across his face, sometimes in his wide eyes, sometimes in his wrinkled forehead, and sometimes in his teary eyes. When I finished I waited for questions and the one he had surprised me.

"About this Albert," he said, "where do you think he is now?"

"Probably still in Mississippi, unless he upped and ran away somewhere," said I, wondering why Albert had drawn Samboy's interest so.

"You mean you never asked Mammy what she knows?"

"She doesn't know anything. Marse Camp sold Albert and she never saw him again. Then Marse Camp sold Mammy to old John. Anyway, the hurt in her eyes was too deep to ask her much of anything."

Samboy seemed content with that. Even though he said he had no more questions, I wasn't quite satisfied with the outcome of our afternoon talk. "If we're going to run away together," said I, "maybe we better make a secret pact."

"I don't know what is a pact."

"A promise. That we'll stick by each other, help each other, and never tell nobody anything."

I could see the eleven-year-old boy in Samboy rising to the surface. "How're we going to do that?" he asked in an excited voice.

"We'll get a thorn and scrape an *X* on our arms. Then we'll put the *X*'s together and let our blood mingle."

Samboy flashed me a scowl and said with unexpected logic, "We've already got the same blood. What's the— "

"All right then, you think of a way to seal our pact. I mean, our promise."

Samboy scratched his head and thought a minute. "All right," he said, "we'll do it your way to make sure our blood mixes together. But we'll do somethin' else too. I'm goin' to show you my secret hidin' place and what's in it."

I nodded, trying to look solemn but expecting some smelly old toad or snakeskin to be in Samboy's secret place. We cut our *X*'s and mixed our blood, then Samboy took me to the fence post at the northwest corner of the patch and started digging by the post with his hoe. "Swear you won't tell anyone," he demanded.

"I've already given you my blood on that, but I'm willing to swear again." I sighed, waiting for toad skins to pop out of the hole.

Samboy dug and dug. The dirt brought up with it a fetid, swamplike smell that made me wrinkle my nose. I guess Dog didn't notice the odor. He kept trying to help, but Samboy wouldn't let him. Samboy dug about a foot and a half down when I heard his hoe hit something metal.

"Is this something you stole?" I asked, suspicion clouding my eyes and my mind.

"Sort of," he said as he reached into the hole. He hauled up a piece of heavy iron chain, eleven links all hooked together and starting to rust from being in the ground. Then he pulled up a lock. Although it was smashed, I could still tell it was a lock.

I rocked back on my bare heels and studied his hoard. "Where did you get these things, boy?"

"I got them in the swamp a long time ago. I brought them here and buried them. Then I went back to look for the bones of the man that busted out of them. I looked and looked, but I never found any bones. I decided that if he broke away from his marster, I could do it too."

I frowned with worry and Samboy added real quick, "Someday. Not right now."

"How often do you look at these things?"

"Hardly ever. I don't want Pappy to notice any diggin' around that post. But I know they're there. And I think about them regular."

"They're your talisman, then?"

"I don't know what is a tails-man. I say they're my voodoo. They keep me going when something bad happens. Like when Paul takes you away to that tree."

Tears jumped to my eyes at that. I touched the chain and the smashed-up lock like they were made of gold. "Can they be my voodoo, too?" I asked in a real low voice.

"If you help me get them back in the ground," Samboy said, always practical and anxious to stick me with part of the work.

At that, I laughed. After he put the chain and the lock back in the hole, I started pushing dirt in on top of them. We danced around on top of the dirt and stamped it down good.

Finally, we cleaned up the weed mess we'd made earlier so Pappy wouldn't start picking up weeds and looking at the ground too close. Samboy grabbed Mammy's jug and we ambled home, lost in our love for each other and our hopes for the future.

chapter five

At this point in my recollections, I went down the row to relieve myself. I remember this homely fact because it gave me a chance to look around the quarters. As I slunk toward the privy at the end of our string of cabins, I listened carefully. All I could hear was snoring. On my way back, I heard the same thing.

I noted that the moon had only half risen, so I settled back into my post at our cabin door. Even though I sure hated to remember the happenings of the trip west, from Mississippi to Oklahoma Territory, I had to admit I'd learned a lot from that journey, especially the importance of planning ahead.

In that respect, I thought, I have to give old John credit. When he was ready to make the announcement about the move to Indian Territory, he set it for a Sunday morning. Word went out that any family that had all its members present at rations-giving would get a chicken. A chicken was a prize that normally came only on holidays.

Instead of sending just one or two people to get our rations, we all left off our usual Sunday jobs of clothes washing and mending and such to hurry to the big house. As we gathered, all puffing and putting our heads together about what this might mean, we saw the dead chickens lined up along the edge of the porch, already starting to get smelly in the sun. Their broken necks hung over the ledge and, in the breeze, their head feathers bobbled this way and that.

"I'm havin' that chicken," Serena announced. "It's the fattest."

"Ha," Tate said, "that one on the end is mine. It's got the most meat."

The mumbling and murmuring got louder and louder until it drowned out the Sunday sounds of breezes blowing and leaves dancing and butterflies fluttering.

Pretty soon, old John strode out on the porch already dressed in his Sunday clothes. On his head sat a stovepipe hat. From beneath his long-skirted coat peeked shiny black boots. "Mornin', folks," he said. "Nice day, ain't it?"

Following old John came Missus Nellie, her hoop skirt swaying and rocking and a brooch at her throat. Saying nothing, Nellie clutched the schoolhouse map in front of her bountiful chest. She stood a respectful few feet behind old John as he commenced to talk.

"Some of you know that things are changing in Mississippi," old John said. He cleared his throat and began again. "There ain't anyplace here for Indians anymore. People are afraid of Indians like us."

Old John's statement and the sight of him and Nellie standing there as gentle as could be drew snickers from the crowd, but old John went on talking right over the top of them. "There's something else," he said and coughed again. "A lot of the big Mississippi planters are getting rich and they want more land for themselves. And there's the wealthy Virginia planters who have worn out their land and are coming to Mississippi looking for more land to destroy."

This time the slaves, almost in unison, sighed, "Oh me, oh my" at the doings of white planters. At that moment, I knew I'd been one of the major news carriers regarding such deeds. I didn't know whether to feel guilty or to be glad I'd helped folks appreciate our Chickasaw owners, old John and Nellie.

Old John seemed sad and about to weep. "Most of the Chickasaw people left years ago. Now it looks like we're going to have to leave, too."

I speculated that old John was remembering his lost brother and family who died on the trail, but the others set up such a hollering that old John had to stop for a minute. He cleared his throat and held up a quivering hand for silence. When we all quieted down, he went on: "I'm going to show you on this here map where we are now and where we're going."

At that, Nellie and her map advanced to old John's side. Nellie handed old John a green ribbon, which he moistened with some tobacco spittle from his mouth and stuck on the map. "This here is our plantation. It's north of French Camp, but closer to Tupelo than Oxford. At one time, this whole area belonged to Chickasaw Indians." John drew a circle in the air over the map with two fingers and everybody wailed and muttered in sympathy.

Nellie handed old John another green ribbon and he moistened that one and glued it to the map a long ways from the first ribbon. "This is where we're going—Chickasaw Nation land in Indian Territory. We got us a parcel of land with a big house and some cabins south of Tishomingo, the capital of the Chickasaw Nation. The Chickasaw Council House is in Tishomingo, along with a bank and some stores, so we won't be very far from civilization."

By then, all the slaves had gone to shaking their heads in wonder and craning their necks to see Nellie's map. Although some just itched to ask old John questions, it was clear he had more to say. "We sold this plantation for a good price, so we can buy wagons and such to get us and our truck out to Indian Territory. I understand some of you may not want to go. For some of you, Mississippi is home. Besides, it's a long, hard trip over a dusty trail with Indians who might not be happy to see us coming. If you tell me you want to stay here, I'll do the best I can to sell you to a good master. If you want to come along, then me and Nellie will be more than glad to have you."

"Are there slaves out there in Indian Territory, Boss?" young Tate yelled out, as brash as always.

"Yes, plenty of Indians and plenty of slaves."

"What are we goin' to do there, Marse?" Willis, the cooper, shouted.

"We're going to grow cotton and corn, just like here, and raise pigs and cows, just like here. One thing will be different. Me and Nellie are thinking about raising cattle for meat. Right now, Texas and Indian Territory are prime cotton-growing areas, but cattle could be our best future. Any of you bucks that want to sign up as trail hands for the trip out west can start learning some of the necessary skills, like riding and roping."

Old John's offer brought wails and sobs from some of the women, but me, I had a plan forming in my head. I turned toward Samboy, who stood next to me quiet as a cotton plant growing in the searing summer sun. I thrust his arm in the air. "Volunteer," I ordered him.

Old John saw Samboy's arm that I waved like a flag. He appeared pleased. "Samboy, I'll be glad to have you as a trail hand. You're young yet, but coming into your strength fast."

Samboy seemed thrilled and dazed at the same time. Old John and Nellie had gone to talking Chickasaw between themselves, so it was plain we'd be getting no more information from them that morning. When old John and Nellie carried on that way, it always sounded to me like a whole lot of wild shoat in the cedar break scared of something, maybe even afraid for their lives.

People began to line up for their rations, still with their eyes on the reeking chicken they had judged the best. All the time we waited in line, everyone talked and tattled about what old John's announcement meant to them.

"I'm goin' for sure," Tate said. "I've heard too many nasty stories about white planters. I'll take my chances with old John anytime."

As we walked home, Becky slipped over to Mammy and asked, "What are you goin' to do, Chloe?"

"Why," Mammy said, "I suspect we're goin'. We know what we got with old John and Nellie, after all."

Next, Serena came along. "You goin' or stayin', Ike?" she bellowed at my pappy.

"Hell, Serena," Pappy responded, "if Samboy's goin' to be a trail hand, then we all got to go along to see how things develop."

Winter, the carpenter who had seen out of one eye since a wood sliver flew up and pierced the other, nudged Pappy. "So you goin', Ike?"

"Winter," my pappy answered, "I'm goin' and you better go too. No planter in his right mind is goin' to buy a carpenter with only one good eye."

Through all this, I saw Samboy busting to talk, but he waited until the rest of the crowd dropped away and we neared our own cabin. Finally, he poked me in the arm and asked, "Why'd you do that to me, Samgirl?"

"It's simple," said I. "If you learn how to ride and rope, you'll be one of old John's main men. You'll get to go places and you'll know everything that's going on. If there's a chance to escape, you'll know about it."

Samboy seemed dazzled at my quick thinking, but I could feel Mammy's disapproval burning through my back. I turned quickly to make amends before the bad feelings got out of hand. "I remember what you told me, Mammy. I'm surely not planning anything immediate in the way of escape. But Pappy always says a person should be prepared."

My pappy looked down at the ground and scuffed his giant bare feet in the dust. "We understand, Samgirl," he said. "We just don't know how we're goin' to get along without you."

I patted Pappy's hand. "There's no saying you and Mammy can't go with us when we run. You wait and see, I'm goin' to think it out real good. There will be a place for you and Mammy in the plan."

"In the meantime," Mammy muttered, "you better shut your big black mouth or none of us will be goin'. Old John will sell us away so fast it'll make your brain rattle in your fuzzy head."

Mammy had a good point. I shut my mouth, but that didn't stop my mind from working. I could picture it already, Samboy the cowboy. Why, we could ride all the way to Canada on his know-how alone.

Everyone decided to go west with old John and Nellie. Nobody wanted to take a chance on the unknown, especially if it hailed from Virginia. Nevertheless, the idea of a move sure upset the quarters. Folks started figuring what they would take, but old John calmed them down. "We got plenty of time," he told them.

That man turned out to be one mighty planner. First, he divided up the families, two to a wagon. I hoped we wouldn't get Becky and Eurias and all those children of theirs. As it turned out, they got a wagon to themselves, with young Tate to help them and ride with them. We had Mose and his wife Amanda, two of the oldest folks in our quarters. They were so old the whites of their eyes had red and yellow splotches in them. Their hair had long ago turned silver and their faces had more wrinkles than the creek bed during dry times.

I sure hoped Mose had forgotten about the pipe-borrowing incident by now. I counted on his memory going bad along with the rest of him. I didn't even know if he ever got that old pipe back after Pappy threw it out the barn window.

Next thing, after old John assigned folks to the wagons, the carpenter and the cooper, Winter and Willis, went to making wooden boxes about four feet wide, four feet deep, and six feet long. Old John said every family would get one to pack their stuff in, but that didn't include food. "I'm not having every family cook its own meals on the trail," John explained. "That's a waste of time. We'll have one wagon to carry the cooking utensils and two or three more to carry provisions. All I need now is three or four of you to volunteer as cooks."

When I saw Mammy's hand shoot up I was glad. Cooks usually got to take home the scraps. It didn't look to me like Mose and Amanda needed much to eat, so I hoped a lot of the extras would come my way.

Next thing we knew, a bunch of giant-bellied wooden wagons arrived at old John's house. Then came the oxen, ugly and mean-looking and carrying huge horns on their heads. Old John told the men to practice and learn to drive teams of the beasts. None of us had ever seen oxen before—everyone in those parts used mules for plowing—so we were scared of the fearsome animals. After Pappy took his turn learning to drive, he said the oxen weren't mean at all. "They're just big and stupid," he added.

Nellie piped in that she needed a bunch of women to sew covers for those wagons. That's when I volunteered. Although I never cared much for sewing, I saw an opportunity. If I learned to sew it might get me somewhere. Maybe I could even make some money sewing once we reached Indian Territory.

"Me, take me," I shouted.

Because I offered before I knew what the job meant, I ended up sewing wagon cover after wagon cover. Every one of the wagons needed two covers, a canvas one on the outside for bad weather days and a cotton one for inside and nice days.

While we sewed, Mammy and the other women readied the cook wagon and prepared food to take along. They made medicine boxes, one for every wagon, and workbaskets so we could sew along the way.

They even packed all the dishes from the big house in cotton seed so we would have seed for our first cotton crop in Indian Territory. The men filled grease barrels to hang under the wagons and practiced with rifles so they could hunt. Even though old John made it clear that the rifles would be locked up except at hunting time, it was extraordinary that he intended to let his slaves handle weapons at all.

During all this, Samboy and Dog did pretty much the same thing—mostly getting in everyone's way. Then the horses arrived and I hardly saw Samboy again. Samboy learned to saddle up and ride, while Dog continued his usual job, except that now he spent all his time getting in my way.

It took us a full four months to get the wagons ready and learn how to handle the oxen. "I'm aiming for spring of 1847," old John told everyone. "When we've loaded the wagons, each will weigh upwards of 1,500 pounds. So be careful with your packing."

In the meantime, I sewed and I thought. Although I usually pondered the possibility of freedom in the new country, gradually my mind turned to the problem of Aggie and her herbs. Maybe I was barren like Paul said, but I didn't want to put it to the test. Because I had a lot of faith in Aggie and even more aversion to having Paul's baby, I decided I better have a chat with Aggie.

I snuck away on a Wednesday night, even though my regular trip was coming up that Saturday. I waited until Pappy snored hard and Dog right along with him, then I let myself down from my bunk and tiptoed across the dirt floor. Despite his open ears waiting to take in every sound, Dog didn't even jerk.

When I reached Aggie's I nearly scared the wits out of her and her mammy, who were already deep asleep. I drew Aggie outside into the light of the glaring moon and whispered, "I have to talk to you."

"I figured it was something important," she mumbled back, "or you wouldn't be goin' through that swamp at this time of night." She pulled her shawl close around her and gave the dark clouds a suspicious stare.

I feared she would go back in her cabin and jump in bed. I grabbed her arm and said, "You know we're going west pretty soon. I won't be able to get my herbs and I ain't having Paul's child."

Aggie jumped at the determination and loathing in my voice. She seemed to forget about the spooky night clouds. "What are you goin' to do, then?"

"I thought on this a good deal. I want you to fix me good, the same way you did my mammy."

Aggie scratched her frizzy head and stared full into the moon's ghostly shine. "I don't know," she said, "you're so young. What if you want babies one day?"

"I thought about that, but the chance of having Paul's baby now is worse than anytning I might want in the future. Besides, after all those stories I heard I don't see why any slave woman would want to have babies."

Aggie's eyes got sad. She nodded. "You come back here at your regular time Saturday night. You tell your mammy you're stayin' all night. You tell her you'll be home early in the morning before the rations-giving so's no one will knows you've gone."

I tell you, after that I was one scared girl. I worried about the matter all the way back along the slave trail. I didn't even hear the night sounds or feel the creepy, slimy things around my bare feet. I worried some more on Thursday, the whole day on Friday, and most of Saturday.

I decided I couldn't tell Mammy about it, so I stuck Samboy with it. "Wait until I'm good and gone," said I, holding his thick arm as tight as I could. "Tell her I'll be back early in the morning. That's all you know."

Samboy seemed irritated and shook free of my hand. "It's plain that's all I know. Unless you want to tell me what you're up to over there all night."

"I'm not telling you now," said I, as I slipped off down the trail, a full hour earlier than usual and without my cornbread. When I reached Aggie's, everything was quiet. No Polly, no Lina, no Martha, no nobody. "Where is everybody?" I asked Aggie.

"They're in their cabins so they don't know nothin' about nothin'."

At that, I got real scared, but Aggie gave me something to drink that tasted like fire and burned the fright right out of me. I felt kind of limp and willing.

Aggie draped a sheet over her table and told me to take my drawers off and lay down. For a moment, I thought of Paul and his blanket and laughed. Then I got mad because it was Paul's fault I had to lie down on Aggie's sheet.

Out of the shadows, Aggie's little mammy appeared. She gave me more to drink. She smelled real clean and comforting to me, like fresh-plowed ground in the springtime. My head rolled one way, then the other. Granny held my hand with more strength than I knew she had in her when Aggie said, "Put your knees up and open your legs wide."

I had a fleeting thought of Paul again, but I didn't laugh. I knew we were about to get down to business. I didn't have time for tears so I gripped Granny's hands and clenched my teeth until they made grinding noises. When I saw Aggie coming at me with a knife and felt Granny squeezing the blood right out of my hand, I wasn't scared any longer. I trusted Aggie to do what she had to do.

I never found out what that was, or what Aggie might have cut and peeled with that knife of hers, for the next thing I knew, Aggie and Granny were wadding rags between my legs to sop up the blood. It seemed to me that it took lots of rags, but finally I quit bleeding so bad.

When she ran out of rags, Aggie packed some raw cotton between my legs. "Here," she said as she passed a bowl to Granny. "Lift her head and try to spoon some broth into her mouth."

That's pretty much how it went the rest of the night. We slept a bit, then Aggie packed some cotton and Granny spooned some broth.

I woke up at dawn because I heard whining. There sat Dog in the open door sniffing at the blood smell in the cabin air. Samboy stood right behind him, his eyes darting around trying to find me in the dark room. "What are you doing here?" I tried to ask Samboy, but no words came out.

Aggie looked up and saw the pair of them and smiled. "Thank the Lord, child. I didn't know how I would get Samgirl back along the trail in her condition. She lost more blood than I knew a body had."

At that, Samboy said, "My pappy made this." He pointed to a litter of sticks and gunny sacking.

It took all of them to get me on that litter. Finally, they had to tie me to it because I kept sliding off. Samboy pulled the litter behind him toward the trail, with Dog at my side looking like he wished he could do something to help. Once in awhile, he lapped up a drop of blood I left on the path. Although I kept going in and out of consciousness, I knew it took Samboy a long time to get me over that track.

Samboy pulled me to the edge of the swamp, then he stopped and whistled. Dog sat by my side and waited. Pretty soon Pappy came and picked me up in his strong arms. "You're home now, Samgirl," he said.

Samboy put the litter on Dog and filled it with twigs. They followed behind. "That's so we can say you and Samboy were picking branches in the swamp when you fell and hurt yourself," Pappy explained.

Inside the cabin, Pappy and Mammy put me on Samboy's bunk and covered me with blankets. Mammy wiped my face with wet cloths and Pappy spooned some broth into my mouth.

"I got myself fixed good," I murmured, "so I won't have Paul's baby between Mississippi and Indian Territory."

Mammy's eyes filled with tears. She leaned down and kissed me on my cheek. "I know. I figured it out as soon as Samboy told us you planned on stayin' at Aggie's all night. We done what we could, prayin' and sendin' Samboy with the litter."

After that, I slipped in and out of sleep for maybe a week. Mammy and Pappy told lots of lies to cover up what I'd done, and they took turns nursing me whenever they could. Samboy did his share of lying and nursing, while Dog hung around my bed like some magic charm that could bring me back to life just by being there.

For awhile, I worried I'd surely die. When I got over that, I worried I was too sick to go west. Finally, I got up and walked around a bit. I started bleeding again so I went back to my bunk. "Samboy," I said as I motioned him toward me, "you make sure to get whatever books you can when they clean out the schoolhouse."

Mammy fed me more and more broth, but I started my trip to the

Chickasaw Nation flat on my back in the wagon, with Mose and Amanda looking on.

We were someplace in western Mississippi when Paul came by to see me. By then, I walked next to the wagon for an hour in the morning and an hour in the evening. Even though I felt stronger, I was in no mood to see Paul, the cause of all my problems and pain.

Paul came sidling up and asked, "How are you, Samgirl? I heard you had a bad accident in the swamp."

I gazed straight into Paul's eyes. He didn't look like a pesky mosquito to me anymore. He looked like a huge, blood-sucking monster who had almost stolen my life, such as it was. I thought a second, then I put on level two of my feeble look—the one where I looked vacant *and* feverish—and raised my hand to my forehead. I let my eyelids flutter and my eyeballs roll sideways. "Oh, I think I'm— "

Paul started to sweat and called Samboy. "Take care of your sister, Samboy. She's about to die or something."

Samboy helped me back in the wagon and I sank down on my pallet. I knew I could use my trick on Paul for a week, maybe even a few weeks. Eventually, though, I'd have to return to being his possession. As fast as I thought that, a shiver shot through me in place of the fever. "Being a slave woman," I muttered, "is agony, misery, torment, and just plain hell." I wondered if the time would ever come when I could lay the burden of slavery down and pick up freedom instead.

After that, I got up and walked a little more each day, but I stayed close by our wagon and out of Paul's way. Mammy carried my meals from the cookfire so I didn't have to join the group to eat. I could always smell her coming, from the perfume of the meat and gravy she carried.

Often, Mammy brought some extras. "I've got some good blood food for you, Samgirl," she would say. Mammy also let some old square nails rust in vinegar, mixed the vinegar with sugar, and gave it to me for blood medicine.

The next time Paul came around to inquire after my health, I took one look at him and fainted. I didn't know myself if it was a fake faint or a real one. I just knew that when I saw him fear and anger flowed through my veins, then I turned weak. Next thing, I grabbed for the side of the wagon and headed for the ground. When I woke up, Paul was gone. I lay on my pallet in the wagon.

That wagon wasn't a hardship for me. Mose and Pappy had fixed it real nice. They put up nails all around for us to hang our clothes and towels on. They stacked the corn-husk mattresses and the quilts right behind the wagon seat. At night, Mose and Pappy and Samboy took their mattresses and quilts and slept under the wagon. Amanda, Mammy, and I rolled out our mattresses in the wagon so we had a nice room all to ourselves. Being a man himself, Dog usually slept outside with the men rather than inside with me.

In the wagon, we also had our wooden box and Mose and Amanda's box of stuff. We also had Mammy's prize possession, an eight-gallon kettle, being some sixteen inches across the top and standing some eighteen inches high, including the legs. We each had a small wooden stool we could sit on outside the wagon at night and take with us to the grub table at mealtime.

Pretty soon, Mammy said, "You got to get around more, Samgirl. You better start goin' to meals."

That didn't turn out too bad because old John's family ate first, and our folks sat down next. I hung real close to Mammy and kept a sharp lookout for Paul, who wasn't around much.

Then I heard from young Tate that Paul had taken to drinking. "Drinkin' real bad, that Paul is," Tate told me.

Liquor wasn't something we had ever seen around old John's house. Nero, who served at table, told us so. "The family has wine at dinner when company comes," he said, "but I never see anything else besides lemonade and tea and coffee and such."

Tate watched Paul real good. "Paul must buy his liquor at our supply stops," he told us. Although old John didn't seem to know about it, I doubted he would stand in Paul's way even if he did know. As far as I was concerned, Paul's drinking was fine if it kept him away from me.

I was happy to get back with the other folks and to taste the food while it was still hot from the campfire, or from those tiny campstoves Mammy and the other women used when it rained or the wind blew too hard to have a fire. Sometimes, Pappy helped Mammy dig a hole in the ground for the fire, so as to beat the wind. Sometimes she wrapped a blanket over her head to keep off the rain, but the campstoves were best of all. Even though they didn't cook much food at one time, the cooks could stand under a wagon flap while doing what they had to do. The stoves also kept the sand and dirt off the victuals. Once, after a windstorm, Mammy said, "The folks who ate the most breakfast ate the most sand. They'll walk around with a heavy craw the rest of the day."

I also enjoyed the food itself. I could have found the grub table by the odors alone. The smells of frying and baking and boiling drifted over our whole camp. Saliva flowed through my mouth and my stomach drew in upon itself, rumbling and grumbling, in anticipation of a fine meal.

On the trail, we ate pretty much what old John's family ate. The cooks turned wild strawberries, currants, or huckleberries into pies; they fried up soda fritters or squirrel or duck meat. When Mammy gave me a plate of fried meat with bread and her good gravy, I smiled. "I'm glad to be alive, Mammy."

Too, I discovered some new faces in our company. Old John had hired a man named Cap'n Jack to guide us to Indian Territory. Cap'n Jack appeared old and dark with scraggly gray whiskers, but I honestly couldn't tell how old or what breed of human he might be. Although Cap'n Jack was as thin as a broom handle, he grabbed a big plateful of food in between old John's family and us. Because he took it off someplace to eat by himself, I didn't get much chance to study him. "I think," I told Samboy, "that Jack is ageless and probably a mix of Indian and Mexican, with maybe a little slave thrown in."

"Who cares?" Samboy asked, always anxious to disagree or dispute whatever I might say. "He's a good trail boss and old John ain't."

I also noticed that old John had bought a blacksmith for the trip, a fine-looking slave named Levi. Levi's quick eyes didn't miss anything. When they turned my way they caused a quivery feeling in my stomach. Levi's eyes stood out against his face and had a sleepy look to them, like he was a lustful man when he had the opportunity. But Levi sure wasn't sleepy, because he saw everything that went on in camp or on the trail.

Levi spotted me the very first time I came to the grub table. After supper, he slid his wooden stool over next to mine. I glanced around. "Can I set here?" he asked.

Samboy had already run off to play with Becky's boy, Tom. Pappy was busy helping Mammy. I smiled at Levi while I sniffed his sweaty, hard-working man smell.

He smiled back and introduced himself. "I'm Levi," he said, "the new blacksmith."

"I'm Samgirl," said I. "I mostly do house jobs. I helped sew all these wagon covers."

Levi gazed around like he was real impressed. "You done a real fine job," he said and smiled some more.

We got to talking. I soon learned that Levi used to belong to some Cherokee folks in Indian Territory, he was probably a bit older than me, and he could read some. "How come they sold you?" I asked.

"My marse is a friend of some friend of old John. He heard old John needed a blacksmith for the trip so he sold me to him. He told me old John would be as good a marse as he was. From the food we get, I can see it's true."

I laughed and said, "These are extra good victuals. Don't be expecting this after we get to Indian Territory."

After that, Levi took to eating regular with me and Samboy and Pappy. He petted Dog and slipped him a scrap or two under the table when he thought no one was watching. But I watched. I began to develop a deep feeling for that man. Every time he walked toward me, my heart jumped to meet him.

Levi never came around the wagon, but he sure proved good company at mealtimes. He told us about Indian Territory—which didn't sound too bad; about himself—which sounded mighty good; and about blacksmithing—which sounded like a lot of hard work.

I could see Levi was taking a shine to me as well. I felt guilty about that, knowing Paul was lurking in the background waiting to pounce on me one of these days. I felt bad, too, because I knew I couldn't have children, but Levi didn't know. I never said anything about anything. I just pushed my guilt into the shadows of my mind and let the feelings grow between us.

chapter

six

We drew near the western border of Mississippi when old John and Cap'n Jack started calling meetings and telling us about the river crossing. Cap'n Jack stood on a fallen log and explained, "We'll take flat ferries made of logs across the Mississippi River near Helena. We'll wait in line until the ferrymen call our group. Then our men will drive the wagons onto the ferries, while the women and children lead the cows on."

Of course, old John had to get his bit in: "Once on the ferries, you all stand real still and keep the animals quiet as the ferrymen pole us across."

Old John said young Tate and Levi—who I noticed were getting real thick with each other—would go on the first ferry carrying slave wagons. They were the strongest men we had, so they could help the wagons off on the Arkansas side. It all sounded simple enough.

We reached the ferry on a Friday afternoon. Crowds of people milled around. I had a hard time breathing because of all the dust and people stench and animal stink. Although other travelers stared at us, they pretty much left us alone. When you think of it, I guess most white folks in their right minds would want to stay clear of a mess of Indians and their slaves. A few poked around us selling stuff and I noticed Paul up the shoreline dickering and making a swap.

At it turned out, we had to camp downriver that night and take a number for the next day's crossing. The smoky odor from the cooking fires mingled with the food aromas to give a sweet, satisfying fragrance to the camp. Everything stayed quiet in camp that night. Paul never came out of his wagon once the entire evening. I hoped he drank so much he ruined his memory and forgot about me, or maybe even ruined himself as far as sex matters went.

In the morning, we packed up and readied ourselves near the ferry, waiting to hear our number called. "The river looks too wide to cross," I told Mammy. "And it's so muddy."

"Hush, Samgirl," she said. "You're the one who wanted to come. Don't go complainin' about it now."

About noon, the youngest-looking ferryman yelled out, "Number twenty-seven. Twenty-seven right here."

It appeared to me that the ferryman about fell in the water when he saw how many wagons we had and how dusky all our people were, including the master's family. He soon recovered himself and started waving and yelling, "Twenty-seven this side. Hold them animals steady, now."

Young Tate and Levi darted and dashed everywhere, keeping things organized and feeling their own importance. Old John and Nellie took care of paying the ferrymen, but I didn't see Paul anywhere. Old John and Nellie's wagon went on first, with Esther and Rebecca inside. The ferryman put rocks under the wagon's wheels to keep it from rolling. That filled the ferry and the man slammed the back shut and away they went.

The second ferry was a bit bigger. "Here comes Paul's wagon," Samboy said.

Even though he drove the wagon, Paul appeared mighty wobbly on its seat. Then came Simon's and Peter's wagon, with Simon driving and looking serious about the whole affair. Then they were off.

And so it went until about half our wagons were gliding across the Mississippi River, the covers I helped sew flapping in the wind. Next thing I knew, I heard a lot of yelling coming from the second ferry. It was more than halfway across and something seemed to have gone wrong.

"Halloo," one man shouted.

"Man off the side," another added.

I jumped up on one of our wagon wheels so I could see over the heads of the crowd, which pushed and shoved and made a noisy hubbub about the whole thing. From my vantage point, I saw Peter do a strange thing—he jumped from the ferry into the brown river. Although I couldn't see Paul or Simon, I supposed they sat on the wagon seats holding everything steady. I soon learned my mistake, for there was Peter hauling Paul right out of that river. Simon reached over the edge of the ferry and grabbed Paul and pulled him back on board.

I saw that Paul had gone real limp. He looked like he didn't care much for all the fuss. Right there on the ferry floor, Simon got on top of Paul and started pushing his chest and trying to pump water out of him. In the meantime, Peter ran around trying to hold the wagons firm. The ferry men tried to slow down yet stay going enough to be out the way of the ferries coming behind.

Finally, Simon hoisted Paul up and threw him in the back of Paul's wagon. Simon climbed up on Paul's wagon seat and Peter jumped on the other wagon seat where Simon should have been. The ferry picked up its rhythm and the whole line started moving again.

You can bet we were mighty curious to know what happened to Paul. "What happened?" Samboy asked me.

"I think Paul fell over the side," I replied.

When we finally reached the other side we heard all about it from young Tate and Levi, who were bursting to tell what they knew. It seems that Paul had been sucking on his jug on Friday night and again on Saturday morning. He was drunk as a sick coon when they started to cross. Thinking he was immortal, Paul went to the edge of the ferry to watch the crossing. He promptly fell in and commenced to drown himself. That's when Peter saw him and jumped in the river and saved Paul's life.

We were also curious about how old John and Nellie would take this. It turned out, however, that Cap'n Jack took charge of the matter.

"You, Simon and Peter," Jack ordered, "take turns drivin' Paul's wagon until Paul comes to himself." After that Simon and Peter were to take turns riding with Paul and keeping him away from drink. Knowing how mean Paul was and how meek Simon and Peter were, I judged the latter an impossible task.

At supper, I pumped Levi for whatever else he knew. "About that Paul," I began, "is he going to be sick long?"

"He'll be all right in a few days. His mammy cried and moaned over him, but he only took a dunk in the river."

I frowned when I heard this. Not that I wished anybody dead, but I sure wished Paul real sick for a good, long time. "How are they going to stop that boy from drinking?" I asked.

Levi pondered this a minute and said, "I don't think anyone can stop Paul from drinking. Not his mammy or his brothers or, leastwise, his pappy. Paul's the oldest and has him a mean streak that scares even old John."

I nodded knowingly. Levi hadn't told me anything I didn't already know. "What do you think will happen to Mister Paul?"

Levi pondered again and looked me in the eye and muttered, "I think we're going to have more trouble with Mister Paul before we reach Indian Territory. I just hope it don't come down on our heads."

Levi's look and his words stirred up my innards something fierce. I couldn't tell if he knew about what Paul did to me back in Mississippi or the truth about my accident in the swamp before we left. I did know how folks like to talk. I bet Levi knew more about me than I wanted him to.

The next day, my heart hanging heavy in my chest, I turned my back on Helena. I thought about our next supply stop at Pine Bluff. God forgive me, I wished we had left Paul behind somewhere at the bottom of the Mississippi River.

We started off toward the trading post at Pine Bluff feeling pretty good. We were out of Mississippi and across the mighty river. The soil was even richer and blacker than in Mississippi, especially as we neared the Arkansas River.

I was feeling relaxed because Paul didn't show his face anywhere. Whether Paul suffered from sickness or shame, I didn't know and didn't care.

After supper one night, Coffee Fred—folks called him that because he looked like the color of Missus Nellie's coffee after she poured top cream in it—pulled out a fiddle almost as old as the river itself and started to pick a tune. We all sang a bit, and when old John or Cap'n Jack didn't come around to complain, we sang a little more. That became the pattern; a good supper followed by some good singing. I even started to enjoy myself.

During meal stops, I helped Mammy with her cooking chores. Almost every afternoon, I drove our wagon some to relieve Pappy. We made about thirteen miles on a good day, at least according to a gadget old John had hooked up to the wheel of the lead wagon. In between driving or whatever, I mooned around about Levi and tried to sneak a glimpse of where he was or what he might be doing. He seemed busy, what with shoeing horses and fixing wagon parts and making new pieces for busted ones. I always saw him at mealtimes, though, and that was just fine with me.

One afternoon, some loud talk ensued between old John and Cap'n Jack about which road we should take across Arkansas.

"I want to head for Little Rock and on north," old John said. His idea was to enter Indian Territory at Fort Smith and drop southward to Tishomingo.

Cap'n Jack had a different idea. He yelled so loud we could all hear him. "You hired me to be boss," he told old John, "now let me be boss."

"But— " old John said.

"We're goin' to take the Great Southwest Trail almost to Texarkana, then we'll follow along north of the Red River for a spell. That'll take us near to your land."

"But— " old John said again.

"It's settled," Cap'n Jack roared, "the Southwest Trail it is."

No one heard any more buts from old John then or later. We did it Cap'n Jack's way and it proved to be a good one. We had plenty of water for ourselves and our animals. It seemed that on every side there lay a river or stream. Cap'n Jack liked to shout out the major rivers as we passed them: "We're goin' over the White River now, folks," he said.

If anything, the soil grew darker and the air clammier. I struggled under the weight of the muggy air and hoped it would be drier in Oklahoma. "Arkansas River comin' up," Jack alerted us.

Even though we sometimes saw other groups of folks moving along that trail, as they had near Helena, most of them left us alone. One day old John decided he wanted to stop and have a chat with the train behind us, which also carried slaves with them. Cap'n Jack went with old John and Nellie. Jack seemed like he wouldn't mind some company and news of home and maybe a strong drink.

When they came back we could tell something was wrong. They appeared agitated, like they had seen the shadow of death.

Pretty soon, old John and Cap'n Jack called one of their meetings. "Gather 'round here," Jack shouted. "We have somethin' to tell you."

We all bunched up, all the while whispering and wondering. Shivers ran down my back when Jack said, "That other train had a bad accident. One of their young'uns wandered away from his folks and went poking around the cookfire. Don't know how he done it, but that two-year-old child dumped himself into a kettle of scalding water and boiled himself to death."

At that, everyone moaned and prayed to send that poor child's soul on its way to heaven.

"Quiet," Cap'n Jack yelled, "all that don't help nothin'. In the morning, me and Missus Nellie will pass out red neckerchiefs, one for every child in this train. If you have children, you tie red kerchiefs around their necks so you can see them all the time. You watch them good, especially round fires."

I thought Cap'n Jack's idea was a good one, but it caused trouble for Samboy. Being he was cowboying for the train, he already wore a red bandanna around his neck. Because Samboy didn't want to be marked as a child, he ripped that red bandanna off before Nellie even passed out the red kerchiefs for the children.

"But, Samboy," said I, "that bandanna's for your protection, so you won't get dust down your shirt and all."

"I'm not wearin' any red rag around my neck that makes me look like a baby," he said. He flexed his arm muscles just to make sure I understood that he was fast approaching manhood.

Mammy overheard us and, as was her fashion, acted right away. She went directly to Nellie, who kindly switched Samboy's red bandanna for a blue one. Mammy came back and, without a word, handed Samboy the blue kerchief. Also without a word, he took it and knotted it around his neck. So we got through that crisis.

After that, everyone watched their children closely. Red kerchiefs flitted all over the trail and the camp. Folks sure hollered if they went near fires, but folks weren't as careful as they might have been about other things.

One morning we were moving along pretty good when up in front we heard a woman screaming. Everyone except the people driving wagons ran forward to help. It turned out that Becky's youngest, a boy by the name of Handy, had fallen asleep and bounced right off the wagon seat. Handy was a strong child with more stamina than most. Yet he hit his head good on the iron-rimmed wagon wheel going down and hit it again on the ground when he landed. He lay on the ground with his eyes closed and his sturdy body limp in the dust.

"Let me at him," Mammy yelled. She scooped up that child and ran with him off the side of the trail and down to the creek. You can bet Becky was hard on Mammy's heels. Mammy laid Handy's head next to the stream and used her hand as a ladle to pour water over Handy's bumps.

After a few minutes, Handy opened his eyes and looked around. "Who you?" he asked.

Mammy sighed but she kept right on spooning. Becky started sobbing with relief, sure now that Handy would live.

After that, Mammy became the unofficial doctor of the train. She treated fevers, rashes, mumps, and measles. Old John said he had tried to buy us a doctor woman before we left, but couldn't find one. Even though we never did find out why old John sold our midwife, I suspected she had fooled around too much with voodoo for old John's liking. He accepted Chickasaw rituals and he borrowed parts of Christianity, yet old John mistrusted anything that smacked of Africa. More than once, old John said, "Slaves' rites amount to no more than voodoo."

That reminded me to ask Samboy about his voodoo chain and lock buried by the post in Pappy's vegetable patch back in Mississippi. I waited until I drove our wagon alone.

"Hop up on the seat with me for awhile, Samboy," I yelled through the hoof noise and shouting of the trail.

This wasn't unusual. Our wagon traveled near the end of the train where we ate a lot of dust, but because no one noticed us, me and Samboy often drove along studying the schoolbooks he'd saved from the trash when we left Mississippi.

This time, though, Samboy appeared hesitant. In fact, he seemed agitated and maybe even angry. "What's wrong with you, boy?"

Samboy scowled at me, the white rings of his eyes standing out in his dusty face. "My cows are the stubbornest ones of the bunch. This here old Bossy is always stoppin' and eatin' grass at the side of the trail instead of movin' her skinny butt toward Indian Territory the way she's supposed to."

I glanced at Bossy; she certainly looked mulish. I had to sympathize with Samboy on this matter. Suddenly I got an inspiration. "Tie the cows to the back of the wagon," said I. "The wagon will show old Bossy who's boss."

Samboy prodded old Bossy and her pals around to the back of the wagon, but he tied only Bossy's head to the tailgate. That was enough; her buddies straggled along behind her. Samboy jumped on the wagon seat with me. "Free of those pests at last."

"But you're supposed to be the big cowboy on this trip," said I.

"Yeah, I'm cowboyin' for milk cows who don't give milk anymore anyway," he grumbled. "Did you call me here just to scold me about cows?"

"No, I want to talk about your voodoo chain and lock. Did you leave them or take them?"

"I speculated about it for a long while," Samboy answered, his voice calmer now that I'd switched the subject away from Bossy and her gang. "I decided to leave them behind. After all, they belong to the man who got free in that swamp. But I think about them nearly every day. And I think about freedom."

At that, I heaved a big sigh and said, "So do I. But it's not so bad on the trail. The food is fine and the work's not too hard."

"That's true," Samboy said, "but we're goin' to be in Indian Territory pretty soon and the food and work will go back to usual."

"That's true," said I, "but, in the meantime, Paul doesn't leave his wagon much these days. Anyway, he ain't back here pestering me."

"That's true," Samboy said, "but you watch out. Paul's driving his wagon again and meaner than ever. I think he's ashamed about fallin' in the river."

I started sweating now and resumed worrying about Paul. "Is Paul drinking again?"

"I don't think so. Simon and Peter watch him pretty close. But they're worried about Pine Bluff. They say he can get drunk again there."

After Samboy left me and went back to his horse-riding, I kept driving. My heart bumped and thumped in my chest. I wished one of those hawks would swoop down from the lazy summer sky and carry Paul off. I knew that would never happen—that I was going to have to deal with Paul myself one of these days. I dreaded that day's coming and did my best to push it from my mind. Instead, I hummed a trail song I had learned, something about green hills and valleys at the end of the road.

"I'm surely hoping for hills and valleys," said I out loud. "This place puts me in mind of the swampland back home."

Sure enough, we made it all the way to Pine Bluff without any more than the usual troubles. A bit of swearing, which made Nellie mad, and some fighting, which made old John mad. And once we had to travel on a Sunday. That night old John read to everyone from his fat Bible, but it wasn't the same as stopping for the day and thinking about God.

Traveling on Sunday made it hard on the women, who used the Sunday stop to wash clothes. They usually hauled out their cooking kettles, found a nice spot on a nearby stream where they could use the rocks as washboards, and away they went. They laughed and talked while they worked and had a break from the usual trail routine. When they finished washing, they laid the clothes over the grass and bushes and low tree branches to dry. They had no thought of ironing on the trail. The sad irons stayed packed away someplace.

I heard there was no creek to camp on that Sunday anyway. Also, Serena, the head washwoman, was bent double with convulsions from something she ate, so she wouldn't have been able to organize the clothes-washing teams. Knowing her, Serena probably thought she was smarter than Cap'n Jack and ate something wild he told us not to eat. Mammy gave Serena a vinegar and lard mixture. I suspected Mammy laughed inside while she did it.

Mammy had to do some other doctoring during that stretch of Arkansas, but it was nothing serious. "Mostly colds or ague," Mammy told me. "I mix melted tallow and turpentine on rags and pin it near the sick person's neck at night to help them breathe."

One time, a rattlesnake bit one of our boys and Mammy grabbed up a young turkey, wrung its neck off, and split it open. She tied the raw turkey meat to the wound, where the meat drew the poison right out and saved the boy's life.

We had one young woman, Dorcas, who turned up pregnant, but it seemed we'd be in Indian Territory well before she had her baby. We also had some mighty sick cows and Mammy mixed up a lard and vinegar remedy for them, almost the same as she had given to Serena.

One morning young Tate had a hard time yoking the oxen to Becky and Eurias's wagon. He went to cussing and kicking the beasts. "Damn you, Tige," he yelled. "Get on, Buck," he added as he leveled his boot at the near oxen.

As a result, the oxen started out fast and upset the wagon. That didn't come to much, except that it slowed us down and gave poor Handy, who was inside the wagon, another bump on his head. Mammy fixed it with a hug and some kisses.

"Thank you, Auntie Chloe," Handy managed this time. Then he wiggled out of Mammy's lap and went back to his little friends.

When we finally arrived at the Pine Bluff trading post, old John and Cap'n Jack bargained for what we needed, but they didn't have much leverage way out here. Pine Bluff had been around since 1819 or so, but it was mostly an outpost for white men who traded with Quapaw Indians. The prices were what the prices were. There wasn't much changing that. Old John and Cap'n Jack had to buy what we needed and pay premium price for it, whether they wanted to or not.

Paul had his own trade deal in mind. That night I saw him sneak around the side of the trading shack. I looked at the burnt orange moon, all ringed with a halo of sweating air, and waited. When Paul slithered back toward camp he carried a jug in his left hand. I knew someone was in for it then. I feared it would be me.

Sure enough, Paul strolled around camp after his supper and spotted me at the grub table with Levi, both of us perched on our little stools chattering away. Paul walked right over to us as bold as a gator in a swamp and said, "Samgirl, come with me."

I gave Levi a sick grin. I felt certain he could hear the terror coursing through my veins. I followed right behind Paul down to the brook. I faced him and waited to hear the bad news.

"Are you feeling well?" he asked real polite, his grey-brown eyes scrunched up with mock concern.

I watched his hard eyes and sniffed his breath. I replied, "Sort of yes, sort of no."

Paul grabbed my right arm. He hauled me up close to his face. His sour breath poured over me and made my stomach sick. "As soon as we get away from Pine Bluff," he ordered, "you're going to meet me after it gets dark. I'll let you know the exact spot."

Way behind Paul's back I saw Simon and Peter looking around and calling for Paul. I decided not to remark on it in case Paul felt shamed and, being as how I was closest at the moment, took it out on me. Paul must have heard his brothers' shouts because he dropped my arm and hissed, "I mean it. You understand?"

"I understand," said I, dropping my head to my chest, inside of which my heart churned and turned all about.

But we didn't leave Pine Bluff the next day. Cap'n Jack discovered we had so many repairs waiting for Levi's hand that he ordered Levi to set up a temporary forge and get to the wagons before we put any more miles on them. That day Levi spent over his shimmering fire fixing everything from broken wagon yokes to iron barrel staves.

I thought God had given me a day of reprieve. I enjoyed the birds singing and the heavy smell of the summer air until I saw Paul head toward Levi with an unsteady gait. Paul drew close to Levi and watched him work for a bit. Next, he baited Levi with insults. "Where do you come from, nigger?" Paul asked.

"From Indian Territory, Marse," Levi replied, all politeness and good feelings on the surface, but I noticed his shoulders laying back a bit farther than usual.

"You think you know all about Indian Territory then?" Paul went on. He stood now with his hands on his hips, just waiting for Levi to make a misstep.

"No, Marse, I surely don't." Levi was all wary courtesy; his manners hadn't slipped a bit yet.

"Then why do you spend your suppertime filling our niggers' ears with twaddle about the territory?"

"I'm sorry, Marse. I won't do it no more."

I noticed Levi had not only pulled his shoulders back, but had slipped into heavy slave-quarter dialect. Although I wanted to walk away and help Mammy with her cooking duties, I seemed incapable of moving. I was stuck to that spot just as surely as if Levi had welded me there.

Behind me, I heard silence beginning to creep over the crowd. I felt other eyes coming around toward Paul and Levi. I wondered where old John and Cap'n Jack had gone to. And where were Paul's brothers, who were supposed to be his keepers?

I watched Paul spread his feet wider apart and ask Levi, "You have a woman back where you came from?"

Levi lowered his eyes and seemed sad. When he spoke, his tone was gloomy. "I had a wife once, Marse, but she died bringin' a baby into this here world."

Paul didn't say anything, but I stiffened sharply. This was the first I'd heard about Levi's wife and baby. Even though I knew it was foolish, I turned feverish with jealousy over Levi's wife. The green pangs of envy raced through my body, making me dizzy. I couldn't see the scene before me in such sharp detail as I had a moment ago.

"You planning on taking one of our slave women as wife, then?" Paul asked Levi, while I stood there ready to faint.

Levi looked up, mannerly yet with anger rising in his eyes. The whites of his eyes shone frosty, even though the sun raged overhead.

He spoke in a terse way that scared me, if not Paul. "Marse, I ain't plannin' on nothin'. You and old marse John make such decisions for me." Levi banged his hammer on the red-hot horseshoe he held on the anvil. I saw the sparks jump higher and higher with every blow. The air hung around Levi's shoulders; not a bit of breeze shifted it one way or another.

Paul turned insolent. His eyebrows arched and a slight smile curved his cruel lips. "How about if I give you a slave gal I also like to use once in awhile? How would that sit with you, nigger?" I sweated now; Paul had come too close to making public a matter that everyone probably whispered about anyway.

Levi raised his head from his work, leaving the horseshoe blazing and sizzling on the anvil. "I'd be glad to take any gal you decide is right for me, Marse." Levi smiled, an empty smile that made his face look like a scarecrow set out to protect the master's corn from scavengers. I noticed Levi's muscles flexing under the back of his shirt, which sweat and grime molded to him.

Before I could return my eyes to Paul, he seized Levi's tongs and swiped that blistering horseshoe right off Levi's anvil. Paul danced around with the tongs and horseshoe held high above his head, taking aim at Levi. Levi saw what was coming and ducked, though not low enough. Paul hurled that horseshoe through the air so it parted Levi's hair where no part should be. I could feel Levi's wound searing my own scalp. I knew Levi would bear Paul's mark the rest of his life.

Not satisfied with that damage, Paul rushed Levi and jumped on his back. A collective gasp went up from the crowd at this rash act. Few planters—white or Indian—would allow themselves to get so enraged and reckless.

Being a smart man who knew he couldn't punch his master's son into mush as he would like, Levi swung around with Paul hanging on. Paul lost his grip and flailed at Levi's shoulders. In that second, Levi leaned over backwards and shook Paul off his back—square into the tub of water Levi had been using to cool hot iron.

By then, the hollering and bellowing of the crowd finally let Simon and Peter know Paul was in trouble. The two brothers came running. They stopped sudden-like when they saw Paul thrashing about in the tub of water. "What now?" Peter moaned.

Simon didn't waste time asking questions, nor did he assume Levi was at fault. Instead, Simon judged Paul as the cause of the mischief. Simon hauled Paul out of the tub and socked him on the jaw, leveling Paul to the ground with that one blow. Simon and Peter dragged Paul out of there like a sack of dead possums.

I retreated toward our wagon, leading Levi along with me.

"Mammy will fix you up, Levi," I babbled into his dazed face.

It didn't take much tugging on his shirt-sleeve to get him going the direction I wanted. At the wagon, Mammy doctored Levi's head with salve, while I sat wringing my hands and praying for Levi. Mammy stopped the burn from swelling anymore, but she told him, "You're goin' to have this the rest of your life, Levi."

"Yes'um, Aunt Chloe," he answered real calm-like. "It looks like Mister Paul branded me good." Even though Levi's eyes had lost their frosty look, I could see he had deep wrath in him against Paul. I knew in my grieving heart that worse was yet to come.

I wish I could say that event was the last disaster during our trip to Indian Territory, but of course it wasn't. The westward trek is a hard journey that frays tempers and breaks stronger men than ours. Besides, we were already at odds among ourselves.

The following morning, we headed away from Pine Bluff going south toward Camden. "Indians once roamed trails here 'bouts," Cap'n Jack told us. "But it's mostly cotton plantin' now."

I glanced at the cotton fields stretching in every direction. Vaguely, I heard Cap'n Jack announce the Sabine River. But mostly I worried Paul would turn up at my side at any moment. I feared he would pull me off into the bush. I had felt so free of him on this trail that I couldn't imagine lying with him ever again. Paul might even murder me. Every nerve I owned leaped and shuddered as I plodded along, head down, breathing dust as I went.

But I didn't see Paul all that day, or the next, or the next. An eerie pall hung over the wagons as we moved along, as well as over the grub table at mealtimes. Even though Levi still sat with me and Samboy and

Pappy at supper, the easy feelings ceased to flow. Talk became sparse. Dog begged in vain for a handout from Levi. After supper, Coffee Fred didn't pull his fiddle out and nobody sang.

It seemed we were all waiting for something to happen, or maybe for Cap'n Jack and old John to call one of their meetings to tell us what to think about everything that had already happened. Eventually, Cap'n Jack and old John did call a meeting, but it was about Camden, a cotton town on the Ouachita River.

"We're goin' down low," Cap'n Jack said. "Camden's near sea level. That means it'll be hot this time of year, hot enough to make people itchy and set anger to flarin'."

"So," old John added, "be polite and stick to yourselves and we'll all stay out of trouble."

"We're goin' to camp there for one night only," Jack added in a quick, hearty way, "to get some supplies. Then we'll get right on the road again." He grinned at us and spit tobacco out of the right side of his mouth, almost hitting poor, hapless Handy with the spittle.

We stopped to fish in the Ouachita River. Because we lacked the proper gear we had little luck. When we arrived at Camden, we did just like old John told us. We camped in sight of a new stage stop being built on Washington Street, but nobody except old John and Cap'n Jack went into town.

I guessed Simon and Peter would keep close guard over Paul, unless he managed to slip away in the middle of the night and return before they discovered he had gone. No one said anything about our troubles. We acted like a normal train going through to Indian Territory.

A day or two, or maybe three, out of Camden and things still went along quiet. We'd be nearing Texarkana and crossing into Texas any time now.

I still hadn't seen Paul. Even when Cap'n Jack called a meeting to tell us how to treat the few Grand Caddoe Indians living along the trail, Paul didn't appear.

"They're real peaceable," Jack said.

"And they're nice people," John added. Then he gave us his usual message, "Leave them alone and we'll all stay out of trouble."

About then, I thought old John should be talking to Paul rather than us. The trouble we caused cussing and fighting seemed very small next to Paul's wickedness. But, as I well knew, old John wasn't much for curbing the spirits of his eldest son.

We headed for Lost Prairie, a small settlement about fifteen miles east of Texarkana. We wouldn't go quite to Texarkana, Cap'n Jack said, but would pick up the Red River and follow it west. Even though I had hopes of making it to Indian Territory without ever seeing Paul again, that wish was soon dashed.

Paul slid up to me after supper and mumbled, "Meet me near the rushes by the creek right after the sun drops down."

I smelled hard drink on him. I knew I would put people's lives in jeopardy if I refused, so I just nodded that I understood. After Paul disappeared, my whole body shook and sweat poured off me like a rain shower. I told Mammy I was going to the rock on the rise to think a bit. Mammy was too busy cleaning up after supper to remark one way or the other.

I planned to sit on that rock and steady myself for what I knew was coming. I climbed the rise real sorrowful-like and sat on that hard rock. I watched the sun start to drop and dusk come on. The twilight dazzled me with its purples and golds and oranges, but I was in no mood to properly appreciate a sunset. I began to mutter and even to cry a bit. I thought about Levi, then Paul; Paul, then Levi. I hated Paul as much as I loved Levi, and that was a powerful amount.

All of a sudden, I went a little berserk. I pictured Samboy's voodoo chain and thought how Paul was my chain. I thought about how I could never have babies with someone I loved, like Levi, because of Paul. Like a sleepwalker, I got up real slow and quiet. I walked down the back of that rise away from camp. I didn't run; I just sort of wandered off.

When night fell, I wasn't at the bulrushes by the creek to meet Paul. No, I meandered around somewhere in southwestern Arkansas with no idea where I was or where I going. I squished my feet into the rich dirt and kept on walking.

I didn't think about Mammy or Pappy or Samboy or Dog or the ruckus Paul might raise in camp. I only thought about getting to the end of the earth and dropping over the side once and for all.

Of course, that wasn't to be. I climbed an old gum tree and slept the best I could. When dawn came, I stuck my head out of the branches.

"Samgirl, where are you?" I heard in the distance.

It seemed like the sounds came from a long way off. I slept a bit. By afternoon I was mighty hungry and thirsty and I didn't hear the calls anymore.

I shinnied down that tree and turned around to find myself staring straight at the flank of a horse.

"You ain't one of old John's," said I. This horse had patches of color—brown and white and tan—all over it. On it sat a delicate-looking Indian woman dressed in buff-colored buckskin. Her black hair hung long and straight down her back. She seemed to have beads everywhere—mostly red and blue. They were on her dress, around her neck, around her wrists, and hanging from her ears.

She stared at me and I stared at her. She drew the pony closer to me and reached out to touch my hair. Then she mumbled something that sounded like "puckachee" and motioned for me to jump up behind her. I figured I didn't have much to lose, so I climbed up on a tree stump and vaulted right on that pony's back as if it were one of our docile, old plow mules from back home.

After that, we rode a long time. Night had started to come down again when we reached an Indian village. I had only known a few Indians in my life and they were all peaceful, so I had no fear of what might happen.

We rode to the center of the village and stopped. Everyone babbled in a language I couldn't understand. Finally the head man appeared. "Hello, little sister," he said and I almost fell right off the back of that horse. He helped me down and held me until my legs were strong enough to stand by themselves.

"Hello," said I back, as I wondered what I'd gotten myself into now.

"Why are you out here all by yourself?" he asked, bowing toward me slightly to better hear my answer.

"Because I'm running from a bad man who wants to— " I stopped at that point, not sure how to express what I meant. I must have glanced down at my body because he gave me a knowing smile and said, "Ah ha." He rubbed his chin and said, "You can stay with us, little buffalo girl, as long as you want. But if your people come for you, we'll have to give you back."

I nodded, hearing my stomach gurgle and grumble at the same time. He laughed and said some strange words to the comely woman who had brought me there. She dismounted and took me away and fed me. Then she took me into her tent, where she showed me to her son. I let that small boy feel my hair. He laughed and giggled until he was almost sick.

She bedded me and him down next to the fire in her tent and covered us with animal furs. I sniffed the air and found a different smell than in our wagon—more herbs and animal odors here—and fell right to sleep. During the night, I dreamt that God let me stay there forever. I woke up at dawn with a prayer in my mouth.

Of course, it wasn't to be either. That very morning I sighted the dust of a wagon train coming along the trail, winding its way through cotton fields and pine trees. Sure enough, Cap'n Jack rode way out in the lead. He came into the village by himself and swapped some politeness with the head man in the funny words all the Indians in that camp used.

The head man pointed to where I sat by the fire of my friend's tent. From his rucksack, Jack pulled some tobacco and calico and other odds-and-ends of trade goods. The head man picked out what he wanted and straightened up. "That's enough pay for keeping your girl overnight," he said. "I thank you for your generosity."

Jack replied "humph" and swung his rucksack over his shoulder. He headed for me. Jack didn't even say good morning; he just seized me by the arm and dragged me off to his horse. Even though my legs felt mighty sore from yesterday's riding, he didn't give me a chance to complain. "You're in big trouble, girl," he told me as we rode off. I waved to my friends behind me and dreaded what lay ahead.

"You're a run-off slave," Jack added. "You know what slave owners do to runaways? They whip them, that's what."

I'd never thought ahead to the consequences of my running away. I shook and trembled. "Unless you have yourself a good excuse, you're in trouble up to your neck," he added.

I had nothing to say as we rode back toward the waiting wagons. I noticed old John and Simon and Paul riding in front of our train. I figured I'd learn the hard way the meaning of all those stories I'd heard at Aggie's, how the lash feels and how much blood it takes to run all the way down to the ground. I thought they might even hang me from one of the tall oak trees along the road. I hid my head behind Jack's back and pretended that we were heading toward the Indian camp and my friend instead.

We reached the train way too fast for me. In that time, I had relived every bit of pain I'd ever experienced in my lifetime and multiplied it by ten. I felt certain my foolishness had brought an end to my strong will, if not to my life itself. I almost fell off the horse when Cap'n Jack reined the animal to a standstill in front of old John.

Cap'n Jack said loud and nasty, "Here she is. Cost me a peck of money and goods to get her, it did."

Old John shook his head and made gurgling noises at the back of his throat. Paul appeared dark, like he had killing on his mind.

Simon stepped forward first. He turned sideways so he could speak to all of us at one time. "Pa, there are some things you don't know that you should know," he began.

I almost fell off the back of Jack's horse again.

"Paul drinks himself insane and takes his bad head out on the negras," Simon continued.

Old John's eyes bugged out. He listened hard while Simon told about Paul baiting Levi and throwing the burning horseshoe at him. Clearly, old John didn't want to hear this. His fine opinion of Paul was going down fast. Already, old John seemed a mite less tolerant of Paul than he had been before we started on the trail. Then Simon told about how Paul always pestered and threatened me and how I had probably run away to escape Paul.

"Is this true, Samgirl?" old John hollered at me. I felt dizzy and decided not to say yes or no. If I said yes Paul would kill me for sure. If I said no, old John would beat me for running away. So I put on my level-two idiot look, kind of stupid and sick at the same time.

Simon took in the situation real fast and said, "She can't say yes, Pa, or Paul will get her later. Why not just let the whole thing lay? Say Samgirl got lost and let it go at that."

Old John looked peaked and like he would fall down right there on the trail and never get up again. He stared at Paul and shook his head as if to clear it. Finally he snapped out, "All right, Samgirl was lost. Cap'n Jack found her and brought her back. Now that's that and I don't want to hear anymore about it."

Old John turned away, but Simon wasn't satisfied yet. "Pa, me and Peter aren't guarding Paul no more. He's crazy. He'll have us dead before we reach Indian Territory."

All this time Paul looked on, his head swiveling back-and-forth, back-and-forth, from one to the other. He appeared stunned, sort of like a little boy, and I almost felt sorry for him. "What am I supposed to do with Paul, then?" old John asked.

Simon thought a minute and replied, "Let young Tate ride with Paul. Tate is the strongest man in camp. He can save Paul from himself."

At that, Paul came back to life. He burst out, "I ain't having any nigger riding in my wagon. I'll ride alone and God damn the whole bunch of you."

Old John's eyes grew big, then teary. He turned his back on all of us. He said not another word about it.

And that's how it came to be that Paul rode alone in his wagon and I ran back to Mammy and Pappy without a cowhiding. Mammy and Pappy hugged and kissed me, Dog slobbered on my bare leg, but Samboy pulled me off behind the wagon. "What's freedom like?" he asked, panting with the thrill of everything I done.

"I was only gone awhile," said I, "but I met some nice folks and slept by a warm fire all wrapped up in animal skins." I wished me and my family were in that Indian camp. "I know one thing now. Running away is going to take some planning. We can't just wander off into the wilderness."

Samboy shook his head as if he understood exactly what I meant. "Look out for Paul," he warned me. "This ain't the end, by a far ways. You know it and I know it and Paul knows it."

I knuckled that child's arm—I could no longer reach his head—and said, "Stick by me, Samboy, and watch out for me."

Samboy never had the chance to guard me. That afternoon, after we stopped to camp, old John and Cap'n Jack went ahead of the train to spot the trail. Paul grabbed his chance. I kicked black clods of dirt near our wagon when I saw Paul coming, hate seeping from his every pore. I could even smell the malice frying in his blood.

"Come here, Samgirl," he said in a voice hard around the edges with fury. Before I knew it, Paul had slipped a rope over my head and tightened it around my neck. He dragged me like a roped calf toward his wagon.

I thought I knew what he had in mind until we got closer and I spotted a big fire going with a long iron thing in its center. "What're you going do to me?" I choked out, that rope wrapping itself tighter around my neck with every word.

Paul didn't answer. He pulled me closer to the fire. He slammed me in the face with his one of his stony fists. He tied me to the wheel of his wagon, muttering all the time, "You're my property. I'll punish you if no one else will."

I shuddered, even so close to the heat of the fire, which annoyed Paul and made him draw the ropes tighter. "While you were gone—I should say lost," Paul growled, "I ordered our blacksmith—you know him, his name is Levi—to make this nice branding iron for me."

He pulled the iron thing out of the fire and I saw a white-hot *P* on its end. Paul walked toward me. I couldn't resist because my hands and feet were tied. I shut my eyes. I felt Paul rip open the front of my dress. The next thing I knew I'd passed out from the shock of that searing *P* on my chest.

I guess I came to when Paul threw a bucket of water in my face. My chest flamed and I was bleary and vague in my mind. I thought I saw Levi coming and there he was, chains in one hand and a hammer in the other. Levi looked miserable, but Paul waved a pint-sized gun at Levi.

Levi moved toward me. He made me a chain bracelet on each wrist and whispered, "Don't worry. I can get them right off again."

Paul pointed the dinky gun at Levi. He ordered him to pick me up and take me back to Mammy's and Pappy's wagon. "Yes, Marse," was all Levi answered.

Levi told me later that as he walked with me in his arms, his tears ran down his face onto mine. But I passed out in his arms and didn't know what Levi felt for me.

Too, I never did hear Mammy and Amanda screaming and wailing when they saw what Paul had done to me. Those women nursed me all night long and pulled my fever down a bit. Even though Mammy used her salve on my burn, she couldn't get the swelling to go down. In between, they talked with Pappy and Mose about what to tell old John and Cap'n Jack.

"I don't think we should tell at all," Mose said. "That old man is goin' to have him a heart attack, then we'll be stuck in Arkansas forever."

"Mose, don't be an old fool. Samgirl has to get to a real doctor," Amanda said. She patted Mammy's hand to show she didn't mean any insult by her words.

"Mose ain't no fool," Pappy chimed in. "There's some sense to what he says."

"No, Amanda's right," Mammy answered. "Samgirl needs some real doctoring and she needs it fast if she's goin' to live."

When dawn peeked into our wagon, Pappy walked away on dragging feet. In a few minutes, he came back, old John and Cap'n Jack following behind. I must have been conscious because I remember old John had tousled hair and Cap'n Jack still smelled of sleep.

"Paul done this?" Cap'n Jack asked, his eyes squinted and his lips tight.

Everyone nodded, but didn't say anything. Old John stood over me, looking wearier than I'd ever seen him. He took my hand real soft-like and said, "Paul did this to you, Samgirl?"

When I nodded, tears sprang into old John's eyes. I couldn't believe old John didn't know what Paul had been doing to me all this time, but I understood that he didn't want to know more than he'd already learned that morning. Old John turned to Cap'n Jack and said, "Where can we find a doctor?"

"We're nowhere, man," Jack replied. He waved his hand at the stands of oak and pine surrounding us. "The only place I know of is the trading post by the Caddoe village, maybe two days ahead."

Old John nodded his head as if he couldn't speak another word. He and Cap'n Jack left our wagon and we started two days' hard driving to reach that trading post.

I don't remember much that happened after that. I guess I mostly sank into oblivion and let the wagon carry me along. On the morning of the second day, Samboy brought me a bunch of wildflowers. "Me and Levi picked them before dawn," he explained. "This afternoon Levi's comin' to take off your chains. Old John said so."

I patted Samboy's hand and gave another pat for Dog's head, but that's all I had in me for the morning. When Levi pushed his black face and sorrowful eyes into the wagon, I smiled a bit. Sunshine broke through the murky clouds in my mind just because he was there with me.

"Old John told me to come take the chains off you," he said.

I nodded and Levi went to work. In a few minutes, he had my wrists free and sat looking at my red, blistered chest. Then he tried to make a joke. "I guess Mister Paul branded us both good, me on the head and you smack on the chest," he said but saw that I wasn't in a laughing mood.

Levi cheered me up considerable, though, when he leaned down and kissed my cheek. A warm, roiling feeling started in the area of my groin. I had never felt such a strange warmth before. Even though I didn't know where that warmth might lead, I knew Levi raised something in me that had never been there before. I smiled at Levi for sure as he ducked out of the wagon and closed the flap behind him to keep out the pesky flies and hot sun.

I guess I dozed off. I didn't even feel the wagon moving, except in my dreams. First, I roamed the prairie riding a wild Indian pony, then I drove a wagon with a span of mules pulling it smartly along. I careened across the West and right into freedom land.

Pretty soon, Amanda tried to spoon some broth in my mouth. I thought I was back in Mississippi, bleeding into Aggie's rags. I woke up enough to see that it was Amanda in the real flesh. I remembered all that had happened to me. A shiver of terror ran through me. I relived the nightmare of Paul branding me on my chest, a nightmare beyond anything I could have imagined.

The third day we sighted a trading post. Cap'n Jack came to tell Pappy, "Yep, that's the one."

Cap'n Jack and Samboy rode ahead to see what doctors or medicine they might have there. When they came back the news proved discouraging. "Just the Frenchy trader's wife and a doctoring book," Samboy told Mammy, "so you'll have to do the best you can with what they've got."

It turned out pretty good. That French trader had a Caddoe wife who knew a lot about doctoring with herbs and unguents. She put a poultice of herbs on my chest that cooled the burning and itching right away. She gave Mammy and Amanda some foul-looking tea to brew and pour into me every few hours. Even though I hated the tea, I drank it. Dog took one lap of it and made it clear he hated it too.

All this time, nobody mentioned Paul. A fear of what was coming next knotted and twisted in my stomach. The tension rose around me until I thought my heart might stop. Finally, I asked Samboy, "Where's Paul? What's old John done to him?"

"Old John didn't do nothin'," Samboy smirked. "Old John's mighty upset with Paul, but he's unable to punish that boy. Old John left it all to Cap'n Jack. Jack fixed Paul. He had Levi make gates for each end of Paul's wagon, like a jail. Paul's brothers have to take turns guardin' him. I heard some yellin' about that, but Cap'n Jack, he shut up them boys with a look."

I relaxed then. I felt a little safer with Paul behind bars and Simon and Peter on guard. Those brothers of Paul's were soft, I thought, yet the two of them should be able to rein him in. Late the next afternoon, I even felt good enough to sit in the back of the wagon and watch from a distance as Mammy helped make supper. She brought me my meal before old John and his family came to the table. "Where's Paul?" I asked, remembering his rank breath on my neck.

"He's in his dungeon," she said with a smug look. "Simon or Peter take Paul's meals there and shove them between the bars Levi made."

I laughed because I knew how happy Levi must have been making those bars. "Serves Paul right," said I. Even though worry was still my traveling companion, I began to believe some justice existed in the world.

After supper, I heard Coffee Fred picking on his fiddle and some folks singing down low. Although I still suffered, I found some peace, too. Just about then, silence fell over the camp, a strange quiet like the kind you hear before a windstorm busts through and changes things forever. The murky air hung still and quiet; Mammy thought it might rain.

I spotted old John and Nellie and the girls circling the main fire, just looking around. Simon and Peter were nowhere in sight. Neither was Cap'n Jack. Along came Samboy and told me that while Peter was guarding the front of Paul's wagon, Paul had used a pocket knife to slash his way through the wagon covers near the back end. Paul was nowhere to be found.

Soon, Pappy ran up with Mammy hard after him. Next came Mose and Amanda, then Levi. "Old John told us to guard you, Samgirl," Pappy explained.

They set about devising a schedule for the whole night. They planned to watch me for the entire night and maybe the entire next day, depending on when Simon and Peter and Cap'n Jack tracked down Paul.

I spent one miserable night. My protectors stood outside the wagon in pairs so that if one fell asleep the other would rouse the sleeping one. I tried to sleep because I knew I needed my strength to throw off the sickness from the burn on my chest, but images of Paul kept running through my mind. I wondered how old John and Nellie had produced such a spawn of the devil as Paul. Simon and Peter, Esther and Rebecca, they all seemed to be normal children. Simon was wise, Peter tolerant, Esther sweet, and Rebecca shy. None of them showed any sign of a mean streak except Paul.

After awhile, I lay thinking and dreaming, dreaming and thinking, and the two mixed together. I saw Paul with devil horns on his head, a great tail out back, and a pitchfork in his hand. One minute, a steaming horseshoe topped the pitchfork; the next a flaming branding iron did so. In the background stood old John and Nellie moaning and praying for Paul to change.

In my waking moments, I reminded myself that Paul was the eldest son and a spoiled one at that. He would most likely get away with however he used me, and the other slaves as well. Even though old John might let Cap'n Jack lock up Paul, old John wouldn't punish his son in any hard way that would stick with Paul.

Dreaming again, I saw Esther and Rebecca looking for husbands. All the white boys ran away because those girls were Chickasaw. Then I dreamed Paul had lost the girl he loved because he was Chickasaw. I saw the whole family pulling up stakes, slaves and all, and moving toward Indian Territory.

Awake again, I knew how old John and his family felt to be judged and scorned because they were different from white folks and had darker skin. I thought about our folks and wondered why coming from Africa and having black skin made us damned among whites. Of course, I didn't come from Africa; I was born in the United States. And I was a pretty nice person. I worked hard and tried to help others, especially Mammy.

Asleep again, I conjured up the worst vision of all. I saw Paul coming to get me one last time. In his right hand, he held a butcher knife and in the left his dwarfish gun. On his face he wore a fiendish grin. I waked up screaming louder than a lost polecat for its mammy.

All my guards came running to my side, those who were awake and those who had been asleep. They calmed down some when they found out Paul was nowhere to be seen. They quieted me down some too, but when I saw dawn peeking its way over the hillside I demanded to get up. "I can't stay down no more," I told them. "I'm exhausted with trying to rest."

We all went outside and started a small fire. Mammy brewed me some of that awful medicinal tea; everyone else had coffee. That's how it happened that we were in perfect position to see old John and Cap'n Jack walking into camp leading a horse behind them. Over it lay Paul's body, still heaving with life but with a bloody rag wrapped around the right arm.

Young Tate followed behind with the rest of the horses. Pretty soon, Tate gave over the horses to another of the men and followed old John's orders to put Paul's body back in his prison wagon.

We all shuffled around in the black dirt and rough grass, restless with curiosity. We figured old John would soon call Mammy for doctoring, but Cap'n Jack came instead. "We need you, Chloe," Jack told Mammy. Leaving Jack standing there with sad eyes, Mammy grabbed her sack of medicine and bandages and headed straight for Paul's wagon.

When Jack said, "That coffee smells something good, Ike," Pappy poured him a cup. We all danced around puzzling what to say to Jack, but Jack himself took the initiative. "I suppose you're all wondering what happened to that boy Paul?"

We nodded our heads yes and waited, then Amanda thought of the fresh cornbread in the wagon and ran to get Jack a piece. She shoved it in Jack's hand and he smiled like he hadn't eaten for days. After Jack chomped that cornbread right down, he seemed ready to tell his story. "You probably know Paul broke out last night," Jack started, not really wanting to talk to us yet having to unload his cares on someone.

"Paul went to the post and bartered for liquor. He showed up at the post again this morning. He started in teasin' the Indian women. Then he traded some junk of his and cheated the men. Next, he went back into the post store demandin' more to drink. The trader's wife—the same one who doctored Samgirl here—told Paul no, but he wasn't having it. He hollered and howled until she called for help. That made Paul so mad he reached right over the counter and grabbed her earring, beads and all. He gave it a good yank and away it came—carrying a goodly piece of her ear with it."

I wasn't surprised at Paul's cruelty, but I was anxious to hear how Paul had ended up slung over the horse's back, so I shushed everyone and asked Jack to go on.

"Paul stood there," Jack explained, "with the earring and piece of ear lobe dangling from his hand when that Frenchy trader walked in. He took one look at Paul and one look at his wife's bleeding ear and took ahold of Paul by the back of his shirt and pants and threw him out of the door right on the hard ground. Paul didn't get up right away. The story flashed like fire among those Indians. When Paul staggered to his feet, a knife came from somewhere and stuck jest as nice as you please in Paul's right shoulder."

As far as I was concerned, the story was getting better all the time. I still wanted to hear what else Jack had to say, so I shushed everyone again.

"That knife stickin' in Paul was just a common trade knife. Any man jack of them could have thrown it. Maybe it was an Indian, maybe the Frenchy trader. No proving nothing. Besides, when me and old John got there and heard the story, old John just shook his head and moaned, 'It's a fair measure of vengeance. They could've killed him.' So I told Tate to put Paul up on the horse and off we went back to camp."

Jack splashed the rest of his coffee out of his cup and into the fire. He walked away just as young Tate came up, looking for Levi, as always. Tate stared at our round eyes and quiet mouths and knew Jack had told us what happened.

"How come you went along with old John and Cap'n Jack?" Levi asked Tate.

"Because I'm strong. They thought they'd need someone to hold Paul down when we found him. Turns out, Marse Paul was down already." Tate seemed happy and sad at the same time. His big shoulders slouched, as if he felt relaxed by Paul's fate.

Levi handed Tate a tin mug of black coffee. It filled the fetid morning air with a steamy smell like a witch's brew. Levi gave Tate a piece of cornbread as well. Tate soon joined our speculating and wishing about what might happen to Paul next.

Cap'n Jack interrupted us by yelling at the camp, "We're goin' to roll, so get movin'." When Jack yelled, he meant business. We all started moving and packing and hitching.

chapter eight

Jack's order surprised us, but I figured old John and Cap'n Jack wanted to get away from those Indians before they decided they needed more revenge. We traveled a hard day, all the time with Mammy riding in Paul's wagon nursing him. We stopped late and the other women cooked supper without Mammy.

At bedtime, Mammy appeared at our wagon looking like a demon herself. Her shoulders slumped low with tiredness. Amanda put Mammy down next to me, but Mammy couldn't be still. She rolled and ranted until finally Amanda sat her up again.

"Mammy," said I, awake and curious, "tell us what's going on up there in Paul's wagon."

Mammy turned wild eyes on me and wailed, "I wished I didn't know doctorin' so I didn't have to tend to the boy who hurt my Samgirl. But I got to do it. I'm so afraid I'm goin' to kill him myself that I'm tryin' to give him my best care. He's one of God's creatures, too."

"I'm not so sure of that, Mammy. Last night, I dreamed Paul was the devil. I'm not so certain that's wrong."

Mammy didn't hear me because she was carrying on about Paul's wound. "That's no plain knife wound," she said. "It swells and I drain the pus out, then it swells and I drain the pus out again. Meanwhile, Paul's whole body falls sick with the fever and cramps and bloatin'. I never saw such a thing."

I shook my head and so did Amanda. "So, what you think, Chloe, really happened to—" Amanda began.

"I think," Mammy answered, "whoever throwed that knife put some powerful poison on it. Paul's going to die one awful death."

As usual, Mammy was right. Paul surely seemed headed toward extinction. Because of his illness, we stayed in that camp with its swampy ground all around and its owls screeching all night.

Mammy spent the better part of the next three days doctoring Paul. She let that pus flood into old cans and a basin and finally onto the bare ground. Meanwhile, old John and Nellie hung around Paul's wagon, praying and lamenting, but it did no good.

On the third afternoon, Mammy came out of that wagon looking as green as a black woman can look. "I can't do no more, Marse John," she gasped. She choked down some fresh air and began to look better. Then she said, "That child of yours is bloated to three times his size. And he smells real bad, like he's rotting. He's out of his head, what with the pain and all. I think he's goin' to explode."

Just then, Mammy got sick to her stomach. She ran for our wagon where we were all sat outside watching and waiting to hear her news. Her usual loose-boned, calm gait had disappeared. Instead, she ran in little hoppity steps, holding her kerchief on her head as she came. When she reached us she gagged back her urge to vomit and said, "Nothin' more I can do, that boy's goin' to die."

Gradually, Pappy got Mammy calmed down. He kept her in the wagon and wouldn't let anyone near her. All she would take was a little water and biscuit. When darkness fell, she slept a bit, fitfully and with her arms pumping as if she were still running away from the sight of Paul.

When three shrill wails pierced the velvet-black sky sometime after midnight, we knew Paul had screamed, probably his last. Not one of us ventured out of the wagon to see what would happen next. We listened good and heard only silence all over the camp, except for Nellie weeping. Samboy poked his head into the wagon. "Cap'n Jack has called for young Tate and Levi," he hissed.

In a few seconds, they ran by our wagon as if death were after them. Next, we heard dragging sounds, like branches being pulled over the ground, and then crackling, like a fire starting. In minutes, a red-orange glow lit up our wagon cover from the outside. Mammy crawled on her hands and knees to the opening and crouched there, her mouth hanging open. It took a long time before she could speak and report back to me and Amanda.

"Paul's wagon is on fire," she told us. "Tate and Levi are adding wood to the fire all around it, so that it's blazin' almost up to the fading moon. Missus Nellie's standin' in the light of the flames like a spook, readin' from her Bible and howlin' at the same time."

I crawled over behind Mammy, while Amanda hid her head under the quilt. When I shoved Mammy aside a bit and peered out I saw a blaze that tried to leap high enough to touch the gray and rose swirls in the early morning sky. Old John set about dragging Nellie out of its reach, but she looked like she wanted to jump right in with Paul. Simon picked up his ma and took her back to her wagon, with the others following like phantoms behind.

Me and Mammy watched that fire until there was nothing left except the iron bows from the wagon box and the iron pieces off the yoke and the wheels. Underneath our wagon, Pappy and Samboy and Mose also watched. Not one of us shed a tear for the boy who was consumed in that unearthly pyre.

The next morning everything went pretty much as it should on a normal day, not that we'd had many of those lately. Although Paul's wagon lay smoking and steaming and the iron pieces stuck out of it like bones, nobody even whispered a word about it.

Then I saw something I'd never expected to see again in my lifetime. Dog came strutting out from under our wagon with his earless head held high and not a trace of fear in his walk. He ambled up to me and sat down next to me, haunch-to-haunch. "Dog," said I, "you sure seem to know Paul has gone off the face of this earth."

Meanwhile, Cap'n Jack bustled around the camp yelling, "We're goin' to move. Get yourselves goin'," with Simon following right behind him. I realized that Simon was now the oldest child and, therefore, in command. I wondered where old John was. Lying in his bed, I supposed, hurting with his grief for Paul.

It turned out old John was in his bed all right, but grief wasn't the only thing keeping him there. Tate told me that after Mammy left Paul's wagon, old John forced himself to go in to see Paul for himself. Tate waitcd by the bars covering Paul's wagon in case old John needed him. Tate heard Paul try to yell oaths from his misshapen mouth at old John and blame him for what had happened.

Tate froze as he glimpsed Paul raise his runty gun in his bloated fingers and aim at old John. Fortunately for old John, Paul only succeeded in landing a tiny bullet in his leg. Tate lugged old John back to his and Nellie's wagon. That left it to Simon to watch over Paul as he died shrieking, his skin spurting pus and maggots. It was Simon who decided to burn the wagon to save the rest of the camp from infection.

Old John had come out from his own wagon and walked with that bullet in his leg to watch Paul's wagon burning. He followed Simon when he carried Nellie back to the wagon. Then he collapsed and didn't rise again. Of course, they called poor Mammy to old John's side to do some doctoring. She judged that his leg had to come off because something yellow was growing around the wound. At that, Cap'n Jack started yelling "Roll 'em" like a lunatic and we were off in a rush for Lost Prairie.

Right away, Old John's new right-hand man and eldest son, Simon, proved he had a cool head in time of trouble and misery. Simon helped Jack get us to Lost Prairie in a couple of hard days of driving without cussing or speaking one cutting word to anyone, Chickasaw or slave. Simon seemed to be everything Paul hadn't been. We were glad of that. We were anxious to see the time of troubles pass on its way.

Of course, we still had old John's leg to worry about. When we reached Lost Prairie, an army surgeon—run away from the Mexican War for a reason we never learned—agreed with Mammy. "That leg must come right off," he said. He seemed unperturbed that we were hundreds of miles away from a hospital or a proper surgeon. "I'll do it myself."

Mammy stood by and so did Simon. Mammy told us later how the army man opened a black leather kit and took out something that looked like a miniature saw. Then he went to sawing on old John's leg until it parted company with old John's body. That army doctor plopped old John's severed leg in a tin pail and carried it off, never to be seen again.

After that, we stayed in Lost Prairie a few more days, while Mammy nursed old John the best she could. In the meantime, Cap'n Jack spent a lot of his time whittling, a pastime he'd never followed before. The children all gathered around and tried to guess what he was carving.

"A whip handle," one speculated.

"No, you fool," another said. "It's a cane for old John."

"Naw," said a third, "it's a wooden leg for old John."

"Fit him as good as can be," Jack said as he put the leg aside and started working on a longer piece of wood. Shortly, Jack handed Simon a piece of rope. "You measure your daddy from the bottom of the foot he has left to his armpit," he told Simon, who went away to do Jack's bidding.

When Simon came back, Jack took that rope measure and used it to make a crutch for old John. "Fit him as good as can be," he declared again to Mammy. He'd asked her to pad the top of the crutch and figure out some way to tie the wooden leg to what old John had left of his own leg.

Mammy padded the crutch all right, but she turned the leg job over to Levi, who devised some leather straps and metal buckles that would do the job nicely. Even though old John still felt too sickly to try Jack's inventions, they were ready whenever he might be.

That could be awhile. Peter drove old John's and Nellie's wagon. He also carried meals to old John and Nellie, which they ate inside their wagon. Simon drove his and Peter's wagon, while Paul's wagon lay smoldering somewhere way behind us.

I always wondered if the Indian, or maybe the French trader, who threw that poison knife ever found the wagon remains and figured out what had happened to the young man who had mistreated the Indian people. The Caddoe woman who had lost the lobe of her ear to Paul's nasty temper might have been glad to hear the news as well.

There was no use, I figured, wondering about the unknown. Still, the world seemed stranger and more threatening to me all the time. It was something I had taken to spending considerable time pondering on.

When I bothered to look around, I could see we were a bedraggled bunch, hardly one that would inspire folks to say "Howdy, welcome." We certainly couldn't blame many of our misfortunes on the hardships of the trail. Old John had never even gotten his rifles out, for hunting game or shooting enemies either one. We had no worry getting food. We had no fuss with Indians. Instead, we had brought along our own supply of enemies and troublemakers, mostly meaning Paul, right with us.

I was glad we would bypass Texarkana and go right up the Red River to Tishomingo. I was about worn out and ready to get to Indian Territory. The *P* brand on my chest especially pained me. In the excitement and anguish of Paul's death and old John's leg, everyone had forgotten about the brand on my chest. I didn't forget. It still hurt and I rubbed salve on it every few hours.

"The worst thing is," I told Samboy, "I bear a *P* brand for a man who no longer lives. I have a mark on my chest for a dead man."

As a result, I wasn't as free of Paul as I had expected to be. He still walked and talked and ate with me every day. At night, sometimes I dreamed I had thought of a way to get that brand off my chest, or I had healed up and the *P* was gone, or an angel of God had come down from heaven and lifted it right off me. When I woke up, the brand was still there.

I went back to driving the wagon a few hours every day. "Mammy," I asked one morning, "can you get me one of those red kerchiefs that Nellie handed out some time back for the children to wear?"

Mammy caught on right away what I planned to do with a kerchief. She went to talk to Simon. He told Mammy to see Missus Esther, who sent me two nice pieces of dress goods, one light blue with tiny red stripes and the other yellow.

Mammy set to sewing hems on the pieces and made me two fine kerchiefs. I tied a kerchief round my neck with the knot behind my neck and the full part hanging right down the opening of my dress so as to cover the *P*. The material made the fresh scar itch until Mammy washed my kerchiefs and dried them in the wind. They got so soft I was able to wear them without noticing.

Levi also treated me with great kindness. That man made me turn to cornmeal mush every time he came around. "You look extra fairly in that kerchief," he'd say.

Levi also brought around little presents when he could.

One morning he marched right to breakfast and held out his hand, palm up. In the center rested a nail bent in the shape of a circle. "This is for you, Samgirl," he said, pride and excitement in his seductive eyes.

I took the round nail in the palm of my hand and examined it. "It's nice," said I, doubt edging my voice.

"It's a ring," Levi explained in a satisfied way. "You put it on one of your fingers and wear it as a decoration."

By then, everybody had crowded around, Samboy and his friend Tom, Mammy, Pappy, Mose, Amanda, even Dog. They swarmed around me and gave me directions about how to wear the ring. I tried the bent nail on every finger. It fit best on the first finger, so Levi closed the nail a bit to make it perfect and said, "Now you got something as pretty as you."

I blushed and thanked Levi. I never thought I'd be wearing a nail on my finger. But then, I never thought I'd be wearing a *P* on my chest either.

A couple of days later, Levi came running alongside our wagon while I drove. He jumped up on the seat with me. He handed me a piece of red ribbon. "Tie this in your hair, Samgirl," he said. He reared back on the seat and grinned.

I squealed and stared at the ribbon he held in his massive hand. "Where'd you get such a thing as a ribbon for me?"

"I traded a man some horseshoeing help for it, back along the trail a bit, but I couldn't give it to you during the misery time." By now, Levi's eyes had softened. They combined affection and amusement, both aimed at me.

I blushed again and took the ribbon from Levi's fingers. When I let my fingers touch his I sensed a spark go through, but I acted like nothing had happened. I was afraid to let Levi know how I really felt way down inside about him, so I half shut my eyes to shield the emotion burning there.

I tied the ribbon in my bristly hair and thought my life wasn't too bad after all. But I knew I would never forget what Levi, and most everybody else, had taken to calling the misery time. The part of our journey where Paul branded me—and later died himself—had burned its way into my mind like a second brand. Even if I ever found a way to get the brand off my chest, I would never get the mark out of my mind.

With old John down, Simon and Cap'n Jack called camp meetings. We didn't see anything of old John or Nellie, but Simon stood right up in front of everything. "You got to watch," he warned us, "for the Indians along the Red River."

"Yeah," Cap'n Jack added, "Texas Indians are warlike and ferocious folks to deal with."

We all laughed at that, given what the peaceful ones had done to Paul. But we were just as glad to stay away from those Texas Indians.

Despite the warnings, it didn't happen that way. Even though we traveled on the Arkansas and Indian Territory side of the Red, not the Texas side, the Indians spilled right over the river and found us as fast as we appeared. Although some had seen black folks before, a goodly bunch hadn't.

Soon, a whole lot of looking and giggling and feeling ensued. Those Indians seemed to think we looked a lot like the buffalo they hunted somewhere on the southern Plains—that our hair was about as tight and curly as that on the buffalo. One of the Indian women even tried to rub the black color right off my arm.

"Those Indians are mostly Apaches and Comanches," Simon told us. "They're great warriors and hunters."

Still, they treated us nice. And good thing, too. I don't know how much more adversity we could have stood up to. They brought us trout, which we didn't know how to catch, although the streams ran with it. And they gave us prairie hen, which sure had tender meat to it. They showed us how to build a temporary bridge over a stream too deep to ford, and they taught us how to make a cradleboard for a baby so we could hang the child right up on a tree branch.

Some of the Indian people could talk with Cap'n Jack. Even though it was clear he didn't speak their language, he knew enough signs and odd words to piece together a conversation. The Indians told Jack they worried about the white folks coming into their land, that the whites used up the land and shot the game and pushed the Indians out of the way.

When Cap'n Jack told us what the Indians had said, we all responded, "Oh me, oh my, what a terrible trouble," and the Indians seemed to like us even more. Even though they couldn't understand our words, they sure caught our tone and meaning.

Pretty soon we left the Indians behind and moved right fast, keeping near the sometimes laggard, sometimes heaving river as a guide. In fact, we moved so fast that we overtook some white folks. Even though they seemed almost as curious about us as the Indians had been, they didn't try to touch our skin or hair. Neither did they compare us to buffalo.

"Where you coming from?" one of them asked.

"Where you goin'?"

"What you goin' to do when you get there?" And so it went until we tired of their questions.

The white folks said they were going to north Texas to farm. We thought it must be wonderful to decide where you wanted to go and to get up and go there. We traveled near that train, and camped near it at night, for almost a week.

In that time, I decided liquor was generally a bad thing. No strong drink had been seen in our camp since Paul died, but jugs appeared real regular in the white folks' camp. The men especially took a swig here and there out of brown earthen jugs, sometimes even before breakfast.

One man carried his jug with him on his wagon seat and swigged regular all day long. That man ran into serious trouble as a result. He yelled at his wife anytime something went wrong, swearing and claiming it was all her fault. He also liked to cuss out any driver who passed him and threw dust his way. He cussed once too often, I guess, when he did it at this swarthy fella called Kirk.

Kirk pulled his wagon crossways in front of the loudmouth man. "You talkin' to me?" Kirk drawled, his beefy hand resting on a knife stuck in his belt.

The two men spit some mean words back and forth and the loudmouth reached for his gun. Trouble was, he was pretty well along toward being drunk, and instead of shooting Kirk, he shot his own foot, which rested up against the footboard of his wagon.

At first, Kirk jumped back. "You sonofabitch," he yelled. Then he realized what the cussing man done to himself and he started laughing until it doubled him over. He was still laughing when he crawled up on his own wagon seat and drove off.

In the meantime, the cussing man's wife cut off her husband's boot with a knife and called for the train's doctor. While the doctor fixed the man's foot, the wife hung out of the back of the wagon and poured the liquor out of every one of her husband's jugs. I never did get to see the end of the matter, but I bet some explosions went off between that husband and his wife.

Too, I noticed that a lot of the white folks did not appear very happy. They seemed to argue about everything. "Let's stop and rest on Sunday." "No, let's keep going." "The northerly trail is best." "No, we'll get ambushed going that way." "You've got more than your fair share of food." "I don't either. You're a liar."

I especially watched two smart-looking young men with their pretty wives. The wives, who were sisters, always had their heads together laughing and talking. The only time the men had their heads together was to fight and insult each other.

After about five days of bickering, the men came near to punching each other. Instead, they got so angry with one another they tore their tent in two halves. The one man took his wife in a southerly direction, while the other man took his wife in a westerly course. Both women wailed and wept as if the other had died as their husbands carried them and their halves of the tent away.

After that, I thought to myself that white folks mostly didn't understand what they had. I tried to explain all this thinking that roiled in my head to Mammy, but she didn't seem very interested. "Go away, Samgirl. You got work to do."

"But, Mammy," said I in my stubborn voice, "I'm trying to figure out why folks act the way they do. Like Paul."

Seeing that she wouldn't be free of me until she answered, Mammy gave me one of the best pieces of advice I ever heard in my life. "It's better not to look back. You ain't goin' that way anyhow. Look ahead and meet folks as they come at you. Avoid the bad ones the best you can and make the most you can of the good."

"Thanks, Mammy," said I with a wide smile, "that helps straighten out my thinking a whole lot."

Mammy took me by my shoulders and said, "I got one more thing to say. Remember, you always got to do what's best for you. Try not to hurt anyone doing it, but take care of yourself."

"Whew," said I, "that's quite a lesson. And you're quite a mammy. I'm glad you're mine."

Mammy smiled all over her face and I went off to look for Dog, who'd been getting into a whole lot of trouble since he found his spirit again.

I bumped instead into Mellisey, from the white train. Mellisey was about fourteen or fifteen, like me, and she was one of the good folks that Mammy mentioned. Mellisey stopped right in front of me and said, "Samgirl, I want you to have this." She shoved something sparkly toward me, her blond curls bobbing and her summer-blue eyes gleaming.

I took it and saw it was a mirror. I stared at Mellisey with awe in my eyes and a croak in my voice. "I ain't ever had one of these."

Mellisey came to my side and pointed to some writing cut right into the mirror near the top. "Can you read this?"

I looked real hard and saw some fine printing. I began to make out the words. "The Lord is my shepherd," I read, "I shall not want. He maketh me to lie down in green pastures. He leadeth me by still waters. He restoreth my—"

Mellisey got so excited she could hardly stand still. Her ringlets sprang about and her cheeks grew pink and she interrupted my reading. "I knew you could read, I just knew it! Papa said no, but I said yes. I was right."

"What is this thing cut in the glass?" I asked her, not caring what her papa thought one way or the other.

"It's the Twenty-Third Psalm, right out of the Bible. I want you to read it and remember me every time you feel upset about something."

I was tempted to tell Mellisey I would be remembering her a lot because I got upset a lot, but I didn't want to chase that smile off her face. Instead, I grasped the mirror to my chest and said, "I'm going to keep this forever. I'll always remember you."

Because of Mellisey, I walked onto Chickasaw Nation land dusty, dirty, and tired, yet strangely content. Even though I was still a slave, Paul was dead and gone. And this was a new place. Anything might happen here. I fully intended to use every possible moment to improve my situation and devise a runaway scheme.

My ownership had reverted to old John Stands-in-Timber and Nellie Mad-Doe. The few times they showed their faces, they didn't seem anxious to criticize their dead son, but they also appeared a mite hesitant to go passing me on to one of their other children. I was just as glad. Although I liked and respected Simon, I was happy to stay where I had begun, with old John and Nellie, at least until my escape plan took better shape.

I figured I had just turned sixteen years old and judged that, all-in-all, I had lived a pretty exciting life so far. What with Paul's treachery and his horrible death, me having Aggie fix me good and Paul branding me, moving to Indian Territory, and feeling what I felt for Levi, I concluded I was probably more than sixteen in my heart, if not in my body. Yet I was almost happy—and surely hopeful—about the future.

I was also real curious about Chickasaw Nation land and old John's new plantation. "I know right where we are," Cap'n Jack said as soon as we hit Indian Territory. After reading old John's charts and papers, he led us straight to old John's and Nellie's new place.

We had spent a good six or seven days before leaving Mississippi fixing and cleaning—we had even weeded the vegetable patches one last time—so we expected to find the same order here. What we saw as we trailed onto that plantation, our backs sore and our spirits worn, was enough to make our stomachs go sour and our hearts quake.

Granted, given one thing and another, it had taken us longer to get to Indian Territory from Mississippi than we had planned, but no place could have fallen into such disorder in a few weeks.

"My Lord, my Lord," was all Mammy seemed able to say.

The big house was run down, to say the least, its portico listing to one side and its pillars to the other. I counted three broken windows on the front alone. Neither had the trees been trimmed; their branches hung every which way and dripped leaves, buds, and pits all over the lawn, which had pretty much gone to seed anyway. The fence sagged and looked about ready to give up the battle and descend the rest of the way to the ground. The front gate had disappeared entirely and the path rested beneath an overgrowth of weeds.

"Uh-oh," I said to Samboy, rolling my eyes, "if this is how the big house looks, what'll the cabins be like?"

"We might as well find out," he answered. Pappy turned our wagon toward the quarters, which lay down a hill, out of sight of the big house. On the way, I noticed that the barns and sheds all stood, but barely. I saw the sun right through the boards of the main cotton shed. I spied branches growing through the roof of the woodshed. I couldn't locate any blacksmith's forge at all.

Pappy drove to cabin number 30, way down at the end of the far-thest row, just as Simon had directed us. Mose and Amanda were to have cabin 29, right before our cabin. What we saw didn't even look like cabins—they seemed more like huts. They were made of boards all right, but they were unchinked and the roofs were nothing but thatch. They stood tiny and miserable-looking.

When we stopped in front of cabin 30, Mammy stepped out of the wagon. Right away, she spotted spiders and bedbugs in that thatch. "We ain't goin' near that place," she said in her stubborn voice, which is probably where I got mine from. "We're living right in this wagon until things improve around here."

"I want to look inside," Samboy said. Off he went with Dog at his heels. Dog came back out first, chasing a large rat or maybe a squirrel. Samboy came out next, dangling a dead mouse by the tail from his fingers.

"That ain't funny, Samboy," Pappy said, seeming afraid that Mammy would take off and run all the way back to Mississippi. But we had no home there anymore; he knew it and she knew it.

Then Samboy stuck his head into Mose and Amanda's cabin and came out holding his nose. When she spied Samboy, Amanda began to wail. Mose went to patting her arm and shushing her, but she wasn't alone. By now a general uproar came from all over the quarters.

Along came Simon and Cap'n Jack, hushing folks as they went. Cap'n Jack waved for silence and got it, except for some sniffling by some of the women. "All right, folks," he began, "so it ain't exactly what we expected. A bit of fixin' and it'll be home soon enough."

At that, Mammy pushed forward and asked, "Can we live in the wagons until that time comes?" Her set face made it clear that she intended to live in the wagon no matter what Simon or Cap'n Jack decided.

"Good idea," Cap'n Jack replied. "Use the wagons for home a little longer. Won't kill nobody to do that."

Simon stepped ahead of Jack, all serious-faced and ready to take charge. He stood even straighter and taller than Paul had when he was alive. Unlike Paul, Simon let his black hair fly and his clothes, too. And Simon's eyes looked at people, instead of at some devilment he planned inside his mind. "You all know my daddy never saw this farm. The land agent said everything was in good shape. The man obviously lied. I'll do what I can to right the situation legally. In the meantime, we better get to fixing and cleaning and making us a home."

Nobody said anything to that. We all stared at each other. We all understood how much work lay ahead of us. Simon heard the quiet and thought what to do about it. "We have to get a room fixed in the big house for John and Nellie, but the rest of us will live in our wagons. We'll all turn to the barns and sheds and fields first and worry about housing later."

We gaped at each other again. We felt pretty good about Simon being willing to share our hardship. The trouble was that the barns and sheds needed more work than we could possibly give them before fall came on. And we'd seen the fields on the way in; they lay choked with roots and dead plants. I spotted a rusted plow sitting beside a falling-down shed, and knew that those fields hadn't had any plowing for quite some time.

"Look, Pappy," I whispered, "a rusted plow over there."

Pappy looked where I pointed and said, "I see," down real low in his throat, somewhat like a growl.

Becky strolled up then, trying to act nonchalant. She said to Mammy, "I don't think we're goin' to be usin' them sad irons anytime soon, Chloe."

"No," answered Mammy, with a stiff smile on her mouth, "but I hope you got a whole big supply of elbow grease and downright guts ready to go."

While all this bellyaching went on, I noticed something strange about Simon. A fiery light burned at the back of his eyes like a fever. Dots of perspiration covered his forehead. His lips drew more tightly together. If I didn't know better, I'd have thought he had a glow coming from around his head and body. He was obviously thinking hard and maybe calling on the Lord to help him in this time of crisis.

Simon bowed his head for a moment, then gazed out at the folks standing and worrying in front of him. He jumped up on a rotten tree stump and flapped his arms in the air. He waited for silence. "We can do this," he shouted, "for old John and for ourselves. We can make this place bloom. It's a challenge. We can meet it."

Some people around me murmured "Hallelujah." Simon went on that way for a few more minutes. He grew louder and so high-flown in his sentiments that he lost most of us along the way, but we kept shouting hallelujah whenever he paused. Even Cap'n Jack seemed stunned, as if Simon had suddenly taken up old-time preaching or backcountry politicking or something.

Fear settled at the bottom of my heart. I knew Simon was out to please his daddy and to prove that he could be far better as eldest son than Paul ever could have been. I turned to Samboy and said, "That boy's changing before our very eyes."

"What do you mean?" Samboy asked. "Simon's just tryin' to get us excited about all the work we got to do on this here place."

"It's more than that," said I, "Simon just found himself a cause. He's out to prove something to old John and to himself. It's going to come down on our heads. And on our backs."

"Naw," Samboy insisted. "That's just Simon carrying on. He's goin' to learn real quick how much we can do and how much we can't."

"There's another thing," I continued, ignoring Samboy's remarks. "Crops were supposed to be in the ground waiting for us. It's getting along in the summer already. How are we going to plant what we need for the winter?"

"Trust Simon," Samboy said, "he's goin' to fix it."

All right, I told myself, we're going to watch Simon and how he will fix life for us all out here in this Indian Territory. At the same time, my faith in Simon melted into the oppressive summer air that hung as heavy around my shoulders as grief at a funeral.

chapter
nine

I wasn't especially partial to Indian Territory. "The soil ain't very rich," I told Samboy. "And the wind carries it right off."

"Samgirl," he said, "don't worry your head about the soil and the wind."

"It's the flatness as well. Cap'n Jack says there's mountains somewhere north of us, but I see only flat land here." I increased my complaints, probably because I was bone tired. "And Jack says there's a lake just south of us, yet I don't see any water."

Samboy looked disgusted. "You're cryin' like a stuck pig and worryin' about the wrong things. You got plenty of work to do just to survive here in Indian Territory."

Of course, Samboy was right. But I didn't care to recall the details of the endless cleaning, fixing, washing, building, chinking, roofing, chopping wood and cotton, hoeing, planting, weeding, cutting rails for fences, and just general damnation we all went through during those first months on old John's plantation in the Chickasaw Nation in Indian Territory.

We grew tired and disgusted and desperate. Most folks figured we had settled at the end of the earth and would never see civilization anymore in our lifetimes. "I didn't know anybody could travel this far and still be in America," Mammy said. She expected to fall off into the ocean any day, even though I tried to convince her that the ocean was a long ways away.

Mammy was also exhausted from all the doctoring she did, night-and-day, day-and-night. She went from wagon to wagon putting salve on calluses and rubbing sore backs. She mixed fennel, butterfly root, and other plants and boiled them up into a syrup for pneumonia and pleurisy—which hit lots of folks because they slept outside at night. She steeped snakeroot for a long time, then mixed it with whiskey to treat chills and fever. She even delivered Dorcas's baby when it finally appeared, all shriveled and wrinkled and looking like a rat instead of a human child.

I helped Mammy as much as I could, but many a day we never got around to the cooking part of her job. The other women had to handle that.

Just like on the trail, no one made supper for their own families. They just prepared breakfast and lunch—usually cold food. At suppertime, the cooks kept working out of the cookwagon, as they had on the trail, and put steaming victuals on the grub table. We all gathered round the table with our stools, while one of the women took some food up to the big house for old John and his family, most of whom still lived in their wagons.

Cap'n Jack continued to eat off alone somewhere. "Here, Cap'n," someone would shout out. "Eat with us."

"No, thanks," he replied in his rough way. "I'll just go over here a piece."

No one ever knew why Cap'n Jack did this. After all, he had stayed with us on the plantation. He helped where he could, mostly bossing work gangs and giving advice on how to do this and that. Simon and Peter worked right alongside him, learning as fast as they could about everything from cotton and corn to horses and hogs.

Meanwhile, old John ventured as far as the portico, wobbling his way around on Jack's crutch. He didn't seem to take much interest in the work going on around him. Once in awhile old John would give

Simon or Peter some advice, or draw some plans on a piece of wrapping paper, but for the most part he left everything in Simon's lap.

I have to give the Chickasaw women credit, though. Nellie set the girls to working right away. "Esther, clean this," "Rebecca, fetch that," was heard morning to night.

Despite the winds and scorching sun, they scrubbed and cleaned and washed and finally hung curtains in the big house. Next, the girls took to making soap and candles out in the yard and storing them in a falling-down root cellar for winter. Nellie even had her girls hanging meat in that joke of a smokehouse. The women saw that the slaves didn't have any time to help with such domestic matters, so they just set to and got it done.

In the midst of all this activity, I began to suspect that Simon's money was starting to run low. "The victuals have gone back to beans and rice, Samboy," I said one evening.

"So," he replied, "the Chickasaw eat the same thing as we do. They're willing to share our hardships."

Through slitted eyes I said, "Then you're admitting that there's hardship on this farm?" Samboy walked away without answering or even grunting.

Soon Simon told us to start breaking apart the wagons. "Use the wood and parts," he said, "to fix the outbuildings. We'll use the strong, whole wagons for storage buildings." Simon made the excuse that the planks he had ordered were slow in coming from the sawmill.

Simon figured out other ways to ease the financial burden. I almost died on the spot the evening Levi told me he was leaving. "Me and Cap'n Jack are goin' to travel back across Arkansas to bring another train through to Indian Territory." I felt as though part of my own body was being ripped away.

"Of course, Jack will make his usual pay." Levi explained all this over a supper of beans and fatback and black-eyed peas, supplemented by some wild onions and strawberries and dewberries that Mammy had gathered. "But my wages will go right to Simon. All I get is housing and food for my trouble."

"You're saying you're going to be gone from here for months to come," said I, with tiny tears in each corner of my wide eyes.

Levi reached over and cupped my big hand with his even bigger one. "I surely am. I'm not happy about it, but Simon says go and I got to go."

"When?" I asked, sorrow pounding through my veins at the very thought of Levi going and me staying. I had heard that love could hurt. Now I knew it for sure.

"A few more days," he replied, "as soon as we get our wagon loaded." He looked as sorrowful as I felt, his sleepy eyes clouded with a hazy film of resignation.

The following morning I volunteered to help chink our cabin, which Pappy had finally gotten around to fixing. First, Pappy had helped Mose and Amanda fix their hut. Then Pappy turned to ours and did a real nice job. He took that hut and put a new shake roof on it. He built a fireplace out of stones me and Samboy hauled back from the field. Pappy said we would use the front part of the cabin for cooking and eating. Then he split logs that he and Samboy had felled with the axes Simon passed out from the provision wagon. With the split logs, Pappy built another room off the kitchen we could use for sleeping. He fixed bed poles in the ground and strung rope strings around.

In the meantime, me and Mammy gathered field grass, because there was no corn in the ground as promised and therefore no hope of cornshucks in the immediate future. We stuffed our mattresses with the grass and laid them on those springs. Next, we aired our quilts and were almost ready to move in, the spiders and bedbugs having gone the way of the thatch roof.

That morning when I took to chinking, I slapped that mud in the cracks so hard Pappy warned me, "Be careful, Samgirl. You're goin' to knock that mud right through into the place where our beds stand."

I just kept on chinking and slapping until Pappy said, "Ah, I've got it. You're mad because Levi is goin' back on that trail."

I felt my face getting hot but I didn't stop chinking and slapping. "No," said I, "that ain't it at all."

Pappy walked over and put his arm, all bulging with muscles, around my shoulder real soft-like. When I finally glanced up at his kind, black face, he said, "I love your Mammy. I understand how you feel about Levi."

The tiny tears jumped back to the corners of my eyes and I nodded to let Pappy know I appreciated his words. He went back to his job and

I stuck to mine. We said no more about the matter of Levi until that night after supper.

We strolled back from the grub table, all stuffed and tired. "Levi's leaving here, Chloe," Pappy told Mammy. Although his voice sounded light, I knew Pappy was trying to get a message across to Mammy.

"I know that," she said. "I heard it from Becky." As if I weren't walking right by her side, Mammy added, "You know, Ike, I bet our Samgirl feels real bad about that."

Samboy perked up his head and stuck in his bit. "Shucks, everybody knows Samgirl's soft on Levi. And Levi's soft on Samgirl."

"Then why is Simon sending Levi off on the trail," I demanded, real sharp and mean, "instead of letting Levi stay here and nature take its course?"

"Because Simon needs the money Levi's goin' to bring in for him," Samboy snapped back. "Everybody knows that. Where have you been, girl? Is your head so much in the clouds that you really ain't been noticing all the fatback and beans we've been gettin'?"

"I know," said I sassy-like, remembering how Samboy thought Simon could improve things. "You said Mister Simon was going to fix everything up for us."

At that Samboy scowled and said, "All right, all right, you were right. Simon's got himself some type of cause. You put it right. It's comin' down on our heads and backs."

"Simon's getting more like Paul every day," said I.

At that, Samboy's head snapped around. He asked, "You mean Simon's been takin' you to some tree?"

"No," I laughed. "Simon will never be as nasty as Paul. I just meant we best not forget our plans. We best be looking out for ourselves."

After Levi left the plantation, I came to my senses. With Levi's soft eyes and beckoning body out of the picture, I could think more rationally. I almost let Levi fall in love with me, I thought, not knowing I could never bear him children.

Even though I still couldn't see much use in bringing children into a slave world, I could see how a woman who loved a man might want to give him one or two babies, and how a man who loved a woman might want some.

The strangest thing about the whole matter was that I had had Aggie fix me so I would never bear Paul's baby, but Paul had never come near me in that way again. Now Paul was dead. Aggie and Mammy were right, I guess, thinking I might want to have babies someday. It was too late to lament that now.

The other thing I realized was that I hadn't been quite fair to Simon. He hadn't sent Levi away to hurt me, only to try to help the plantation. So I tried to think of a way I could make it up to Simon. I thought about the sewing I had learned before we came west, but I couldn't think of a way to turn that into cash.

Pretty soon, I noticed our cows had started giving milk again, now that they were free of the trail, yet nobody had time to make butter and cheese from that milk. So I went to Simon. "I'd be willing to give those cows and their milk a try if you'd get me a dairy book or two." When I said maybe we could sell some of the butter and cheese for cash, he brightened right up and showed some enthusiasm.

"Why, Samgirl," Simon said, his eyes shining and his lips pulled back from his long white teeth in a wide grin, "that's a brilliant idea. I'll do far better than a book. I'll apprentice you out to another plantation and you can learn firsthand."

"All right, Marse Simon, whatever you say," said I, figuring in my heart that if Levi was gone I might as well be gone too.

Pretty soon, Simon sent me, not to another plantation, but to a dairy near Tishomingo. I worked there every day of the week except Sunday. I slept on a cot in a back room. On Saturday afternoon, Samboy came for me. We rode back to Mammy's and Pappy's cabin doubled up on a plow horse's back. On Sunday afternoon, Samboy turned that horse right around and we went back to the dairy. Dog always smiled when I got home and whimpered when I left.

I went along this way for ten weeks. I liked Tishomingo less and less. It was too bustling and too busy for me. "People there are more anxious to make money than to enjoy their lives as free men and women,"

I explained to Samboy as we trotted down the dusty road toward home one Saturday.

"What do you mean? They're free. What could be wrong with that?"

I cocked my head behind his back and tried to think of an example. "Take the new sawmill, for example. They had some kind of boiler there that they fired up for power. One day the mill owner was overseeing things and cussing at his workers. The boiler blew up and tore that man's legs right off. When they hauled what was left of him into the office he said, 'God have mercy on my wife and children.' He never spoke or breathed again. They buried him on the hillside in a box made of black walnut sawed from logs that once grew on that very hillside."

"Serves him right," Samboy said without much interest in that example or in hearing others.

Despite its frantic pace, however, I learned a lot in Tishomingo, both about human nature and especially about the dairy business. I discovered how to use a churn and a cream skimmer and a separator and so on. I also realized we would have to put money into equipment for the plantation before I would be able to run a dairy there. When I broached the matter to Simon, I was relieved to learn that he was way ahead of me on that one.

"Don't you worry, Samgirl," he told me. "I've arranged to trade your labor in the Tishomingo dairy for some basic implements and supplies we'll need back at the plantation."

When my tenth week at the dairy ended, I came home in a wagon surrounded by a churn and such. When I got back to the plantation, Simon waited for me, his hair hanging in his eyes like a little boy. "I have something to show you, Samgirl," he said, a smile spreading across his gaunt face.

Simon walked me up the rise toward the big house. On the top of the hill I saw a new stone building built into the ground with a pole shed coming off one side. It was my dairy. I thought I'd better strike while Simon felt in a giving mood, so I asked, "Can I have that Isaac boy to help me mornings carrying cans of milk and his sister Jessie in the afternoons to help with the cheese and such?"

"Isaac and Jessie it is," Simon replied. "Samgirl, you can have almost anything you want."

I was tempted to say, "How about freedom?" but I knew that would get me no place.

Besides, I had plans. If I helped Simon make some money now, I wouldn't feel guilty stealing myself and my family from him later. Too, I intended to take whatever supplies we needed when the time came to run. In the meantime, I would train Isaac and Jessie to take over the dairy after I left. Isaac was about nine and Jessie about eleven, so they weren't doing much heavy work around the farm yet. I planned to raise them right up in the dairy business and then disappear.

I schemed in other ways as well. I goaded Pappy not to break up our wagon for wood. "Pappy," said I, "settle that wagon against the back of our cabin and store things in it—like firewood."

"But, Samgirl," Pappy said in a cranky voice, "that wagon has good wood in it. I won't have to bring down so many trees if I bust the wagon up."

"Pappy," I explained, "remember those plans I said I would be making. This wagon is part of those plans."

Then Mammy put her bit in. "Put that wagon on the side of the cabin, Ike," she said. "It'll be easier to get wood and stuff out of it if it's on the side."

Real gentle-like I told Mammy, "If that wagon ever disappears from the side of the cabin, people will notice right off. If it's in the back, no one will miss it for a long time."

"Oh," Pappy and Mammy both said, shaking their heads and probably wondering what kind of a daughter they had brought into this world.

Finally, Pappy and Samboy hauled that wagon around the back of our cabin. They took the wheels and the yoke off and stored them in the bottom of the wagonbed. Pappy put planks over the wagonbed and we used the top of the planks to store firewood.

I also convinced Mammy to roll up the wagon covers and stick them under our beds, the canvas one under hers and Pappy's bigger bed and the cotton one under Samboy's bunk. Yes, I still slept in the top bunk. Now Samboy was too big to take a chance on a top bunk that might come off the wall with the weight of his muscles and all.

One day, Serena strolled along with her usual prying eyes and big mouth. "Why're you wasting your wagon that way, Ike? You could just as easily store that firewood right on the ground."

"We like it this way, Serena," Pappy said, his eyes crinkling at their corners.

"And," Mammy added, "what if we got to move again, Serena? Don't look like there's too much money around here these days. We might need that wagon."

That set Serena off onto another tirade. "That Marse Simon," she muttered, "drives himself too hard. He drives us even harder. We're all goin' to break down like old, busted mules afore long."

Serena started in on me next. "You and that Levi," she said, "you sellin' cheese and him hirin' out on the trail. Pretty soon Marse Simon's goin' to have me washin' clothes for the whole neighborhood. What you want to work that way for, anyhow?"

"Serena," said I, "shut your mouth. You don't understand nothin'. If me and Levi bring in money this plantation just might make it. You want to get on the trail again and go live someplace else?"

Serena reared back, but she recovered from my smart mouth real fast. "I only want to move if I can get away from the likes of you, Missie Samgirl," she said as she flounced her two hundred and fifty pounds of lard away from our cabin. Even though I hoped she'd never come around again, I knew we couldn't be that lucky.

In the meantime, I had other things to worry about than Serena. I kept busy training Isaac and Jessie in the dairy, and smart learners they turned out to be. Isaac showed up early every morning and lugged and toted milk cans and whatever else I wanted. Although Isaac ran to plumpness, after a few weeks working in the dairy he began to slim out. His features became sharper and it was clear he would be a good-looking boy.

Jessie was different from Isaac, fairer-skinned, slender, and real shy. The first few days Jessie jumped around that dairy like a beetle on a hot hearth every time I spoke to her. Even though I tried to gentle down my deep, booming voice, that child almost wore me out with her bouncing and squealing. After awhile, though, we adjusted to each other and I found that Jessie was a willing apprentice. She had more curiosity than a hound dog on the hunt. She wanted to know "what's this?" "what's that?" all afternoon long.

It's a good thing we were willing to work so hard, because Simon came around every hour, it seemed. "How's things going, Samgirl? When will you start selling butter and cheese and things?"

"Pretty soon, Marse Simon. Pretty soon."

By November, I had things pretty well in place. We made our first extra butter and cheese for sale. Simon went out of his mind with joy. He brushed his hank of forehead hair out of his eyes and let his face relax a bit. "Samgirl, you're one smart gal."

"Are you going to let me go out on the road and sell this stuff, then?" I asked, ever hopeful.

Simon had other plans. "No," he said, "you stay right here and keep this dairy humming. Make as much as you can. I'm sending Esther and Rebecca out in a special buggy. They'll go from farm to farm, and plantation to plantation, selling what they can."

I was real shocked when I first heard Simon's plan. I could hardly believe he intended to send two young ladies to do his hawking and selling for him. Then I realized he was right; he needed every slave at home working as many hours as they could stand up and keep going. And it was different here than in Mississippi. We lived among Chickasaw here. Esther and Rebecca were Chickasaw. They could go out selling without danger to themselves or loss of face for the family. Nor could they get lost. One look across the prairie and they could see which road would lead them home.

Off the two girls went in a buggylike affair with a special compartment in the back. Every Tuesday and Friday morning, despite rain or wind or a glaring sunshiny sky, Isaac loaded that compartment with butter and cheese and then Esther and Rebecca made the rounds of the neighborhood. Although I never saw the money they brought back, one Friday afternoon Simon came to the dairy with a dead chicken swinging from each of his fists. "This one is for you, Samgirl," he explained, "I hope your family enjoys it."

I took the chicken and looked at it hard. I almost laughed as I thought back to the time me and Samboy stole one of old John's chickens and tried to cook it. This time I would let Mammy get the feathers off her own way. I would just do the eating.

"This one is for you, Isaac and Jessie," Simon continued, "I hope your family enjoys it. You've worked real hard."

Isaac said, "Thank you, Marse Simon," but Jessie just smiled her sweet, shy grin at Simon.

What Simon didn't know—and he certainly wouldn't have been handing out any chicken to me if he had known—is that I regularly skimmed some cream off the top, so to speak, for my own purposes. I always made sure I was in that dairy before Isaac in the morning and stayed after Jessie in the afternoon so I could set aside some of our makings for myself. I hid them under my dress in a special sack Mammy had devised for that purpose and I took them home.

Sometimes we ate those extras; sometimes we gave them to such others as Mose and Amanda, or to Becky and her brood, or even to Serena to keep her fat mouth quiet. More often, we traded them on what I called the black market. I used that term in a joking way. I meant that wherever there were slaves there was also a network that ran from plantation to plantation. An axe might turn up missing, or a horseshoe, or a few nails, or whatever. In fact, some planters started putting brands on their tools so they could track them down when they wandered away.

Little by little, I started to trade dairy products to build a cache of things we'd be needing when we ran: nails to reinforce the wagon, iron rims for its wheels, shoes for the horses I intended to liberate from Master Simon, extra blankets, bits of cloth, and so on. In return, I would give butter or cheese or maybe some cream. Slaves on other plantations seemed mighty glad to have it and never said a word about it.

They ate their trade items right down, but, on our end, my new goods created a storage problem. "Where do you expect me to put all this truck?" Pappy asked.

"Under the beds, Pappy. In the rafters. Wherever you can."

We filled every inch under the beds and under the wagon and under the firewood in the wagon. Pretty soon, we had more stuff than we had firewood. Next, Pappy built a ceiling in our cabin with an attic above where we could put some of the lighter items, such as the wagon covers and such. Then he built a false wall between our kitchen and our sleeping area to store more stuff in.

Our cabin grew smaller all the time, but no one knew it except us. Master Simon never came into the cabins. Any visitors we had always stayed in the cooking room, or more often outside on our tiny porch or on the dirt area Pappy had fixed with cut-off log stools. So none of our friends noticed much either. Those that did thought we were junk collectors, or maybe saving up nails for Levi, if he ever came home.

Levi finally showed up right before Christmas. Frosty air pressed against my shoulders with a threat of snow. Although I didn't like the chilliness, we certainly needed the moisture snow would bring; the fall had been unusually dry.

Despite the icy wind, I broke out in a sweat when I saw Levi swinging down the trail toward the big house. "It's Levi," I shouted out loud. In my joy, I announced the obvious to no one in particular. I forgot all my worries and ran toward him. Then I remembered my fears and stopped, pushing down the affection and the need I had in me for Levi.

Levi marched right up that road and took me in his hard-muscled arms. "I'm finally home, Samgirl."

I ducked out of his hug and drew back. "Come see my family, Levi," I panted. "They've all been missing you."

"And you, Samgirl? Have you missed me?"

I ignored his question and took off down the hard-packed dirt road to the quarters, Levi right behind me all the way. Half of me hoped he wouldn't stay for long; the other half hoped he would stay forever.

Usually, Christmas wasn't a big celebration on our plantation, being that old John and Nellie were really Chickasaw and hadn't grown up with Christmas. We usually got a half-day off work. We went to the big house and got a chicken per family, some extra molasses or sorghum, and a piece of pork from a newly slaughtered hog. After that, we listened to old John—I supposed this year it would be Simon—read from the Bible. Then we'd go home and have a good supper and rest up a bit. But this year Levi made Christmas a celebration for me and my folks.

"Samgirl," he said as soon as he got to our cabin door, "I've been thinking about you. I brought you some presents. I traded my labor along the way and picked up a thing here and there, but I'm saving them until Christmas."

That set me and Samboy to making gifts for everybody. Samboy carved a wooden ladle for Mammy and a prod for Pappy to use with the mules. I made Samboy a cheese with a picture of a horse stamped in it and one with a picture of a cow for Levi. What Levi brought beat all. As I look back, I know it wasn't much, but it sure seemed grand to us then.

On Christmas Day snow feathered over the hard, lumpy ground, covering and softening the bleak landscape as best it could. Levi showed up about ten o'clock, presents in his hands and pockets.

"For you, Samgirl," Levi said, relishing every minute he could drag out of the gift giving, "I brought some sugar candy and a new kerchief for your neck." I almost cried at that, knowing that Levi understood the pain my brand caused me and tried to help me hide it.

"For you, Samboy," Levi added, "some molasses sticks and a pair of spurs I made myself." Although Samboy looked like he would faint with delight, he rallied and put the spurs right on the cheap boots Master Simon had given him for riding horses.

"For Aunt Chloe," Levi continued, "a yellow scarf to tie around her hair. And for Ike, an iron hoe that won't break in this lifetime."

Everybody oh'ed and ah'ed. I gave Levi his cheese and he seemed real pleased. "You learned all this while I was gone?" he asked.

My face heated up and I nodded yes.

"So we're both bringing in money for Marse Simon," he said, pride popping out all over his face.

That's when the bad part of Christmas came. "You ain't going anymore, are you, Levi?"

"Not until early springtime, Samgirl. Then Marse Simon is sending me back on the trail again. This time I'm going down into Texas, where I've never been before."

"Oh," was all I managed to say. I fought back tears that scorched the back of my eyeballs and battled to get out. I didn't understand my own feelings. I had decided Levi was not for me. But only my head had decided; my heart was going along its own path.

Mammy tried to cover my distress by giving Levi a special corndodger she had made him with green peppers in it. She'd baked it in her old iron skillet with a lid; she set it right on the fire and heaped it with coals. Pappy gave Levi a clever knife that we'd traded butter for. Samboy gave Levi a bowl he'd carved out of wood and filled with colorful seeds and nuts and such.

Levi looked at everyone with tears rimming his dark eyes. "I thank you all. I'm glad to be home."

By the time that was all over, I had straightened out and remembered the part about Aggie fixing me good and not being able to have Levi's babies. I twisted my lips into a smile to show I didn't care if Levi went away again. At the same time, my eyes and the rest of my face stayed in mourning for Levi's return to the trail. We got on with eating the good supper Mammy had fixed and with making the most of the only time to rest that Simon had given us since we first arrived way back last summer.

After Levi left for Texas in the spring, I knew it was for the best. Besides making a poor wife for Levi, I had my own future to consider. I wanted freedom more than I wanted anything, even Levi.

I decided it was time to move on to the next part of my plan. "I have to get rid of that *P* brand on my chest," I had once told Levi. "No matter where I run, that brand will mark me a runaway slave for patrollers and slave-catchers."

I had hoped Levi could make an iron that would somehow cover the brand. He said he could, but pointed out that the *P* would always show through because that scar tissue was older and darker than whatever we put over the top of it. I also asked him about cutting that piece of skin right off. "If you cut deep enough to get the *P* off, Samgirl," he said, "you'd probably lose so much blood you'd die."

After Levi went back on the trail, I was left to my own devices to think up ways to get rid of that hateful *P*. I finally concluded that the only way to hide it was with a worse burn than the first one, a burn that would cover a good part of my chest and that people would naturally turn their eyes away from. That way, if the *P* showed through a bit, no one would notice anyway.

I knew I could get scalding water in the dairy because we used it to wash our equipment. The rest of my plan turned out to be harder. Because I didn't want to burn my whole chest, I had to figure out a way to protect a good part of me while exposing another part. I finally decided I would cover with butter the part I didn't want to burn. Then I would tie a pig hide over my breasts with a stout rope. That would leave the top part of my chest exposed.

It took me awhile to trade for the hide and the rope, but I gradually collected what I would need. In the meantime, I used my time alone in the dairy to practice ladling cold water on the *P* on my chest and seeing how far the water would splash. I decided that I'd better cover my shoulders and arms. That took more trading to get more hide and rope.

I even drew on my sewing skills, because I made some of that hide into a jacketlike affair I could slip over my shoulders. When I practiced with that and the cold water, though, I still found lots of the water splashing where I didn't want it going. Clearly, I had to take Samboy into my confidence and ask for his help.

"Samboy," I started one morning when we went out to get wood for the cooking fire, "what would you think if I tried to get rid of this *P* brand on my chest?"

Samboy's eyes sprang wide open and he asked, "Why do you want to do that? You cover it good enough already with a kerchief."

"What about when we run away?" said I. "Patrollers and slave-catchers will know right away I'm a runaway slave."

"Oh," said Samboy. He took a minute to digest that thought. "All right, but how you goin' to get rid of that *P*?"

I explained to Samboy about my conversations with Levi and my experiments with hide and rope. "You got any ideas, Samboy?"

Samboy pondered until Mammy started yelling from inside the cabin for her wood. We ran fast and stopped her yelling. I could see Samboy thinking, thinking in that head of his. After breakfast, such as it was, Samboy said, "Let's pile up some wood so Mammy doesn't run out anymore." Mammy grinned as we headed outdoors.

On our way to the shed, Samboy said to me, "I think what you got to do is make a tight dress out of hide. You could put it on first, then wet it with cold water so it would shrink tight to your body. We could have a jagged hole cut in the front and throw the scalding water just on that part. Then we could burn the *P* right off you."

I was so tickled with Samboy's suggestion—which improved on my own earlier attempts—that I tried to grab him by the neck to hug him, but he had grown bigger than me and he ducked away. "Don't forget Mammy's wood," I yelled after his back. But he had already left and I had to haul the wood in the house myself.

That's how Samboy became my assistant in the *P* prank, as we called it in code so no one would know what we were up to.

chapter ten

In a strange way, I was happy to remember the next part of my story. It reminded me how much pain I had gone through to get our runaway scheme in place and how set I was on seeing freedom. I shifted position on the cabin doorsill and watched that moon inch its way across the August sky.

First, I recollected how difficult it had been to get the supplies we needed for the *P* prank. Finding a suitable piece of hide, as well as the needle and thongs to sew it up with, took me and Samboy most of the summer. In fact, it was October before I started stealing minutes here and there to make that dress. I worked at the hide dress in the dairy, mostly late at night, and hid the dress during the day in a special hole in the wall that Samboy carved out.

"I sure am glad," I told Samboy, "that your job as a cowboy means you can carry such things as a knife and that you've been so smart as to learn to whittle."

"Just don't tucker yourself out working so late at night," he replied.

"Shush. You don't know anything. Working late into the night fits into my scheme. When I tell Mammy and Pappy I'm going to sleep in the dairy overnight they won't think anything of it."

"Ha. Mammy and Pappy ain't as feeble-minded as you think. You better try it a few times to see how it goes."

So I tried it a couple of times. Pappy didn't say anything one way or the other. Mammy made me a special corn-husk mattress to use in the dairy.

By November, I felt ready. Me and Samboy picked a Saturday night so I could recover over Sunday. We had both forgotten how sick I was when Paul first put that mark on me and how much doctoring it took from Mammy and that French trader's wife to get me well. I had a hard time explaining to Mammy and Pappy why both me and Samboy had to work in the dairy on a Saturday night, but by then Simon was driving us all so hard I could use him as our excuse.

"Me and Samboy has got to help Marse Simon with his money problems," said I, feeling bad about at my lie but knowing it was necessary if I was ever to free myself of the damning *P* on my chest. "You know Mister Simon wants to get all he can out of this place," said I, not looking Mammy or Pappy in the eyes.

Pappy bowed his head. I noticed tiny curls of gray in his hair. He said, "I thought Simon proved himself to old John long ago. This is our second summer. We have cotton and corn in the ground, along with a bit of oats and millet and tobacco. We're doing all right on meat too, seeing as how there's always duck and quail, especially in the fall. In between, there's everything from polecat meat to bear meat. We got a peach orchard in from those peach stones Simon had sent from back East. And we got a well dug and the spring opened up. But Simon's not stoppin'. He's just pushin' himself and us on and on and on."

"Maybe things are worse than we think," Samboy said, glad to shift attention away from our plan to stay at the dairy all night. "Or maybe Simon's just greedy."

Mammy shot a sharp look at me and Samboy, but she seemed too tired to argue much further. "Go then. But remember, Samgirl, you're human too. A body can only take so much."

Anyway, we left the cabin and went on our way to the dairy with an extra quilt for Samboy. I also spirited away some of Mammy's salve and the kerchief Levi brought me last Christmas to cover the burn when we finished. I planned on telling Mammy and Pappy about it later when the deed was done, and telling people in the quarters and the big house never. I would just keep wearing my kerchief as always.

"All right," Samboy said, after he laid out my mattress and his quilt and put Mammy's salve on the counter where he could reach it right away. "Get your hide dress out."

I scrabbled in the wall and pulled out my dress. It was really more like an apron, because I didn't have enough hide to cover my back, but I'd decided it didn't matter. "The only problem," I told Samboy, "is that I was never able to test it to see if it would shrink right. I was afraid I would never get it off again."

Samboy scrunched his forehead and said, "That's all right. If it doesn't shrink right, we won't go on."

I greased myself with butter and put on the apron. Samboy doused me with water. At first, the hide didn't seem to shrink so Samboy poured on more. I shivered. The apron got tighter. When it clung to me we rubbed more butter all over the hide, except for the cut-out part on my chest.

"Practice first with cold water," I instructed Samboy. I showed him how I leaned forward and splashed the water up on my chest with a ladle. When he learned that, I told him, "You got to keep the scalding water coming until my skin starts to swell. There's no use burning it a little bit, we got to do this right."

When Samboy hit me with the first splash of boiling water I cried out. He wanted to stop. So I bit my tongue and grabbed my knees harder. I told him to keep the water coming. After the second hit, I sank down on a wooden stool, but kept leaning over that steaming pot of water. He doused me again and I went into shock. Now I froze into position and he did it again, I don't know how many more times because I could no longer count.

It turned out that Samboy nursed me all night, putting cold cloths on my head and salve on my chest. When Pappy stopped by during the morning after the rations-giving, I was still out, so Samboy had to own up to what we had done. Pappy carried me back to the cabin and got me to sitting up with my eyes open. I sat unmoving, like a fatback hog who had eaten a whole winter's worth of feed.

When I focused on their faces I saw that Pappy and Samboy looked real alarmed. They shifted their eyes back and forth toward each other and let them roll toward the ceiling. "Mammy's not here," Pappy explained to me, "she said with you and Samboy gone it was a good time for her and Becky to work late in the weaving room. She and Becky said they were goin' to make that loom go bump, bump all night."

I couldn't say anything. It seemed real strange to me that Mammy would object to my working in the dairy and then go work all night herself. But my woozy mind couldn't pursue the puzzle.

Samboy chimed in, "Maybe you better go get Mammy. And bring Becky, too, so she can help."

Pappy seemed double-worried. He rubbed his forehead and let a creeping uneasiness show at the back of his eyes. "I don't know why Chloe ain't home yet. She's been gone all night and half the day."

Samboy appeared to believe Pappy had had too much of a shock for an old man—old, that is, from Samboy's point of view—so Samboy volunteered to fetch Mammy. "I'll find her," he said as he ducked out the cabin door.

Me and Pappy waited, but Samboy didn't come back. Finally, Pappy carried me into the sleeping room and put me in Samboy's bunk. Dog curled up at my feet, whimpering and moaning like he could feel the hurt himself. Pappy sat on a stool by my bed and patted my hand while he kept watching the cooking-room door. When he heard Samboy come in, he jumped up and went through to the front room, the cooking and eating room.

Pretty soon, Pappy returned, carrying Mammy in his arms. He laid her on their bunk. Becky and Samboy followed right behind. Because I couldn't speak, I raised my hand and Becky saw I wanted to know about Mammy. She came to me and said, "It looks like you and your mammy's minds think alike, Samgirl. Your mammy's left breast's been throbbing and hurting. It's full of funny kinds of bumps. The doctor woman next door said it had to come off. So your mammy and I cut it off, last night in the weaving house."

I felt murky in my head myself, so I couldn't quite take in what Becky had told me. Samboy and Pappy both had to explain it to me again before I got it fully into my mind. I could only wonder who would nurse me and Mammy now.

A big argument started on that very point. Samboy said, "We got to get Marse Simon to bring a regular doctor in here right away." He paced up and down that little sleeping room, pushing everyone back against the walls to avoid his big feet.

"Think what you're sayin', boy," Pappy said, shaking his head. "We're walkin' the knife-edge of danger here. If Marse Simon gets a doctor, that doctor's goin' to tell him Samgirl wanted to cover her brand and Mammy tried to get rid of a sick breast. Marse Simon's goin' to be powerful mad about all that. He's goin' to say Samgirl and Mammy should have left themselves alone."

"He's goin' to be madder yet," Becky added, "about all the days of work he loses out of these two while they's gettin' well again."

That's how it came about that Pappy asked Simon to have Eliza sent over from next door. She was the doctor woman who said Mammy's breast had to come off. Pappy told Simon that me and Mammy both had terrible fevers and maybe even something bad like cholera. Just as Becky had predicted, Simon was upset about our lost workdays, but he was even more worried about the other slaves catching what we had. Simon sent in Eliza and quarantined us all, including Pappy, but not Becky, right in our own cabin.

I didn't like Eliza. She was bony and tense and didn't know how to smile. Still, she knew how to use herbs and poultices and that's what me and Mammy needed. Eliza stayed with us a week, sleeping on a pallet on the floor near me and Mammy, while Samboy and Pappy slept in the cooking room.

"Simon will pay my master," Eliza said when she left. Still, we gave Eliza all the payment we could, butter and sewing needles and such.

Me and Mammy stayed down a few more days after Eliza left, then we each got up a little bit at a time. Samboy and Pappy had been doing the cooking in the morning and at noon. In the evening, they brought supper back from the grub table. Now Mammy started helping some. She couldn't carry anything heavy and I guessed that her time for work in the weaving house and the loom room was over.

As I went out about the quarters a bit, I learned that other things had changed, especially up at the big house. Wouldn't you know, Esther and Rebecca had found themselves Chickasaw husbands as they peddled that butter and cheese. Esther planned to get married and move right down the road; Rebecca's future husband would take her almost to Tishomingo. So we had a couple of weddings coming up.

Then I found out Peter had found himself a wife, also a Chickasaw. We were going to lose two young women and get us back one. Some talk occurred as to whether Peter could marry before his older brother did, but Simon didn't care one way or the other. "Go ahead, Peter," Simon told his brother. "Get married. Your new father-in-law will pay for your wedding. I'll stand the cost of Esther's and Rebecca's."

What did Simon do but throw one huge wedding in the spring for both couples. Folks came from all around to see them say their vows before a Christian Chickasaw preacher named Joe Grey Mule, and to eat and drink with them afterwards. It all made a lot of work for the slaves—three weeks just to clean the house from top to bottom and get the yard in order—although Mammy and I missed most of it, being as we were both still sickly.

It also made a lot of expense for Simon, even sticking two weddings into one the way he did. Simon didn't hand out any big wedding gifts of slaves or land, either to Esther and Rebecca or to Peter and his bride. With money as tight as it seemed to be, the celebration proved expense enough, including as it did such extras as beer, wine, baked chicken and ham, and rows and rows of pies and cakes.

After the wedding, we all expected things to tighten up even more. Sure enough, we hadn't seen Levi for almost a year when Simon made a crushing announcement: "You're old enough to go on the trail, Samboy. Get yourself ready."

Samboy was only fourteen, yet Simon thought him skilled and strong enough to work with the best cowhands. Besides, on the trail Samboy could make some wages that would come right into Simon's waiting pocket.

I fled to my bunk when I heard the news. I lay like a piece of fatback, feeling heavy, sodden, dull. I hurt, I brooded, I moped, I muttered. "Besides losing Samboy, I'll no longer have a partner in my runaway scheme." I buried my head in my corn-husk mattress and grumbled some more. "Here it is the spring of 1849. We've been in Indian Territory for almost two years and haven't made a whole lot of progress on the freedom business."

When Samboy finally mounted his horse to ride off, I started crying like water gushing from the pump, especially when I saw the metal tag with the year and a number on it Simon put around Samboy's neck on a leather thong. I squeezed my eyes shut and tried to think of the future. I held back my tears and caught my breath. "Watch out, Samboy, and learn everything you can. Maybe we'll run away to Mexico instead of Canada. That'll mean going through Texas. You study everything good, the trails and the forts and so on."

Samboy nodded his head and I knew he understood. That was one smart boy—who was about to become a man. He would come back smarter yet, if I knew my brother.

After that, Dog and I became almost inseparable. With Levi and Samboy gone, Pappy working in the fields, and Mammy going about her doctoring and little else, I felt bereft—like the last row of cotton at picking time. If it hadn't been for Dog, I would have laid down in my bunk and stayed there.

As it turned out, my chest burn healed real good, with lots of scars and no trace of the hateful *P*. As soon as I felt strong enough, I went back to the dairy with Dog trailing behind. I couldn't do anything heavy; I just supervised Isaac and Jessie and gave some orders here and there.

Seeing I was not as useful as I once had been in the dairy, Simon put me to doing pickup jobs, such as rubbing the sprouts off Irish potatoes. I wasn't too fond of these jobs, so I worked slow. "Maybe I'd work better," I hinted to Simon, "if you moved me to the big house to help Dolly Lee."

I liked Dolly Lee, Peter's new wife. Also, I thought working in the big house put me near some useful information and even some supplies. "I know how to sew and how to manage other slaves," I reminded Simon. "I could do lots of other tasks that needed doing."

Simon thought about it. It seemed Dolly Lee had come from a plantation with plenty of slaves and older sisters to supervise them and didn't know how to do much of anything. Finally, Simon gave in. "You can supervise the dairy mornings," he said, "and supervise Dolly Lee afternoons."

This was where Dog and I parted company. I wasn't bringing a slave-quarter cur into the big house. Dog took it philosophically, as dogs usually do. Dog walked to the big house gate with me and was waiting at the cabin door when I got home.

I missed Dog, but I liked Dolly Lee a good deal. She was smaller and whiter than anyone else in old John's family. Dolly Lee blushed a lot and her whole face turned rosy pink when she did. I urged Dolly Lee to dress in light blues and greens and yellows so she looked like a flower, especially a camellia.

Dolly Lee was just about my age and she was the first friend I ever had. I knew that slaves were not supposed to become friends with their mistresses, but it was different with me and Dolly Lee. We could laugh and cry and complain together. Besides, she didn't know how to do most of the chores, so I taught her how. As she felt more useful around the big house, she liked me more and more.

Dolly Lee and I took over the big house without much trouble. Nellie didn't mind giving up household leadership to Dolly Lee. Nellie was getting old and tired, what with nursing old John all the time and him still refusing to try Cap'n Jack's wooden leg or go any farther than the portico on Cap'n Jack's crutch. Nellie had her hands full with old John, as well as with having Esther and Rebecca visit her once a week or so.

Besides, Peter spent most of the day helping Simon one way or another. That left me and Dolly Lee pretty much alone to run the house the way we wanted. By now, nobody lived in their wagons anymore, including old John's family. Only the slaves continued to eat supper at the grub table. Old John's folks ate in the dining room of the big house. So Dolly Lee and I had a cook and a few house servants to deal with.

They were also easy to get along with. "I'm happy for you to choose the menus," Cook told Dolly Lee. "Less work for me that way."

The others let her tell them when to spin yarn, knit, or clean the house. It made it easier on them if Dolly Lee took charge. They had less planning and thinking that way, and less blame if things went wrong.

Dolly Lee would spend the morning dressing, fussing, ordering meals for the day ahead, and opening this cupboard or that with a key on the ring she had inherited from Nellie. From those cupboards, Cook or the house servants would take the wine, silver, or linens they needed. Then Dolly Lee would lock up the cupboards again.

By the time I reached the big house in the afternoon, Dolly Lee was ready for some serious work.

"Teach me to sew," she begged, so I taught her how to do coarse sewing. In return, she taught me some fancy embroidery work. I also taught her how to make soap and candles and rag rugs and she showed me how to sew patchwork quilts. By the time we finished those afternoons, both Dolly Lee and I were tired. She had more knowledge to her and I had more polish to me.

Not that the big house matched the one old John and Nellie had had back in Mississippi. I described it to Mammy and Pappy after dinner one night. "This house has a nice portico, all right, and a carved front door with colored glass in it. But when you come in you see a plain, dark center hall with a straight, narrow stairway leading upstairs. Around the hall hang some huge pictures of old people who all look like full-blood Indians."

Mammy and Pappy shook their heads in unison. "Imagine," Mammy said. "People's pictures on the walls."

"I don't like those pictures," I said. "I go here and there and every whichway, but anywhere I go those Indians always look straight at me and watch me work."

"What else they got in that house?" Pappy asked.

"Well," said I, "on the right-hand side of the hall is a dining room with a serving area behind that and a kitchen behind that." In Mississippi, old John's folks would have considered it common to have the kitchen right in the big house. But this wasn't Mississippi.

"On the left-hand side," I continued, "is a parlor with the family sitting room behind it. And that's all—no fancy receiving rooms or ballrooms or anything. The furniture is sparse. Only rag rugs cover the floor. The curtains look to me like old bedsheets. Right out the parlor windows you can see the log cribs and a corral for the riding horses."

"I like horses," Pappy said.

Mammy frowned. "But, Ike, anybody knows horses ain't supposed to be right outside the big house windows."

"Why not, Chloe?" Pappy asked, scratching his head and furrowing his forehead.

"For one thing, they make a mess. And—"

"Mammy," I interrupted. "Don't you want to hear about the upstairs?"

When I had Mammy's and Pappy's attention again, I went on. "Upstairs are four bedrooms, directly over the four downstairs rooms. The big front one is for old John and Nellie. The other front one for Peter and Dolly Lee. Two stand empty, but Dolly Lee hopes to fill one with a baby pretty soon." In fact, I never saw a woman who wanted a child so bad. Nearly every week she thought she might be in the family way.

In the meantime, Dolly Lee took to entertaining. Sometimes she had ladies for tea, or other planters for dinner, but the best party she ever gave was a quilting. To her friends' houses she sent messengers, each carrying a small bit of cotton with a note asking that it be spun and reeled. The women were to bring the spun cotton to Dolly Lee's hanking.

When the women arrived, Dolly Lee and I had two quilts stretched on frames. All her friends took to quilting for the rest of the morning. They stitched and talked until quilt patterns took shape right on the frames.

There must have been thirty women; at noon they all stopped to eat. Cook and her helpers set up long tables in the yard with plenty of food for everybody: turkey, chicken, pork, vegetables, pies, and preserves. By late afternoon, the women's husbands and sweethearts started to arrive. They soon cleared the parlors of furniture, either pushing it back against the walls or shoving it into the front hallway.

After that, everybody danced, everything from a waltz to a Virginia reel. Coffee Fred's fiddle music tweedled its way through every bit of the big house until 5 A.M. In between, more food appeared. Around midnight, Cook served pound cake and coffee and tea. Pyramids of pound cakes filled the tables.

Dolly Lee heard about it later from Simon. "I don't approve of such frivolous expense, Dolly Lee," Simon said in a hard, tight voice.

Dolly Lee told me Simon had hollered and pushed sheets of figures under her nose until little tears trickled down her cheeks. At that, Simon relented. He even apologized. But Dolly Lee had seen the seriousness of the situation.

After that, we spent most our time working downstairs and talking away while we worked. Sometimes, when old John and Nellie rested out on the portico, we sat and sewed in the upstairs hallway, which had sun and breeze both. It was one of those afternoons that me and Dolly Lee had the most surprising conversation I ever had in my life.

"You know," Dolly Lee said in a low voice, like she was about to tell me a secret, "I don't believe in slavery."

"What?" said I, sticking myself with a needle in the process.

Dolly Lee lowered her voice even more and said, "I don't believe in slavery."

I'd recovered by now so I asked, "But, Dolly Lee, you got slaves in your daddy's home. And you got them here in your husband's home."

Dolly Lee jiggled her head of pale brown curls. The gold streaks glimmered in the sun. "I know that," she said. "And I appreciate all the work they do. But I still don't believe in slavery."

"What's your daddy say to that?" I asked, thinking the sky must have fallen on Dolly Lee's head when her daddy heard her views on the very thing that allowed her to live in luxury.

"I never told my daddy," she answered with a little pout to her lips. "I was afraid he'd be angry with me. That he'd blame it on the fancy Chickasaw female seminary where he sent me to get finished."

I didn't know what *finished* meant, but I had far more interest in the slavery issue anyway, so I pursued that. "What's Peter say about all this?"

"That's one of the reasons I love Peter. He doesn't believe in slavery either."

I stopped sewing altogether. I held my needle in midair, in front of my open mouth and bugged-out eyes. "What do you mean, Peter doesn't believe in slavery? He owns slaves, doesn't he?"

"Not really," Dolly Lee said with a dainty toss of her head. "Papa John owns the slaves and Simon drives them. Peter just helps because he has to."

I grew cagey now. I worried that perhaps Dolly Lee suspected my runaway plans and had set out to trap me. Yet I knew the woman didn't have one devious bone in her body. Finally, I said, "Why don't you and Peter go off on your own and start a farm without slaves?"

"We can't because we don't own any land." About then, Dolly Lee sounded real put out. "Peter is the youngest son so he won't get much when Papa John dies. I'm only a girl. I have my dowry, but I won't get any land."

I made a sign across myself for Dolly Lee talking about old John's death that way, then I asked, "What's a dowry?"

"You know, that's the money and jewelry my daddy gave me to bring to my marriage. He wanted to give me some slaves too, but I wouldn't take them. Peter didn't want them either."

"What are you going to do, then? Will Peter just go on working for Simon forever and— "

"No," Dolly Lee interrupted. "Peter went to old John and asked him to make Simon give us a share of the farm's takings. So we have a little money coming in. Someday we can buy our own land. Or maybe some day we'll go west on the trail and find us a farm."

All of this came as a huge shock to me. Hot coals seemed to burn their way through my body, changing every particle of me as they went. First was the idea of slave owners who didn't approve of slavery. Second was the notion that folks other than slaves had plans to change their lives in some drastic way. Third was the thought that Peter and Dolly Lee wanted to run away too.

I was not so stupid that I would tell Dolly Lee my plans. Besides, I remembered my pact with Samboy, sealed in the vegetable patch back in Mississippi, that we wouldn't tell anyone anything, except maybe Mammy and Pappy. I did, however, see Dolly Lee as an ally. At least, she might lend me books and get me the map of Texas that was a linchpin in my runaway scheme. Maybe she could even help me with the puzzling matter of those special permits carried by free blacks.

The question of the map was an easy one. I simply told Dolly Lee I wanted to know more about the area where Levi and Samboy worked, as well as the territory around it, and she went and ripped a page out of one of her books for me. It was a good-sized page with Indian Territory, Texas, and part of Mexico, just what I needed.

The free-black passes proved to be another thing. I didn't quite know how to edge around to that topic until I found out that Dolly Lee's oldest brother, Eustis, did some patrolling. I had always showed lots of interest in her family anyway, so I just started asking questions about Eustis. "How old is Eustis?" "Is he married?" "Do you like him?"

In the course of talking about Eustis, Dolly Lee told me what she knew about patrollers and passes, which wasn't very much. In the meantime, Dolly Lee turned curious about the whole business of patrolling. She promised that next time she went home to visit she would find out more from Eustis.

As it turned out, Dolly Lee did better than that. "I'm going home next week to visit my family, Samgirl," she told me one afternoon. I could hear birds twittering and feel the stifling summer air hanging low and bothersome around me. "Peter says I can take you with me, if I like. Do you want to come?"

That was like asking a crocodile if he wanted dinner, a slave owner if he wanted more slaves, or Simon if he wanted more money. "I'd love to go if Mister Simon says I can," said I, holding my excitement in check as best I could.

"Of course, we must ask Simon for permission. I don't think he'll want me traveling alone. Even though my daddy will send a carriage for me, I should have a female companion."

By the next morning, it was settled. It seems that Simon had a soft spot in his heart for Dolly Lee and refused her little, except maybe expensive quilting parties. I hoped Dolly Lee would wait a good long while to air her views on slavery in front of Simon.

Dolly Lee got me a real dress for the occasion, a brown-checked cotton with a long skirt. "This dress is very seemly for a lady's companion," she said.

"It's my first real dress," said I as I swirled around in front of her pier mirror, holding the dress in front of me.

From getting into her daddy's carriage to coming back and getting out again, I enjoyed that trip more than I can say. Dolly Lee's home was a larger plantation than old John's, with a bigger big house, a fancier dining room, more well-bred people, and more slaves than I had ever seen before.

There was no doubt in my mind that Dolly Lee's family were dignified Indians and had an elegant home. We drove up to it on something Dolly Lee called a carriage drive. I saw four massive white columns with a porch below and one above. Around each porch wound a lacy, black wrought-iron railing that came down the sides of the steps right to the ground. The house windows went from the porch floor to its ceiling. Each had an immaculate green shutter at its sides. The front door was hand-carved, with pieces of stained glass at its top and black-and-brass carriage lights at each side.

In front of the house stood two stone statutes of ladies. "Who are they?" I asked Dolly Lee.

With her tinkly laugh she said, "One represents virtue and the other patience."

Curling around them and lining the walkway in front of the house grew green bushes, all clipped in squares to set off the refinement of the house itself. The crawlspaces beneath the porch were even covered with wooden lattices, painted to match the green shutters above.

I said to Dolly Lee, "Why, that porch ain't no fit place for rations-giving on Sunday mornings."

"No," she said as she laughed again. "We have a special side porch for that. It also has a door for the house slaves to enter when they're working in the big house. The door goes into a separate hallway near the kitchen so they can slip right in and out again."

"I can hardly wait to see the inside," said I. I sat up ready to jump out of Dolly Lee's daddy's carriage.

Inside, the house seemed filled to bursting with fine rooms, like a dining room and a ballroom and a bunch of parlors. Each one had plump furniture that sucked people right into their depths when they sat down. Of course, I was never allowed to sit in that furniture, but I saw Dolly Lee sink right into the chairs and sofas. Mixed in with everything were pier mirrors and vases and candlesticks and silver coffeepots and lamps with fancy shades and such truck as I'd never seen before and wasn't likely to see again.

I liked Dolly Lee's ma and her two sisters, who were pleasant and always dressed in the very latest styles. I could tell they wore expensive dresses. Almost every evening after supper—except that Dolly Lee's family called it dinner—the one girl played tunes on a huge black piano with gold lettering across the front, while the other one sang and later recited verses.

The funniest, and also the saddest, thing that happened while we stayed at Dolly Lee's parents' house was that they had a ball in her honor. Now that wasn't funny in itself, but one of the men who had traveled from a distance asked to have his boots shined. I told Samboy about it later and he turned indignant. "A slave named Loye put those boots on his own feet to shine them," I told Samboy. "Loye went dancing around and got the boots stuck good on his feet. When Dolly Lee's daddy found out about it, he bought the gentleman another pair of boots. The sad part was that Dolly Lee's daddy ordered Loye to have fifty lashes for his foolishness."

"That's downright mean," Samboy said. "If Loye had his own boots he wouldn't be dancing around in someone else's."

"Still, I learned a lot from that visit," I reminded Samboy.

Most important, from my point of view, were our conversations with Eustis. One evening, Dolly Lee and I sat in the family parlor sewing, she up near the white marble fireplace, me back in the dusky corner as suits a house slave. Eustis came in and took to talking with Dolly Lee. It seemed he'd just been out the previous evening patrolling.

"What do you do, Eustis, on patrol?" Dolly Lee asked real subtle-like.

"I'm sure there's a more suitable topic of conversation, my dear," he replied, real pompous-like.

Dolly Lee didn't let him go. "But, Eustis, I seldom see you now. I'm truly interested in your doings."

That's all Eustis needed to hear. He sat down and started spilling his innards, all in polite parlor language, mind you, but spilling his innards just the same. "Well," he said, "we stop every colored person we see on the road, or anywhere else, and ask for a pass. If they have a proper pass, we let them go on their way. If they don't have a pass, we inflict some punishment and take them home."

At this, Dolly Lee acted perplexed and asked, "What kind of pass?"

"Well," he said, "sometimes they have a pass to go from their plantation to do some work on another, or maybe a man has a pass to visit his wife on another plantation, or maybe it's a free black with manumission papers."

Dolly Lee smiled at Eustis and said, "That's so interesting. What are manumission papers?"

"Well," he said—I could see that Eustis couldn't talk about this subject without saying "well" first—"it's just a little piece of paper with the person's name on it, where he was freed, and a legal seal."

Dolly Lee gazed at Eustis and said, "I know what you mean, a seal like Daddy puts on his bills of sale and land deeds."

"How do you know that?" Eustis laughed. "What did you ever have to do with Daddy's bills of sale or his land deeds?"

Dolly Lee pouted; it was clear she took objection to Eustis's tone. "I have such a seal on my dowry paper," she said, "and I watched Daddy put it there."

Now we're getting somewhere, I thought to myself, but Eustis had tired of the conversation. "I hope you have your dowry paper in a safe place," he said.

"Oh, yes," she responded, "it's in a safe place. Peter sees to all that. He's very careful about legalities."

Eustis appeared satisfied. He strolled to the table to pour himself some amber liquid out of a crystal decanter. Although I didn't know what the liquid was, Dolly Lee had told me about crystal and decanters when we first arrived.

From there, the talk fell into pleasantries about this cousin and that. I started to doze off. "Your girl is going to fall right on the floor," Eustis said, so Dolly Lee excused us and we went upstairs.

"That was all very interesting," she said as she repaired to bed and I curled up on my cot in the anteroom. "Sometime I'll show you that dowry paper and the seal."

I tried not to seem too curious about patrollers and passes and all. I had lots of questions about this legal seal business. I had never heard of a seal. Among the Chickasaw I knew there were no such things as deeds and dowries and seals. Their word served as their bond. Still, despite my full head, I fell asleep in minutes.

chapter

eleven

When we got back to old John's place, Dolly Lee showed me the dowry paper. She then asked Peter to put it in a safe place, where she had assured Eustis it already was. Dolly Lee was a loyal person, I concluded, always protecting and helping the ones she loved.

I studied the seal. I felt confident I could get Samboy to whittle something that would press a mark into paper like that. It would be harder getting the paper and the ink.

I forgot about that problem, though, when Dolly Lee told me why we had taken the trip to her daddy's house. "I'm in the family way," she said. "Peter and I are going to have our first child. I wanted to tell my family about it myself. Now I want you to help me fix one of the back bedrooms as a nursery."

I was anxious to help Dolly Lee fit up that nursery. I would have laid down in the mud for her and let her walk over me. But it wasn't to be. By fall, I'd been pushed out of the big house entirely. First, despite Dolly Lee's and Peter's objections, Dolly Lee's daddy sent a personal maidservant to brush Dolly Lee's hair, dress her, and bring her breakfast. Next, along came a midwife who visited regularly and gave Dolly Lee a whole bunch of orders about eating this, walking that way, sleeping so many hours, and on and on.

In a way, I was glad to see all this help coming. By now, Dolly Lee deserved the title of Missus, because she could manage everything. Still, that baby just grew and grew in Dolly Lee's belly, putting an awful strain on Dolly Lee's slight-framed body.

At the same time, I was sorry to see myself jostled out of the big house. By fall I was back in the dairy. "You're growing stronger every day," Simon told me. "You could be making money in the dairy instead of coddling Dolly Lee up at the big house."

At least Dog was happy; he followed me everywhere I went once again.

That fall always stuck in my mind as a miserable one. I had no one to talk to, except Dog. Mammy wasn't very well and Pappy used up his extra time caring for her. Levi and Samboy were still gone. It appeared they would miss Christmas again.

Sure enough, that holiday was about to pass with just the four of us to celebrate—that is, me, Mammy, Pappy, and Dog—when a wonderful thing happened. Dolly Lee's baby made its appearance smack on Christmas Eve. The work bells rang and rang. When we all ran to the big house to see if it was on fire or someone had died, we learned that someone had been born instead. From the steps Simon announced, "Every one of you get the whole of Christmas Day off from work. I'm giving out extra rations to boot—all in celebration of the first baby in this family."

Dolly Lee had a boy she named Eustis Lee, part for her brother and part for her mother's Lee-side of the family. I figured it was for the best, since old John and his bunch relied on the Bible for naming babies. If it had been up to them, we would have had another apostle, that's all.

A few days later, Dolly Lee called me to the big house to see the baby. He appeared as small-boned and fragile as Dolly Lee herself. Dolly

Lee seemed perky, sitting right up smiling and petting the baby. "Isn't he beautiful?" she cooed.

He *was* beautiful, but that was the last time I ever saw Eustis Lee up close because along came a wet nurse, then a special nursemaid.

Somehow, Simon talked Dolly Lee's daddy into giving him the nursemaid, whose name was Luwina, so she and little Eustis Lee would never have to part. When Esther came home that spring with a baby, and Rebecca followed in early summer, Simon didn't reciprocate for what he had received from Dolly Lee's daddy. He firmly refused to give them a wet nurse or a nursemaid or anyone. I heard he thought their husbands should take care of those needs, even though he had accepted all kinds of help in the same situation.

Next thing, Simon turned his attention to his unmarried slaves. He married—or as near as slaves were allowed to marry—Luwina to young Tate. Not long after that, Simon pressured Tate and Luwina to produce an offspring. I heard Simon say to Tate, "The master's family is increasing at an unbelievable rate, but I can't afford to buy any more slaves. You negras are going to have to give me more babies. I'm looking to you and Luwina next."

I thought to myself that Simon's words must have put the pressure on Tate and Luwina until I found out that Luwina was already pregnant. At the end of the summer, Luwina gave Tate—or Simon, depending on how you look at it—a baby boy. They named that baby Dido. He would be raised right near Eustis Lee.

I didn't see it coming, but Simon started on me next.

"How old are you, Samgirl?" he asked me one Sunday morning when I came to get our rations for the week.

"I'm not sure, Marse Simon," I lied.

"I checked my father's records and I make it eighteen this year of 1849, sometime this past summer."

I should have known better than to fib to Simon. I smiled and said, "Eighteen sounds about right."

"I was thinking about marrying you to Tate, but now that I've hitched him up to Luwina I'll have to look for someone else. Trouble is, everyone's coupled up pretty good at the moment."

I sighed with relief, but fear clutched my heart when he went on, "When Levi comes back, I think I'll marry you to him. He's a likely man—and you're a likely woman. I think I'll see lots of babies from that union."

I grinned and thrilled inside, all the way down to the soles of my bare feet, at the thought of marrying Levi. Then reality returned, with a rush colder than the cold spring water I used in the dairy. In my panic, I said something inane like "Sho' 'nuff."

I walked back to the cabin, my feet dragging in the dust. I was against marrying Levi anyway, seeing he didn't know about Aggie fixing me good, but this was a terrible turn. If Simon married me to Levi and I didn't have babies, Simon might sell me away from everyone I loved.

Now I didn't want Levi to come home for sure. I did want Samboy, so we could get going on our running away. Even if everyone else refused to go with me, I'd have to run before I could be sold away for being a failure as a breeder, a real barren wench.

I decided I would impress Simon—and maybe get him to leave me alone for awhile—by expanding our dairy business. Since Esther and Rebecca had married and no longer took the milk-and-butter wagon on its route twice a week, most planters sent their slaves to our place to get what they needed. I figured that if we could produce fancier butter and more kinds of cheese, we could sell them even more.

As I expected, Simon liked the idea. He bought some wooden forms with designs to make special butter to be served for company and a book telling how to make various types of cheese. He even bought some cheese cutters so we could slice and dice the cheese ready to use for appetizers and such.

Soon our dairy business grew. Then I had another idea. While I was at Dolly Lee's, I'd noticed that her daddy's cook liked to put tiny frilled papers on wild turkey, duck, prairie chicken, and pigeon legs. I'd even seen Cook's helper struggling to form those paper circles—*papillotes,* they called them. "If you buy me some paper and scissors," I told Simon, "me and Jessie will give it a try."

"Who wants paper feet on their roast bird?" he asked. "It's an insane idea."

"I saw them at Dolly Lee's house. Maybe they'll make money for you."

Either Simon was getting grasping, or he had more money squeeze on him than I appreciated, because within two days Jessie and I had our paper and a special pair of scissors each. Even though making those silly paper ruffles turned out to be a lot of painstaking work, we stuck to it. We only sold a few at first, then gradually they started to go to the same people who bought the cheese already chopped up for canapés.

Simon was happy, but I was tickled to death. Now I had the supply of paper I needed to make freedom passes. All I wanted was for Samboy to come home.

Samboy came home right after first plowing started. Samboy looked mightier and more powerful and more immense than Pappy in his prime. Samboy was only fifteen in age, yet he was a man in stature. Samboy was also a man in experience. He had drunk liquor—which he didn't like—and laid with women, which he did like, and come out on the winning side in a lowdown, dirty knife fight that made a scar across his left cheek.

He had also been nearly to the southern border of Texas and ridden over a good part of the country between Indian Territory and Mexico. He had branded cattle and roped steers and met a free black cowboy he could hardly wait to tell me about.

I didn't know why Samboy seemed so excited about this cowboy until Samboy and I finally ran off into the fields alone after supper his third night back. Twilight had long ago tinged the field with purple and dark had come down hard, with only a sliver of moon to lighten things up a bit.

"See," said I to Samboy, "Simon is working us hard and late. I know his family's growing, but we've got this place going pretty good now. He could slack up a bit. If he doesn't, he's going to have some worn-out folks. Besides, we can't produce any more cash for Simon. He gets your wages and Levi's and money from my dairying business. What next?"

Samboy answered, "Simon wants to buy some beef cattle. Remember? Old John said he intended to try cattle once we got to Indian Territory."

"I don't see any cattle," said I. "Only cotton and corn and horses and hogs."

Samboy seemed real impatient and frustrated. He switched the subject. "I've been workin' on my end of our runaway plans." He stopped and stood up real tall as though he expected me to say how wonderful he was.

Instead, to bring him down some, I said, "What do you mean, boy?"

My strategy failed to take effect. Samboy stood straight and said, "I mean I got a fella who's willin' to help us. Providing we can get ourselves into north Texas. He don't want to come up here because he's a wanted man for helping slaves escape."

"Who's this?" I scoffed. "Your free black cowpoke?"

Samboy responded, "His name is Albert Camp." He waited for me to twig to what he was really telling me.

"And?" said I.

"Albert Camp," Samboy repeated very slowly, emphasizing each sound.

"Why does that name sound familiar to me?" I asked.

Samboy lost his patience. He yelled at me, "Because you've got a half-brother named Albert who was born on the Lamar Quimby *Camp* plantation back in Mississippi!"

All I could think to say was, "Oh."

"This Albert is our Albert," Samboy added. "I met him on a trail drive and we liked each other right away. When I heard his name I started asking questions. I found out he's our half brother."

"Oh," said I again, "that's why you didn't want to tell me when Mammy was around; you were afraid to upset her."

Samboy smacked his fist to his forehead and said, "You sure got slow in the head while I was gone."

We must have walked across the moonlit fields another hour. The early spring air settled on our shoulders like a balmy veil.

Samboy told me that Albert was golden brown, like Mammy, but that's where the resemblance ended. Rather than being soft and curved, Albert was tight and hard, bone and sinew from one end to the other and not an ounce of fat along the way. "Albert's wanted in Indian Territory," Samboy explained, "because he ran away from the Cherokee owner Lamar Camp sold Albert to when he was just a child."

Albert had run away when he was younger than Samboy was now. He had learned to ride and shoot and herd cattle with the best of them. He stayed away from Texas cotton country, which held lots of slaves and could always use another one. Instead, he roamed over the wilds of west Texas. In between earning his living, Albert occasionally helped other runaway slaves to freedom in Mexico.

"Albert is ready and willing to help us," Samboy finished, "but I don't see how we're goin' get from here to north Texas. He sure ain't comin' here to get us. That's our part to do."

Then it was my turn to tell Samboy what I'd accomplished in the way of our plan. Of course, he already knew about the wagon behind the house and the goods hidden in the house, and me burning over my brand, but he didn't know about Dolly Lee and the map she'd given me or how she'd gotten her brother Eustis to talk about patrollers and passes.

Samboy about fell on the ground laughing when I told him about making the ruffled paper feet for turkeys so I could get some paper. He agreed he could probably whittle us a passable seal for our "papers."

"I take it back, Samgirl," he said as he let his eyes run over my face. "You're not slow in the head at all."

"I got something else worrying me," said I, puckering my forehead and squinting. "Simon wants me to marry Levi when he gets back and have lots of children. You know I can't do that."

"But Levi's not here, right?" Samboy asked in a superior tone.

I seethed and glared at him. "Right, but what if he comes back tomorrow? And Simon marries me and Levi the day after that? Then what?"

Samboy turned gentle. He said in a deep, dust-roughened voice, "Springtime's coming on, Samgirl. Maybe Simon will keep Levi out on the trail to make more wages, then bring him home in the fall to marry you. That means we got to get ourselves out of Indian Territory and into north Texas sometime this coming summer."

I nodded. In silence, we turned back to the cabin to break the news about Albert and our summer plans to Mammy and Pappy.

Nothing in life ever works out as slick as you plan it, and that's the way it was with Levi. He marched into the quarters in late May or early June of that same year, 1850, just when he should have been herding cattle all over Texas.

I almost jumped up and grabbed him around the neck. Then I remembered Simon's plans for me and treated Levi real cool instead. It was torture for me—I wanted to kiss Levi, to seek shelter in his arms, to feel his strong grip protect me, to let the roiling warmth in my groin start again.

It was also torture for Levi. I could see the hurt in Levi's eyes and hear it in his words. "I know I've been gone a long time," Levi told me. "But I remembered you the whole time."

Inside, my heart turned to cold porridge. I forced myself to say, "I'm older now, Levi. And different."

The impatience in his eyes glittered and stung me deep. "You're still living with Aunt Chloe and Uncle Ike. I don't see any man hanging around."

"No," said I, "there's no man, but I got other things I want to do in my life."

"Like run the dairy for Marse Simon?" Levi asked. He moved a few steps back from me and raised his shoulders into a wary pose.

I realized how silly it seemed to say yes, but I couldn't tell Levi about our running away plans. That would really be something, wouldn't it? I would ask this fine man to endanger his life for me and my family, then, *if* we did reach freedom alive and well, he would find out he had a half a woman, one who couldn't bear him free babies. I forced a smile and replied, "I like my position. I think of ways to make money and Simon lets me do them."

Levi watched me like his heart was breaking behind his eyes and said, "I want you to be happy, Samgirl." That made my heart shudder somewhere down deep.

Levi wasn't done with the matter, though. In the days that followed, I felt him watching me like a flock of geese circling in the sky looking for a pond to land on. He must have had a talk with Simon, or Simon with him, because one evening Levi asked me to go for a walk. On one level, I fell prey to my own curiosity—some would say nosiness—and agreed to go. On another, I couldn't stay away from Levi and the chance to be alone with him.

When we got way down by the canebrakes, Levi said to me, "I think I understand your coldness, Samgirl."

"How's that?" I asked, wondering what Levi could have come up with to smooth over the rift between us.

"Marse Simon say he wants us to hitch up and have lots of babies. I know how you feel about bringing babies into a life of slave misery. I can see why you don't— "

By now, tears were sliding down my black cheeks, making them shine like an oil slick on water. "I'm sorry— "

"No, I'm sorry," he said. "I should have known something was wrong. You're not the kind of gal to play with a man."

I glanced up at Levi through a fringe of wet eyelashes wondering what to say next, but he kept going.

"I told Marse Simon I want to go back on the road. That anybody can make him slave babies, but I can make him money."

"What did Simon say to that?" I asked. I felt ripped down the middle, one half of me wanting to jump into Levi's arms and the other half holding myself far away from him.

"Marse Simon thought for awhile and then he said, 'Yes, that's right, but I've got a lot of work for you to do right here. You get busy here shoeing and repairing. I'll think about you and Samgirl. In the meantime, maybe you'll make up the bad feelings between you two.' "

I shook my head in wonder. Not many slave owners would care one way or the other if a man and woman liked each other, if they wanted slave babies produced.

As if that wasn't enough, Levi had more to tell me. "Simon also said 'You're right, Levi. You can make money and I don't suppose you would make too many babies if you didn't like the woman I paired you with or she didn't like you.' "

"Levi," I sniffled, "I like you."

Levi took my large hand in his huge one and kept on walking. "I know you like me, and I like you, but I understand about the babies. Remember, I saw my wife die bringing a baby to life. If she wasn't a slave, she would've had a proper doctor. She might've lived."

"That must have been horrible," said I. "Where is that baby now?" I held my breath waiting to hear his answer, fearing he would tell me the baby lay dead along with the mammy.

"That baby's now a little girl. She still lives with the Cherokee folks who sold me to Marse John. She's north of here, with her grandmammy and grandpappy, but I don't know how much longer they're going to live. If I were a free man, I would bust my back working to buy that child out of slavery."

I stopped on the path and stared straight at Levi. "If I were a free woman, I'd help you." My heart bammed so hard against the inside of my chest, I was sure he could hear it.

Levi gathered me in his powerful arms. He folded me to his chest, blocking out the twilight, the trees, everything. For a moment, I felt safe and hidden. When he pulled me back from his chest and leaned down to kiss me, I kissed him back. My body arched to meet his. I molded myself against his hardness, especially against the hardness I felt in his loins.

I considered telling Levi the truth about Paul and Aggie and everything when we heard an explosion, like a boom of thunder, from the woods ahead. Levi dropped me and ran, me right behind him. In the woods, we found Simon and Peter and a couple of the rifles old John had brought from Mississippi.

"Are you all right, Marse Simon? Marse Peter?" Levi shouted at them.

The two men turned around, looking surprised, and said, "We're fine. We thought we would learn to use these rifles to hunt. That way we could bring meat to the big house without expense."

Levi seemed doubtful, especially as Peter held his rifle upside down. He would shoot off a toe or two if that gun went off. "Pardon me, Marse Simon and Marse Peter," Levi said, "but I learned how to shoot on the trail. Maybe I can help you."

The two men looked relieved. They leaned their guns against trees, Peter's with the barrel pointed into the ground. I knew it was time for me to skedaddle. I gave Levi a lame wave and headed back along the path. Chance events had saved me from my own weakness.

After that, we heard lots of booms from the woods and even saw an occasional squirrel or possum come into the quarters with Levi. Although Levi told me that Simon and Peter had caught themselves a deer, their family alone enjoyed the venison; we didn't taste any of that meat.

Levi and I seemed to have an unspoken agreement that we would block Simon's plans for us. Every time Simon came around, Levi and I always went two different directions or did two different things. When Simon talked to me about it, I used my vague look. He soon gave up.

For the moment, I didn't have to worry about Levi or my feelings for him. I hoped he would be back on the trail making money for Simon when my family was ready to run. I told myself it was better that way, that I would never see Levi again in this life.

In the meantime, I had discovered that the rifles and ammunition were stored in the main barn. And I had found out that Samboy, like Levi, had learned how to shoot on the trail and would know what to do with the rifles when the time came.

You can believe that was one busy summer. I went back to the dairy business full steam so I could borrow dairy products to trade for the goods we still needed. I figured we were ready for things like boots and clothes now.

At the same time, Samboy found a cave somewhere by the scraggly trickle of water we called a stream. "Pappy," he said, "let's haul the wagon from the back of the house to the cave."

"What for?" Pappy said, suspecting a joke.

"We can work on it there. Get it ready for a runaway trip."

The cave Samboy had found was just big enough to hold the two men, the wagon, a few tools, and some supplies. Best of all, the cave was private. In it, Samboy and Pappy could repair the wagon in secret. The two men took that wagon away in the middle of the night just as quiet as could be. No one even noticed the wagon's disappearance for three days.

It was Serena's big nose that found it out. She came late that Saturday afternoon and said, "I see the wagon is gone at last. What it'd do, Ike? Rot away?"

Pappy jumped right in, his face smiling and his mouth laughing, but his mind working hard. "You know, Serena, we decided we didn't need that decaying hulk anymore. Bugs and crawlers lived in it. Me and Samboy just chopped it up and hauled off its poor, sick pieces."

"Humph," Serena said, her hands on her hips and her nose in the air. "I told you to do that when we first came here. But no, that smart-aleck Missie Samgirl had her own ideas."

I wished I could whap Serena in her fat, nosy face. Instead, I said, "You sure were right, Serena. Simon made a good go of it here. It looks like we're all staying for one long time."

That set Serena off lamenting Simon's faults and how the work was breaking her back. "I can't keep up with it now," she moaned. "If any more babies come to that big house, I'll have to have a helper, what with baby napkins and all. That Marse Simon said, 'You don't need no helper, Serena, you're a strong, stout woman.' "

"My, my," Mammy said, shaking her head, "what are you goin' to do, Serena?"

And that's how the matter of the wagon's disappearance was noted in the quarters and just as soon forgotten. We stacked the firewood in the shed Pappy had built and let weeds grow right over where the wagon had always sat.

At the same time, Samboy and Pappy took to going fishing late every evening in that pitiful creek. They would eat supper with me and Mammy, then load a handful of nails in this pocket and slide a piece of iron down a pant leg, then off they'd go into the heavy dusk, fishing poles over their shoulders, acting like they had not a care in the world. Given the sad state of that stream, no one seemed surprised when they seldom came back with fish. Just to make it look good, Samboy told around how happy he was to be home with his pappy after so many months on the trail and how he wanted Pappy to himself for a bit.

chapter twelve

Samboy and I had used one of my pieces of paper from the turkey feet to sketch out a wagon plan. We decided on a false bottom, where we would store the rifles we took from Simon and where we could pad up a bed for Mammy. Me and Mammy worked on repairing and restoring the wagon covers we had saved from the trip between Mississippi and Indian Territory. It was clear to me that Mammy had never recovered from the breast cutting. Still, I was set on her seeing freedom.

As much as she tried to help us, Mammy moved slowly and accomplished little. Her chest scars seemed to be growing inward and pulling her with them. Anyway, we knew that Mammy would have to ride. I was glad I'd had the idea of hiding Mammy in the wagon's false bottom.

"She'll suffocate down there," Samboy said.

"No," said I, "you and Pappy fix it so she'll have an air vent."

"She'll choke to death from the dust coming up from the ground," Pappy added.

"Then you better fix her compartment good. No air and dust coming from the bottom, but fresh air coming down to her from its top."

"Why can't she ride in the wagon on a pallet the way you did when we left Mississippi?" Samboy asked.

"Because I've got a plan," said I.

Samboy and Pappy locked eyes and looked worried, but they hitched their stools closer to mine and prepared to listen.

"Patrollers and slave-catchers," I started, "will be looking for four runaway slaves, two women and two men." I stopped and let that sink into their minds.

"Yeah," they both agreed and nodded their heads.

"But what if there's only three runaway slaves and they're all men?" I gave them a sly smile and they knew I had a scheme.

"How are you goin' to do that?" Samboy asked scratching his head. "Putting Mammy in a compartment only gets one woman out of sight."

"Oh, oh," Pappy murmured, seeing already what I had in mind.

"I'm going to dress and act like a man," said I. "You, Samboy, are going to teach me how to ride a horse proper so I look like just another cowboy."

Samboy appeared doubtful, but Pappy said, "Samgirl's big enough to look like a man. She has the muscles from working in the dairy."

And, I thought to myself, I don't have to worry about my women's monthlies anymore, not since Aggie came at me with that knife, and my breasts ain't grown much since I was eleven. But I didn't say these things to my brother and pappy.

"What about when you have to say something?" Samboy asked.

"I've got a deep voice," said I. "I've also got my moronic look. You and Pappy can explain I'm not too smart in the talking department."

"What's your moronic look?" Pappy chimed in. I showed what I'd practiced in secret for so many years; the two of them almost fell off their stools laughing. Finally, they calmed down and admitted I made a first-class moron.

It was settled then. Mammy would ride in the compartment, where she could rest. Me, Samboy, and Pappy would take turns driving the wagon and riding horseback. We would dress like cowhands on our way across Texas.

"What are we goin' to say if somebody asks *why* we're ridin' across Texas?" Samboy asked. "We ain't likely to be in Texas just roaming around."

"We'll have two stories ready," said I. "We all three will wear little metal identification tags like you wear around your neck when you're out working the trail. We can say we're hired-out slaves taking supplies to our party and got lost. Then we ask directions. You must know some trail bosses' names by now, Samboy."

Samboy smiled in slow admiration and said, "I know names, but where we goin' to get the tags?"

"You're going to have to think up some story to get Levi to make you some extras. Tell him you're afraid you're going to lose one while you're away, or that you got a gal you want to take along, or some such."

"What's the second story?" Mammy asked, showing more interest than I'd seen in her so far.

"We're going to have free-black passes. Me and Samboy are making them. We got ink and paper and everything. When we get far enough down in Texas, we'll take our metal tags off and say we're free blacks. If anyone wants to see our passes, we'll hold them up at a distance. We'll say we're afraid that if anyone gets too close, they might dirty up our passes and we can't afford to have anything happen to them. When we get to Mexico, we can say we're free blacks and show our passes."

Mammy grinned at me and patted me on the back. "You sure are a thinker, child," she said. "And, from our Mississippi trip, I remember how to pack a medicine kit and some victuals."

"Don't forget your iron kettle," Pappy laughed. "You don't want to go nowhere without that stout kettle."

"There's only one thing that bothers me," Samboy said. "How are we goin' to get away from here without being noticed?"

"Yeah," said I, "that bothers me too. I'm still thinking on that part."

After that, I thought and thought, but leaving Simon and the rest without being seen seemed impossible. I joked to myself that we couldn't sneak away without setting something on fire. At first, I laughed at that idea, but eventually I got serious about it.

Pretty soon, I cozied up to Nero, trying to find out what the big house had planned in the way of social events that might lend some distraction. "Well," Nero said, "Dolly Lee is in the family way again. She's goin' home to visit her family."

"Does that mean baby Eustis Lee and his servants will go along with her?" I asked.

Nero nodded. "Peter's goin' as well. The whole troupe of them's goin' this time."

Then Pappy told me that Simon planned on bringing in some early cotton while his brother was gone so that he could drive the slaves hard without Peter interfering and complaining. I finally made out that all of this was going to happen at the beginning of September, although I couldn't get any exact dates.

"Be ready any time," I told Samboy and Pappy and Mammy. "We'll go as soon as we see our chance." Then I heard a whining and noticed Dog looking me smack in the eye.

"Yeah, you're going too. What would cowboys be without a dog? So you be ready too. You're going when I say we're ready."

Dog appeared relieved. Anyway, he went over and curled up on his straw mat and fell asleep.

"You still haven't told us how we're goin' to cover our leavin'," Samboy said.

"I'm still thinking," said I, not feeling ready yet to bring up my idea that we might use a fire to cover our departure.

Finally, I decided we would have to set our end of the quarters on fire. After all, we lived way down at the end of the last row, stuck off by ourselves with the woodshed between us and the place where our wagon lay hid and waiting. Although it was a dangerous scheme, I hoped it might look like we had died in the fire. At any rate, by the time Simon figured it out, we would be in our wagon and off Chickasaw Nation land.

The only problem was Mose and Amanda next door. Although I surely didn't want to set them on fire, it was likely to happen. Mammy helped me with that part. "Child," she said, "I'll find some bedbugs and put them in Amanda's wall. Then I'll go over there and spot the bugs. Amanda will wail and moan, like always, and I'll offer to chase the bugs away for her. I'll tell her and Mose to move down to their daughter's cabin for a few days while I take care of the bugs."

"Mammy, you're one smart woman," said I. I thought a minute, then went on with more details. "Samboy and Pappy can plow a firebreak between our cabin and theirs. Maybe we can even turn part of the spring through so the fire won't jump from our cabin to theirs and from theirs to the rest of the quarters. Everybody will be so busy bringing in the early cotton and letting Simon drive them from dawn to dusk that they won't even notice us doing such things."

Pappy helped too. From the main barn, he brought some coal oil and stored it in our woodshed. We planned on torching our cabin, woodshed, and maybe even part of the woods. At the end of August, we started setting the scene among the other folks in the quarters.

"It's so dry," Mammy told Becky. "We built our woodshed too close to our house. We don't like living so near to that woodshed. We're afraid it's goin' to go up in smoke one of these days."

"It's so dry," Pappy told Mose. "I think I'll make part of the spring come down here between the cabins. What if there's a bad fire and we need water?"

"Here's an extra bucket of water," Samboy said to Levi. "The sparks going up from your fire make me real nervous."

Everyone shook their head and agreed. Everyone, that is, except Levi. "We never had a fire in the quarters," he told Samboy one evening after we left the grub table. "What you got in your mind?"

"Nothing," Samboy said, but I sensed him starting to weaken. I knew he hated to leave Levi. I poked Samboy in the back. "We ain't had a blacksmith working here night and day either," said I in a loud voice from behind them.

Samboy perked up and added, "No, Levi, you've been gone so long. And it's a dry summer. We've had lots of sun cooking and baking everything."

I couldn't see Levi's face, but, knowing that man as I did, I feared he realized that there was more behind our words than just fretting about the quarters. Maybe he had noticed the box of rifles and ammunition missing from the barn, or maybe he'd been spying on Samboy and Pappy when they went on their fishing trips to the dried-up creek.

That Saturday morning, Levi came around our cabin before dawn. He fell in step with me on my way to the woodshed. I startled and prickles ran over my shoulders and down my arms.

"What are you doing here?" I asked Levi. I tried to keep my eyes large and timid—like a doe—yet I knew they showed worry around the edges at what he might say back.

"I'm just looking over the situation. I want to see just how dry it is down here."

I backed into the woodshed to make sure Levi couldn't see the coal oil we had stored there. I started throwing some sticks at his feet so he had to pick them up. Then I pushed him out of the shed with my body and an armload of wood.

Levi dumped his burden of wood on our porch outside the door. He twirled around and ripped the kerchief right off my neck. I stiffened and turned into a statue as he stared at the scars covering the *P* brand.

I looked deep into Levi's eyes. The whites had gone ashen. Even Levi's black skin had a chalky cast to it. I thought he might fall down in the dust as he took in the red web of scars covering Paul's brand. But Levi held himself steady and said, "Since that time we walked in the woods together, I knew something was different about you, but I didn't know what. You kept fussing with that neckerchief of yours, so I thought it might be the brand. I know you've always wanted to get rid of that *P*. Tell me the truth of what happened."

I decided to be honest with Levi about the matter. I told him how I hated that brand more all the time, how I felt Paul was still with me everywhere I went, and how me and Samboy plotted to burn the *P* off with boiling water.

"You done a good job," he said. "But you got a nasty-looking chest. Doesn't it hurt?"

"Not anymore," said I, my hand springing to the still-raw scars. "At least, not most of the time."

"Why do you keep it covered?" he asked, his eyes narrowing. "Nobody can see the *P* now."

Then I had to tell Levi about falling sick afterwards and how I didn't want Simon to get angry about the time I'd lost at work, and how I said I was down with a fever instead.

"What about your mammy?" Levi asked. "She's different too. She seems to be getting smaller and sicker all the time. What's wrong with her?"

I told Levi about Mammy's breast and how she had said she had a fever along with me. I could see Levi was thinking of more questions, but Mammy saved me. She poked her head out the door and said, "Morning, Levi. What're you doin' here? Are you the one who kindly put this wood here for me? Or did you just come by to see Samgirl? Or is it Samboy or Pappy you're wantin'? You want some breakfast? You goin' someplace special today?"

I had seen Mammy do the same thing to Pappy when she wanted to confuse him and get his mind on something else, and it always worked. Sure enough, it worked with Levi as well. I pushed down a laugh as Levi, with great energy, backed away from our porch and Mammy. He didn't even try to answer any of her questions. Like Pappy at such times, Levi looked dazed and like he had forgotten his own questions, at least for the time being.

I was getting anxious about the whole runaway scheme. For one thing, Levi made me nervous. Even though he didn't come around again right away that day, I could feel him watching me from a distance. I decided I better find out some specifics about when Dolly Lee and Eustis Lee planned on leaving. I knew we better get on our way as soon as possible.

The following morning, there was Levi again, hanging around too close for my comfort at rations-giving. After rations-giving, he gave me the eye and a sign, but I ignored him. He ambled off, looking back every few seconds.

I waited until everyone had started toward the quarters. I walked right up to Nellie and Dolly Lee and said, "I miss working in the big house and serving Dolly Lee. I hear Dolly Lee is going on a trip. I came to offer my help."

Old John was nowhere in sight and Nellie looked like she just wanted to get back in the big house and be left alone. She mustered up a nod and a smile for me before she shuffled through the front door. Dolly Lee smiled at me and said, "I miss you too, Samgirl. But my daddy sent so many servants for me and Eustis Lee, and Simon says you do such good work in the dairy, that I never get the chance to call you up to the big house."

I grinned as my love for that woman pounded in my chest. I said, "What about now? Can I help you with your packing?"

Dolly Lee seemed sad. Her mouth formed a little pout and her forehead a frown. "No, we're all packed. We're leaving first thing in the morning. I can't even ask you to come around in the morning to wave us away. Simon says you'll all be busy in the fields, or keeping things going while everyone else brings in that early cotton."

I knew I would never see Dolly Lee again so I kneeled down before her and lifted my kerchief from my scar. Dolly Lee grabbed the porch rail and said, "Who did that to you?"

"Peter's brother, Paul, did it. Peter once saved Paul from drowning in the Mississippi River. Later, I ran away. When they brought me back, Paul branded with me with a *P*. Then Paul sickened and died along the trail to Indian Country. After we got here, me and Samboy burned away the brand with boiling water. Now I got these scars."

"Why didn't you show me that before?" asked Dolly Lee, looking so pallid that I pulled the kerchief back in place, but stayed kneeling in front of her.

"Because I didn't want Simon to know what I did," said I, my wide eyes begging for her understanding. "I got sick and lost lots of days of work. I was afraid he'd be angry."

Dolly Lee turned tender and soft, as if she knew I was telling her something even bigger than about the burns. "Why are you telling me now?" she asked in a whisper.

"Because I never want you to hate me," said I. "I want you to know that if I'm ever bad it's because I got reason to be."

That sweet woman put her tiny hands under my elbows and raised me to a standing position. "I could never hate you," she said. "You're a slave and have a hard life. You must do what you have to do."

At that, I took my prize possession—the mirror with the Twenty-Third Psalm carved into it that Mellisey had given me on the trail—and shoved it into Dolly Lee's pale hands. I remembered I'd promised Mellisey to keep that mirror forever, but I thought Mellisey would understand why I wanted to give it to Dolly Lee. Besides, that mirror had a slim chance of making it across Texas to Mexico with me. "Remember me kindly," said I to Dolly Lee.

Dolly Lee grasped the mirror to her chest. Then she smiled at me and pushed me off the porch with one of her sisterly hugs. I waved and went on my way rejoicing. I believed Dolly Lee understood what I had planned and had given me her blessing in doing it.

That afternoon, I worked without one word of complaint. I knew our escape drew closer and that Dolly Lee would do what she could to hold back the patrollers when the time came. I didn't really expect Dolly Lee to be able to help much. I thought she might weep, or say something against slavery, or pretend sickness to add more confusion. Just knowing she was on my side gave me confidence.

By late afternoon, as I sat on the porch rubbing Dog's scruffy head, I glanced around to see how likely my plan was to succeed. "We seem to have everything in place," I told Dog. Samboy had told me the wagon waited in the cave, the box of rifles in the secret compartment, the rest fixed up and ready for Mammy. He had packed some dried meat and fruit, along with some nuts. He had put our clothes and bedding in the wagon and he had hidden our identification tags and free-black passes in a metal box under the food.

We had to take as much as we could in the wagon because we had no money. Samboy had a few dimes and two-bit pieces that he had earned doing extra jobs along the trail and he understood how money worked, which was a whole lot more than the rest of us did. Still, we had little to spend buying supplies. We knew we would have to trade something we had for what we needed or work for it.

"I'm ready, too." I knuckled Dog's head the way I used to do Samboy's when he was a boy. "Yep, I'm ready." I had learned just enough about horses to stay in the saddle. I suspected I'd learn a lot more on the trail, but I planned to start off by driving the wagon. I'd put together a man's outfit from Samboy's and Pappy's clothes, along with a pair of boots that Samboy traded butter for somewhere on a neighboring farm.

Mammy also was ready. She had her medicine satchel packed and her kettle sitting empty and waiting. We had decided to dump fresh victuals into the kettle and haul the whole thing to the wagon instead of packing the kettle and the victuals separate. Samboy and Pappy would carry the kettle, Mammy the medicine bag, and I would come last after starting a fire in our cabin and woodshed.

The only thing left was getting the bugs into Mose and Amanda's wall and getting Mose and Amanda to move down to their daughter's cabin. I concluded we had a day or two or three yet. I wanted Dolly Lee and Peter settled at her daddy's house, and Simon and all the slaves good and tired from the fields, before I went setting any fire and running toward freedom.

Then I noticed Dog and realized we hadn't planned on how he would get to the wagon. I sure didn't want him running the wrong way at the wrong time. "But are you ready, Dog?"

I studied him and decided he had a right to see me torch our end of the quarters. After all, he was a slave too. He had paid for his master's ownership and his wrath with an ear. Besides, I needed somebody with me. I couldn't do it all alone. For a brave girl who had been planning for years to run away, I seemed to have a bad case of the jitters.

I found Pappy and asked for his help. "Can I have an old piece of rope?"

"What do you need rope for? What've you got in mind now?"

"Dog's going with me," I replied as I tied the rope around Dog's neck. That dog sat up as smart and alert as could be, listening to every word. When I walked him on the rope to the woodshed, he followed along without griping. When I ran back toward the cabin, he sprinted right along with me.

Of course, Serena came by at that moment and stuck her nosy nose in. "Why are you runnin' that dog around on a rope? He goes every place you go anyway."

"We're playing a game, Serena," said I. "It's called bogeyman. I tell Dog what person is my enemy. Then we run and try to wipe him—or her, whatever the case may be—out of this life."

"Girl," she said, "you've never been right in the head since you were little. Now you're teaching that poor dog to act mean."

"No, Serena," said I in a firm tone, "I'm teaching my dog to protect me, to chase away people who don't treat me right."

At that, Serena did a double-take and started to back away. "Wait until morning, Missie Samgirl," she yelled at me. "There's goin' to be so much work around here you won't get to sit high-and-mighty in your dairy. Even you're goin' to have to work so hard you'll come home and fall into your bunk at night. You won't be havin' time to teach that poor dog nothin'."

Just then, Dog growled and eyed Serena. She turned around and walked away from our end of the quarters at a smart clip, while I patted Dog on his earless head. I knew he understood the whole plan. After all, I concluded, he had been in on the whole thing from the day me and Samboy dug up those chains in that Mississippi vegetable patch.

Serena was wrong. I didn't have to go into the fields, but Isaac and Jessie did. They had to carry water and help feed the workers so the work would keep going as long as it was light out. Although their absence made more work for me, I was glad there were few people around, just Serena washing clothes and grumbling up at the big house, Cook preparing the night supper for the family, me in the dairy, and old Mose watching over the barn.

Mammy stayed in the quarters. No one bothered her now except when they needed doctoring. The rest of the time Mammy sewed or worked her slow way through taking care of us. Following my orders, Dog also stayed in the quarters, watching out for Mammy until the right time came to run away.

I figured the best chance would be Wednesday sometime after midnight. "I want lots of muddle down in the quarters," I told Samboy. "Everyone will scatter about and try to fight the fire in the dark."

"Yeah," Samboy agreed. "People'll be numb tired from the day's work. They'll be flying around in their nightclothes at that."

I passed the days turning out more butter and cheese than ever. I had to have enough to sell the servants who came to pick up their goods. I also had to supply Simon and his workers. Still, I was one nervous girl. My teeth chattered and my nose ran and my head burned. In between that, my hands shook and I dropped stuff all over the floor. My body even smelled rank with the fear of it all. I had never been so afraid of doing anything in my life, not submitting to Paul that first time, not running away along the trail, not having Samboy throw boiling water on my chest to cover my brand.

I was surprised I was so scared. I had to admit that part of my upset had to do with Levi. Even though I wasn't fit to marry that man, I didn't want to leave him either. To think I would never see Levi again made me feel near to throwing up. I would never know how it felt to lie with him, to be his woman, to be his beloved.

At the same time, I certainly felt glad to leave Indian Territory. For one thing, I had developed a strong aversion to Indian Territory weather. It was too hot or too cold and usually too windy. Mammy was always complaining about the wind. "That dratted wind blew away my wash-tubs again," she'd say. The tubs were made of ash or white oak and very lightweight. Other times she'd say, "That wind ripped our clothes right off my line."

For another thing, I was glad to see the last of Simon. Not only was he increasingly stingy, lately he had taken to involving himself in politics, opposing something called the Full Blood Party. Maybe because Simon wasn't a full-blood, he resented them more than most. He was even getting funny about Christianity. "Absolutely no," he said when we asked if we could have Sunday school in an old wreck of a log corncrib that wasn't doing any good for anybody. Sometimes I played with the idea of setting fire to that crib as well.

Last, and more important than anything, I was overjoyed finally to be making my bid for freedom. I knew it was going to be a hard way to go, but suffer what I would, I had to give it a try. I'd rather lose my life trying for liberty than keep on living as a slave. I'd rather set my feet on the path toward the hereafter than remain on God's green earth in bondage to another human being.

Every evening after supper, I checked everything in our cabin over, but I wouldn't let Samboy and Pappy go near the wagon. I didn't want anybody, especially Levi, discovering our secret and putting a crimp in things now. I also quizzed Samboy and Mammy and Pappy: "What are you carrying?" "When are you going to run?" "Where are you going?" "Who's going to stay behind to start the fire?" I carried on until no one would answer me anymore.

"Will you shut your mouth?" Samboy finally snapped at me. "The only one you got faith in is Dog. You don't pester him half to death."

"Oh, yeah," said I, eyes blazing and mouth pursed. "For your information, we're still practicing on his rope."

At that, Samboy and Pappy gave me their usual argument about taking Dog with them and leaving me free to start the fire. Their voices got louder and louder until I worried they would give away our plans to everyone in our end of the quarters.

"No," I interrupted, "Dog goes with me. I ain't having it any other way."

"What if somethin' happens to you two?" Samboy asked, a dark look turning his face sour.

I stared at him with pinched lips. Finally, I said, "Then you and Pappy and Mammy run. Me and Dog will stay here and cover this end."

At that, Mammy leapt from her stool and grabbed me around the waist, hugging and crying, crying and hugging.

"We can't do that, Samgirl," Pappy said, watching Mammy clutch me in her tired arms.

"You better do that," said I, "or we'll all be in the soup."

Samboy said, "She's right, Pappy. If it comes to that, we got to run without her. But," and he kicked me in the shin, "it ain't going to come to that. You got those matches from the big house and a flint as backup. You're goin' to start that fire slick as anything and by that time, we'll have the wagon out of the cave, the mules hitched, and the horses saddled. Mammy will slide right into her bedroom and off we'll go. Right, Samgirl?"

"Right, Samboy," said I, as I kicked him back in his shin.

The next morning, so early it was still black outside, Mammy got up and turned loose her box of crawlers into Amanda's wall. She waited for dawn to start and then went to Amanda's door. She rapped and called out, "I spotted a crawler by your window, Amanda. Open up before they get in your bed. If they ain't already in."

Amanda's grey head poked itself out the door, with Mose right behind. "You know how I hate those things," she said.

"I know," said Mammy; then she screamed and jumped at an imaginary insect on the doorsill. "That's why I came to help. You and Mose go to your daughter's cabin after watching over the children and the barn today. I'll be home here. I'll get the bugs out. You can come back in a day or two to a clean house." Mammy stared Mose hard in the eyes. "You goin' to do what I tell you, old man?"

"Yes'um," he said, "we're mighty glad to have your help. You're a good woman, you are."

We went back to our cabin to eat breakfast, then Samboy and Pappy set off to the fields. Mammy and Dog stayed home, while I went to the dairy to tremble and shake one last day through my work. One last day as a slave, I thought to myself. After that, I would be a runaway—contraband with a price on my head. I hardly dared let myself think it, but after that I would be in Mexico with my family and we would be free.

chapter thirteen

That night, after hours of lying in the cabin doorway and recollecting the events that had brought me to make an actual run for freedom, I understood the hugeness of it all. I'd spent nearly my entire life working up to this point. If my scheme failed, my whole family could end up whipped, maimed, or even dead.

Instead of scaring me, this hardened my determination even more. I was glad I'd had the time to spend watching the moon and remembering everything that brought me to this moment.

Finally, I saw the moon reach its peak. It seemed to perch an instant before its drop. "Mammy," I called in a low voice.

"Yes, child." She answered so fast I knew she hadn't been sleeping.

Mammy woke the others. They worked as quiet as ghosts loading the kettle with the cornbread Mammy had made and wrapped in clean rags. They added some greens and fatback and other victuals until the kettle was almost full. Then Pappy saw it would be a trial for Mammy to carry the medicine bag, so he tucked it in the side of the kettle as well.

Pappy and Samboy struggled off past the woodshed and into the woods with their load, Mammy following right behind. That left me and Dog alone in the cabin. I planned to set our woodshed and bedroom afire first, low enough to burn slow, yet high enough to burn sure. I moved on stealthy feet around the bedroom, scattering handful by handful the sawdust Pappy had put by. I wanted to give my folks enough time to get to the wagon, find the animals where Samboy had staked them, and start hitching up.

After a bit, I tied Dog's rope around his neck and the other end around my waist. "It's time. We're going," I told him in a shaky voice.

I crept out of the cabin, as low to the ground as I could get, toward the woodshed. We slipped inside and, with fluttering hands, I sprinkled coal oil around. That's where my troubles began, for a tiny drop of coal oil splashed in my right eye. It burned like I had lit it with a match. I squeezed that searing eye shut and let it pour tears down my right cheek, while I kept on working.

All the time, Dog stood at the end of his rope near the door, watching to see if anyone was out in the quarters. When I finished with the shed, I decided I better set the sawdust in the cabin afire first. I didn't trust the things they called matches, so Mammy had conserved a few coals from the breakfast cooking-fire. I snuck back to the cabin and laid the coals in the sawdust.

Then Dog and I slid to the back of the woodshed and tried to light a match in the coal oil. Sure enough, it fizzled and went out. I tried another one, with the same result. Now I sweated a rainstorm because I heard the beginnings of cracklings from the cabin. I threw the matches down and turned to the flint. As soon as I struck it, the coal oil ignited. So did the matches. Fingers of fire started to grasp the bottom of the woodshed.

"Come on, Dog. It's time for us to hustle right out of here."

We headed for the beginning of the trail. I had practiced the route only once with Samboy. I hadn't wanted to draw any more attention to us than necessary, so I had not gone as far as the creek and the cave and the wagon. Now I moved with the aid of only one eye and not much moonlight. Dog was no help because he had never seen the entire course either.

I went as fast as I could, keeping my one good eye on the ground and the other closed against the inferno burning my eyeball out of its socket. A hanging branch, which I didn't see, whacked me in the head and threw me off balance. "It's Simon. He's caught me already," I thought wildly.

I slipped on the loose dust and the undergrowth of the track. I landed on my left arm with a crack I thought would awaken all the forest creatures and the quarters both.

I tried to get up, but dizziness overtook my head and forced me to hold onto the ground to stay conscious. While Dog slurped my face and whined, I hoped Samboy and Pappy and Mammy would have the good sense to run without me. "Quiet," said I. "We got to take our licks now, whatever they are."

Pretty soon, I heard Dog chawing on his rope. I thought he wanted to get away and run with them, instead of lying there to get burned up in the fire with me, or get beat half to death for trying to run away. But, no, Dog had his own plan. He ate right through the rope like a chicken supper and ran off looking for Samboy. Maybe that dog's earless head heard better than most, or maybe his sense of smell could find anything—man or possum—but he must have gone right to Samboy.

Within minutes, Samboy and Pappy scurried back along the track. "You're comin' with us," Pappy said.

"Yeah," Samboy added. "Even if we have to drag you all the way to Mexico."

This time, they hauled me away instead of Mammy's kettle. When we reached the wagon, with me hanging upside down over Pappy's shoulder, I could see poor little Mammy holding all the horses by their bridles. Pappy put me over the back of one of the horses and Samboy tied me to the saddle. I didn't have the heart to tell them I was blind in my right eye and carrying a broken bone or two in my left arm.

Samboy mounted the other horse and Pappy got on the wagon seat, while Mammy slid into her hiding place in the wagon. Even though we spoke not a word through all this, we each knew what we had to do. Mine was to bear the stings of pain without complaining. I did, at least for awhile.

We pulled out slow and quiet. The only sound I heard was the whooshing of the stick-and-leaf drag that Pappy had fixed at the back of the wagon to erase our tracks.

Dog followed me, jumping up to lick my hanging-down face whenever he could. That dog not only saved my life, but now he kept me from giving in to unconsciousness along that first stretch of trail. From my position, I couldn't see any flames flaring up in the night sky. I prayed like a lunatic that I'd set the fire proper and that it had flamed its way through our woodshed and cabin, and had even reached the edge of the woods, but wasn't touching anything else in the quarters.

Maybe Samboy saw that I had injured my arm, because instead of letting it dangle, he had draped it across the saddle. Even though that helped a bit, I gave in to blackness now and again. Maybe I hallucinated, for I seemed to hear shouting and bells ringing from afar. I finally concluded that I was having one of my irritating dreams and shortly it would be time to wake up and go to work in the dairy. Pretty soon, I came to my senses a tad and detected Samboy walking along aside of me.

"So that mutt of yours turned out to be the real hero," Samboy hissed. "He saved your big black ass."

I looked upside-down and sideways at Samboy through my one good eye and whispered back, "Yes, and now you're trying to kill me by hauling me out of here dangling upside down over a horse's back, a horse I don't even know."

"I guess you're all right," Samboy muttered, "if you can be so smart in the mouth."

"Oh, I'm all right," I snarled back, "I've just got one blinded eye and one broken arm."

"I know you're hurtin', but we got to get to the first stopping point Pappy and I plotted out before Mammy can work on you."

"What do you mean, plotted out? Are you telling me you and Pappy have been this way before?"

"Well, we couldn't let you do all the plannin'. We got a nice safe place picked out where Mammy can set to doctorin' you."

At that, I let myself pass out and wait for that nice safe place to come along.

I have to give Samboy and Pappy credit. We headed southwest away from Simon's plantation and toward Texas. "We're goin' to cross the Red River," Samboy said. "We'll head into western Texas, so as to stay away from the cotton-planting areas. We'll make our way through ranching country instead. If anybody asks, we'll say we want to hook up with the rest of our outfit."

"You're pretty smart for a cowpoke," said I.

Samboy grimaced at me. "Then we're going to head west of the trading post at Fort Worth. We'll camp there and send out word to Albert. Then we'll drop down to somewhere around Camp Eagle Pass where we'll ford the Rio Grande into Mexico."

"Sounds easy to me," I answered. Of course, Samboy didn't tell me we had to cross hills and rivers, deserts and plains, and get through thousands of Comanche Indians and millions of buffalo to reach Camp Eagle Pass and the Rio Grande.

It was probably a good thing Samboy didn't tell what we had ahead of us. I might have quit at that first place in Indian Territory. I was bent into the shape of a saddle and a horse's back by the time we stopped. It seemed all the fiery pain in the world burned its way through my body. Samboy and Pappy lifted me off without breaking anything else, although I felt like more of my bones would snap when they straightened me up.

"We can't take a chance lightin' a fire," Mammy said. "You'll have to have cold beans and cornbread."

"Could I have some water," I croaked, "to help get the cornbread down?"

As we ate our meager fare it started to rain. "Feel that, Chloe," Pappy told Mammy. "The Lord is with us."

I held out my hand, palm up. Soft drops hit it like angel kisses. "No trail left for Simon's men to follow now," said I as I licked the raindrops from my lips and savored their sweetness.

In the meantime, Samboy got our metal identification tags hung on leather thongs around our necks. At least, he did on everyone's neck but Mammy's. Samboy already had his own tag and he had lifted two more from Levi's shop, but he had been unable to get one for Mammy.

"If anyone sees her out of her hiding place," Samboy said, "we'll explain she's along as our cook and doesn't need a tag." It was illogical, yet we hoped it would work.

Next, Mammy set to doctoring me, with Dog licking my good hand the entire while. It must have been about noon because the sun bore down from the sky to where I lay next to the wagon on the sweltering ground. Heat swirled down from the sky and steamed up from the ground. I felt like the center of a pot of stew boiling in Mammy's fireplace back home.

"Hold still, Samgirl," Mammy said. "I'm making a poultice. It's goin' on your eye whether you like it or not."

The poultice cooled my eye down some. "Now we've got to do something about your arm."

I scrunched away from Mammy. "My arm's just fine. It'll grow back."

"It'll grow back crooked, that's what," she said. "Samboy, sit on your sister."

Samboy sat astride me and held me down, a job he seemed to mind not at all. "Now, Ike," Mammy said, "when I say so you jerk Samgirl's arm that way." She pointed to the right and Pappy nodded.

Instead of a crack, this time I heard a pop. When I came to again, Samboy whittled me a green-wood splint. Mammy tied it on my arm with rags and fixed me up a sling to keep that arm close to my body until the bone healed.

"You can do this, Samgirl," Mammy told me. "You're young and strong. You're goin' to mend right away."

I stared Mammy right in the eye and said, "I'm young and strong, but I'm getting beat up pretty fast. I'm only nineteen. If I keep going at this rate, I'm going to be an old, patched-up woman long before my time."

"Quit whinin'," Mammy said in a hard voice. I knew she wanted to help me pull myself together. "Get goin' instead."

I did my best to follow Mammy's orders. I felt fortunate that I had a good right arm to drive the wagon with and a good left eye to watch the horses with. "Let's get going right now," said I.

But, no, Samboy and Pappy and Mammy thought I should have some rest. That's when the Indians appeared.

First they weren't there and then they were. We were aware of shadows moving around our pitiful camp and soon the phantoms came over the rise and out of the trees and became Indians. They stood silent as deer around our wagon and us. Strange blue and yellow stripes made their mouths stand out from the rest of their faces.

"They're Chickasaws," Samboy said. I thought they were unlike any Chickasaws I'd ever seen.

"What do we do now, Samboy?" Pappy asked, gulping so hard we all heard him.

"Nothing," Samboy said. "They got us. We ain't goin' nowhere except where they want us to go."

Pappy whispered, "Should we shoot Samgirl and Mammy? So they don't come to some horrible end at the savages' hands?"

Samboy laughed and said, "No, Pappy. They're not savages, they're Chickasaws."

That didn't settle my mind any. I was awful upset to think that we'd gotten only one day away from Simon's plantation and here we were—already captured by Indians. I was even more unhappy when the head Indian showed the most interest in me, pointing to my splint and the poultice on my eye. Pretty soon, he ordered the women to tug me up on a travois and off they set, the head Indian leading the way, the women dragging me along on a travois behind a horse. Samboy and Pappy and Mammy and their captors brought up the rear.

After an hour or two of traveling, we bumped our way into a village, all tents and dogs and children and fires and such. A lot of ruckus ensued, including a good deal of hollering and barking. People seemed to be running everywhere, but a few followed my horse as he hauled me right up next to the main fire. The women took me off the travois and laid me on the ground, then set to getting kettles of water boiling in the fire.

I glared at Samboy out of my good eye and said, "They're going to boil us alive, right? Including Dog, right?"

Pappy shook and Mammy sweated, but Samboy laughed. He laughed and laughed until I concluded he'd gone mad with fright. Finally, he choked and said, "It's a pushofa dance."

"That's nice," said I, certain now my end was near. "They're going to dance before they eat us."

"No," Samboy said, "I mean it's a medicine dance. They're goin' to try to cure you. They're sure that buzzards did you in. See all those men goin' off to kill buzzards? And see the women coming with buzzard feathers? They're goin' to tie them on those poles to warn off the evil in your body."

"Humph," Mammy said, finally perking up a bit. "I never saw such doctoring in my life."

I can tell you we all watched the proceedings with some interest and much doubt. I still wasn't sure Samboy hadn't told us it was a medicine dance just to ease our passing in those boiling pots. But the women soon put corn, meat, and salt in each pot. Wild turkey went in one pot and deer in another and squirrel in another and so on. The cooking smells came up out of those pots and hung around our heads. As sick as I felt, I could hear my stomach grumbling. It looked like—or I should say, it smelled like—we would have quite a feast.

Pretty soon, the old people circled around me and began to chant an up-and-down singsong song. In the background, two young men pounded on drums, tom-toms I guess they called them. When the other men returned to camp, dead buzzards hanging from their hands and their shoulders and their horses, the place began to reek. For a few minutes, dead buzzard smell made my head dizzy. When the men walked away after showing off their kills, the boiling turkey and deer and rabbit aromas swirled around me again, going right up my nostrils to my brain.

"My Lord, my Lord," Mammy wailed when things livened up even more. The hunters put on head feathers and breechcloths and danced around me and the fire. The women guarded me so nothing could come between me and the fire, even Dog.

"They want to make sure the fire burns the evil right out of your body," Samboy explained.

"I don't need any more fire," I answered. Still, I was in no position to protest.

Next, along came a young woman with mussel shells wrapped clear from her waist to her ankles. She danced to the beat of the tom-tom. She kept perfect time with the tinkle of the shells. I almost jumped off my pallet when two of the men grabbed the poles with the buzzard feathers and leaped across the fire with loud screams. I was glad when they disappeared into the forest, to find some more wicked buzzards, I guessed.

The Indians also passed around gourds full of liquid, first made out of grapes and persimmons, but pretty soon laced with liquor. After awhile, the women ladled some of the victuals into a big dishpan and gave each person a horn spoon. Everyone dug in but me. A mean-looking medicine woman fed me. "She's giving me poison," I mouthed at Samboy.

"Shut up," he mouthed back. "Eat."

This went on the rest of the evening and the entire night. First the dancing and screeching and jumping over the fire, then the running into the woods with poles, next the drinking and eating. I don't know how many times the cycle repeated itself, because I felt better and managed to sleep here and there. By morning, I was ready to get on the road again. But everyone else had collapsed with a hide or a blanket, plumb tired out from the night's proceedings.

I settled down as well, since it seemed clear to me that we weren't going anyplace that day. I thought to myself, at least we're safe; no civilized person would come into this camp with buzzard blood and painted-up Indians lying around everywhere. So I fell asleep.

By late afternoon, most of the Indians were awake and up, setting their camp to order. They seemed pleased to see me looking better. Some even urged me with hand motions to get up and walk around a bit. Now that I knew they didn't plan to eat me, I liked those people a good bit.

Mammy and Pappy stuck pretty close to me though. "Those Indians are strange ones," Mammy said.

"Yeah," Pappy added. "I wonder what they're goin' to do next?"

At suppertime, we all ate some more out of the dishpan, this time the leftovers of last night's feast. There seemed to be a lot of packing going on, as if we were going somewhere.

"They're goin' to see us to our Red River crossing," Samboy told us. "We leave at dawn tomorrow."

"How did you find that out?" asked I, suspicion ringing in my voice.

Samboy flashed me a proud grin. "From the head man. I know a few of his words and he knows a few of mine. We get along just fine."

"How are we goin' to repay them for what they've done?" Pappy asked.

"I don't think they expect any pay," Samboy answered. "Unless something comes up that we can help them with."

The following morning, right at dawn, we headed west. We wanted to dip into Texas nearer the panhandle than the cotton-planting area. We left behind the children and dogs and many of the older women. Along our sides, a fair number of men and women rode. They fanned out around us, acting as our advance and rear and side guards. At stopping time, we all came back together around a single campfire where the women cooked some of the tastiest food I'd ever eaten in my lifetime, stews and rabbits and bread fried over the fire.

"Sure tastes good," I told Samboy as we stood by the dying fire. "But what's that hollering about up at the head man's place?"

Samboy frowned. "You're in trouble again, Samgirl. One of the head man's sons want you for a wife."

I let a peal of laughter fly out of my mouth. "A wife. Don't be silly, Samboy. I don't want to stay here and marry a Chickasaw. I'm running away from Indian Territory and the Chickasaw."

Samboy wasn't smiling. He didn't say a word. His serious eyes bored into my face until it turned hot. Beads of sweat formed on my temples. "You know I can't marry that head man's son, Samboy. Say it."

Samboy's eyes turned resigned. "I know it. We all know it. But the Chickasaw don't know it. This is a serious matter, Samgirl. It's goin' to take some negotiatin'."

I shrugged my shoulders. "Well, you can do that for your own sister, can't you? You know a few of their words and signs. Just tell them how the— "

Samboy held his hands in my face, calloused palms facing me and hiding even the sky from my view. "We have to give proper heed to this. How would you like it, Missie Samgirl, if I proposed marriage to some woman and she laughed like a swamp loon?"

"Oh," said I as I ducked my head in shame. "I didn't think of it that way. What do we have to do?"

Sam flung his hands around the camp. "See them women unpackin'? We'll stay here for as long as it takes. I got to take Pappy and Mammy to the council fire tonight for some smokin' and palaverin'. But we won't talk bride prices until tomorrow—or the next day."

"Bride prices?" I shrieked. A few of the Chickasaw women working nearby turned around to look at me. In a more subdued voice I asked, "The head man's going to buy me for his son?"

"Not exactly. He wants to compensate Pappy and Mammy for the loss of your labor. He'll probably put up a few ponies."

Now I was really put out. "Only a few. Does he realize how strong I am? How hard I can work? How much I— "

Samboy kicked a stone into the embers. "Quit bein' ridiculous, Samgirl. First you don't want to marry the head man's son, then you're worried they ain't payin' enough for you. Which is it? Are you goin' with us or stayin' here?"

Samboy's question brought me back to my senses. "I'm going with you." Then another worry grabbed my mind. "How long will this take? What if Simon's slave-catchers find us while we're sitting here smoking and palavering?"

Samboy laid one of his hamlike hands on my shoulder. "I thought of that. But the rain wiped out our tracks. How will they know which way to go?"

"Simon's not stupid. He'll send some north and some more south. Any idiot can see that Mexico is closer than Canada."

Samboy's face fell. "There's nothin' we can do about it now. We can't insult the Chickasaw or we *will* be in the soup."

My fears of the Chickasaw popping us in their cooking pots on that first day flashed across the back of my mind. "What would the head man do to us, Samboy?"

Samboy puckered his forehead. "Let's just say this. It'd be a lot easier havin' them lead us to the Red River than chasin' us there."

I pictured the two scenes for a minute. "All right, smoke and palaver but make it as fast as you can."

The next morning I woke up to the sound of boot heels scraping in the sandy dirt somewhere near my head. I squinted into the sun and made out the shape of old John's youngest son, Peter, standing nearby.

"You sure sleep late, Samgirl, now that you're free," he said as if he had just seen me yesterday.

I sat up, pulled my legs up to my chest, and wrapped my good arm around my knees. "I been sick, Marse Peter. I hurt myself running away. The Indians did a healing dance over me. Now the head man's son wants me for his wife." After this tumble of words I had to gasp for breath.

Peter had stopped kicking his boots in the earth, but he looked confused. "You mean these Indians aren't holding you hostage? You aren't their captives?"

"No, we ain't captives, Marse Peter. If you're planning on ransoming us to take us back to Marse Simon, you're likely in for disappointment."

Peter squatted in front of me and looked square into my eyes. The sun backlit him, making him look like an avenging angel. "Take you back to Simon? Why would I do that?"

I rubbed my eyes clear of sleep and took another look at Peter. Yup, it was old John's youngest son, in the flesh. "Because we belong to your pappy and your brother. That's why you'd take us back."

Peter guffawed, loud and hearty, and stood up. "We're runaways ourselves. Me and Dolly Lee and Eustis Lee. We're on the runaway trail to California. I took the little money we had saved and— "

"Where's Dolly Lee and Eustis Lee?" I squealed as I jumped up and grasped Peter's arm.

"Don't knock me over, Samgirl," Peter complained. "You don't know your own strength."

I dropped my hand to my side while Peter brushed himself off and made sure I hadn't broken any of his bones. "Where's Dolly Lee, Marse Peter?" I repeated.

He waved his hand toward a bunch of giggling Chickasaw women. "Those women have got Dolly Lee. They can't seem to believe she's a Chickasaw. They're poking and prodding her hoops and stays and corset and who knows what else. I can't understand how— "

I never heard Peter's last words. I was already flying toward the circle of women, intent on tearing Dolly Lee from their grasp.

After me and Dolly Lee exhausted ourselves hugging and laughing and looking at each other, we settled down under the skimpy shade of a tree, Eustis Lee playing with a hide ball that the Chickasaw women had given him.

"See that boy, Samgirl?"

I studied Eustis Lee's sturdy legs and flailing arms. "He's a good one," said I, wondering what was coming next.

"He doesn't look a bit like my brother Eustis, does he?"

I didn't know whether Dolly Lee wanted me to say yes or no. "I don't remember your brother's looks very well, Dolly Lee. That was a long time ago when I saw him."

"Yes," Dolly Lee sighed. "And so much has happened since then. It's funny how you think you know something and you really don't. Or you think you love someone and you really don't."

I matched Dolly Lee's sigh with one of my own. I didn't know where this line of thinking was going and I wanted to be in the right place when I found out. I hummed my favorite hymn under my breath, so as to make me hold my tongue until Dolly Lee found hers.

Minutes passed and I couldn't stand the silence anymore. I peered under the brim of Dolly Lee's bedraggled straw hat. "You look mighty peaked to me, Dolly Lee. Those circles around your eyes make you look more like a coon than yourself."

Dolly Lee gave a little groan and pulled Eustis Lee to a sitting position at her side. He sighed and fell asleep with his head in Dolly Lee's lap.

"This running-away business is hard work, ain't it?" I prompted her.

"What happened before the running-away was the hard part, Samgirl." A dainty tear formed at the corner of each of Dolly Lee's eyes and started to leak out. "After you ran away, Simon sent for Peter and me at my daddy's house. When I heard you and your family escaped I got excited and yelled, 'Let them go. Let them go.' Daddy looked at me real hard and said, 'What do you mean, girl?' "

When Dolly Lee paused, I whispered "uh-oh." I patted Dolly Lee's sunburned hand until she felt strong enough to go on.

"I told my daddy I didn't believe in slavery," Dolly Lee burst out. "He turned purple and pounded the table. He said I was like some other Chickasaws, that I'd probably even marry a black man if I weren't already married. He said he never wanted to see my face in his house again."

I pulled Dolly Lee to my chest and let her sob for a bit. "He'll get over it when he wants to see Eustis Lee and the new child you're carrying," said I.

Dolly Lee looked up, her eyes glowing with a loathing I thought she was incapable of feeling. I was glad it wasn't me she hated.

"The next thing that happened," Dolly Lee went on, as if she hadn't heard me at all, "was that Eustis grabbed me by the arm and pulled me into the parlor. He said, 'I'll talk some sense into her, Daddy.' When I repeated that I didn't believe in slavery, Eustis slapped me full across the face."

Dolly Lee stopped to take in a great gulp of air. "I fell on the very table that held his brandy decanter. Glass flew everywhere and the table splintered beneath me." Dolly Lee threw her arms around my neck and wailed, "I lost the baby, Samgirl."

I held Dolly Lee with fierce arms. "You and Peter will have more. You're young and strong and—"

Dolly Lee pulled back. Her light hair hung straight and lank from her battered bonnet. "No, Samgirl. The doctor says we won't have any more children. That's why we want the child we have to grow up someplace that's free of the malice of slavery."

"Lord amighty," said I. "That's a lot of bad news to be coming in one bunch, Dolly Lee."

"That's not all, Samgirl." Dolly Lee swiped at her eyes with a limp lace handkerchief. "When we got back to Simon's, he blamed me for your running away. He said I gave you notions."

I chuckled. "You helped me out, Dolly Lee, but it wasn't your idea."

For the first time, Dolly Lee smiled. Her lips curved up, her cheeks filled out, and even the circles under her eyes retreated. "I know. The map of Texas you asked me for. I remembered. I got so mad at Simon I told him I tore a map for you out of my schoolbooks." She paused and let one hand fall to caress Eustis Lee's head.

"So Simon knows which way we went?" I asked.

"No. I told Simon I gave you a map with Kansas and Iowa and Minnesota on it. I told him you were heading straight to Canada and he was going straight to hell."

I choked on Dolly Lee's words. A full minute passed before I said, "You did that for me? You told him we went to Canada?"

"Yes." Dolly Lee looked pleased with herself. Some of the little-girl sparkle had even returned to her eyes. "Yes, and the next day Peter told Simon we were headed for California and that we expected a wagon, a team, and some supplies for all our hard work."

I glanced over Dolly Lee's shoulders to see if I could spot a familiar-looking wagon and team. Sure enough, a small wagon rested at the edge of the clearing, its hobbled mules grazing nearby. "And Simon gave them to you?"

Dolly Lee nodded. "He said they weren't to help out Peter and me. He gave them to his only nephew, to Eustis Lee." Dolly Lee caught Eustis Lee in the crook of her arm and dusted a light kiss on his damp forehead. "So the only people I plan on writing to back home are Mama and my sisters. I miss them but I've got Peter and Eustis Lee. And now I've got you, Samgirl. You and your family must come to California with us. There's no slavery there."

My heart danced in my chest, yet I knew there had to be flaws in Dolly Lee's plan. It sounded too simple and perfect. "Let's talk to the rest about it later, after Pappy and Mammy are done smoking and palavering with the Chickasaw head man."

chapter fourteen

After hearing about Dolly Lee's telling Simon we went to Canada, I kind of relaxed. "Take your time, Samboy," said I. "Smoke and palaver all you want. There won't be any slave-catchers coming this way now, not with Dolly Lee telling Simon we went to Canada."

Samboy snorted, kind of sharp and disgusted. "You said it yourself, Samgirl. Simon's not stupid. Any idiot can see that Mexico's closer than Canada. With Dolly Lee and Peter leaving for California so soon after our escape, Simon might even think we planned to meet up—to go on to California together."

"Then maybe we should do just that," I snapped. I had planned to bring up Dolly Lee's suggestion at a better time, but the trap was sprung now. I held my breath and waited to see if Samboy would stick his foot in or not.

"Do just *what?*"

"Go on to California with Dolly Lee and Peter," I said in careful, measured tones. "There's no slavery there."

Samboy's eyes turned cool and bitter. "No, there's no slavery in California now. But what if the government changes its mind? We'd all be slaves again."

"Well," I said, after considering this possibility, "the Mexican government could change its mind as well. Then what?"

Samboy stuck his face into mine. "Then what nothin'. The Mexican government won't change its mind. California might."

At that point, Marse Peter moseyed over and poked his nose into our conversation. "If you're talking about Dolly Lee's plan to go to California together, wipe it out of your mind. People don't specially like black folks in California, whether they be slave or free."

I turned on Marse Peter with all the fury of dashed hopes, combined with the knowledge that I would never see Dolly Lee again. "People don't specially like Indians in California either," I screamed in Peter's face. "And you're an Indian."

Peter stood calm before my assault. "True enough. But neither I nor Dolly Lee look like Indians. Even these Chickasaw don't believe we're Chickasaws. We look French. And Dolly Lee speaks French. We're going to pass ourselves off as Frenchies from Louisiana. You remember the Frenchy trader back in Arkansas, don't you, Samgirl? The one with the Caddoe wife."

I froze. Why would Peter bring up such a painful thing, I wondered? I studied Peter's face for a sign of Paul-like meanness, but I couldn't find any. "Are you chasing us away from you and Dolly Lee for our own good, Marse Peter?" I whispered.

Peter nodded. "I'm not takin' you along. It would be too much like the old days, which is exactly what I'm trying to leave behind." He sucked in a deep breath and went on. "Look at you, Samgirl. Ever since you laid eyes on me you've been calling me *marse*. I'm not your master. I'm not anybody's master. And I don't want to be anybody's master ever again."

"But, Marse Peter— " I began in a strangled voice.

"What if Simon or Dolly Lee's family changes their minds and sends someone for us?" he yelled over my weak words. "What if they decide we planned this from the first? You'd be back in Indian Territory and slavery in no time at all."

In a smug tone, Samboy said, "That's what I told her. But she won't listen to me." Samboy looked down on me, eyes glistening, nostrils wide. "Study on it, Samgirl. Are you willing to throw away all our years of planning to be with Dolly Lee? She's a sweet woman, but you got your own life to live."

Tears rose in my eyes and my voice cracked. "You're right, Samboy. And you too, Marse—um, Peter." I searched my right forearm for the tiny scar that remained from the day Samboy and I swore ourselves blood conspirators. "See this mark, Samboy?"

Samboy peered at the faded scar. When he realized what it was, he let his mouth and eyes break into a smile. "I got one, too. As soon as I convince the Chickasaw head man you can't marry his son, we'll be on our way."

As it turned out, Mammy was the one doing the convincing. It seems that Samboy interpreted and signed, but all the head man did in response was to increase the number of horses he offered for me. Strained to the breaking point, Mammy burst into tears accompanied by wailing that would have scared the swamp animals back in Mississippi.

"Samgirl's my only daughter," she moaned. "I can't leave her behind. I won't leave her behind."

She rose, nearly touching the flames in the head man's fire. She thrust out her hand and waggled her fingers at him. "If you take my daughter you'll surely meet a terrible fate yourself."

Pappy stood up behind her and tried to wrap his arms around her shoulders, but Mammy threw him off. "There's all kinds of slavery," she screamed at the sky. "I've seen some of the worst. But this is the— "

Pappy drug Mammy off, while Samboy did his best to interpret for the head man. The head man didn't want to hear what Samboy had to say. With trembling hands, he waved Samboy off. Samboy concluded that the head man either thought the spirits had touched Mammy—a special state to be sure—or that she had the power to consign him to the flames. In any case, he dropped his son's suit immediately and told Sam we would set out the very next day.

That news nearly killed me and Dolly Lee. We clung to each other and cried. Peter tugged at Dolly Lee. "We've got to be on our way to California. The Chickasaw are splitting off a small party to go along with us. They'll get us started toward the proper trail."

At the same time, Samboy tried to loosen my grip on Dolly Lee. "The rest of the Chickasaw are taking us to the Red River." Finally Samboy bellowed, "Let go of Dolly Lee right now."

In fright, we dropped our hold of each other. Peter led away Dolly Lee, while Samboy took me in the opposite direction. "Look at it this way, Samgirl," he told me. "You'll always have the memory of a wonderful friend, no matter what happens to us on the road ahead."

"Yes," I sighed, "and Dolly Lee still has the mirror with the Twenty-Third Psalm that I gave her. Do you think that makes some kind of spiritual bond between me, Dolly Lee, and Mellisey?"

Samboy stopped in his tracks. "Who's this Mellisey?" he asked, and gripped my arm until it throbbed. "We don't need no more friends. We need to get goin'."

I cast my sweetest smile at Samboy. "I got all the friends I need," said I. "You and Dog."

We traveled with the Chickasaws for three quiet, peaceful days. On the morning of the fourth day, we had headed for the Red River when shouting erupted first from our right side, then from the left. The words were in English: "Pull them up. Stop your wagons." I nearly fell off the wagon seat when I saw white men dressed as Indians swoop down on our guides and on us.

"White Indians, they're called," Samboy shouted to me. "They steal, rape, kill, whatever, and the Indians get the blame. They mean big trouble for us."

By then, I'd recovered. I yelled at Samboy to get in the back of the wagon and break out one of the rifles. "Shoot those thugs off," I ordered him.

Samboy swerved his horse around the back of the wagon and jumped toward the tailgate. I saw Mammy helping him into the wagon. Samboy made it and soon had a rifle in his hands. With Mammy passing ammunition, Samboy shelled the white Indians. "Don't hit any of the real Indians," I shouted at Samboy, who didn't appreciate my advice.

"I already know that," he hollered back between shots.

Some of the white Indians caught on real quick that Samboy had fired over their heads, hoping to scare them off. Two of them bore down on our wagon. "Here come two outlaws," I warned Samboy, who reloaded as quick as he could.

By now, I had a hard time keeping the mules steady. The wagon rocked from side-to-side, bouncing Mammy and Samboy around so hard they could barely stay upright. I glanced back just in time to see one of the white Indians riding straight toward the back of the wagon. Samboy hid the rifle behind his back and waited.

I had to turn around and give the mules some direction, but I heard a shot from the back end of the wagon. In a moment, I saw the white Indian flash by my seat. He swung from his horse's side, one foot stuck in the stirrup, his face blown into a bloody pulp and his brains hanging loose, all from Samboy's blast.

That was the first man I ever saw killed. I had to lean off the side of the wagon seat so I wouldn't vomit all over my clothes. I managed to hold the reins steady and we kept going, rocking and swaying, with Indians swirling around us on horseback. They shouted and hollered. It was hard to see which were the real Indians and which the white ones.

Samboy could see. He roared at me, "Slow the mules down."

I pulled the team up a bit and heard another blare off the end of the wagon. This time the white Indian wasn't lucky enough to die immediately. Samboy's shot grazed his shoulder. That left him to die at the hands of the Chickasaw who jumped on the back of his horse. The Chickasaw reached around and slit that man's throat with a knife. Blood spurted out and the man slumped forward. His Chickasaw passenger vaulted off and bounced back onto his own horse.

That was the second person I watched get killed. I had nothing left to be sick with. I just kept on driving. Meanwhile, the death of those two white Indians proved somewhat discouraging to their comrades, who rode off as fast as they had come, but with far less bravado and whooping.

We and our friends pulled to a halt, also feeling pretty subdued. "How many did we lose?" I asked Samboy.

"The head man says a few Indians wounded and two dead ponies. Nothing stolen, no one raped, nobody killed."

"Mammy," I squealed, "you lost a whole chunk of your hair."

Mammy fingered her scalp where the patch of hair had been. "Bullet must have taken it clear off my head," she said, her brown eyes dark with wonder, "but I never even felt it!"

After that, the Chickasaws crowded around me and Samboy and pounded their fists on our shoulders and arms. "That's their way of thanking us for running off their enemies," Samboy hissed.

"I'm glad they're happy." I felt I had aged a hundred years in less than an hour.

We traveled for several more days along the north bank of the Red, waiting to cross into Texas at a safer point. Finally, we calculated we were across the Red from Wichita Falls, where we thought it safe to ford the river.

Dog seemed to understand that we would soon leave his canine friends behind. He cavorted and played around the camp to near exhaustion. I could see his earless yellow head running this way and that, his bony yellow butt bouncing in the air, his yellow jaws smacking over the supper leavings.

Samboy sat with the head man one last time. The head man made it clear to Samboy that the Chickasaw wouldn't be crossing the Red with us. It seemed they feared Texas Indians, Texas whites, and about everything else that Texas had. They were even afraid of the Red and what it carried.

In his own dialect and with his hands waving, the head man told a chilling story: "My people used to leave cut firewood on the banks. The captain of a small steamboat stopped and picked up the fuel. He left liquor and such in return. A few weeks back the captain overfired his boilers. He blew his passengers to pieces."

Literally pieces; even I could understand when the head man described, along with hand motions, the heads and arms and legs he saw flying from the ruptured boat.

None of this made me too confident about either the Red or Texas, but I was feeling better physically and ready to get on with it. After all, I was headed for freedom now.

As it turned out, freedom was a mighty hard thing to come by. Even though we forded the Red River without incident, except for getting good and wet, I was naive about what we had waiting on the other side. It took hours to ride just a few miles. My seat was sore, my back ached, and my head felt like it would split apart. To relieve the boredom that made us sleepy and almost knocked us out of the saddles, we sang—tunes from the quarters, hymns, even burial songs.

We talked some, too. But the one thing we didn't talk about was the thought that haunted all of us every minute of every day—that our delay had given Simon a chance to get men on our trail. We carried a fear with us that caused nightmares, and daymares, too, if there were such things. After a while, we stopped singing. Nobody said so, but we all knew we had turned quiet so we wouldn't give away our whereabouts.

In the meantime, we fought our way through prairie grass that reached the top of the wagon wheels and sometimes higher. Some places I rode through grass over my head. "I don't know where we are, I can't see where we've come from, and I don't know where we're going," I complained.

"Shut up," Samboy said.

I shut up, but I felt lost in a sea of grass, swallowed by a sea of grass, and, eventually, like I was drowning in a sea of grass.

We surely drowned alone because no people seemed to live in that part of Texas. From afar, we saw an occasional Indian scout, or even a camp. None of those Indians appeared to have the least interest in us. We never saw a ranch or a cowboy or a white person of any kind. Of course, what we dreaded most was the sudden appearance of a bunch of patrollers, armed with guns and knives and orders for our arrest, or slave-catchers, who would return us to Simon at any cost. But they didn't ride down upon us through that curtain of waving grass.

Soon, we discovered another truth: water was too often a rarity, a precious commodity to be savored whenever we happened to find it. Even then, the water we found often looked murky and thick. We had to hunt for alum to clear the stream or try to catch rainwater, which there wasn't much of that particular year. We located one puny river, all brown and red. "It looks so red," I muttered. "We've turned back on ourselves. It's the Red River again."

Samboy said, with a certainty that relieved my mind, "No, it may be a branch of the Red, but it ain't the Red itself."

That tiny river wasn't good drinking, so we went on and camped by a gulch. At first I thought it was a dry gulch, then, about twenty feet down, I spied a fine spring of cold water bubbling out. "We're goin' to tie a rope around you and lower you down to the water," Samboy said and I reluctantly agreed.

I went down that gulch wall grumbling all the way. "Hold tight to that rope," I yelled at Samboy. At the bottom, I untied the rope from my body and a wooden bucket from my belt. Then I tied the bucket to the rope. I handed bucketful after bucketful of water up to them waiting at the top, until my healing arm ached and throbbed.

"I can't do any more buckets," I finally shouted. "You must have watered the whole prairie by now."

"All right, Samgirl," hollered Samboy back to me, "we're ready to pull you up."

I came up that wall a lot faster than I'd gone down, especially after I spotted a huge, hungry-looking bobcat perched in a dead tree—he'd been watching my every move without my noticing him at all. I heard Dog whining above me. I realized he'd been eyeing that cat the whole time, planning to attack if necessary, even if he had to fly through the air twenty feet to do it.

"We're sorry we wore you out, Samgirl," Pappy said when I came up over the edge of that gulch. "Are you all right?"

I looked at Pappy. I looked down behind me at that bobcat. I decided to say nothing; we had enough problems already. "I'm all right, just tuckered," I said and sniffed my way toward Mammy's cooking fire. I saw we were about to eat the last of our fresh meat, given to us by our Chickasaw friends.

In addition to our troubles with grass and water, we weren't dressed sensibly for the climate. Me and Samboy and Pappy had cowboy boots near to our knees. "These boots are cookin' my feet faster than the fireplace back in Indian Territory baked your mammy's cornbread," Pappy said.

To get some relief, we rode and drove the wagon without boots, just our bare feet, which had soles almost like leather anyway.

We also wore the same flannel shirts most cowboys wore year-round. That fall the humidity was extra dense, though it stubbornly refused to rain. It clung to those shirts, turning them into near shrouds. The flannel grew heavier and heavier, stuck to our backs, and caused rivulets of sweat to stream down our necks and shoulders and backs. We ripped off our bandannas and opened the front of our shirts to get the breeze that didn't exist on the prairies that particular fall.

At least the men didn't have to carry the weight of whiskers. Samboy and Pappy kept their beards cut short so my lack of whiskers wouldn't be as noticeable. Every evening, Mammy used her tiny sewing scissors to clip their chins down so it looked like about two days' growth. I made up for my lack of chin hairs by practicing my moronic expression. In case anyone came along, I planned to stare and drool until they couldn't stand looking at me.

The only one who didn't complain—besides Dog, that is—was Mammy. Samboy and Pappy had fixed up the inside of the wagon with their usual cleverness. Down both sides they had built in boxes of supplies, supposedly for the cowboys we were hunting. Actually, the boxes were fake. Each line of boxes had a hidden door that opened, on the right side, into a storage area where we kept guns and ammunition and, on the left side, into a miniature bedroom for Mammy.

"You done a real good job," Mammy told Pappy and Samboy. "I can leave the door near the wagon seat open. I get good air without anyone seeing me. They'd have to come right into the wagon and look real hard."

Pappy and Samboy preened. They had also put a nice, fresh corn-shuck mattress in that room of hers so she could nap a bit as we fought through that tough prairie grass. Still, I knew something wasn't right with Mammy. In fact, I knew Mammy was dying. Even though I didn't want to know, I knew. She had never been herself since the breast-cutting day. Because I felt guilty about dragging Mammy out here on the prairie, I apologized to her.

"Mammy," said I, "I'm so sorry I brought you to this land of agony when you're not feeling yourself. I told you back in Indian Territory we'd wait until you were strong enough to travel."

Mammy gazed at me with sad eyes and said, "Samgirl, I'm as strong for travel as I'm ever goin' to be. Remember, I told you in the swamp the day we went to see Aggie for the first time that I'm older than your pappy. And I birthed four children and seen two of them taken from me, one way or another. I'm not strong, yet I want to see freedom just like the rest of you. If I don't see freedom, I want you all to have it. I would never stand in the— "

At that, I wrapped my mammy in my arms, muffling the rest of her words. She seemed to be shrinking before my very eyes. "You've got to eat more," said I. "I'm going to tell Samboy to take a rifle and go hunting tomorrow."

I sensed Mammy smiling against my chest: "Samgirl, you take care of me good and I'm goin' to see freedom yet."

I wasn't ready for such a big responsibility, so I tried to turn it over to the Lord. Each night I prayed to the endless black sky. Each day I offered up pleas to a wide and deep blue sky, asking that Mammy be allowed to live to see freedom.

It seemed like I prayed day and night for months before we reached a stopping point to the far west of Fort Worth. "It's only been somethin' over a week," Samboy snorted when I told him. "I'm goin' to take the long ride into the trading post this mornin'. I'll leave a message for Albert."

"When'll Albert show up?" I asked. I realized that, despite all my planning, we'd need Albert's help to succeed.

"How would I know?" Samboy looked tired and exasperated. "It could be days or weeks or even months before Albert shows up. We'll wait a week and then go on. Albert will catch up with us when he can."

I added to my prayers that Albert would show up real fast. First of all, I wanted Mammy to reunite with her son before she died. Second, I wanted to get on our way. I was beginning to feel real peculiar out here in all this grass and almost no people.

I turned out to be ignorant for lamenting the lack of people. When they came up they brought aggravation. Even though Albert didn't arrive, others did, carrying prying eyes and questions with them. On our second day of waiting for Albert we heard, or maybe felt, some iron-girded wagon wheels groaning over the prairie in our direction. They were a bunch of Alsatian immigrants, headed for forty acres of farmland for each family down by Castroville on the Medina River.

"We're hired-out slaves," we told them and they believed our story. They spent a great deal of time saying "tsk, tsk" about the metal identification tags we wore around our necks and bemoaning the evils of slavery—about which they knew next to nothing—before they finally went on their way.

Next came a bunch of Indians with a young leader named Victorio, along with his wife and their little children. By then, I was laid so low with the frying Texas sun, and irritated with my cursed flannel shirt rubbing against my chest scars all day, that I bared a good part of my chest as a regular thing. I wasn't a pretty sight. The Indian women took one look at me and put their hands over their children's eyes. Just to ensure that they left us alone, I adopted my moron expression. Added to my scars, my vacant eyes and slobbering lips drove them right away from our camp.

We all laughed about it over supper that night. "This is easier than I thought it was going be when we were out there struggling our way across that prairie," said I.

Pappy nodded and added, "You're a mess all right, Samgirl. You'd scare anybody away."

That's not quite what I had in mind. I had hoped someone would compliment my cleverness. I turned to Samboy. "Good thing I developed that idiot face, ain't it?"

"Yeah," Samboy grinned, "but I want to show you something." He went to the wagon and pulled out the map Dolly Lee had ripped out of her schoolbook for me, seemed like it was years ago. "This is Fort Worth," Samboy said, pointing to the map. "See how it's way up at the top of Texas. Mexico is way down at the bottom. And see how much we got to go yet?"

I studied that map. I gulped and said, "Samboy, you sure have improved in geography. I see we've got a long distance to travel yet. Still, things ain't going too bad."

"No," Samboy agreed, "things ain't going too bad."

On our fourth morning of waiting, already feeling like wilted summer flowers in the beating fall heat, we heard hoofbeats coming our way. I admit I'd gotten cocky and careless, and thus was the major cause of our downfall.

Three men rode right up to our fire without even saying howdy. They looked like I always believed slave-catchers would look. Two of them were white, the third a black man with thin, cruel lips and hate in his hard eyes. I suspected he was one of those I'd heard about who preyed on people of his own kind.

"Howdy," Samboy started out. "We're glad to see you. We're looking for Aron Ashworth's cowpokes. We're hired-out slaves and we're supposed to be taking supplies to them." Samboy had especially picked out Aron Ashworth because he was black and his cowboys were black. It seemed logical that we would be working for a black outfit, taking truck to them.

"Aron Ashworth," one said as he spit his tobacco juice into our fire and made it sizzle. "He's that nigger rancher in Orange County. No account, if you ask me."

Samboy threw back his big shoulders and tried again. "Yessir, but Ashworth owns some 2,500 head of cattle. We've got to relieve his cowboys with these supplies. Have you seen their camp? Or heard of their whereabouts?"

"I don't know 'em or seen 'em or care about 'em," the man said, as tobacco spittle dribbled down his grizzled chin. "How do we know you're hired-out slaves, anyway?"

Samboy pointed to his identification tag and Pappy to his, while I tried hard to put on my idiot's face. The black man glanced my way and asked, "What about him? The one with the chest scars?"

"He's not right in the head," Samboy answered, "but he's got a tag. See it around his neck."

I fingered the tag. I also made the mistake of meeting the black man's eyes and letting my dislike show through the film of stupidity with which I tried to shade them.

That man slid down off his horse and came at me. His hand whipped up and tore down the front of my flannel shirt, exposing the little bit of breasts I had.

"She's a woman," he growled. "If she's truly a hired-out slave, why is she dressed up as a man?"

"We're trying to protect her since she ain't too smart," Pappy said. "We thought— "

The black man turned toward Pappy and spit in his face. "I don't want to hear nothin' from you. This gal's a runaway, or you wouldn't be hiding her under men's clothes. You're helpin' her run away."

"No, no, that's not it," Samboy protested, while I prayed Mammy had the good sense to stay in her hiding place in the wagon. Mammy stayed hid; I was glad she didn't see my troubles.

One of the white men slid down off his horse and neared me. He tweaked my breasts. "She's a gal, all right," he snickered. "What say we take her in and put her on the block? See what she'll bring? And maybe use her a bit ourselves along the way?"

The other white man tipped his head back. He let out a peal of laughter that, to my ears, sounded like a death knell. I had gotten this far only to be taken prisoner by some of the dirtiest, smelliest, foulest men I had ever had the misfortune to see.

The black man strolled over to his horse and unsheathed his rifle, which he held on Samboy and Pappy. The mounted white man pulled me up behind him on his horse. When I struggled a bit and acted like a solid lump of coal, he whacked me a good one across the face with his riding whip. "Shut up, bitch," he growled. His blow opened a slash of skin down my cheek and across my lip.

Samboy held Dog by the bristling hairs on the back of his neck. With his eyes, Samboy warned me to go along and bear it, that he and Pappy would rescue me as soon as they could.

That rescue couldn't come soon enough for me. I was on my own with those three monsters until the time of deliverance might come. They rode hard out of our camp and didn't stop all day. At nightfall, they camped. That white man threw me to the ground, still with my shirt front hanging and my chest bare to any who had the guts to look. The black man tossed a tin plate of beans my way. I caught it and poured its contents into my mouth, still acting the imbecile.

When the black man finished eating and headed for me, unbuckling his belt, I knew I had to act fast. I started to simper and moan, all the while scratching myself down below. "Hell," he hissed through teeth stained near as black as his skin by too much tobacco, "I'm not takin' a chance on her. I had the clap once. I'm probably goin' to catch worse from her."

When I heard that, I panted and sniveled and reached out for him. I motioned him to come to me. I smiled a lopsided grin and let my eyes go toward the bridge of my nose.

"I wouldn't touch her with a butt of my rifle," said the other white man.

The one I had ridden with all afternoon seemed nervous, like he itched. "I ain't havin' her on my horse tomorrow," he said, "one of you can take your turn haulin' her into the slave-tradin' place."

That's how it came about that I escaped rape at the hands of those scoundrels. Instead, I spent a calm night, even though I couldn't sleep, wondering whether my rescuers would get to me before the auction man did.

It was a long night, with a bloated harvest moon lighting up the camp and my tormentors, but not showing up any rescuers sneaking toward me across the prairie.

Morning came and with it no more salvation than the nighttime had brought. The three of them ate without giving me anything, even water. At noon, we stopped for coffee and beans. As we neared Fort Worth about suppertime, they decided that none of them wanted me on their horses any longer, so they tied a rope around my neck and made me walk behind, choking all the way on the grit their horses' hooves raised.

I smelled the trading post before I saw it, all cooking grease and strong drink and tobacco odor combined. About ten feet from the post sat a rickety wooden building with a sign that seemed about ready to topple off into the Texas dust: "Slaves Bought and Sold Here."

Chills ran up and down my spine as I remembered every detail of every auction-block story I'd ever heard in Aggie's quarters or anywhere else. The best I could do was keep my fool's smile in place and hope for the best.

Within minutes, the three men turned me over to the auction man. "We'll split down the middle whatever price you get for her," the leader said. The auction man agreed with a nod.

He shoved me into a slave pen, open to all who cared to look and to the shimmering sun as well. He didn't bother to give me any food or water.

I crept to the far corner of the pen, which was empty. A miserable-looking hunk of man huddled in another corner, apparently dying from scurvy or ague or some other terrible disease. He and I were the auction-master's wares for the day. Unless someone else turns up, I thought, I'm clearly the prize bit of merchandise to go on the block today.

That thought turned out to be another bit of arrogance on my part. The auction man let us sit all day in that pen; he'd decided to wait for something better to come along. After a supper of beans and black coffee that I swear the man had laced with sawdust, I spent a night nestled against the wreck of a slave man in his corner. We gave the other what little warmth we could muster. For our bodily needs, we used yet another corner. Since the auctioneer hadn't given us much in the way of food or drink, we didn't make too many trips to that place. It stunk just the same and flies buzzed over it, day and night.

fifteen

Late the next morning a wagonload of white folks came into Fort Worth to trade for goods. The auction man came out and looked us over. "I'm goin' to put you on the block this noon," he spat at us. He ordered his boy to go up and down the miserable dirt street shouting, "Fine breeding wench to be auctioned at noon. Be there to get a bargain."

There it was again, I thought to myself. I was supposed to breed and produce slave babies. I almost wished a stingy man would buy me, only to learn his mistake the hard way. But that would lead to a life of misery for me. I changed my thoughts. I spent most of my time hoping to see Samboy and Pappy and maybe this Albert Camp riding into the post.

At noon, only a few people sat in the auction house. When the man, with his greasy fingers and sour breath, put me on the block, he got only a few half-hearted bids. He tried to whip up some interest: "What am I offered for this portly, strong young wench? She's never been abused and will make a good breeder."

I wondered how that man could say such things, given my swollen, cut face and the scars on my chest, which were clearly visible because he had tied only a cotton loincloth around my hips. He appeared about to try to stir up some enthusiasm again when the back door flew open. Because I faced the door and looked right into the sun, I couldn't see who came in. All I could hear was some child calling, "Mammy, Mammy" in a raggedy voice.

Within seconds, I could make out the outline of a man hauling that child—a wizened, old-lady-looking girl—down the center aisle. As they got closer, I realized the man was Levi. My mouth went as dry as an old, parched field that had felt the heat of the sun for too many months. My hands trembled like a cotton plant in gusting winds and my eyes burned as if the winds had lifted the soil of the fields right into my face.

Instead of understanding that Levi was here to save me from the auction man, I only thanked the Lord that I had lived long enough to see Levi one more time. Then my senses returned somewhat. I noticed another man with Levi. "Albert Camp," I whispered under my breath.

Albert came right up to the auctioneer and shoved a paper under his nose. Clearly, the auction man couldn't manage much reading, so Albert yanked the paper back and said: "This here paper says that Aron Ashworth has lost a hired-out slave by the name of Samgirl. This man is her husband, Levi, and her daughter, Gracy, come to identify that very woman there on the block as the very same Samgirl named here in the paper."

At that, Levi rushed forward saying, "Samgirl, Samgirl," while the child Gracy kept calling "Mammy, Mammy" and staring right at me. The auction man dropped my arm like it was an ear of corn fresh out of Mammy's fire and hot enough to scorch his fingers to the bone. In the meantime, Albert flashed a tin badge and said, "I'm Aron Ashworth's patroller and I want his hired-out slave back."

Albert sure knew how to stage a bluff. By the time he finished huffing and hollering and blowing, there wasn't one person left in that slim audience of bidders. Albert marched up to the auctioneer and slapped two twenty-dollar bills into his grimy hand. "Here, sir," he said, "a finder's fee. I'm sure my marse will be much obliged."

At that, Albert grabbed my arm and jerked me toward the door, where Levi and little Gracy had already stationed themselves. I'm sorry to admit it, but I acted like a true moron for a moment and stood gaping.

I suppose I was so relieved to have Levi back in my life—and to have been saved from the auction man—that my brain failed for a little while. I came to my senses quickly, though, and ran to Gracy, screeching, "Gracy baby, Gracy, it's me, your mammy."

I noticed Levi smiling just as Albert hit us from behind, forcing us out the door and onto the waiting horses' backs. We were out of that wretched excuse for a town so fast I almost forgot I was still wearing only a loincloth. I drew Gracy close to my front, face-to-face, and rode with her as my warmth and my clothes. That child snuggled into my chest and never even paled at the sight of my scars. Because Gracy had never known her own mammy, she quickly accepted me as the real thing.

Only later did I remember my three captors and think how angry they would be to receive only twenty dollars for me, half of the finder's fee Albert had paid the auction man.

We rode straight through the rest of that day, all night, and part of the next day to our camp; Samboy and Mammy and Pappy and Dog had waited to see if we got out of town dead or alive. When we reached the camp, Mammy hugged me half to death, then held me back as if she couldn't believe what stood before her eyes. "You ain't got no clothes on, child. Ain't you ashamed? And in front of all these men."

Levi unbuttoned his shirt and draped it across my shoulders, which sent waves of love through me and across me and over me. He said to Mammy, "We weren't thinking about clothes, Aunt Chloe, just about getting away. Maybe we better get busy feeding Samgirl before she wastes away to near nothing."

Everyone laughed at the idea of me approaching nothing, then we all grouped around the fire to hear Levi's story. He took Gracy on his knee and began, "I knew you were up to no good, Samgirl, when you started talking about your cabin and woodshed burning down. When it really happened, I knew you all had run."

Shame at deceiving Levi burned its way up my neck and across my face. Quickly, I changed the drift of the conversation. "Did Simon know?" I asked, afraid to hear the answer.

"At first, Simon didn't know you ran. He thought you might have burned up in that cabin fire. But he's got the slave-catchers after you now, even though Dolly Lee came home and begged him not to do it."

"I know," said I. "We met Dolly Lee and Peter along the trail. They were running away themselves." After that, there was no help for it. I had to tell Levi all about the time with Dolly Lee. Finally, I studied Levi and asked, "Was anyone hurt? Did anyone else's cabin burn?"

"No," Levi replied. "There was a whole lot more smoke than fire, especially after it started to rain. We came running fast enough to save the other cabins, but not to save yours. That's why Simon thought you went up with it."

"You knew the truth, Levi, didn't you?" Samboy chimed in.

Levi stared at Samboy a long, quiet moment before he answered. "I knew. My feelings were good and hurt. I didn't understand how you— like my own family—could run away without letting me in on it, or maybe taking me with you."

"But," I started, while everyone else tried to talk at once and reassure Levi. I clamped my arms across my stomach, where I felt Levi's pain the most.

Levi waved his hand and said, "It's all right. I figured out you were afraid to trust anybody, even me. I decided I'd run away on my own and find you. It was easy with all the confusion going on. Simon wanted people back in the fields and he wanted Peter and Dolly Lee back home. He sent special messengers to Dolly Lee's daddy's house. Old John about had a heart attack over it all and Nellie cried for days. I just walked away as nice as you please."

"Where did Gracy come from?" I busted in, impatient to learn the whole story as fast as possible.

"I thought as long as I was running, I'd get my little girl. So I headed north instead of south. I hid in the trees until I saw Gracy walking down a path near the quarters. Then I just ran out, clapped my hand over her mouth, and ran back into the trees with her."

"What about Gracy's grandmammy and pappy?" I chided Levi. I remembered how he had said Gracy's grandmammy and grandpappy took such good care of Gracy and adored her so.

"Gracy told me they're dead." He shot me a defiant look. "She was glad to see me and run away with me. We headed south, traveled back by Marse Simon's farm, and here we are."

"How could you know we headed west of Fort Worth?" Samboy demanded, a put-out look on his face at having our plans so easily discovered.

"I'm a cowboy, too," Levi said. "I know Albert Camp, too. I know Albert's your half brother and I know his home base is somewhere around Fort Worth. So it didn't take me and Gracy too long to find you. That's when I learned about Samgirl and met up with Albert and you, Samboy, and we rode off to the trading post to see what we could do."

At that, Albert joined our circle. I suppose he stood about six feet, two inches tall and carried some 180 pounds of mostly muscle on his sparse frame. His eyes were heavy-lidded, much like Levi's. His full mouth chewed on, yet never smoked, a tightly rolled cigarillo. When Albert spoke, he did it with the same economy that characterized his motions. "I'm especially glad to see my mammy again," Albert said now.

Mammy studied him and said, "Albert, you're my first-born baby. As much as I love Samgirl and Samboy, I've got a special place in my heart for you. I watched you go down the lane that day Marse Camp sold you and I cried and cried. I thought I'd never ever see you again."

"But here I am," Albert said he took Mammy's work-worn hand in his hawklike, leathery one. "With my mammy at last."

I was overjoyed to see how Mammy perked up after that. As tired as we were from our Fort Worth misadventure, we got away fast, Mammy in her hiding place and the rest of us taking turns riding horseback or driving the wagon—except for Gracy, who mostly rode with me. Although that girl was about six or seven, she didn't say much. She just clung to my chest or my arm or my leg or whatever part of me she could get hold of at the moment. Although Dog wasn't too happy about this development, he soon learned to treat Gracy as a miniature Samgirl. When he couldn't follow me, he followed her.

I'd given up the idea of traveling disguised as a man, for it surely hadn't saved me from our three attackers. I'd put on a dress again and was traveling as Levi's wife and Gracy's mammy. I pushed to the back of my mind what all that might mean until I had more time to think about it. As far as I could see, it was a dream I might as well enjoy while it lasted, for it could never come true.

Albert thought we should head west again before we turned south, so as to avoid any more encounters with slave-catchers. "Give up the hired-out slaves story," he said, "and go on as free blacks."

Unlike his usual restrained self, Albert had reared back and laughed out loud when he saw the free-black passes me and Samboy had fixed up: "Those are first-rate," he said. "Seals and everything."

Me and Samboy puffed up our chests and went on our way rejoicing. We would willingly follow our half brother, Albert Camp, anywhere he told us to go.

Albert said we had to move fast and swing wide of Comanche country. "The Comanche war trail reaches all the way from the High Plains in the north to Big Bend in the south," he warned us, "with Big Spring at its middle. If we stay east of Fort Concho and west of the hill country we'll probably get through all right."

It was Albert's "probably" that bothered me. I was growing more attached to Gracy, and she to me, every minute. I didn't like the thought of losing her to Comanche Indians. I also had heard the Comanche cooked up dogs and ate them. Dog wasn't much, but he had turned leaner and rangier and stronger from walking. He had solid muscles and good teeth and a loyal heart. I didn't want to see him end up in a Comanche cooking pot.

I figured the rest of us could fend for ourselves, despite Albert's horrifying stories around the campfire every single night. "The Comanche are the bravest, toughest, most ferocious Indians on the southern Plains," he told us every single night. "The Comanche are the best warriors and hunters in the world," he told us every single night. "The Comanche always get their enemies," he told us every single night.

I grew tired of listening to Albert and his Comanche stories, so I got a bit careless. Then we came across the skull. It was an ox skull, I guess, bleached as white as the whites of Levi's eyes in his jet black face. On it these words were written in charcoal: "Lost 14 to the Comanch. Beware."

Underneath the warning, some macabre-minded dunce had drawn a skull-and-crossbones. "As if we haven't already understood the message from the words alone," said I, then I remembered that lots of folks couldn't read.

The skull did its job—it scared me good. I listened a little more carefully to Albert's campfire tales and prodded him about means of defense. "What can we do," I asked, my eyes thoughtful and forehead puckered, "if the Comanche come swooping down on us?"

"I think," he said, "our best bet is to stand still and let them look us over. They seldom kill a quarry without checking its worthiness. Maybe they'll find us wanting and go on their way."

Not too promising a strategy, I thought to myself, yet it's all we've got at the moment. Five adults, one scrawny child, and a lean yellow dog; who'd want that for prey?

The Comanche attacked us in a laughable episode. At least it was laughable for them. At the time, it scared the bodily fluids right out of us. I mean that literally. Samboy wet his pants and he was the only one who admitted it. If everyone had told the truth, I bet we had more than one pair of damp drawers in camp that afternoon.

When ten or eleven braves rode in, I knew immediately that they were a war party. "They're going to take our scalps," I moaned, "and leave our bones to whiten in the midday sun."

"Shut up," Samboy hissed. "They're probably a huntin' party, lost or something."

We all froze in place, Gracy hanging on my chest as usual and Dog at my heels. Albert waved his arms, making a sign of peace, I guessed, or what he hoped the Comanches would interpret as a sign of peace. Actually, he looked like a windmill in the middle of Texas, waving-and-creaking, creaking-and-waving.

Albert yelled, desperation tingeing his deep voice, "We are just passing through. We go to MEX-I-CO."

"I understand your words," the head man replied.

Albert did a double-take. "You speak English?" he asked, sounding like a complete jackass.

"Better than you do," the head man responded.

"In that case," Albert said as he tried to regroup and act like the mighty leader we all believed we had in him, "we're just passing through. We're going to Mexico."

"So I see," the head man answered. "You're runaway slaves?"

"Yes," Albert admitted. "We're looking for freedom."

"There's no freedom where the white man walks," the head man told Albert. "He takes the air out of the sky, the nourishment out of the ground, and the life out of the earth's true people."

With that, Albert could see that we had friends in the Comanche, or at least that we and the Comanche shared mutual enemies. Albert invited the head man and his buddies to dismount and take a seat near our fire. There they palavered for hours.

Finally, the head man rose and said, "Besides, you have women and a child with you. We do not harm women and children. Only white soldiers do that. Nor do we harm dogs," he added, looking directly at me, as if he could read my thoughts.

After the Comanche departed, we sat around shaking and taking deep breaths for awhile. Then Albert said one of the most profound things I ever heard come out of his mouth: "It's sure strange how we all blame white folks for our problems. Yet I've met a few good ones in my time."

"Like Mellisey," I murmured under my breath.

"Yeah," Samboy said more loudly, his head nodding and shaking, "there are some good white folks—like the abolitionists Samgirl read about. We need to find some of those."

Samboy's statement led to a lot of questions. During the next few days, I recited what I remembered about the abolitionists. "But they're mostly up north," I warned. "I don't think we can count on finding them down here."

The next morning I peeped an eye out of my blanket to see that the Comanche had returned. "Samboy," I whispered, "where are you?"

Next to me, Samboy sat up and looked where I pointed. "I thought we were shut of them," he said.

Meanwhile, the half-dozen or so Indians squatting around our fire ignored me and Samboy. They fastened their gaze on Mammy. "Not again," said I. "They want to trade ponies for Mammy for somebody's wife."

Albert was way ahead of us. He marched to the fire with smiles dripping from his lips and eyes. "Ho," he said, or some such. "We're glad to see our friends."

I nudged Samboy. "How does Albert do that? He's so steady. He ain't even asking them what they want."

Samboy shushed me. "Albert knows what he's doin'. You don't march right up to an Indian and say 'What you want?' You take it slow and easy, polite-like."

In a few minutes the Indians left the fire and headed toward their horses. Albert motioned us to take their places in a circle around him and the fire. "The Comanche got a sick girl back at their main camp. They told their folks there about Mammy bein' a healer. They come here this mornin' to fetch Mammy and take her back there."

"At least they don't want to trade ponies for Mammy," said I.

"How long is this goin' to take?" Samboy asked, ignoring me.

Albert scratched his head. "Near as I can tell it's half a day's ride to the main camp. What happens after that depends on Mammy."

All eyes turned toward Mammy and fastened on her unruffled expression. "What's wrong with the Indian girl?" she asked Albert.

"Fever, rash, out of her head most of the time." Albert's forehead puckered into a frown. "I don't like it. The Comanche medicine man can't bring the girl out of it. They think Mammy can."

"We got any choice in this?" Pappy asked. He wrapped an arm around Mammy's shriveled shoulders.

"I'll put it to you this way. If we help the Comanche, they'll help us in return. If we don't try to help, they might cause trouble for us somewhere down the trail."

"That ain't the thing of it at all," Mammy broke in. "A girl's dyin'. If I can help, then I got to try."

Levi's deep voice caused all heads to turn toward him. "What if the Indian girl dies? Will the Comanche blame Mammy?"

Albert considered this a minute before he answered in a somber voice. "I think them Indians will give us credit for tryin' to help."

The matter appeared settled. Mammy rolled up her blankets and snapped her satchel shut. "Let's get goin', then."

When we came to the Comanches' main camp we caused a stir everywhere. Folks and dogs came running like we were some kind of saviors. Dust roiled up from the dry ground, mixing with the shouts of the people and the barking of the dogs. Neither the people nor the camp looked like the Chickasaws we had so recently left behind us.

Two women in fringed, hide dresses helped Mammy off her horse and led her toward a hide tent, Pappy following like a lost pup. "Everything will turn out fine," I assured Samboy.

Then he spoke the fear we had all hidden so well. "We can't be startin' and stoppin' all the time, Samgirl. First it was you, now it's Mammy. Simon's men will be on top of us in no time."

Albert, who stood behind us, added: "At this speed, Simon's men will get to Mexico before we do. They'll be waitin' at the border for us, just as nice as you please."

"No," said I. "Mammy will heal the girl and we'll be on our way again."

But my faith in Mammy turned out to be a little overstated. "That girl's ravin' out of her head," Mammy told us that evening. "It's goin' to be days afore I get her to talkin' straight."

"We got days," Albert lied. "You do your best, Mammy."

"There's somethin' else," Mammy said. "The Indian medicine man wants me gone. If I heal the girl, no one will trust his medicine ever again. He wants to keep the girl sick."

Albert's fingers tapped against the side of his tin supper dish. Pretty soon, the tapping turned into drumming. "All that means is we got to take turns standin' guard over that girl. If Mammy tries to make her well and the medicine man tries to make her sick, this could take months."

"We ain't got months," Samboy said. "Stop that drummin', Albert. You're janglin' my head."

Like a preacher, Albert raised his hands in the air. "Steady now, folks. We're all gettin' edgy. We'll take turns standin' guard over the girl and Mammy will do her best at doctorin'. I'll tell the Comanche we're keeping the evil spirits away."

"That ain't so far from wrong," Levi said. "What next? This running-away business is getting more complicated all the time."

What was next was that Mammy tried to urge us on our way without her. The next afternoon she told us, "The head man said he'd send me along to catch up later."

Pappy acted first. "I ain't goin' without you, Chloe." He stamped his foot on the ground and added, "And that's that."

"Well," said I, "I surely ain't going because I'm Mammy's helper."

Albert and Samboy exchanged glances. "We're Mammy's sons," Albert said. "We're stayin' where our mammy stays."

At that, Levi hoisted Gracy into his arms and looked at all of us. "We ran to Texas to catch up with you. We're surely not leavin' you now."

"That's that, then," Pappy said. "We're stayin' right with you, Chloe, until you're done with what you got to do."

The tears that glazed Mammy's eyes made them stand out like shiny stars in the night of her dark face. "Then we got work to do," she said. "Samgirl, I need some herbs. You boys set to cuttin' wood for a fire. I'll need lots and lots of wood. Ike, you help me with the poultices."

"What about me?" Gracy asked. "I wants to be a helper, too."

With one hand, Mammy pulled Gracy to her side, where the child stuck her face into Mammy's grimy apron. "You, Gracy, are goin' to be the best helper of all. You goin' to pick and pull these leaves for me into tiny bits."

Gracy poked her nose out. "Them leaves?" she asked, pointing to a bowl of herbs near Mammy's feet.

"Them leaves," Mammy said. "They'll make Missie Gracy's hands smell good." Mammy swung her free hand at us. "Scoot now. You got jobs to do."

Even with guarding Mammy's patient and helping with Mammy's doctoring, we could see that we would have time on our hands. "We can't sit around worryin'," Albert said more than once.

Levi had already solved the problem for himself. He went out trapping with some of the Indian men. Soon Samboy was riding an Indian pony without a saddle.

Next, Albert announced that it was a good time for me to improve my cowboying skills. "You got to learn to ride better and to shoot, Samgirl. We could be doin' that while we lay up and wait for Mammy to heal that Indian girl."

To my joy, Albert took on the task himself, chewing his cigarillo and concentrating on me real hard. Although Samboy had always boosted me into the saddle like a sack of dried corn and pretty much left me to fend for myself, Albert seemed determined that I learn the basics. He started by introducing me to my horse, the same broad-beamed Appaloosa that had carried me this far.

"This is Dan, Samgirl. He's yours for the trip, so you got to learn to care for him."

Albert took my hand and ran it over Dan's body. "These are the withers, here's the rump, and these are Dan's hocks."

I pulled my hand away from Albert's as if from a hot cookstove. "They look like shoulders and heels to me. Why not just call them shoulders and heels?"

Albert jammed his worn cowboy hat back on his head. "Samgirl, are you with me or against me? I'm tryin' to teach you somethin' here."

I felt sorry for Albert having to deal with a person as stubborn as I was. "All right, Albert, Dan's got withers and hocks. What else do you want me to know?"

I ended up regretting asking that question. The next thing I knew, Albert had me cleaning out the bottom of Dan's feet and learning all the parts of the saddle. Through all of this, a growing number of Comanche boys and girls stood around, watching and giggling.

When we progressed to tightening the cinch to hold the saddle on, both Dan and I resisted. "Don't be so timid," Albert roared. "Pull that cinch up tight or you'll be on the ground afore you know it."

"But Dan snarled at me," I protested. "And look at his tail thrashing around. He doesn't like the cinch."

Albert turned and walked in a circle three times before he could answer me. "No horse likes a cinch, Samgirl. You want to be on the horse's back or the ground?"

I considered this for a moment and saw the sense of Albert's line of thinking. "I want to be on the horse's back," I muttered.

"Then pull hard," Albert bellowed.

I grabbed that leather strap and yanked. Even when Dan turned his head around in my direction I kept pulling. "He's snarling at me again," I told Albert.

Albert made a fist and punched Dan in the belly. A whoosh of air replaced Dan's snarl and the cinch strap tightened and held. "Oh," said I. "That's how you do it."

Albert just shook his head and said, "Now mount."

"But Samboy always helps me up." I sensed we had more cowboying lessons coming.

Albert held a stirrup toward me. "Put your left foot here and shove off with your right foot. When you get up there, swing your leg over the saddle and sit down."

I followed Albert's instructions and landed with a resounding plop. Dan started and I grabbed the saddle horn with both hands. "I did it, Albert."

This time Albert slid his hat forward toward his eyebrows, but I could still see his eyes laughing at me. "You did it, Samgirl, but a couple hundred pounds hitting Dan in the back is goin' to spook him."

Well, naturally I was insulted by Albert's description of my weight, so the rest of the lesson didn't go very well. The next day we seemed to have more patience with each other, and Dan seemed to accept his fate. Within a few more days, I could take care of Dan and myself passably well. I didn't even have to punch him in the belly to get the cinch tight. I just sort of sweet-talked him, telling myself all the time that Dan's snarl was really a horse smile.

"You're doin' good, Samgirl," Albert told me in a grudging voice. "Let's try some runnin' now in case you need to go fast."

With his mouth, Albert made a noise at Dan and the fool horse took off in a seesaw gait that I can't describe. Pretty soon I yelled "whoa" and pulled Dan's reins to one side just like Albert had showed me. I nearly went over Dan's head when he stopped. "What was that all about?" I asked Albert. I noticed a vein pulsing in Albert's left temple.

"That's a canter, Samgirl." Albert wiped his brow with a dirty kerchief that had been hanging out of his back pocket. "Let your a— um, I mean—your bottom go with Dan's back. Think of it as a rocking chair."

"Fastest rocking chair I ever sat in," said I.

"Try it again," Albert said as he signaled Dan with his lips. We were off again. I heard Albert shout, "We haven't even gotten to the gallop yet."

I didn't care. I was letting my body sway with the rocking chair called Dan.

The shooting lessons, which usually followed riding and drew a bigger audience, didn't turn out nearly as well. Although I showed more natural talent for shooting than for riding, I didn't like anything about it. "The smoke stinks," I howled at Albert after my first shot. I dug my fists into my eyes to try to clear them.

"Step back after you shoot, Samgirl," Albert advised me, clearly amused by my lack of common sense.

On the third day, I called it quits. "I don't want anymore shooting lessons, Albert. It's smelly and makes me cough. My eyes water. My trigger finger hurts and is turning black. I don't— "

"Calm down, Samgirl. Shootin' may not be what you want it to be, but it'll protect you when you need it."

I shook my head. "So I can't shoot the rattles off a snake or hit a squirrel between the eyes. I know enough to hit something big, like a bear or a slave-catcher."

"All right, Samgirl." Albert hung his head in mock defeat. "I've got other things to do than argue with you."

"What?" said I. "What else you got to do?"

Either Albert didn't hear me or he ignored me, because he just kept going, his back getting smaller in my view. Finally, the Indians broke their circle and followed Albert, anxious to see what he was up to next.

Through all this, I think Samboy had a twinge of jealousy or two, but he was so proud to be Albert's half brother he wasn't prepared to quibble.

I could also tell that Levi felt some envy over my growing affection for Albert. I tried to keep my distance from Levi and didn't get around to discussing the matter of Albert with him. I felt happy to see Levi, yet I still puzzled about this business of not being able to bear him any babies.

chapter sixteen

Finally, on the fifth day Mammy told us the Comanche would let us go. "The girl's fever broke last night," she said. "I taught some of the women how to make poultices and tea."

"What about the medicine man?" Albert asked. "I ain't seen him around lately."

Mammy laughed and smiled. "He's my friend now. I set him to working alongside of me and showed him stuff out of my satchel. He taught me some herbs and roots I didn't know about. Now we're both smarter than we was before."

"You mean we could have quit guardin' that girl days ago?" Samboy said, his face puckered up in accusation.

"No, Samboy," Mammy said as she rubbed the hard muscles in his arm. "I told the medicine man it was the guards keepin' away the evil spirits that really done the trick. So you're guardin' turned out to be good."

Samboy relaxed. "What else did you have to do, Samboy?" I asked. "You didn't have anything to do but eat and ride ponies anyhow."

Samboy patted his belly and smiled. "I'm surely ready to get on my way now. Tomorrow, Albert?"

"Tomorrow," Albert replied, looking like one relieved man.

The next morning, we left the Comanche's main camp behind and veered farther west, hoping eventually to turn south and reach Camp Eagle Pass with no more scrapes. Albert had said no to an Indian guard. "We're in a hurry to get on our way. And we want to do it quiet-like," he explained to them.

We all followed Albert like he was Moses, come to lead us to the promised land. But as we moved along, heading steady to the west, I came to believe that every blade of grass I had seen on the prairie had turned into a buffalo here on the plains. This part of Texas was wild all the way, with thousands of greasewood trees. Most of all, as we swung toward west Texas, buffalo surged around by the millions, no, by the billions. "The ground is black all the way to the horizon," I told Levi.

"Look behind you, Samgirl. The land's dark all the way back to the sky."

At least the grass-grabbers, who ate shortgrass this time of the year, had leveled the growth so we could see where we were going. I found it hard to believe that such monstrous animals could live on grass, but there they were, grazing in the morning and night and being their curious selves in between.

I kind of liked the huge beasts, especially when Albert brought one down, skinned it, and cooked up its various parts in Mammy's smoke-blackened kettle. "They taste good," I remarked, "but the live ones are so nosy." A lot like Serena, I thought. "And they act skitterish, ready to jump this way at a spark of lightning or run over the side of a gulch at a crack of thunder."

"What's on your mind, Samgirl?" Albert asked.

"I'm afraid they'll jump this way, or run that way, and we'll be smack in the middle of the trail they intend to use at that particular time."

As usual, Samboy pooh-poohed my fears. "Me and Albert have been out here before. We've seen the buffalo stampede, but it's easy to spook them away. Ain't that right, Albert?"

Albert nodded. After that, I watched carefully as Albert threaded his way around a herd, or went out of his way to avoid them. We got by all right until the night a cracking, banging, wrenching, drenching thunderstorm hit our part of Texas. We had camped in the center of low, already nibbled grass and a few greasewood trees—which were really more like overgrown bushes—because we didn't want the buffalo coming around and eating our camp out from under us. We backed the wagon up against two or three of the trees so the wind wouldn't catch it.

As always, Gracy and Mammy and I bedded down inside the wagon and the men grouped themselves around the fire outside. The horses, tied to the other trees, nickered us right to sleep that night.

Within a few hours, we sat up wide awake, watching lightning bolt toward our wagon and turn the canvas cover into what looked like a thin sheet of parchment. "Them greasewood branches look just like witches' fingers against the cover," Mammy said.

The first drops of rain that hit looked like pebbles plopping down on the wagon top. At first we weren't too alarmed because the air carried the sweet clean smell that comes with the first few raindrops. It had been a gritty, dirty day with no waterhole on our way. We had to restrain ourselves to drizzling a few drops of water each out of the canteens and down our dry gullets. We didn't even boil up any coffee at suppertime.

With the water drops splashing, I yelled to Gracy, "Let's go. Have you ever played in the rain?"

She squealed and we jumped out the back of the wagon. Ignoring the lightning and thunder, we cavorted around like two lunatics, getting our nightdresses wet clear through to the skin. We turned our faces up to the sky and let the raindrops bounce off our noses. We laughed for the sheer joy of it all.

A dash of lightning interrupted our frolic. It streaked across the sky, lighting our camp and something else we hadn't seen: a milling herd of buffalo ready to bolt just as soon as the leader picked his direction, which looked like it would be the very spot we had already chosen to use. I threw Gracy up on the tailgate of the wagon. "Stay here until I come for you."

I ran shrieking toward the men. "Buffalo," I shouted into the wind and rain. "They're going to trample us." Even though I must have looked like a lunatic as I ran at them, the men sprang out of the bedrolls and rushed for the horses.

"Circle the horses and grab the rifles," Albert commanded the others. "We'll shoot into the air and force those crazy beasts away from our camp."

I grasped a rifle and stood with the men against the oncoming current of 2,000-pound bodies. They came at us as one, a roiling tidal wave that could destroy all in its path. We fired into the air at first and finally into the midst of the maddened brutes, but we couldn't reload fast enough to do much good. "Keep firing," Albert yelled. "It's our only chance."

The fierce beasts kept coming. They simply wanted to flee the savage cracking sounds coming from the sky and splintering over their very backs. Despite our efforts, the horde rolled on, eyes flashing yellow in the storm. Their damp coats filled the air with the odor of wet, rank wool and flesh.

"God, please help us," I prayed out loud when the leader veered slightly to our left, taking part of a greasewood tree with him. The rest also swerved, missing our camp but trampling our wagon. They threw Gracy free. In fact, I found Gracy swinging from a branch of the only greasewood tree still standing, Dog right under her cringing next to the trunk. Gracy didn't even cry; she simply waited for me to find her and get her down and hug her to my grisly-looking chest.

Mammy was a different matter. "Mammy," I moaned. "Where are you?"

When we sorted through the wreckage of the wagon, we found iron wagon bows and wheel rims pounded flat by buffalo hooves, wooden wheels in a thousand splinters, and Mammy, within the remains of her hiding place, smashed and broken almost beyond recognition. Only parts of her skin remained, holding her shattered bones in one place and letting us know she was our dead mammy.

I went crazy when I saw Mammy lying all torn and tattered in what remained of the wagon. I didn't let Gracy go from my chest while I tore around the rubble that had been our camp, screaming to the skies as I went. "It's my fault my mammy's dead," I sobbed. "And the evil buffalo. Why did they kill my mammy?"

Finally, Pappy forced me into a sitting position against a tree stump, Gracy still clinging to me like a baby sloth hanging on its mother's chest. "This ain't your fault, Samgirl," he said.

"Yes it is," I gulped. "I planned the whole thing, didn't I?"

Pappy reached out his hands. He put one hand on Gracy's shoulder and the other on my head, patting and rubbing at the same time. "Your mammy was in pain every minute of every day. The only breast she had left to her was full of lumps. The sting and ache pulled at her body and her spirit every one of her livin' moments. I know she was happy to die fast, with noise and power and glory trampling over the top of her."

I shook my head and wailed, "I know Mammy was sickly, but I wanted her to feel freedom. I promised her that—"

"You're not God," Albert boomed. "You can't promise anyone anything. Mammy got to run away. She saw Texas and her firstborn son, think on that."

I swallowed hard and nodded, feeling a bit calmer in my heart now. Then Samboy, as he had a way of doing, settled the matter. "Besides," he said, "Mammy felt freedom, even back in Mississippi. She was never a slave in her heart. That's why she carried her head so high, at least until her scarred-up chest started pulling her down. She was always a free woman, and one of God's children, in her soul."

I bowed my head into the soft, warm place where Gracy's shoulder met her neck. I sucked in her little-girl smell, still clean in that spot from our dance in the rain. I thought about how most of us had some freedom in our souls. Perhaps, as Samboy said, Mammy had a greater portion of freedom than most and that's how I had gotten so much freedom in my own soul.

"All right," I hiccuped, "I'm going to get up and go on. I'm going to quit whining and get on with it. That's what Mammy would say."

I felt tough then, but I wasn't so strong when it came to burying Mammy under what was left of the greasewood trees. Samboy and Pappy fixed up a coffin out of bits and pieces of cracked boards. Levi salvaged some iron to bind the casket. Albert dug a hole and Gracy searched in vain for any flowers, or even weeds, that had escaped the stampede.

Me, I sat crying into Mammy's iron kettle. It was clear we couldn't take the kettle with us. We'd have to bury it with Mammy. Albert had fixed up some leather strings behind the cantles of our saddles so we could each carry a rifle and Samboy had piled the few goods we had left on the mules' backs, but that kettle would have to go into the ground with Mammy.

"Think on it, Samgirl," Pappy told me. "Your mammy would like to have her kettle with her forever. Why, she'll probably tote it right up to St. Peter's gate and offer to make supper for him and his helpers."

I gulped and smiled and said, "All right, Pappy. I'm willing to leave Mammy's kettle with her and a small part of me as well." I pulled off the little nail ring that Levi had given me so long ago, that I'd worn ever since. It was the most precious thing I owned. I dropped the ring into the kettle where it made a hollow, plunking sound. When I glanced at Levi I saw he understood. His eyes had gone soft and wet.

Everybody started searching for some part of themselves to add to Mammy's kettle. Pappy shuffled by and dropped his battered pocket-knife in with a plunk. "Bye, Chloe," he whispered. "I'll see you in heaven soon."

And so it went. Samboy put in his favorite whittling knife, Levi the tiny hammer he carried in his saddlebag, Albert his handwoven leather lariat, and Gracy the only button off her only dress. Even Dog dropped in a hunk of buffalo bone. I pushed Mammy's kettle, so full of the ones she loved and those who loved her, to the graveside where Albert lowered it in.

"Now I'm ready to leave Mammy," said I and turned my face south, determined never to look back again. I wanted to remember Mammy as I had known her once—brown and round and smiling and loving.

The Comanche had traveled light, hunting along the way, and so could we. Our wagon and most of our supplies were gone. We would live like the Comanche on the move.

The result was that I ate more meat than I ever had. I once thought I'd be in my glory days if I could eat meat all the time, nothing but chicken, turkey, deer, squirrel, possum, duck, rabbit, pork, whatever. It all sounded so delicious and like I could never eat enough of it to satisfy me in a lifetime. But meat was *all* we ate now. I was good and sick of it.

Since Mammy died, Albert and Levi had been doing the cooking. For one thing, they were strictly meat-cookers. For another, our fresh food was long gone. Even the cornmeal and dried peaches had disappeared longer ago than I could remember. Anyway, any supplies that hadn't been eaten had been trampled by the terrified buffalo during the storm.

"We can't trade," Albert said. "We've got no goods or money."

"Who would we trade with anyway?" I asked. "I'm not anxious to trade with the Comanches. I'd rather keep my distance from them."

For once Samboy agreed with me. "Your plannin' and supplies got us this far, Samgirl. Now we'll have to live off the land."

Because it was deep fall we sometimes came across some nuts or berries. Most of the time, one or another of the men went out hunting or trapping. They came back with prairie chicken, wild turkeys or hogs, deer, squirrel, possum, duck, or rabbit. Albert and Levi fixed the meat well enough, frying it right over the fire or putting it in a pot to boil. True, it wasn't the same as Mammy's, but the real problem was that it soon tasted dreadful without some greens or potatoes or fruit with it.

After the first few days of our meat diet, my stomach turned tight and hard. I had a constant pain hanging somewhere near the bottom of my intestines. As far as passing waste was concerned, it hardly seemed worth the time to try. What we needed was some of the cornmeal we had relied on—and often complained about.

Gracy turned her head away and whimpered when I tried to put a tidbit of meat in her birdie mouth. "Look at this, Gracy," I'd urge her. "It's the moistest, best bit of all."

Gracy usually turned sad eyes on whatever I offered. Sometimes she ate a piece and always had hiccups later. She just mooned around the camp after supper, looking like a piglet who couldn't find her mammy's teats. I could see how Gracy longed for a piece of cornbread with molasses on it, or maybe some wild strawberries with honey.

I spent hours trying to remember what garlic smelled like when Mammy broke it open. "I'll never smell garlic again," I told Samboy.

"That wouldn't be all bad," he said. "You and garlic don't make good company anyway."

I flounced away from my brother, flinging hurtful words over my shoulder as I went. "None of us are going to live long enough to get to a place that has freedom and food too."

I could see the men were all losing weight, despite their grunts of pretended pleasure and words saying how happy they were to have another squirrel or coon. Pappy's muscles had already turned flabby around the edges and Samboy had dark circles under his eyes. Albert appeared more gaunt than ever, with his last chewed-up cigarillo hanging out of his mouth. Levi would never be taken for a blacksmith. We were a sorry-looking bunch.

"Can I go off the path—such as it is—a ways to look for berries?" I asked Albert one morning.

"No," he shouted at me with an exasperated look on his face. "You're so worried about food. You want to become some Indian's next meal yourself?"

Samboy tried to break the tension by teasing me: "See, Samgirl, you should have learned to cook from Mammy when you had the chance."

"I could cook," I grumbled back at him, "if we had something *to* cook."

Levi chimed in then. "I think I'm getting scurvy."

"What's that?" asked I. "It sounds like a fungus growing on your skin."

"No, it's something sailors get when they're too long at sea. Your body ain't getting enough fresh stuff. Pretty soon, your gums start to bleed and you feel kind of weak."

At that, I hugged Gracy closer to my chest. We both had bleeding gums and I surely felt weak most of the time. The real shame of it was that if Mammy had been with us, she might have been able to tell us which grasses and roots we could eat to make up for the lack of foods we were used to. Now that Levi had mentioned scurvy, I could remember Mammy talking about something called scurvy grass that went in with the pot with other greens. I wondered if it could help us and if we were walking right on top of it and didn't know it.

Gradually, we stopped talking as we rode along. We had to conserve our energy to get to the next stop and to hope it would be a better place than the last. Samboy turned so cranky that he twisted his horse's ears to make him stand still at saddling time. Albert was the worst; he seemed to take all the blame for our troubles on his own shoulders.

"If I were a real trailhand I would know how to survive out here in nowhere Texas." He waved a thin hand toward the grasslands that stretched away from us on every side.

"You're a real trailhand," Levi said. "Why, you're the best roper I know. I've seen you throw overhanded head catches and heeling catches and even a backhand slip catch. And you can— "

"We haven't got any cows to tend now," Albert broke in. "What I mean is I don't know how to feed myself out in the wilds. I always relied too much on the cookwagon and cookie to fix up a plate of beans and greens and meat."

"It ain't your fault, Albert," Pappy piped up. "You're doin' the best you can."

"My best ain't good enough, especially since you're all my family."

Samboy roused himself enough to say, "We'll get there, Albert. You'll see."

Albert glanced back. He saw Samboy riding crooked on top of his horse, sort of leaning over to the left. He turned his horse and rode back to Samboy and said, "What's wrong? You want some water?"

Samboy couldn't answer. He just reached out his hand for the canteen. Instead, Albert opened the canteen and tipped it into Samboy's mouth. "See, that," he said, "a few drops. If we don't find proper food and water we're goin' to be dead and these horses with us."

Then Albert got the idea to let his horse have his head because he might be able to sniff out some water. As he walked along behind his horse, Albert ordered us, "Let up on your reins and see what happens."

What happened was that Albert's horse found a water hole all right, except that a herd of thirsty mustangs already surrounded it. They neighed and brayed, stamped and shuffled, kicked and pranced so that we couldn't get within a quarter mile of the water hole. As we sat with our tongues dangling out and wishing for water, Gracy pointed to the ground and saved our lives. "Dere," she said. "Water's down dere."

I looked and saw nothing but thousands of horse tracks that had nicked the ground beyond recognition. "Where, child?" asked I, thinking Gracy had gone out of her head at last.

"Dere," she said again. "In them little holes."

I looked again. The horses' hooves had dug so deep into the dirt that some water had come to the surface and filled in the hoof dents. The holes and their water sat at our feet like tiny springs, just waiting to rescue us.

We slid down and quickly learned the art of drinking out of horse "springs." We each took a tin spoon out of our mess kits and spooned drop after drop of water into our mouths. Our horses and Dog also drank, but without spoons.

I credited the wild horses with saving our lives, and also that Gracy child. Had she not looked down, our horses would have found the water anyway, or so Albert said, but Gracy seeing the water made her more dear to me than ever. "You're not as foolish as you look, Gracy," said I, teasing her.

"I know it. That's what my grandmammy used to say."

I learned from Gracy's answer that certain bantering goes on season after season and is handed down from generation to generation. I prayed we'd all be around long enough to hear Gracy use that same joshing on her young ones.

Maybe the worst thing of all was the heat. It seemed to get drier and hotter, flatter and dustier, as we veered southward. I didn't know it would be so hot and humid in Texas in November. The vegetation had turned dry and brown; wilted grass, wilted leaves, wilted everything seemed to surround us.

Overcast days gave us our only relief. Even then, the clouds seemed to hold the heat to the earth and stew us in our own sweat. Everyone was utterly wrung out with the heat. I fashioned a sling affair around my waist. In the front, it held Gracy in the saddle next to my crotch, because I feared I would weaken and let her go. In the back, the sling held Dog on the horse's loins. Dog fared better than most of us, but I could see he wasn't going to make it without some help.

"That's the first time in my life I saw a dog ride horseback," Albert said. "I don't— "

"She'd never leave Dog behind," Samboy interrupted. "Dog is Samgirl's best friend."

I turned around and stuck my tongue out at Samboy. The joking didn't stop my worrying. Everything around was arid and seared, the ground and the grass and especially us. Even though I could feel the sunburn on my face, I had no salve to treat it with. Because the buffalo had destroyed Mammy's medicine satchel, we had no way to doctor any illness or injury.

One afternoon, we poked along, drooping off our horses. We let the sultry air push us farther toward insensibility, and the horses along with us, when a roaring sound forced its way into our minds. "What would make such a roar way out here?" asked I.

"Look," Albert said, "see that grey cloud on the horizon? That doesn't mean rain coming, it means a prairie fire."

"It's a long ways from us," Samboy said in a hopeful way.

"Yup," Albert agreed, "but prairie fires move a hundred miles an hour. It'll be here directly."

We all stood dumb and dismayed at this news. Finally Samboy asked, "What do we do now, Albert?"

"We don't have any water," Albert replied in his maddening calm, terse way, "so we can't fight it. We don't have any plows or shovels, so we can't dig a firebreak between the fire and us. The only hope we got is to outrun it."

I almost laughed at that, given the state of ourselves and our animals. We couldn't outrun a pack of rats if they were so foolish as to want anything we had left. "We ain't running no place," said I. "We ain't got no run left in us."

Albert nodded and thought a minute. "There's one other thing we can try. I saw it done once and it worked. That fire will burn toward us in a long, thin line. It'll eat up this spot where we're standing in seconds and zoom right on past us. What we got to do is wait until the fire's almost to us. Then we ride into it as it's going past us. That means it won't be chasing us. Instead, we ride right through it and get on its other side."

"Samboy," said I, hope pounding in my chest, "what do you think?"

"I think we ain't got a choice."

"Me, too," said Levi and Pappy at the same time.

I bent my head into the place I liked in Gracy's neck and whispered, "We're going for a wild ride, right through a wall of fire. You ever done that before?"

"No, I rode through tall grass with Pappy," she answered in her squeaky, little-girl voice. "I rode in pouring rain with you. Nobody ever took me through fire."

"I'm going to take Missie Gracy through fire in a few minutes," said I, as I watched the fire fill the horizon with shooting, jumping red-and-orange pillars of flame. It came at us with more thunder and speed than the buffalo had. Only it smelled different. It destroyed the air and turned it to acid, unbreathable by humans or animals.

"Albert," said I, already feeling sickly with the acrid smell, "should we put our blankets over our heads?"

"Yes," he said and then added with a grin, "you're not as foolish as you look, Samgirl. Let's cover the horses' heads too. Spur them on hard into that blaze. We'll either die in it or see each other on its burned-out side."

We all yanked our blankets out of our saddle packs, while Pappy and Levi jerked the two remaining pack mules up next to their horses. We couldn't speak, the din was too great. It sounded like you had put your head in an iron kettle with someone hammering on the outside; like the thunder from every storm in the world had come together in that one place; like the earth was cracking and caving in on itself.

I ducked into the tent I'd made with my blanket over my head, over Gracy, Dog, and the horse too. I had pointed Dan at that line of fire. "As soon as I feel it burning its way toward us," I told Gracy, "we'll walk forward, nice and steady, no panic or rush."

"I'm goin' too, ain't I?" Gracy asked.

"You're going too, Gracy," said I as I wondered if this meant the end for all of us. I reached back and scooted Dog nearer my body.

I almost started out too soon. The heat of the flames burned so intensely I thought I felt my skin starting to bubble and my hair to singe. Gracy had put her face smack into my chest scars and said nothing at all. Dan gave a high, piercing whinny that shivered its way along my spine. When he saw I wasn't going to give way he held steady.

When I couldn't hear anymore because the roar made me deaf, couldn't breathe anymore because smoke clogged every pore in the blanket, couldn't think anymore because I was sure my horse was dying under me, I urged Dan forward, a step at a time.

Dan either understood our strategy or, more likely, got a hotfoot, because he started trotting along right smart. Even though he had been one of Simon's sturdiest horses, I didn't know Dan had it in him. I prayed that Gracy would hold her breath long enough, but I didn't have ample breath myself to remind her. I felt nothing behind me so I also prayed Dog was still there.

Dan walked us through a tunnel of hell itself, a black passageway with Satan's crimson lights streaking up from the ground, with the Devil's own smoke cutting us off from anything living, with God's salvation beckoning from the other side. When Dan stopped, I drew back the blanket from our heads and gulped in the sulphur-and-brimstone smelling air. "We're alive, Gracy."

She came out of her cocoon and gasped at the air. Although it was far from pure country air, it was breathable and life-giving.

As my eyes cleared of smoke and grime, I saw before me nothing. Every blade of grass, every mesquite bush, every greasewood tree was gone, stripped right off the earth as if they had never existed. The soil itself was black and scorched and smoking, giving off strange, steamy fumes that made it look like it would explode and fling itself toward the sky. The air hovered somber and still around my head. Not a bird chirped or crossed the sky, not a small creature moved or perhaps even lived. The sun itself seemed pasty in comparison with the fire that had just laid bare this part of Texas.

"We survived," said I to Gracy, "but for what? We didn't have much before. We got nothing now."

I slid down off Dan. I felt the most sorry for him, for he had singed hair and burned patches up his sturdy legs right to the bottom of his belly. His hooves were cracked and charred, like they would take a long time to grow healthy again. As I studied Dan, I dragged Gracy and what was left of Dog with me.

"You seem fine, child."

"Yes, Mammy," she piped.

I had the idea Gracy could survive anything, as long as she could dive into my chest while it happened.

Dog huffed and puffed like an old yellow cigar trying to get itself lit. "Ain't you had enough fire and flash for one day?" said I to Dog. "Looks like you better get yourself a breath of air, even if it is putrid."

I turned my face back to Gracy and said, "That dog ain't going to hang round me anymore if I keep on getting him involved in this fire or that. He's going to find someone less fire-minded than me."

I stood there and thought about what I would do if I had to survive out there alone with one child, one dog, and one horse. Then I heard coughing and hacking behind me. As Albert and Samboy stumbled toward me I sighed. "You all look the worse for wear," said I.

"You should see yourself, especially your hair," Samboy said. "Dog has more hair on his tail than you've got left on your head."

Suddenly I felt worried and asked, "Where's Pappy and Levi? Why aren't they with you?"

"Because they're busy stripping the little bit of stuff we got left off the pack mules. Those poor animals are fouled with smoke and got to be put down."

A shot, followed by a second one, pierced my consciousness. The sudden noise robbed me of whatever particles of good sense I had left. I screamed and kept on that way until Samboy slapped me across my right cheek.

"Don't do that to my mammy," Gracy squealed. "She didn't do nothin' to you."

At that, we all laughed. We must have appeared a fright, as bad as the Chickasaw Indians that "captured" us our first day out in Indian Territory and had blue-and-yellow stripes painted around their mouths. Except that our stripes came from sweat drizzling its way down through the soot on our faces and making us shades of brown, black, and blacker yet.

chapter seventeen

After the fire, the air hung sluggish and oppressive over the burned-out land. The odor of smoke gagged us. "We'll never get the stench out of our skin and hair," I complained to Samboy.

"You're alive, ain't you," he snarled back.

We staggered along beside our horses, praying to find some water. The fire had come at us from the north and burned its way south, leaving both those directions stark and bare. So we walked to the west and planned to turn south again as soon as we got out of the fire-scarred zone.

I had put Gracy in Dan's saddle. Gracy was so skinny and shriveled Dan probably didn't even know she was there. Dog and I tottered along next to Dan. Night plummeted down as we finally sighted grass at the edge of the scorched earth. I'd like to say we speeded up, but we were unable to do anything more than move at a crawl.

We got to the grass, bore south, and practically walked into a tiny spring bubbling and singing in the unburned earth. Albert had sense enough to keep the horses and Dog from drinking their fill all at once, but he let us go to it.

"I got to frow up," Gracy said.

Pretty soon, we all vomited into the grass around that spring. When our stomachs settled a bit, we tried again. This time, we used our spoons just as we had to get the water out of the horse tracks. I gave Gracy a spoonful of water, then myself, then Gracy, and so on until we could hold it down.

About then, I thought how glad I felt that Levi hadn't heard Gracy call me Mammy. I didn't want him getting any ideas about how far my masquerading as his wife and her mammy was going to go. In spite of everything we'd been through together, I still worried about not being able to bear him babies. I no longer had Simon pressuring me, but I was sure Levi would want some free babies because he was so sweet with Gracy—whenever he could get her away from me, that is.

Levi was a natural pappy. He just seemed to have a feel for the right thing to do or say around children. I had noticed that back on Simon's plantation in Indian Territory. When Levi was at home and not out working on the trail, he always had little children hanging around his forge, asking him this and that and going away with a nail or a bit of scrap metal. I watched Levi shape tiny pieces of iron into forms, like cabins and dogs and horses, and give them to the children.

Once I asked Levi about it. "Why do you let the children bother you?"

"They're no bother," he said. "I love children whether they're short or tall, tubby or lean, mouthy or mild. Why, those children lighten my day."

"How do they do that?" asked I, doubt hanging in my eyes.

"Let me think," he said. "One day I told them I was going back on the trail pretty soon. One girl asked me if that was the trail to her grandmammy's house." At that, my heart flopped over. I knew it was the only trail that child had ever seen.

"Another time," Levi went on, "I mentioned Peggy, one of the house slaves, and one little boy piped up, 'What kind of name is that?' he said. 'Who would name their sweet baby such a thing?' "

"What's wrong with the name of Peggy?" I asked. I had always liked the name. I thought it sounded romantic and lighthearted.

"Seems he was hearing it slightly different. He thought we called her Piggy. He sure got angry over the unfairness of giving such a name to a sweet woman like Peggy."

I giggled at that. I saw where maybe I should pay more attention myself to the girls and boys milling around the quarters, getting under everybody's feet and asking "what's this?" or "what's that?" all the time.

When Levi showed up in Texas with Gracy, I knew he doted on that child. After all, he had risked his own life to go pluck her out of slavery and take her with him to Texas. Levi wasn't a reckless man. He had told me himself, "I know having a child along might slow me down and maybe catch me up, one way or the other." Yet Levi still stole that girl away and hauled her toward Mexico.

Besides that, after supper at night Levi would take Gracy on his knee by the campfire and tell her stories that he made up right out of his head, about possums and crows and other creatures. I always noticed the way Gracy gripped Levi tight, like she feared he might disappear from her life again. When I saw Gracy do that to Levi, jealousy burned in my throat. I was never sure if I wanted Levi to myself or Gracy to myself.

It would be a miracle, I thought one night, if I could have them both to myself. "Such a dream could never come true," I said out loud. "Not only would Levi want free babies, but he would want a son." As much as he loved Gracy, I could just picture what that man could teach a boy.

Anyway, I glanced around quick-like, afraid that Levi watched me and read my thoughts. I was lucky; Levi had left the fire, headed away from the camp to go scouting for food. From the sag of his back I could tell he was using his last drop of energy. From his hand trailed a trap he had devised out of vines and young, green twigs. He had learned a lot from the Comanche. Now Levi obviously hoped to spot a squirrel or rabbit.

"Good hunting, Levi," Albert called after him. "The game should be good. It probably ran here to get away from that fire."

It didn't take long for Levi to drag back into camp, such as it was. His trap hung from his hand, as empty now as when he left. Them animals must have skittered farther away from the fire than Albert thought. In his pockets, Levi had some nuts and currants. We had to content ourselves with those for supper.

"At least we have clean, cool water to drink," said I in an attempt to make the best of the situation.

"Yeah," Samboy said. "Try chewin' water."

Still, we made the most we could of the water, drinking it and filling our canteens and washing in it. Why, I even gave Dog a bath to try to turn him back into a yellow dog instead of a dirty grayish one.

I gazed around and could see that everyone else felt more dead than alive, too. Levi kept his distance from me, though once or twice I caught him watching me sideways. I wondered if he held back on purpose. Maybe he didn't care that much about me after all. Or maybe he let Gracy do his work for him. If so, she did a good job. I felt more and more like she was a child of my own womb and he was my husband for real.

After our pathetic supper, Gracy went to Levi for her story. That man managed to dredge one up from somewhere in his depths. "I'm goin' to tell you a tale about a brave girl. She rode right through a flaming wall of fire. She came out again on the other side. What do you think about that?"

Gracy grinned up at her daddy, but I had half a feeling that Levi meant me rather than Gracy, that he was praising me for my courage. In spite of that, jealousy soured my saliva because Dog had gone over there too, nuzzling Levi's hand and trying to get a pat on his earless head, which, despite my washing him, still had coal-colored spots here and there.

I felt happy when Gracy and Dog returned to me, although I was not so happy for Levi's aloneness. When we settled down to sleep—no, we didn't have a campfire—I laid on my side as usual. Dog snuggled up to my back and Gracy nestled into her customary place at my stomach. All had fallen quiet around us when Gracy piped up, " 'Night, Mammy. I love you."

Did Levi hear? I bet he did. Did Levi grin? I bet he did. Did I grin? Yes. And no.

The following morning, we straggled out of our fire-stinking beds. We longed for the smell of coffee or the odor of frying bacon to lure us from our threadbare, singed blankets.

"There's nothing but water," Albert said, "so you better drink your fill."

We also watered the horses. I wept inside that I had nothing—no salve or grease of any kind—to put on Dan's blistered legs. I also watched Samboy and Pappy with a close eye to see what hurt they might have suffered. What I saw made me shudder. Although Samboy limped and lagged about, his youth showed through. Pappy limped and lagged about, but he looked like an old man.

For the first time, I saw my pappy as a man of advanced years, years filled with love for Mammy and us to be sure, yet also filled with aching, breaking work in some other man's fields. Those years had forced a lack of self-respect on Pappy; how could a man honor himself when he was all the time taking orders from someone else and being called nigger? White folks' hatred and fear of Pappy and his kind also marked those years, along with patrollers and slave-catchers waiting to punish the least trespass of white peoples' rules. And death tinged those years, first the death of the slave baby Mammy and Pappy didn't want and, more recently, Mammy's ruin by lack of medical care and by the hooves of storm-crazed buffalo.

I slipped over next to Samboy and whispered, "We got to keep better watch over Pappy. He's aging fast, as we go along this trail to freedom."

I noticed Samboy didn't look too sturdy either, but he pulled himself together and said, "You're right, Samgirl. I'll try to watch out for him better. But he's a strong man, he's going to get through this."

A chill tickled its way along my backbone. "Samboy, you're young. You don't realize what Pappy's gone through in his lifetime. I bet that fire was harder on him than we think. Why, he couldn't have much breathing room left in his lungs after all the years he's spent working in ginning rooms and corn-shucking houses, with all that dust clogging the air."

I knew Samboy tried hard to understand. He answered, "I hear you, Samgirl. You got to have hope. He's our pappy, he's going to take care of us for a long time yet."

I turned away from Samboy, knuckling his arm the way I used to do when he was younger, and strolled over to where Pappy struggled to lift his saddle to his horse's back. "Let me help with that, Pappy," I said and right away saw I'd made a mistake.

"I can saddle my own horse, Samgirl," he said. "I'm not dead yet."

"All right, Pappy. I'm just trying to help. How are you feeling this morning?"

Pappy broke into coughing and his eyes got red and teary. In a minute, he said, "I feel just like everybody else, real bad. I'm starving and cranky. I don't think we're ever goin' to reach the promised land after all."

This startled me and made me think I was right to worry about Pappy. "We're somewhere in south Texas, Pappy. I believe the worse is behind us now."

Pappy snapped back at me, "You're wrong, Samgirl. It's goin' to get worse yet. We're all goin' to die if we don't do something pretty soon. We don't got food. The horses can't carry the weight of us no more. We're almost out of ammunition. We're goin' to drop dead right here in south Texas. The buzzards will feast on our hides. Nobody will even know or care about our passin' from this life."

Pappy gasped for breath after such a long speech. I asked, "You miss Mammy, don't you?"

Pappy studied me with his rheumy eyes and finally muttered, "Yes, I miss your mammy. I'm ready to join Chloe anytime now."

"Pappy, Pappy," I murmured as I threw my arms around his bony shoulders. "You still got us. We love you and— "

"I know that, Samgirl. I love you too, but I want to go. I want to be with Chloe."

At that, I hugged Pappy and went back to my own preparations. As I pulled Gracy to my chest, I almost cried. I hoped and prayed we would find decent food so Pappy would rally and look at the world with a brighter eye.

We started out that morning, leaving the blackened land behind us, moving southward with little hope showing in our demeanor. We each straggled alongside our horses, except for Gracy, who now rode on Levi's horse. As puny as Gracy was, my horse seemed too tuckered to carry any more than his saddle.

I walked behind Albert, who held his usual place at the front of our wretched procession, chewing a weed now that his cigarillos were gone. I got to thinking about what drove that man. He could go back to cowboying. He had no reason to stay with us now that Mammy had died. Pappy and Levi weren't kin to Albert. Too, me and Samboy were only half-related to Albert, who hadn't even known about us during his growing-up years.

The lay of Albert's shoulders, low and dejected-like, told me he wasn't in any mood for conversation but, being me, I started anyway. "Hey, Albert," I said from behind him.

"No, you ain't goin' off on your own in search of food," he replied in a snarling voice.

"I don't want to search for food. I'm getting real used to being skinny. I kind of like it."

At that, Albert glanced back and half-grinned. "What do you want then?"

"I want to know why you're doing this," said I, as bold as the white-and-yellow daisies that used to pop up every springtime by our cabin steps back in Mississippi.

"Because you're all my family," he said.

"Actually," said I, "Pappy's not your pappy and Levi's not your brother. And me and Samboy are only half to—"

Albert turned quick, like a snake, and hissed, "Blood ain't all there is to it. You're all my family through love. I got no one else in the world and I love no one else in the world."

"Oh," said I, thinking over his words and taking them into my heart. Then I tried again: "You think we're going to make it to Mexico?"

This time Albert didn't look back, he just said, "I'm not God. Only He knows if we're goin' to make it."

Like a bee at a flower, I kept pestering Albert: "What are we going to do in Mexico if we make it?"

I saw Albert sigh. He said, "I got a friend there. He works for a *rico* who owns a big ranch. I believe the *rico* will hire us, maybe even give us some land to plant, like he did my friend."

"Where's this *rico* located in Mexico? Have we got to go far to find him?"

"He lives near Monterrey," Albert answered, seeming resigned now to my badgering him when he was half-dead already. "South of Saltillo. It's a ways from the border, but we'll be traveling as free blacks once we get into Mexico."

"If," I pressed even more, "we're going to get to Mexico, we got to do something about our sorry state. We need food and— "

"What you got in mind, Samgirl?" he asked in that same despondent tone, his shoulders dragging lower toward the ground all the time.

"How about if we send Levi into the next settlement and he offers to do some blacksmithing in exchange for food?" I suggested.

"You know we're trying to stay away from towns. What if they turn us in, or put us on the block, or, worse yet, kill us outright?"

"They may do one or all of those things to us, but if we don't give it a try we're going to drop dead right here and be eaten by buzzards. Even Pappy says so."

Albert sighed again and said, "All right, we'll give your idea a try. That is, if Levi is willing."

Satisfied, I dropped back a bit. I offered to take Levi's place by his horse's and Gracy's side. "Albert wants to talk to you," I told Levi. "We got a plan."

Levi simply nodded and moved up toward Albert. In a few minutes, I saw them with their heads together, arguing and pointing, pointing and arguing. A few more minutes and Levi came back. "I'm willing to go into a settlement," he said. "It's all we've got left. Or else we're going to die right here and never taste freedom at all."

My scarred chest burst with pride. I told Levi so. "You're a good man and a brave one, Levi. We'll all pray until you come back to us."

"Hold on, Samgirl. It might be days before we see a town. We might die before we get there."

"Then I'll start praying now. I'll pray we find some folks and find them fast."

Levi glanced at me sideways and said, "I've got something else to say to you."

I thought to myself I had big trouble now, that he wanted to talk about me and him and Gracy. I soon learned I was mistaken. "I'm afraid," Levi began, "your pappy ain't goin' to make it."

"Why do you say that?" I asked, as beads of sweat popped out all over my forehead and neck.

"That fire did Ike no good. He's rasping and coughing like he can't catch his breath."

"I know," said I, my head hanging low. "I know and— "

"He misses Aunt Chloe something fierce," Levi added. "He wants to die himself and join her in heaven. Ike's certain that Aunt Chloe went straight to heaven, kettle and all."

"I know that, too. I talked to Samboy about it and he said we have to have hope, that— "

"Yes," replied Levi, his throat strangled with tears, "we've got to have hope."

That night Levi trapped a rabbit, so we ate meat once again, along with the water we had brought from the little spring. We also ate the weeds we tore from the ground in handfuls and chewed the best we could. If I'd been in a better mood, I would have laughed. There we sat like a small herd of starving cows, shoving grass into our mouths as fast as possible and nibbling our cuds afterwards, trying to get every bit of flavor out of the weeds.

The next day we didn't see any sign of people, settled or traveling. Late that afternoon, Albert walked to the top of a rise. "I see what looks like smoke wiggling up into the sky," he said. "But it's some distance away."

That night we were even more desperate; we ate rattlesnake meat and weeds and water. I was surprised we were alive at all. "I've cut off the snake's rattles with my knife, Samgirl," Albert told me. "Do you want them for a necklace?"

I looked at Albert's hopeful eyes and thought a minute. "No," I finally said. "I don't want to carry a memento of this starving time along with me."

I didn't sleep much that night. Instead, I thought about the kitchens and pantries and larders in that hamlet ahead. I dreamed of beans and bacon and greens and garlic and fruits and cornbread and molasses and every other type of food I had ever tasted or even heard about.

Gracy and Dog must have dreamed about food too. They fidgeted all night long. We no longer fit together because we were all bones instead of curves. Their twisting and turning just made it worse. I almost fell asleep once or twice, but then my sharp-edged hip bumped Gracy awake, or that infernal dog banged my backbone with what I called his knee, being as I had no other word handy to describe that part of a dog.

Dog had gotten to be as much of a spectacle as the rest of us. I knew for a fact what the expression "bag of bones" meant. Dog was little more than a skeleton with yellow hair on its outside. He limped, he stumbled, he staggered, yet he never once whimpered or whined. "See," I told Samboy. "I always knew Dog had a loyal heart."

By mid-afternoon, we came into sight of the village. "It's almost as ragtag as we are," Albert said in a hopeless tone.

We made camp along a stream and rested, gathering any last bits of energy and will we might have left in us. We washed up Levi the best we could, and sent him into town to offer his services in exchange for victuals.

In the meantime, Albert and Samboy went in search of food. Me and Pappy prayed for Levi, while Gracy and Dog slept away their hunger.

Levi came trudging back again about suppertime, carrying two small cotton sacks, one in each hand. He appeared sassy, yet at the same time drawn.

First things first, I thought to myself, so I took the sacks and drew out their contents. We immediately tore into some flat things made out of cornmeal. "They call those *tortillas*," Levi said.

Beans we set to boiling in our only pan, while we placed some cooked rice wrapped in corn shucks in the coals to heat. At the bottom of one sack I found some tobacco leaves for Albert and some salve for burns, which we spread over the horses' legs and our own blisters.

As starved as we were, we forced ourselves to eat slowly and carefully. We had learned our lesson about vomiting at the spring a ways back. Besides, we wanted to savor the food and each luscious flavor. I thought I detected a bit of garlic, but something hot overwhelmed it, something I had never tasted in my life.

"That's called *jalapeño*," Levi said, acting real smart about everything. "And the doctor-woman that sent the salve is called a *curandera*. When you're done stuffing your faces, I'll tell you all about the folks in the town."

After we finished, we all lay back on the ground and admired the twilight drifting down over our hillside of peace and food. Albert had rolled his tobacco in a green leaf and sucked on his crude cigarillo. I noticed that Gracy still clutched a tortilla. Even though she couldn't eat another bite, she wasn't about to let that tortilla out of her grasp. Dog had a grain or two of rice clinging to his whiskers and seemed real satisfied.

Pretty soon, one by one we sat up and eyed Levi, waiting to hear what more he had to say. I also prayed, thanking the Lord for bringing him back to us unharmed. I decided that, when the right time came, I would talk to Levi about babies. I'll find out, I promised myself, how he feels about wanting more children and having a son and so on.

Levi knew we were ready to listen, so he said, "They're poor people, but they're willing to help us some. At first I thought they wanted to kill me because they ran around squawking some strange words I couldn't fathom. I kept hearing a few words over and over, like *Tejano* and *Tejana* and *Español*. Then they took me to the priest, who teaches school in a raggedy little room at the back of an adobe church. He talked real good English and he explained them to me, and me to them."

We all busted in at once with questions. Levi raised a big black hand in our faces. "Let me tell it first," he said. "The priest told me that *Tejanos* are Texan-Mexicans. They hate Anglos—white people—for driving them off their lands and taking over their pastures. They also hate Anglos for what they did in the Mexican War."

I thought this was getting complicated, but I nodded and waited for Levi to go on, which he did. "When I told the priest we were slaves running away to Mexico and freedom, tears trickled down his cheeks. 'You're going to my homeland, which I left years ago for this mission,' he said and cried a little bit more."

Levi stopped to take a drink of water. We glanced at each other with wondering eyes until he was ready to continue. "Then that priest told the folks—who all tried to jam themselves into that one little room—

that I wanted to work, that I'm a blacksmith who needed to earn food for my people."

I couldn't restrain myself any longer; the subject of food was too crucial to me. I busted in, "What did the people say to that? Did you work? Are more victuals coming?"

"They said they already got a blacksmith and they're poor, which I already knew. They said they'll give us what they can, that we should camp here for a few days and eat and rest up some."

Albert could contain himself no longer: "Where are we, man? How far to the Rio Grande and the Mexican border?"

"We're in an area they call New Sonora, after old Sonora back in Mexico. They say it ain't really a town, just a bunch of *peons* who work for a *rico* and try to raise some corn and cows on their own."

Despite his fatigue, Albert jumped up and began to dance, or at least as much of a dance as an indrawn man like him ever learned to do. "Did they say anything about caves?" he asked when he stopped twirling around.

Levi pondered a minute and said, "The priest drew a map with a piece of charcoal on the school wall. He said something about caverns or caves . . . a grotto, I think he called it."

"I know where we are," Albert near-shouted, almost losing his green cigarillo from his mouth. Because our map had fallen to pieces long ago, Albert snatched up a stick and scratched a map in the dirt. "We're here, north of the Rio Grande. If we let the horses recover, or trade them for better ones, we've got about a week's travel to get to Camp Eagle Pass where we can cross into Mexico."

I looked around and saw lots of glowing eyes. What a difference some food and the promise of freedom made, I thought.

The following morning Albert announced that he, Levi, and Samboy would go into town and do whatever work they could in exchange for the rice and beans and tortillas the *Tejanos* would share with us. "Samgirl, you and Pappy and Gracy will stay in camp. Do what you can to patch our tattered clothes and blankets. Wash up everything for the final distance ahead."

Before leaving, Albert warned me, "You can poke around for berries and such, but stay close to camp. We can see you up near the top of this hill. If you need help, tie a piece of light-colored rag on a tree branch. We'll come right away."

Me and Gracy found some berries and some dandelions, which we picked and boiled up over a tiny fire. Pappy didn't do much of anything. He just lay around, once in awhile working on a bridle and trying to mend it. We ate rice and beans at noon and were mighty glad to have them.

The day passed without mishap. When Albert and Levi and Samboy came back that night, toting more small sacks, we gobbled our plain supper and offered thanks to God for it and our lives.

Things went on this way for four days. Mornings and afternoons, Albert and Levi and Samboy helped the *Tejanos* in whatever way they could. Although bone-thin and exhausted, between them they managed to shore up the priest's tiny schoolroom and whitewash the church and clean up the town square and dredge out the well; things the people of the town didn't have time to do because they were so busy making a bare living.

On the fifth day, our menfolks planned to patch the roofs, which were mostly thatch or red tile, replacing worn spots and repairing leaks. They would also help the priest decorate the church for Christmas, which the *Tejanos* started celebrating near the beginning of December.

In the meantime, I grew worried about Levi. He had perked up and seemed stronger. I had forgotten how portly he could look. "You spend a lot of words," I told him, "praising the women down below. You're always saying how nice they keep their houses, with peppers and such hanging on beams outside to dry in the sun."

Levi missed my point. He just went off describing the women's shawls, which he insisted on calling *rebozos*. Just in time, I remembered we'd be on our way soon and leaving those women behind us.

When it hit me that there would be more of those women where we were going, my stomach turned with jealousy. I felt as green as a new spring twig. In despair, I reckoned Levi could find a fertile wife from among such women. I started to think that maybe I shouldn't talk to Levi about babies after all. "Anyway," I muttered, "I have plenty of time before we reach Monterrey to worry about that."

I also decided that I'd like to see those women for myself. The evening of the fourth day, I convinced Samboy to stay in camp with Pappy the next day, while Gracy and I went into town in his place. "Levi and Albert can work on the roofs," I argued, "while Gracy and I help in the church with the Christmas decorations."

"There isn't that much more we can do in town anyway," Albert chimed in, a proper cigarillo dangling from his lips. "Samgirl and Gracy might as well go in and meet the people who helped them."

"Yeah," I added. "I'd like to say thank you to those people." I didn't mention my desire to see the *señoritas*.

Fortunately for me, Samboy gave in gracefully. "I've been wantin' to spend some time with Pappy anyway. So you go on into town tomorrow in my place, Samgirl."

eighteen

On that fifth morning, we made a merry procession marching into town: Albert, Levi, me, and Gracy. I hoped that the young women would see me with Levi and give up any ideas they might have about him. That's why I made Albert and Levi come to the church with me before they began working on the roofs. "Now, remember," I told them before they left, "at noon you come right back here so we can eat together." I wanted all the women to see me with Levi in the tiny, dusty plaza.

My morning went just fine. At the priest's direction, I rearranged candles and hung bunting and laid out the crèche. By then, Gracy had finally lost her shyness. She joined me in grouping the little figures in the crèche and sprinkling straw around.

The sun hung high overhead and lit the church's only window when Albert strode in. "Levi will be along in a minute. I've finished my roofs and he's almost done with his. I came to help you here."

The priest and I turned startled faces toward Albert. "That's like an answer to a prayer," the priest said. "We wondered how we would hang this glass star—the Star of Bethlehem."

"The ladder broke," Gracy piped up by way of explanation. "The star hangs way up there. By the window. On that rusty hook."

Albert peered in the direction Gracy pointed. He studied the situation and said, "Don't worry, *padre*. I'll get a long pole. We'll attach the star to it. Then I'll reach up and fasten the star on its hook."

After Albert left to search for a pole, the priest fondled the star in his shriveled hands. "This is the only beautiful thing we own," he said. "Town artisans made it years ago, in the way their fathers taught them back in Mexico."

I ran my finger over the blue and gold glass. It had an etched surface. Metal edging, maybe copper, girded each segment of the star. I touched the sharp point of each metal-edged portion of the star. "It will be beautiful on Christmas Day."

I searched my mind for inspiring words, but Albert interrupted before I found any. "I've got a pole," he announced as he waved a long, warped stick in front of him. "Hook the star to its end."

With difficulty, I finally perched the pointed star on the end of what Albert insisted on calling a pole. To my mind, it was little more than a piece of dried cane.

Albert raised his pole slowly toward the ceiling, balancing the star on its tip, chewing on the cigarillo in his mouth. He had almost transferred the star to the rusty hook when the pole swayed and he lost his balance. He reeled backward and then regained his steadiness.

I held my breath as Albert once again veered toward the hook, intent as a hawk on its prey. I pried Gracy from my chest: "You stay over here. It's safer between these wooden pews."

Again, Albert had almost gotten the star secured when his balance failed entirely. He fell on the dirt floor, the sharp-edged star following directly behind him.

I screamed. Gracy ducked down into the pews. "Dearest God," the priest yelled as he rushed forward to throw himself between the star and Albert. Despite the priest's efforts, a sapphire point of star, edged with tarnished copper, plunged into Albert's side. Blood spurted out around the glass, dulling its magic hue to a sick, muddy color. Albert's cigarillo lay, unlit, on the dirt floor next to his inert body.

I pushed the priest out of the way. "Go get one of those *curanderas*,"

I shouted at him. I fell to my knees beside Albert, who appeared bewildered and near to stupor. "Lie still," I ordered him. "I'm going to pull the star out of you and stop the bleeding."

I had confidence in myself. Often enough, I'd watched Mammy perform a similar operation with wounds involving tools. I seized the top portion of the glass star and yanked. It almost jumped from Albert's side.

I placed the bloody star on the pew nearest me and turned back to Albert. Because his entire side bled, I couldn't see any way of applying a tourniquet. I put one hand on each side of the wound and pulled it together to stop the bleeding as best I could.

By then, people crowded around us. "Let us through," the priest shouted in Spanish. The crowd parted and a *curandera* knelt down beside Albert.

"She says it's a clean cut," the priest translated, "but we have to watch for infection."

I stepped back to watch, as I'd done whenever I assisted Mammy. Now that it appeared Albert would live, I studied the *curandera*. She appeared old and wrinkled, not a smooth-skinned, attractive young woman as my jealous mind had thought.

The woman packed Albert's injury with herbs and bandaged it. She found a bump on the back of Albert's head, which she also wrapped with a clean rag. Next, she rolled him over on his back.

"My leg, mother," he moaned. "I fell on my leg."

At that, Levi pushed forward. "I can help," he offered. "I'm strong. I can pull on the leg bones if you need me to."

The priest interpreted Levi's offer for the woman. She nodded and motioned Levi how to place his hands, much as Samboy had pulled my arm for Mammy early in our time on the trail. When Levi yanked, Albert shrieked. "Even God is against me," he moaned. "He aimed his own Son's star at me. He doesn't want me to see freedom land."

"Hush," the priest told Albert. "You're hysterical." He pulled a jug of altar wine from its hiding place and poured some into Albert's mouth. "You'll see freedom land. Because our star harmed you, we'll ensure your safe passage away from this place."

Albert said no more. Several men carried Albert out of the church and loaded him on a cart. As an ancient donkey pulled the cart and

Albert toward our camp, I recalled my journey on a litter along the swamp trail home from Aggie's. "I know how you feel," I whispered to Albert, but he didn't seem to hear me.

Late that night, I slept fitfully, Dog at my back and Gracy at my front, when I dreamed I heard the sound of horses' hooves right through the earth my head rested on. When I shook myself and forced my eyes open, I saw two men coming, one with a huge hat, the other wearing a drab, long dress. They looked so strange, I was certain I still dreamed and had not yet awakened.

Fortunately for us, the riders were the town's mayor, or what they had that passed for a mayor, and the priest. Although we all jumped up and tried to make them welcome, they shushed us and pulled us toward the darkest part of camp.

"We have visitors in town," the priest began.

"*Malo gringos*," the other man added.

"He says they are evil Anglos," the priest translated. "They are rough men who are hunting runaway slaves."

Albert, still swathed in bandages but with his cigarillo restored to his mouth, turned as pale as a black man could and asked, "Do they want us in particular?"

"They have a fistful of papers," the priest replied, "notices about runaway slaves."

"Did they read any of them out loud?" Albert asked. Although he still lay on a pallet, he propped himself up on his elbows.

"No, they learned the townspeople could speak only Spanish and I spoke very little English to them, so they posted two notices on the front of the church. Then they went off to make camp for the night."

This fit with what I had heard about slave-catchers. Most worked much like bounty hunters. They collected announcements about runaway slaves from sheriff's offices and other public buildings. From these, they picked out the slaves with the highest prices on their heads. Then they went after those runaways, hanging notices as they went. If they captured the slaves, they returned them to their owners and collected the rewards.

The priest rummaged around under his black dress and pulled out two crumpled announcements. "I'll read them to you, if you wish."

The first one the priest read by the light of the moon had nothing to do with us. It described a couple—she a cook and he a cooper—who had fled from Arkansas just two weeks ago. The other one had each of us in it, except Gracy and Albert. Simon must have been truly angry about our running away, because he described every one of us in detail, from the part in Levi's hair that Paul had made that long-ago day with the burning horseshoe, to the *P* on my chest—Simon had never seen the scars Samboy and I had made to cover the *P*. Neither, of course, did he know that Mammy no longer traveled with us or that Albert Camp guided us.

Simon also offered a handsome reward: $100 for Levi, whom he called a prize blacksmith; $100 for me, whom he described as an excellent dairymaid and a likely breeder; $60 each for Pappy as a fieldhand and Samboy as a young cowboy; and $45 for Mammy as an old doctor woman. That meant the slave-stalkers could realize $420 if they returned Levi, me, Pappy, and Samboy to Simon. We had no way to know what price might be on Albert's head in Indian Territory for helping slaves escape. The $420 alone was enough money to make the meanest, greediest slave-catchers eager to find us and haul us back to the Chickasaw Nation and Simon.

I sighed and said, "Oh, me, we've come all this way and Mammy is dead. Now we're going to be caught."

"No," said the priest, "we have a plan. The grotto lies not far from town. Few people know about it. It stays warm all year around and is dry. We can easily hide you and your horses in there until those men leave. I'll hasten their departure. I'll tell them people told me they saw some black folks heading toward the foothills of the Guadalupe Mountains looking for a place to hide. I'll suggest that perhaps you intend eventually to go to Presidio to try to cross into Mexico."

Albert thought a minute, obviously drawing a map in his head. Despite his battered condition, he smiled, winked at the priest, and said, "That'll get the slave-catchers going in the opposite direction. They'll go west while we go south. Maybe they'll even tangle with some Comanches."

The priest stood over Albert and peered down at him, his wrinkled face intent. "Do you see now that God does not hate you? The Star of

Bethlehem hit you for a reason. You and your people would have been in plain view when the slave-catchers arrived in town. Because of your accident, you had already returned to the secrecy of your camp."

Albert nodded. "But will I be able to travel?"

"You will have time in the cave to regain some of your strength. Make the most of it."

After that, we packed up our few belongings and crept along behind the priest and mayor to the caverns. Once there, we huddled into a dark corner. The two *Tejanos* soon departed, leaving their horses behind in case we needed them to escape on short notice, along with two more sacks of provisions and even firewood.

Before they hiked back to the village, they nearly suffocated under our hugs and kisses and thank-yous.

At the last moment, Gracy topped us all: "I loves you and so does God," she said. "He smiles on you good now."

Even though we lit a tiny fire, we could hardly see each other in the half-dark. The only thing that gave us a hint of fresh air and light was a natural opening in the rock ceiling in the back of the cave.

Things started out pretty good. We had full bellies and faith in the priest and his people. We slept for a few hours. When we awoke we ate *tortillas* and cold beans.

"Let's sit in a circle and hold hands," I suggested. "That way we won't feel so lonely." As usual, Dog settled on one of my parts, this time my feet, and proceeded to put them to sleep. We took turns telling stories: first Albert and Levi about the Texas trail, then Samboy about his mishaps as he learned to cowpoke, then me about my time at the dairy in Tishomingo. Only Pappy and Gracy remained silent, willing listeners as we prattled on.

"I'll check the air shaft," Samboy said after a couple of hours. "I think it must be about noon—time to eat again. Are you hungry?"

"I don't really know," Albert replied. "I feel kind of mixed up."

Gracy decided the matter: "I'm hungry, Mammy," she whispered in my ear. Hearing the mention of food, Dog also perked up. He opened one eye and cocked his head in my direction. So we ate what we guessed was our midday meal, *tortillas* and cold beans. But no one complained.

We passed what we made out to be the rest of that day, as well as the next, in the same way. As he chewed on a limp cigarillo, Albert said, "Eating, sleeping, and swappin' lies is all we're good for."

"It's passin' the time, ain't it?" Pappy growled at Albert.

"The priest will come for us soon," said I with more hope than I felt inside. I went to fussing with Albert's bandages, rewrapping them as well as I could in the near-darkness.

"Leave me alone, Samgirl," he said as he rolled on his side away from me. "Just because our mammy was a healer don't make you one."

I pulled back, stung by Albert's remark. "I know you're hurting, Albert, so I forgive you for your sharp tongue."

"Don't forgive me nothin', Samgirl," he replied. "Just leave me be."

We settled down to sleep without another word passing between me and Albert—or between anyone else either.

When I awoke a few hours later I sniffed the dank air pushing in on me. "I feel like an abandoned child," I whimpered to myself.

I noticed that the cave wasn't quite as warm and dry as the priest had said. "This is going to do Pappy no good," I whispered to Samboy who had sat up at the sound of my voice.

Samboy nodded. "But Pappy's perked up some, what with the food and rest and clear air. He'll get through this."

I didn't say any more. I could hear Pappy coughing and gurgling low in his throat so we wouldn't notice. But I noticed. I spent the rest of the night worrying about him.

I also dreamed of priests riding in the moonlight, caverns where snakes and bats kept me company, and of slave-catchers who hauled me back to Simon, who would beat me and the others until our blood ran onto Chickasaw Nation dirt and turned it into a maroon mud of misery and hopelessness.

The next morning the priest still didn't return to tell us it was safe to go. "What do you think, Albert?" I asked. "I guess the slave-stalkers didn't believe the priest. They didn't go off toward the mountains after all."

Albert's eyes looked scared and weary. "Calm down, Samgirl. We'll have to wait and see."

For hours and hours, I played with Gracy and chewed on dry tortillas and listened to Pappy's cough turn into a croup deep in his chest. I also nursed Albert the best I could.

That was one stubborn man. "Give me back my cigarillo," he snarled when I removed it from his mouth.

"No, you got to sleep now."

"I'll sleep with it in my mouth," Albert said as he aimed glinting eyes right at me.

"Have it your way, then." I gave in and pushed the worn plug between his lips.

When he awoke, Albert seemed even grouchier. "The priest believes the Lord is on our side," he told me. "But He could have chased us out of town without piercing me with a star."

"What does it matter?" I asked Albert. "The accident saved us from slave-catchers."

At that, Albert took umbrage and raised himself to one elbow. "What does it matter? It doesn't matter to you. It isn't your side and head and leg that hurts. It's mine and— "

I reached out with one hand and pushed Albert flat on his mat. "You're going to live," I said in a callous tone.

"Humph," Albert replied. "No thanks to you."

Samboy and Levi also squabbled. "It's a trick," Levi announced to Samboy. "That priest put us in here to trap us. He'll sell us back into slavery himself and use the money to fix up his church and school."

Samboy shot Levi an unbelieving look. "Did the priest seem like a liar and a cheat to you? He's spent his life in poverty to help these people."

"Yeah," replied Levi, "and he's sick of it. That's why he's going to sell us."

They also quarreled about whether the grotto was truly a holy place, placed bets if Albert would live or die, and poked some bugs that looked like sand beetles with sticks to make them race each other in the dim light of our miserable fire. At first, I turned my head away from those two men, whom I loved so much. I couldn't believe they were acting so mean and childish.

"Gracy," I ordered, "you stay away from Samboy and your pappy." I didn't want Gracy to hear her own pappy say such hateful things.

As I listened to the men's voices grow louder and nastier, I realized we all hung on the edge of despair. We sat in a murky cave in limbo, not knowing our fate. The villagers could have ransomed us by now. Perhaps the slave-hunters circled the cave at that very moment, preparing to capture us and take us back to Indian Territory and to Simon.

I grew harsher with Albert. "Quit worrying about whether God's on your side or not. You'll know soon enough. Just worry about getting strong enough to walk out of here—if and when that time comes."

I even snapped at Gracy. "Don't pull at me with your fingers, child. They're like sticks." I felt bad about that remark because it was true. Despite our recent week of feeding, Gracy remained little more than a loose collection of bones.

chapter nineteen

Finally, on the fourth day, as near as we could tell living in darkness, the priest tiptoed into the cavern. "Are you still here?" he whispered as he groped his way toward us.

"We're still here, *padre*," Albert muttered, "but we're anxious to be on our way to freedom. What's happenin' out there?"

As the priest led us and the animals out toward the sunlight, he explained, "Those men scouted this entire area before they came around to believing me. They finally headed toward the mountains this morning."

When we came out of the cave, sunlight hit us and made us blind. We wandered around blinking in the daylight and bumping into each other like fools. When we could see again, the priest said, "I've brought some supplies for you. I'm afraid it's not much. It's all we could spare."

"Any bullets?" Albert asked, hope in his voice.

"No, I'm afraid we have nothing like that. Here is a knife our blacksmith fashioned. Maybe it will be of some use to you."

Albert took the knife and slid it into his saddle pack. When he mounted up, he said, "*Padre*, your place in heaven is certain. We'll never forget you and your people."

I glanced at Levi to see if he had the sense to look ashamed for his suspicions. He looked flustered, certainly, but so did we all.

The priest seemed unaware of the doubts and mistrust we had felt as we waited in the cave. "Kiss the ground in Mexico for me and I'll be well repaid," he said. He waved us off in a southerly direction.

By no means were we strong, but we felt restored enough to make our final push toward the Texas-Mexican border. Besides, we had supplies. It was rice-and-beans, beans-and-rice every meal, yet nobody complained. We had learned our lesson about food. After eating grass, we were glad to have any victuals at all.

We were also thankful for the horses the priest and mayor had pressed upon us. We were able to spell our horses, who stepped along lively enough after their rest, yet still had not fully recovered from their pain. Good thing, because Albert pushed us hard. "Those slave-chasers will see through the *padre's* story sooner or later," he said. "They'll turn back south, right where we were headed toward the Rio Grande."

"Albert," I protested, "nothing more could possibly happen to us now. Everything has already happened! The rest of the trip will be— "

"Don't be foolish," Albert interrupted. "Things are getting hotter for runaway slaves every day. And this is Texas. The land itself will destroy us if it can."

I said nothing, praying that Albert was wrong. Surely we had suffered enough; we'd already paid a dear price for freedom.

Albert broke into my thoughts as though I'd spoken aloud. "What we've gone through don't guarantee us freedom. We still have a ways to go . . . if we make it at all."

I clenched my teeth and took Gracy back in the sling with me. Soon I burned up from the sun. I perspired a river and got too weak to hold onto Gracy. Because I feared Dog couldn't keep up and would soon be left behind, I also boosted him up on that horse and into the backside of the sling. We moved along right smart. I could imagine Dog's bones jiggling about on Dan's loins.

Most of all, we drove ourselves and let fear eat away at us. Each day, with fear of the slave-catchers goading us onward, we rode until long after nightfall and camped with our horses circled around us. "We can't chance a fire," Albert said each evening.

Fortunately, the *Tejanos* had had the foresight to know we would do this, so they had precooked everything. We were up again before dawn and on our way while the sky still appeared inky, except around the edges where the sun gave a few pinkish signs of its coming.

Within no time, I turned as jittery as the buffalo, ready to jump this way to run that way. If Dan stepped on a twig, cracking it with his hoof, I feared the slave-hunters rode at my back, firing over my head to stop me. Dan and Gracy and Dog soon caught my dread and took it into themselves. Every so often, they jiggled and twisted and drove themselves and me into agony.

"Stay still," I ordered but the jiggling and twisting continued. We jogged along like one big parcel of nerves, ready to explode at the slightest indication of trouble coming our direction.

The men were just as bad. Despite his injuries, Albert had taken to leaping on and off his horse. In between doing that, he rode like the devil himself chased us, or ran instead of walking. Samboy took to sweating all the time. He sweated in the noonday sun; he sweated in the evening breeze; he even soaked his bedroll with sweat as he tossed and fought off nightmares. Levi began to mumble, complaining about this, warning about that. Like Samboy, he kept it up awake or sleeping.

Pappy was the worst. He coughed and crouped day and night. Even though the priest had brought some of the *curandera's* medicine for Pappy, it was like pouring honey into an old rusted kettle. It did no good at all. Besides, Pappy choked the syrupy medicine back up as often as not. At the same time, Pappy took to twitching and trembling and quivering. At first, I thought it was worry that set him dancing as if he had fire ants in his britches, but then I remembered Mammy's talk about spasms and how they could shake the life right out of a person.

All this took its toll on us. "This is almost as bad as the days when we nearly starved to death," I thought to myself. Of course, we weren't quite starving, even though our supplies ran low, but I worried something worse was going to happen.

Until Albert used his last bullet to scare away a wild boar, I feared that he, the only one of us who wore a sidearm, would shoot his own leg in his jumping around.

"You wait and see," I told Gracy, who half-slept and cared little what I was saying. "One of us will ride right over the top of another. In our hurry, we'll cause a horse to misstep and fall, crushing one of us under it."

We grew more and more haggard as we pushed southward, hardly speaking to each other, except for Levi's eternal muttering that made me certain of his approaching insanity. Gracy said not a word. In fact, I often doubted she still lived. If it hadn't been for her occasional agitated jerkings, I would have stopped and dug her grave.

Worry also tore at our insides. Albert no longer chewed anything, cigarillo or weed. Instead, he bled from the right side of his mouth— just a trickle, mind you, but blood just the same. I worried he had torn open the puncture wound in his side.

The whites of Levi's eyes turned chalky, while Samboy lost three teeth in as many days. My stomach roiled and burned from morning to night and from night to morning.

I remembered once when I was a little girl back in the schoolroom in Mississippi, the schoolmaster had read us a story about a headless horseman. "This story's about a rider who dressed in a black shroud and terrorized everyone he could find," he intoned. Now I pictured a troop of headless horsemen behind us, riding as swiftly as the buffalo to catch us and kill our dreams of freedom.

I wasn't even convinced we were headed in the right direction. I figured I better not say anything to Albert, for fear of my life. I was mistaken, though. After days of riding—I don't know how many because only God counted—we came in sight of Camp Eagle Pass. I about jerked off Dan's back when Albert threw up his hands and ordered us to stop.

"I didn't want to tell you this earlier," he said, a sure sign of bad news coming. "We can't go into Eagle Pass itself. Even though a lot of the white soldiers there don't like slavery, they're bound by law to turn us in if we appear. The same with the soldiers at Fort Duncan, a few miles upriver, and the miners at Camp California, about four miles up, who are going to the gold fields."

Of course, we still had our free-black passes with us, but Albert didn't think they'd work here. "No," he said. "We'll travel down the river a ways, build ourselves a raft and cut some poles. Then we'll get across that river at the calmest spot we can find."

Even though it'd been dry in Texas, snow and rains in the San Juan Mountains could swell the river at any time. "The Grande is one strange river," Albert said, "sometimes quiet, nothing more than a desert stream. At others, it floods. In fact, some folks call the Grande the Rio Turbid."

I felt hope once again. I hugged the stick that was Gracy and said, "Let's go while we got the last bit of life in us to build that raft."

We had to ride quite a ways downriver before Albert felt safe enough to stop. We found a stand of cottonwood trees surrounding a pool of oily-looking water. Even though cottonwoods only grow where there's water, this water looked unfit to nourish human or tree. The horses set to work, though, stripping the silvery leaves off the cottonwood trees. After the desert scrub they'd been eating, this proved an unexpected treat.

We set to work chopping and tying logs together with anything we could find—vines, bits of rope, rags. Even though it didn't look like a very river-worthy craft to me, especially for the surging waters that lay between us and Mexico, I went on working and kept my mouth shut. The raft only had to carry people, for we had hardly any supplies left and we planned to swim the horses across.

"What are we building this raft for?" I grumbled to Samboy. "Why don't we just stay on horseback and let the horses get us across?"

Samboy nodded his head in Pappy's direction. "Look for yourself, Samgirl."

Pappy could hardly stand up, much less chop and tie. Blood shot through the whites of his eyes. Saliva dribbled down his bearded chin.

Pappy must have realized we were building that raft for him, because he pulled me aside. He asked me to shoot him dead, like a horse that had gone down with a broken leg. Even though it sounds unbelievable, it's what my pappy said to me that day. "Samgirl, I want you to take this rifle and put its last bullet through my head so I can join Chloe at last."

"Pappy," said I, "I can't kill my own pappy. I can't put a bullet through your head or kill you in any other way. Besides, I want you to go with us to the freedom place."

At that, Pappy sank on the ground and lay there in a heap, his head almost in the Texas dust. I patted his shoulders and walked away with no feelings left in me at all. I was dead at my center, as if I had shot that bullet into my own heart.

"Albert," I said, "we've got to go. Pappy's dying. We've got to get him to freedom."

"We've got to go anyway," Albert said, as he adjusted the bandages that still encased his chest. "I was just out scouting. I spotted two riders coming fast this way."

At that, Samboy took Gracy and strapped her to his back. We assumed that Dog could swim the river on his own. I got on the raft with Pappy. Although we had planned to tie Pappy on for safety, now there was no time. There was no time to search for a calm place, either, as Albert had said we would. We had to take the river as it was and that wasn't good.

Samboy went into the river first, horse and all. Then Albert and Levi pushed me and Pappy in, raft and all. "Me and Albert are staying behind a bit to fight off the slave-catchers so you can get a head start," Levi shouted.

"No," I screamed, "no, we need you! We're almost there!"

Levi didn't hear me. Two slave-hunters rode hard into what remained of our camp. As they came, they shouted oaths and curses into the air. I cowered on the raft with the muddy Grande pounding underneath, pulling me and Pappy farther away from shore. I watched Levi halt one man by putting the rifle bullet Pappy had wanted for himself smack through the man's forehead.

That left Albert and Levi unarmed. The other man seemed to know it. Because Albert and Levi were worth bounty money, the slave-hunter didn't want to drop them where they stood, although he could easily have done so. Instead, he came at them with his pistol in one hand, rattling some chains and collars in his other.

I sweated and prayed as the man threw the collars at Levi. He motioned for Levi to yoke one collar around Albert's neck. Albert must have signaled Levi to obey because Levi snapped the collar shut. The hunter moved toward Levi, all the while hollering for Albert to chain up Levi. Albert waited a bit, as if he couldn't drag his sore leg any further, letting the scum inch toward him. The man hurled a chain at Albert's injured side, but the thick wad of dressings saved Albert from harm.

When the man grabbed for Albert, he bent down, whipped the *Tejano* blacksmith's knife out of the wrappings on his chest, and slashed the slave-catcher across the neck. To make sure, Albert poked the knife in his enemy's breast three or four times.

I saw a surprised look on the hunter's face before he collapsed. He hung poised in midair for a minute, as though wondering where the pain had come from, then crumpled down on top of what had been our campfire. "I hope that fire-pit still had hot coals in its center," I shouted into the air, so full now of the river's noises that I could hardly hear myself.

After that, I didn't see any more. The dun-brown river had a menacing energy that claimed all my attention. Pappy and I hit a run, with its fast-flowing water carrying us along. Next we swirled around, caught by a pirouette of water from below the surface. We went in circles faster and harder than I ever saw Mammy beat any cornmeal mush and that was hard and fast enough to make you dizzy.

Pappy seemed woozy and confused, then his eyes cleared and he said to me, "I love you, Samgirl."

Before I realized what he intended, Pappy rolled over twice to the edge of our unfinished raft. He made one more roll and plunged toward a pool of deep, dark water about ten feet away. He disappeared in the murk that was the Rio Grande, so fast I never even saw the bubbles of him going down. "Let his head hit a rock," I prayed, "so he feels no pain drowning."

"Here Pappy comes, Mammy," I whispered, "take good care of him. You too, God. He was a good man, the best pappy any child could've had."

Tears blinded my eyes. The emotions I thought were dead pounded in my chest, demanding to be let out in moans and screams and sobs. But I had a more immediate problem—hanging on to the raft myself. I clutched at the logs until my skin broke and my fingers bled. "Samboy!" I screamed, "Samboy!"

Samboy couldn't hear me over the rushing water, but he must have sensed that I faced serious trouble. He slowed down and appeared at the raft's side, muddy water jumping and flipping around him. Behind him he yanked my horse, Dan, whose mouth bubbled with foam and fear.

"Get off," Samboy yelled, "let go. Grab on to Dan instead."

With that, Samboy tossed Dan's reins high in the air. I released my death grip on the raft. When the reins came down on top of my near-senseless head, I rallied enough to grab them. Dan did the rest. Like a tugboat, he towed me along behind him through what seemed like mile after mile of thrashing water, topped with froth and lather.

Dan dragged me right up the shore on the Mexico side. I lifted my head enough to shake it and try to clear it. I saw Samboy lying belly-down in the dirt, Gracy still tied to his back and lying face down on him. Being her, she quietly waited for someone to undo her. Dog, looking cleaner than I'd ever seen him, nuzzled at Samboy's and Gracy's faces. Although I could see Gracy breathing, I feared Samboy had died.

I crawled up beside him and said, "Samboy, are you alive?"

"No," Samboy answered in a raspy voice. "Are you?"

"Barely," said I, ignoring his feeble attempt at humor, "but I think I've got a couple of broken ribs."

"Where's Pappy?" he asked.

I started to howl, which further convinced me I'd cracked some ribs in that river. When I calmed down, I told Samboy about Pappy's suicide.

Samboy's smile startled me. Samboy had realized more than I knew about Pappy. "Pappy drowned in the river of freedom," Samboy said, "and he's heading toward Mammy. He must be one happy man."

"Yes," said I, grief edging my voice, "Pappy's happy now."

I helped Samboy unstrap Gracy from his back. We pulled our soggy selves farther from the water's edge toward a stand of puny trees. We curled against each other. The sinking sun still gave enough heat to warm our skin and dry what little clothing we had left. At the same time, fat red-and-green birds welcomed us to their country with raucous noises.

We nestled in the grit and the wispy, strawlike grass. We slept right there the rest of the evening and night, Gracy against my stomach and

Dog at my back. I don't know whether I cried or slept more those next hours, for I feared I would never see Levi again. I never even felt the jabbing of the mosquitoes that left welts all over my body.

When dawn woke us, Albert and Levi sat beside us. "We're here," Albert said. He still wore the slave-catcher's collar around his neck, along with a few soaked bandages on his body. Most of the dressings had departed from his chest somewhere during crossing. Levi sported an open gash down the left side of his face, which had stopped bleeding. Little more than dried blood held the wound together.

Retching tore at my insides when I saw Levi's wound and felt his hurt. I crawled toward him. I cradled his damaged face to my damaged chest. "Poor Levi," I crooned. I heard Levi's pulse pounding in time with my heartbeat, the two of us locked in an embrace that no one else could share or even understand.

When I finally drew back and moved away from Levi a bit, I twisted toward Albert with a question on my sorrowful face. "How did this happen? Who did this thing to Levi?"

It turned out that a third man had followed the first two into our camp on the Rio Grande. The man wasn't part of the team. Rather, he had let the first two take the chances, intending to grab the runaway slaves for himself later. When he saw the two fall, he had rushed Albert and jammed his arm upward, causing Albert's knife to go flying. Levi caught the knife and set on the man, who had a knife of his own. After the man cut Levi's face, Levi returned the favor by piercing his attacker's neck, much as Albert had done with his assailant.

At that moment, I had seen and heard more about bloodshed and death than I could stand in a lifetime. I started to whimper and whine. Levi took me back into his arms. I shivered along my entire spine and tried to crawl inside Levi himself.

"It's all right. We're in freedom land now," he said low-down into my ear. When his warm breath started me shivering again, he dusted light kisses over my neck and my face. He keened over every mosquito bite, welt, and bruise he found.

I pulled myself away from Levi, straightening my backbone and arching my neck until I sat proud and tall on the bank of the Rio Grande. "But we got to get all the way to Monterrey yet," said I, illogic clouding my brain in this time of sorrow and joy, despair and hope. "And I don't have my mammy and pappy to help me do it."

Levi gathered me back in. He patted me on my nearly naked back and said, "There, there. I'm going to help you."

I pulled away again. I stared right at Levi and his battered face and hollered, "You don't want me. You want those *señoritas*."

"For God's sake, Samgirl," Samboy interrupted, "can't we settle this later?" He stood up, took hold of my arms, and tried to pull me free from Levi.

At the same time, Albert sat real quiet, waiting to see what would develop. "No," he said, "let's get it over with now."

"I want you, Samgirl," Levi told me in a sudden shout. "I love you. So does Gracy."

In the face of Levi's emotion, I calmed down. My voice turned low and sly. "You may love me now, but you won't when I tell you about Aggie and her knife."

At that, Levi's eyes grew wide and his nostrils flared. He got up and stomped in a distracted circle. "You mean to tell me," he shouted, "you've been pushing me away because of what Aggie did to you?"

"How do you know about that?" I screamed at him and jumped to my feet myself. "*How do you know?*"

Levi glanced at Samboy. I followed his gaze and also looked at Samboy, who sat on a fallen, rotted log with a stupid grin on his face and a shrug on his shoulders. "I didn't think it was a secret. I told Levi lots of things along the Texas trail. After all, we came near death together many a time."

My mouth still hung open when Levi grabbed me in his viselike grip. "Don't blame Samboy. I should've figured it out myself. I thought there was somethin' funny about all this. Back at Simon's, I concluded you didn't want me because you were afraid to have slave babies. Then I found out from Samboy you can't have babies at all. If I hadn't been so busy with this running-away business, I'd have put it all together for myself."

I stood quiet and still, barely even breathing. Levi positioned me directly in front of him and stared into my eyes. "Do you love me, Samgirl?"

I swallowed hard and looked into the sharp rays of the rising sun. I nodded. "I've loved you a long time, Levi. I was afraid you wouldn't want me because of what Aggie did."

"How did you get your mind so fixed on babies?" he asked.

Now it was my turn to shrug my shoulders. "As far back as I can remember, everybody talked about babies: Aggie and her friends, Mammy, Pappy, Dolly Lee, Simon. I knew Simon wouldn't want a barren wench like me on his plantation. I thought you wouldn't want me either, given the way you dote on children."

Levi gave me a deep look. He smiled in a soft way. "You're right about one thing, Samgirl. I do love little ones. But me and you got a child already," Levi said. "We've got Gracy. I don't need any more children. I just need you."

I let Levi fold me in his arms. I leaned against his chest. Then I pulled back from him, my eyes piercing his and my shoulders drawn back with anxiety. "I'm not sure I can bear it. In one day, I've gained freedom. Now I have you, too."

The tension hung in the air between us like a cloudburst about to break. Gracy brought me back to my senses. A clawlike hand slid into mine. "You got me, too, Mammy," Gracy said. "You got lots of work ahead fattening me up, like you always say you're goin' to do."

I grabbed up Gracy and hugged her in between me and Levi. Samboy sat looking perplexed. With a grin, Albert said, "If that's settled, can we please get ourselves off this shore and a little bit farther into freedom land?"

Albert grabbed a piece of dead wood and pulled himself up, using it as a crutch of sorts. "All right," he said, "I admit it. The priest was right. The Lord seems to be on our side."

chapter twenty

We were lucky. In Peidras Negras—which lay on the Mexico side of the Rio Grande across from Camp Eagle Pass—we met up with some white folks, Claudia and Walter Bonham, who had fled the United States because they hated slavery. In that dusty, fly-ridden little border town, they had been helping runaway slaves who bobbed up out of the river the way we had.

Claudia and Walter seemed to be hanging around the sheriff's office when we straggled up the street. We looked for all the world like a bunch of lost souls. "Where you folks going?" Claudia shouted.

"We got trouble now," Albert mumbled. He yelled back, "We're going to the church—to see the priest. To give him a greeting from his friend in New Sonora in Texas."

"Step along faster, folks," Albert urged us. "Look like you know where're you're goin'."

"Maybe that woman can help us, Albert," I protested. "She has a kind face. She's not a slave-catcher."

We all stopped, Albert included. I grabbed my chance and shot the woman a shy, scared smile. "We're lost," I mouthed at her.

She walked toward us, clearly ready to herd us with her umbrella. I could see no other use for the umbrella unless, like folks back in Mississippi, she used it to keep the sun off her head.

"Don't be afraid of me," she said in a shrill voice.

Walter ambled behind. "We'll help you if we can," he added.

Albert's shoulders dropped, but inside me, I knew that everything would turn out all right now. Within minutes, the Bonhams gathered us up and took us home with them.

Claudia stood at least five-feet-nine and was scrawny. When she piled her black hair in a bun on top of her head, which she usually did, she appeared even taller. That woman had a heart of pure love. She took in every stray that came along, be it dog or cat or slave.

Gracy described me as a black woman, but she called Claudia a "clear" one, meaning white-skinned. After a few days, I grew convinced that Gracy's word really described Claudia's soul.

Walter was only five-feet-four, a fluffy man—not fat, just fluffy. He wore a funny little mustache that looked like someone had drawn it under his nose with a grease pencil. He loved Claudia like the dickens and folks in need almost as much. What Walter lacked in physical strength he made up in spiritual grit. To Walter, nothing seemed beyond hope. Like Mammy had, he would just say, "Let's get going."

First, Claudia and Walter patched up me and Levi. Then they gave Levi the tools to get Albert's neck-lock off and we all helped rebandage Albert's side. Although he seemed to favor his game leg, he could walk.

Finally, Claudia and Walter fed us lots of plain and nourishing food. It was about then I began to feel freedom. I felt it in my head and my heart and in the one place it had always been—in my soul.

I let freedom put a grin on my lips and a gleam in my eyes and shimmer on my skin. I let freedom put starch in my shoulders and vigor in my hands and lightness in my feet. I let freedom give me the strength to think of Mammy and Pappy and wish they were here to savor liberty themselves. I let freedom fill me with faith that Mammy and Pappy had found a better place yet, a place where everyone was free. I let freedom turn my eyes heavenward and thank God for what we had.

I even let freedom transform the way I saw myself and the world around me. When everybody gathered together, and with Claudia and Walter listening hard, I said, "No more Samgirl for me. Now that I'm free, I want to be called Samantha." Everybody cheered.

That started a trend. Samboy said, "I'll be called Sam, if you please." Albert said, "I ain't using Camp as my last name anymore, so I'll have to find a new one." Levi said to me and Gracy, "We're going to have find a last name that suits us all."

It looked like Dog was the only one stuck with his name, because he didn't object. He just went around licking everyone's hands and feet and whatever other part of them he could get at.

Next, the Bonhams got me and Levi married in a regular, legal way. They did it right on Christmas Day with the Mexican sun shining and beaming down on us like it couldn't stop smiling. It was Christmas and summer at the same time. It was also my wedding day, a day I thought I'd never see in my lifetime.

Even though we seemed an odd pair, with my ribs taped and his face sewed up and Gracy standing in between us holding our hands, the marriage took just the same.

We had no rings, but Levi gave me a hug and whispered, "I love you, Samantha."

Shyly, I hugged Levi back. "I love you, too, Levi. Always will."

"Me, too," Gracy chirped. "I loves everybody."

Afterwards, we even had a bit of a wedding feast, courtesy of Claudia and Walter and the good people of the town who helped the Bonhams out with donations when they could. We gobbled down rice and beans and tortillas, along with some pork that tasted like honey and a drink called *mescal.* "That tickles all the way down," I giggled. The liquor also warmed my belly faster than Gracy herself did by hanging against me.

I don't remember much about the rest of the night and what happened in the cushion of soft summer air and fiesta music. I do remember that lying down with Levi in our own bed was a warmer, wider, more stirring experience than I could ever have believed. During the long-ago nights when I spied on Mammy and Pappy in their bunk, I had sensed waves of affection spiraling through our cabin. Still, I had no idea of the overwhelming power of love and sex linked together.

When I allowed myself to give two seconds to remembering what Paul had done under that willow tree back in Mississippi, I laughed. He and so many others like him had mired themselves in ownership and lust. Later, I almost felt sorry for Paul and all he had missed in his short life.

Before New Year's came, the Bonhams helped us get down to Monterrey to find Albert's friend. "Monterrey is far enough away from the United States border," Walter assured us, "so no slave-stalkers will take the chance of following you there."

"A few of them," Claudia added, "venture into Mexico after slaves, but they don't go very far."

I hoped they were right. We had seen enough slave-catchers to last a lifetime.

When we arrived in Monterrey, the *rico*, just as Albert had hoped, gave us each a small parcel of land to work on shares. The land wasn't much, but it was our salvation.

Samboy—I mean Sam—took one plot for himself, while Levi and I took another. Albert claimed a third. "Let's make some wooden markers," I suggested, "for Mammy and Pappy."

"I'll carve their names on the markers," Sam volunteered.

"And I'll find some rocks to hold the boards," Albert chimed in.

Albert also helped us plow and such. Yet in a few weeks his feet turned itchy. Despite the pain in his wound, which would never let him be, and a leg that occasionally turned gimpy, he wanted to follow the cattle once again.

"I'll be on my way soon, folks," he told us one sunny afternoon.

Sam's face fell. "I was afraid of that," he said.

For days afterward, Sam begged Albert to stay. "Don't go," Sam pleaded. "Stay here with us."

Finally, Albert answered Sam. After shuffling around in the dust Albert clapped his right arm around Sam's shoulders. He chomped on the cigarillo that had returned to his lips. "I'm not cut out to be a farmer, Sam. Ever since I escaped Lamar Quimby Camp's farm back in Mississippi, I've liked being on the go."

"But you got family now, Albert," Sam noted, his eyes begging Albert to change his mind.

Albert drew Sam close to him. "Will you work my land for me, Sam? You watch it for me and get something growin' on it. I bet Samantha and Levi will help. Then next time I come, maybe I'll look at those pretty crops coming out of my land and I'll settle down on it."

Sam nodded his head. He dashed the back of one hand against his eyes. "You love those cows better than you do us."

Albert thought a moment before he answered. "You might turn out to be wrong. I might get down the road a piece and feel my family pulling at me so strong, I'll turn around and come home."

"Sam," I said in gentle tones, "if Albert's got to go you better let him get on with it."

"So go," Sam muttered to Albert. "But come back soon."

That's how it came to be that Levi and Sam and I promised to work Albert's patch of land for him as best we could until he was ready to settle down for good.

All our patches were dry soil with too much sand and not much water nearby to help it out. Even though it would yield crops slowly, it looked like paradise to us. We were willing to give all the energy we had—and some we didn't even know we possessed—on getting that land to bloom.

After we got settled in tiny adobe shacks with mud-and-thatch roofs, I undertook to learn how to cook properly and how to dry peppers in the sun and hang bulbs of garlic from the open, wooden rafters in the ceiling above my kitchen.

"We don't eat grand but we eat regularly," Levi liked to say. "You're one good cook, Samantha."

We frequently thought back to the time we sat on the hard Texas dirt and ate rabbit and grass that we pulled right from the ground. We agreed we never wanted to see such hard times again.

"You know what," said I one gentle spring night as we rested in front of our shack, "this farm looks a lot like Simon's farm, and the work feels a lot like Simon's work, and the food—except for the hot peppers—tastes a lot like Simon's food. Yet at the same time, it's different."

I stared at the silver moon for a moment and knew it was the same one I had seen back in Mississippi and in Indian Territory out west. I felt more philosophical than I ever had before. "Having freedom sure changes the way a person sees things in this life," I said.

Levi took my hand, Gracy crawled on my lap, and Dog sat on my feet. So lightly that at first, I thought it was a lightning bug or some other tiny insect, Levi brushed his thumb against my palm. When I realized it was Levi, the warm feeling swirled its way out from the center of my body, downward to the tops of my legs, upward to my breasts. I knew now what such sensations meant and where they would lead.

When Gracy's head tipped sideways, Levi scooped her up and carried her to bed. In the moonlight that filtered in one of our shack's few windows, Dog settled down beside her, for he had taken to sleeping with Gracy now that I seemed to prefer Levi. I undressed and slid into our bunk. I threw back our quilt. "I'm waiting for you, Levi."

Levi shucked off his clothes and scrambled into bed beside me. Levi kissed my neck. I ran my hand down his lean hip. The quiet evening, broken only by night birds and crickets, turned into something the two of us shared and glorified.

Later, I slipped outdoors while Levi slept, snoring away his tiredness from the work he had done today and storing up strength for the labor to come tomorrow. In the moon's glossy shine, I fell down on my knees and lay my cheek on the fresh-smelling soil, still warm from the day's sun.

"Thank you, God," said I, "for giving me this ground, where I've finally been able to lay my burden of slavery down and take up freedom instead."